I march across
interspersed with to
lamplight in the distance.

Obscured by the surrounding shrubbery next to the base of a conifer is a blue tarp. I press my free hand against the brown bag, feeling the warmth radiating from the container of broth. Good. I'd hate for the soup to be cold.

A gust of wind pushes me sideways. From somewhere overhead comes a loud crack like the bone of some gargantuan creature snapping. A widowmaker thumps to the earth. Gasping, I nearly drop the soup and freeze in place. Overhead, the trees sway in the wind, branches creaking and groaning. I scamper toward the encampment.

About half a dozen tents surround the base of the tall conifer. A wide man with hunched shoulders moves around the camp. I smile. It's Joe.

Dragons Walk Among Us

by

Dan Rice

This is a work of fiction. Names, characters, places, and incidents are either the product of the author's imagination or are used fictitiously, and any resemblance to actual persons living or dead, business establishments, events, or locales, is entirely coincidental.

Dragons Walk Among Us

Cover Art by *Debbie Taylor*

The Wild Rose Press, Inc.
PO Box 708
Adams Basin, NY 14410-0708
Visit us at www.thewildrosepress.com

Publishing History
First Edition, 2021
Trade Paperback ISBN 978-1-5092-3655-8
Digital ISBN 978-1-5092-3656-5

Published in the United States of America

Dedication

Dedicated to Crystal, Alex, and Anders who allow me to write. And Diana Rice, for reading every chapter I've ever written.

Chapter 1

The buzz of conversation echoes inside the gymnasium of Cascadia Prep High School. People admire the photographs hanging on the walls snapped by students from across the school district. I stand in front of my image, a black-and-white portrait of a homeless veteran named Joe. The LED lighting is awful for viewing photographs, especially a black and white. It makes my photo look like it's a split tone. It's not.

"I see tons of photos, and that's a grand slam," Haji says.

"Thanks," I reply, but I know the gangly boy only says so because he's my friend.

Then again, maybe he's right. The bad lighting doesn't detract too much. The glow of the fire Joe sits beside is reflected in his wise, sad eyes and highlights the seams etched into his face from years of living on the streets. He isn't much over forty, but he looks sixty. I turn away from the photo, unable to look at it for long. Joe is more than a photographic subject. He's a friend.

"Allison, what's wrong?" Haji asks.

I blink my moist eyes. "Nothing. Let's look at the other photos."

Haji escorts me around the gym, offering his criticism and approval of the photographs mounted on the walls. As the editor of the *Cascadia Weekly*, our school's online news source, he claims to see dozens of photographs every week from student photogs and insists I'm the best. My shots of high school sporting events around the city grace the site's pages practically every week.

We've gone about halfway around the gym when I spot Leslie Chapman surrounded by admirers. Leslie is a junior and is everything I'm not, popular and beautiful and tall. Not just tall for a girl either, she's tall period, like six feet at least. In the most generous terms, I'm only five foot two inches. When she sees me in the crowd, her blue eyes slide right over me as if I'm invisible. I veer away.

"It's Leslie," I hiss to Haji.

"I don't know what she has against you," he says and follows me.

"Leslie likes being the best at everything," I say, struggling not to clench my teeth. "It's not enough for her to be the captain of the cross-country team and a 4.0 student. She wants to be the best photographer too. She just wants me to be the girl she makes fun of at cross-country practice."

"Well, you're the best," Haji says. "She has to accept that."

I smile, feeling a spark of confidence. I'm glad Haji takes my side. In his words, having the two of us as his top photojournalists for the school news site is a sticky wicket.

The high-pitched voice of a district official pipes from the speakers mounted high on the walls. She summons everyone to gather around and face a podium at the front of the gym. Hardly anyone is glued to their phones. I shift my weight on my feet and rub my hands together.

"Don't worry," Haji says. "Your portrait of Joe is just as good as anything else on display, better than most. Even accounting for my bias, I'd say you have a great chance at winning."

"I don't know. What about that shot from the goalkeeper's perspective? Diving. Hands outstretched to block the ball. That's pretty dope."

"Nah."

I elbow him in the ribs.

"Hey." His smile shows off his tea-stained teeth. "It's a dope shot, okay. Amazing, but yours is better. Yours captures something extra special, the whole enchilada."

I give him a toothless grin. "Thanks for saying so."

"I'm totally serious."

"I believe you."

"That smile says you don't."

"Whatever." I roll my eyes.

"Silence, please. Silence," the official chirps, her clipped movements as birdlike as her voice.

A relative quiet falls over the gym as people finish maneuvering. The official spouts a boilerplate speech about the importance of education and a free press and how the contest is the synergy of these two crucial aspects of civil society. I tap my foot against the floor. Haji has pulled out his phone and is texting. So is about half the crowd. I stifle a sigh. All my dad allows me is an archaic pay-as-you-go flip phone. He is such a dinosaur about some things.

Once the speech ends, teachers are summoned to the podium to announce the winner from their schools. Just as I said, the photo from the goalkeeper's perspective is a winner. It takes first place in the sports category. Next up is the documentary category. I rock back and forth on my heels.

Third place goes to a boy I don't recognize from a high school up north. His image is of the grisly aftermath of a street race gone wrong. The twisted metal is hard to look at, knowing that three high school students died in the accident.

I sigh when second place goes to Tammy Nguyen, a girl I know from elementary school. Her colorful picture of the lunar new-year celebration in Chinatown deserves recognition. I wave to Tammy, although I don't think she sees me in the crowd.

"Next, I'd like to call up Mr. Eldridge to give out the first-place award in the documentary category," the district official says and stands aside for the Cascadia Prep teacher to take the podium.

Mr. Eldridge, his bald head gleaming in the light, stands behind the podium and adjusts his glasses on his hooked nose. He peers out over the crowd, squinting. I'm sure his gaze pauses on me. My breath catches in my throat, and my eyes go wide. Am I the winner? Then his head swivels away. My gaze flicks to Haji. He gives me a thumbs-up.

"First place goes to an extremely talented photojournalist," Mr. Eldridge says in a voice raspy from years of smoking. He's always entreating his students not to take up the habit. "Please, join me in recognizing Leslie Chapman for her amazing photograph entitled Blaze at the Museum."

"No way," I whisper as the gymnasium erupts in applause.

Everyone is clapping.

Everybody loves Leslie.

I hang my head. Haji pats me on the shoulder, and I look up. Leslie, holding the first-place plaque, stands next to Mr. Eldridge. She smiles, showing off blindingly white teeth. I swear, she must whiten them every day.

As much as I hate to admit it, Leslie's photograph of the fire that destroyed a museum in downtown Seattle is brilliant. The shooting flames reflect off the building's metallic skin, making the metal and fire seem alive. I guess my photo isn't as excellent as I thought.

I wish I am anywhere but here, like at cross-country practice. At least then I could stare longingly at Jason as he bounds over the ground like a gazelle and talk to Dalia with her neon pink hair bobbing in time with the patter of her feet.

The district official escorts Leslie from the podium. The urge to pee hits me. Too much coffee. I'm about to make a beeline for the bathroom when the official returns to the mic.

"We have one more award. Mr. Eldridge, please do the honor of announcing the grand-prize winner."

Grand-prize winner? I exchange a puzzled glance with Haji, who shrugs.

"The grand prize goes to a young lady with a professional eye for photography. It's been a real treat to teach her. Allison Lee, come on up. Her photograph entitled Joe was chosen by the judges for the grand prize because it captures something quintessential about the subject."

My jaw goes unhinged. I utter a squeal before clamping my mouth shut and covering my face with a hand. Haji beams, and people clap. I maneuver through the crowd to stand next to Mr. Eldridge by the podium. He shakes my hand and gives me the plaque. It's shaped like Washington State with a camera etched in the upper left-hand corner on the Olympic Peninsula. Across the top of the state, it reads *1st Annual High School Photojournalism Contest*. Below that, *Grand Prize* is etched across the state, followed by my name at the bottom.

Staring across the crowd, I don't feel absolutely horrible having so many people watching me. I barely notice Leslie standing up front, her eyes narrowed in a drop-dead glare. At the back of the gymnasium, my father smiles and waves at me. I wave back, delighted that he made it to the ceremony to watch me take home the grand prize.

Mr. Eldridge shakes my hand again. "Excellent work, Allison. You really deserve this award."

The district official smiles and ushers me off the podium. I reenter the crowd and head straight to the bathroom. I'm floating in the pristine water off a tropical paradise. Life can't get much better than this. It's like all my greatest dreams are coming to fruition. The only thing that could make it better is if an editor from a major newspaper materializes out of the crowd to recruit me as a staff photographer.

I enter the girls' locker room that smells of deodorizer and scoot past rows of lockers for the stalls. I balance my plaque on the toilet paper dispenser while I get down to business. I shut my eyes, not quite believing that I'm the grand-prize winner. I can't wait to tell Dalia and Jason and Joe.

I stop at the sink to wash my hands. The door to the locker room creaks open. I look in the mirror both to admire my green hair and to catch a glimpse of the interloper. I clench my jaw. It's Leslie staring at me balefully.

"Congratulations on—"

"Your photograph is fake." Leslie snarls. "Just like you. Fake. Fake like your hair. Ugly like your slanted eyes."

I freeze, the lukewarm water cascading over my hands. The words remind me of a fact I try to ignore. The reality that my face is a mixture of Asian and Caucasian features. My cheeks pale as Leslie marches across the locker room.

"You don't deserve this." She snatches my plaque off the counter. "Your photo isn't documentary or photojournalism. It's a portrait of your friend."

She looms inside my personal space, scowling down her nose at me. The standoff might last for five seconds or five minutes for all I know. With a scoff, she twirls away and strides for the exit, pausing to deposit my plaque in the trash can.

Chapter 2

I slink from the locker room into the gymnasium with the grand-prize plaque clamped in my hands. It's moist from the paper towels discarded in the trash can. Leslie is nowhere to be seen, and the people who deign to notice my presence either smile politely or offer enthusiastic congratulations. I mutter the bare minimum of acceptable platitudes, suspicious that they know what happened in the locker room and approve.

Haji intercepts me at a side exit from the gym. I give him my leave-me-the-hell-alone stare with no effect. Smiling, he waves my dad over, calling that he found me. I almost make a break for the exit, but I don't because then they'll know that I'm upset.

"What's wrong?" Haji asks.

"Nothing," I say.

"If we hurry, we can make the 7:05 bus," Haji says.

Narrowing my eyes, I look at him quizzically. Haji's eyes widen.

"You forgot." He gives me a concerned smile. "We're meeting Dalia at Noodle House. You still want to go, right? She'll want to congratulate you in person for winning the award. Congratulations, by the way. Your picture is totally lit. Just like I said."

"Ummm…yeah, of course, I'm coming." Haji says something to me, but I'm busy plastering a fake smile on my face. "Hi, Dad. I'm thrilled you made it."

It's not that hard to pull that off because I'm glad he made it, although thrilled might be an overstatement. Jason being here, on the other hand, would be thrilling. If only…

"Congratulations, Allison," Dad says and embraces me. "I'm so proud of you."

My cheeks flush. "Thanks, Dad. Haji and I have to catch the bus. We're heading to Noodle House for dinner."

"Just wait until we tell your granddad. He's quite the photographer too, you know," Dad says, squeezing me even tighter.

"Don't you have to teach that evening class tonight?" I squirm in his arms.

"I do." Dad breaks the embrace. He glances at his watch. "Let me call you a car. You said Noodle House? In the University District?"

"That's okay, Dad. We're going to catch the bus," I say.

"It's dark out and raining." Dad takes out his phone and opens the vehicle hailing app. "A car will drop you at the front door."

I notice the glint of his wedding ring, and annoyance sparks through me. I don't know why he still wears it. She abandoned us nearly sixteen years ago after cursing me with her genetics. If it wasn't for her, people like Leslie wouldn't target me for how I look. For all we know, my mother is dead or back in China. I don't really care which.

Stifling my irritation, I glance at Haji, who nods his head in approval and gives me the thumbs-up.

"Okay. Sure, Daddy, we'll take a car this one time," I say.

"There. The car is on its way. It will pick you up in front of the school." Dad's expression turns serious. "Listen up, you two. There have been some assaults on the university campus and the surrounding area this week. Be careful."

"If someone assaults me, I'll bludgeon them with this." I heft the grand-prize plaque.

"Allison," Dad says, "I'm not joking. You could get hurt."

"I'm not joking either." I want to take a practice swing with the plaque, but the gym is too crowded.

"Don't worry, Mr. Lee. We'll look out for each other," Haji says.

Five minutes later, we're in the pleasantly warm backseat of a well-kept-up sedan. The driver is all business and seems to know his way around Seattle. The vehicle is a hybrid, making me feel a little better about not taking the bus. As a rule, I prefer public transportation. Dalia is one of the organizers for the local climate marches, so I'm super aware of human civilization's environmental impact. You know, like how the typical passenger car emits 4.6 metric tons of carbon dioxide per year. 4.6 tons! Multiply that number by 1.2 billion cars worldwide, and you begin to understand why the planet is warming.

"What's bothering you?" Haji says. "You've been uptight since coming out of the bathroom."

I sigh. "I don't want to talk about it."

"Come on, Allison. It's me, Haji. I'm in your corner."

"I said, I don't want to talk about it." Especially not in front of the driver.

"Fine, be that way."

In my peripheral vision, Haji's fingers dance over his phone's glowing screen.

"Do you have to do that?" I ask.

"Do what?" Haji says without looking up.

"Text Dalia."

"Who says I'm texting Dalia?"

Sighing, I stare out the window at the bright lights of the city. A motorcycle making a distinctive thump, thump, thump rolls by. In my pocket, my ancient flip phone buzzes. I fish it out and flip it open.

"How sweet, you did text Dalia."

"It's not my fault you won't talk to me," Haji says. "Now you'll have to talk to her."

I read the text twice, my lips curling into a smile. My dream boy is joining us for dinner.

A few minutes later, the car pulls up in front of the noodle joint. We thank the driver and pile out into the pouring rain. By the time we reach the restaurant's door, my hair feels like it's matted down. Haji pulls open the door to allow me inside. The place is crowded with college students armed with large spoons slurping soup from big bowls. The scent of cooking ramen from the kitchen is mouthwatering. I spot Dalia by her wicked neon-pink hair. She waves to us from a long wooden bench at an equally long wooden table. Standing on my tiptoes, I do a quick survey of the crowd and frown. Jason isn't here yet.

I follow Haji to the bench and sit down next to Dalia. Haji sits across from us.

"Congratulations, Allison," Dalia says, all smiles. Even in the dim light, her golden nose ring gleams. "Is that your award? Let me see."

I set my plaque on the table.

"That's so cool."

"Thanks," I say.

"I really should have skipped cross-country practice to come," Dalia says.

"No, no. It's okay." Dalia is training extra hard to make varsity this year.

"So," Dalia says and rotates her torso so she faces me. "Haji told me something is bothering you."

"Spill the tea," Haji says.

I shut my eyes, racking my brain for a viable excuse not to discuss this right now. I need time to process what happened. Opening my eyes, I spot Jason by the front door.

"Jason," I call and wave to him. I whisper to my friends. "I can't talk in front of him. Not about this."

Jason lopes over, dodging a waitress carrying a steaming bowl of ramen. With a broad smile, he greets us and sits down next to Haji. I try not to stare too longingly at Jason, but it's hard. Just being in his presence sets my heart thrumming like a plucked guitar string.

"Allison, can I see your award?" Jason asks.

I slide the plaque across the table to him, and our fingers brush together as he takes the award. My fingers erupt with electric sparks at the contact.

"Your photo is so dope. You deserve the grand prize," Jason says and passes the plaque back to me.

My hands become clammy, and I will myself to not blush.

"Should we order?" Dalia asks.

"I know what I'm ordering," Jason says.

Haji nods in agreement.

"Spicy ramen every time," I say.

"Oh, you like it hot and spicy," Jason says.

Dalia waves over a harried waitress to take our order. I ask for two bowls of spicy ramen, one to eat in and one to go.

"For Joe?" Haji asks after the waitress moves on.

"Yeah, he loves the ramen, and I want to talk to him about the photo contest," I say.

We talk about school until the waitress arriving with our food puts the conversation on pause. As we slurp ramen, Dalia guides the discussion to the upcoming homecoming dance. My knees clatter together in a frantic rhythm. Will Jason ask me to the dance, or should I ask him?

"Is everyone going?" Dalia asks.

"I'm attending as a reporter," Haji says between mouthfuls of soup.

I notice Haji staring at me. I meet his look and flash him a saucy smile. His gaze darts back to the soup bowl.

"I am," Jason says.

I swallow the spicy concoction in my mouth and choke. My hand goes to my chest as I cough on the gob of noodles lodged in my throat.

"Are you okay?" Dalia asks, voice shrill.

She raises her hand, ready to pound on my back. The boys jump up. I hold up a hand to keep everyone at bay. With a final heave that makes my chest throb, I manage to dislodge and swallow the noodles.

"I'm okay," I gasp. God, I'm such a klutz. Why did I ever think Jason would want to go to the dance with me?

The boys sit down, and Dalia lowers her hand.

"You're sure you're okay?" Dalia asks.

I nod and pick up my soup spoon. There is an awkward silence as we recover from me nearly choking to death and get back to eating.

"So, Jason, you have a date?" Dalia asks.

"I do." Jason sets his spoon in the bowl. "She asked me today."

"She asked you?" I ask.

I hold the oversized soup spoon in my hand like it's a club. Jason smiles, his gaze dropping to the table.

"I was going to ask someone else, but then she asked me. I couldn't say no."

"Just tell us who it is already," Dalia says.

"Leslie Chapman."

The spoon falls from my hand and plops into my bowl of half-eaten ramen. Soup splatters across the table. My eyes feel like they're bugging out of my head.

Leslie Chapman asked Jason to the dance?

He said yes?

Oh my God.

Blinking, I rub a hand across my brow. "Wow."

I look around the table, searching for a sign that what Jason said was my imagination. Dalia's face is ashen. Jason looks apologetic, maybe, I don't know. Haji continues slurping soup.

I stand, grabbing my jacket and plaque. "I think my to-go order is ready."

I rush to the front of the establishment, retrieve my order in a brown paper sack, and pay the cashier in cash. I turn to leave to find Haji by the door.

"Can I tag along?" he asks.

"I just want to be alone right now."

I push open the door, and cold air blasts my face. Rain pelts my coat, and a gust of howling wind blows back my hood. I pull my hood up and hold it in place. Cars whizz by on University Way, headlights highlighting the heavy rainfall.

My tears intermix with the rain while I wait for the light to change at the intersection of 42nd and Little Tahoma Avenue. Why am I crying? Over Jason? If he is dumb enough to date Leslie, he isn't worth my time or tears. Doesn't he realize she is a racist mean girl? Maybe that's too harsh. How could he know? I should've asked him out sooner.

I'm such an idiot.

The wind dies down. I release my hood and wipe the tears, not wanting Joe to see me crying. A big truck roars by just before the light changes, leaving the stench of diesel exhaust in its wake. I cross the intersection and scramble up the low retaining wall separating Tahoma University's grounds from the sidewalk. I march across the dark swath of wet grass interspersed with towering Douglas fir toward the lamplight in the distance.

Obscured by the surrounding shrubbery next to the base of a conifer is a blue tarp. I press my free hand against the brown bag, feeling the warmth radiating from the container of broth. Good. I'd hate for the soup to be cold.

A gust of wind pushes me sideways. From somewhere overhead comes a loud crack like the bone of some gargantuan creature snapping. A widowmaker thumps to the earth. Gasping, I nearly drop the soup and freeze in place. Overhead, the trees sway in the wind, branches creaking and groaning. I scamper toward the encampment.

About half a dozen tents surround the base of the

tall conifer. A wide man with hunched shoulders moves around the camp. I smile. It's Joe.

I'm about to call out to him when I smell a strange mixture of eucalyptus and menthol and sweat on the wind. It's the kind of odor I'd expect to roll off guys at a crowded dance club. I scan my surroundings for the source of the scent.

A figure stands behind me in the gloom.

"What are you doing?" I ask.

The stalker strides toward me, raising something about a foot long overhead. A club?

My muscles tense like springs under immense pressure. Dad warned me about attacks on campus. I back away, a scream rising up my throat. The club whirls through the air too fast to avoid.

Chapter 3

A steady beeping drags me into consciousness. My head is gripped by a pounding headache, and I'm stiff as a mummy. A groan escapes my dry lips.

"Allison, thank God! You're awake."

"Daddy." The word comes out as a croaked whisper that burns my dry throat.

"I'm right here, baby. I'm right here."

His warm hand takes mine. I'm with my dad. I try to open my eyes, but my head is locked in a tightening vise. The effort only makes my head hurt more.

"Allison, can you hear me?"

I don't recognize the voice. It's distant, fading, as muddled as my mind feels. I'm just so tired.

****

An oddly familiar beeping wakes me. I shift my cramped body. Ouch. Moving makes me feel like I'm slamming my head against a brick wall. *Ugh.* I'm lying down on a soft, cushy surface. Fabric covers me. Bedsheets? I'm in bed? How in the world did I end up in bed?

I draw in a deep breath, and my eyes flutter, never quite fully opening. A harsh scent hangs in the air like the antiseptic odor of a recently cleaned high school bathroom. Where the hell am I?

My eyes blink open, only something isn't right. I don't see anything.

17

Nothing.

At.

All.

"Help," I say, sounding like I'm speaking with a mouthful of toffee.

I try to stay calm, but my body is reacting. Pulse reverberating. Breathing rapid. I'm so hot underneath the sheet I want to tear it aside.

I raise my voice. "Help!"

Fear slams into my brain like a baseball bat. My eyes are wide open, but all I see is the most intense darkness I've ever known. Absolute black.

"Help me!"

"What? Allison, you're awake. Thank goodness. I was really worried when you woke up, then drifted off right away," Dad says groggily.

"Daddy, I can't see."

"What? Can't see?" Dad says. I can hear his shoes tapping against the floor. A hand touches my wrist, fingers cold yet comforting. "Don't worry. A nurse will be here any minute. I'm sure the doctor will be called."

"Why can't I see?"

He enfolds my wrist. "Allison, you were hit on the head. I'm so glad you're awake."

My stomach clenches into an icy knot. "Where am I?"

"You're in the hospital."

"Are you serious?"

I hear a door slide open and heavy footsteps against the floor.

"Thank goodness. It's the nurse," Dad says.

"Hello, Allison. My name is James, and I'm your—"

"I can't see!"

****

"Do you notice any light or shadows?" Dr. Clarissa Maywood asks.

"How many times do I have to answer that idiotic question?" I say through clenched teeth.

Dad massages the back of my hand. "Allison, don't be so waspish. Dr. Maywood is here to help you."

I groan. "I'm sorry that waking up blind in a strange bed after a two-week coma has put me in such a wonderful mood."

"I know it is frustrating, Allison. It is not unheard of to have vision problems after taking a blow to the head," Dr. Maywood says. Her voice is calm, and her words are clipped. "Now, can you answer my question?"

"I can't see anything."

Something about Dr. Maywood is annoying. My image of her is of a tall, beautiful blonde woman much like Leslie Chapman. I don't know why—maybe it's the click of the high heels against the linoleum?

"Is there anything you can do?" Dad asks.

"I am going to order some tests," Dr. Maywood says. "And we will go from there."

I listen to her walk away, feeling like I am drowning, my fingers slipping from the life preserver.

Dad pats the back of my hand. "Just hang in there, baby. Just hang in there."

I pull my hand away. "Just hang in there? I'm blind. I'll never be a photojournalist. Never. My life is ruined."

"I know it's hard, baby, but you need to try to stay positive. I think that's for the best."

Stay positive. Easy for him to say. He can see. Why can't I see? I'm still trying to put that together, but there are too many missing pieces.

"Dad, what happened? Dr. Maywood said I took a blow to the head, but I don't remember any of that."

Dad takes a deep breath. "You were attacked on the university grounds."

"I…I remember taking soup to Joe," I say. Did I give the soup to Joe? I try to remember, but that only makes my head hurt more.

"Someone hit you with something against the side of your head. Maybe a lead pipe or some kind of cudgel. The police aren't certain. You're lucky to be alive. If it wasn't for Joe…he heard your scream. He stopped the attack. Then he called the police, using your phone."

I try to recall the attack. I can't. My head feels like it's being used as a bongo drum.

"What's wrong? Your head?"

I nod.

"Try to clear your mind. The doctor said you might have severe headaches, especially if you spend too much time deep in thought."

He takes my hand again.

I squeeze his hand in return. "Thanks for being here, Dad."

"You'll get better," he says. "You'll get better."

I try to quiet my mind, but I want to remember what happened to me. I need to know why I'm broken.

I don't know how much time has passed when I hear the nurse's voice, James I think he said his name is.

"Allison. Mr. Lee. We're going to run some tests

now."

Casters roll across the linoleum.

"Can I stay?" Dad asks.

"Sure you can," James says. "We just need to slide in next to Allison."

"Dad, please don't go," I say.

"Don't worry, baby. I'm not going anywhere."

Chapter 4

I lie on the hospital bed with my eyes open. I'm on my back, so I'm probably staring at the ceiling, but I can't be sure. I still can't see a thing, and every ounce of energy has been squeezed out of me by one and a half days of tests. One and a half. I must have been wheeled through miles of hospital corridors from one test to another. Techs visited my room to attach electrodes to my head. No one tells me anything since the tests must be interpreted by a doctor. My life is one big cliffhanger.

Dad is in the room with me, pacing judging by the footsteps against the floor. I'm supposed to learn the test results soon, so I'll either be overjoyed or devastated.

Now I know how a death row inmate feels. You pine for the stay of execution but expect the lethal injection. That's what permanently losing my eyesight is to me, an immediate, irrevocable death sentence. How can I pursue my dream of becoming a photojournalist without sight? It's so depressing I want to throw up the salad I ate for lunch.

The door slides open, and high heels click against the floor.

"Allison. Mr. Lee," Dr. Maywood says. "Good afternoon."

I swipe the air with a hand. "Daddy."

His warm hand takes mine. "I'm right here, baby. Everything is going to be okay."

The tremor in his voice tells me he is just as afraid as I am.

"You are looking better, Allison," Dr. Maywood says. The clicks of her high heels intermix with the beeps of machinery. Someone leans against the bed. "Any change in your eyesight?"

"No."

"Do you see light and shadow?"

I sigh. "I don't see anything. Just...just indecipherable blackness."

The weight eases off the bed.

"Do you have the test results?" Dad asks.

"I do," Dr. Maywood says. She pauses.

"Am I permanently blind?" I clench Dad's hand like it's the only thing preventing me from plunging down a bottomless chasm.

"It is premature to jump to that conclusion," Dr. Maywood says as clinical as a computer. "All the tests are inconclusive."

"Inconclusive? I need my vision back."

Dad rubs the back of my hand with his thumb.

"Allison," Dr. Maywood says. "We have no reason to believe your vision loss is permanent. For now, I suggest you stay in the hospital for observation for a few days or until your vision returns. If we do not see any change in your condition for the better, I will refer you to specialists for more tests."

"Could it be neuropathy of the optic nerve?" Dad asks.

"I have visually examined the nerve. It does not appear swollen. The MRI is inconclusive."

"You don't know what's wrong with me." I feel like a whirlpool is sucking me down a drain. I'll never again photograph sporting events for the *Cascadia Weekly*. God.

"Do you have any questions?" Dr. Maywood asks.

Neither of us have questions, and the doctor leaves. I fight back tears. It's one thing to anticipate execution. It's entirely more terrible to be strapped into the electric chair and have all the hope you've clung to vaporized.

Dad releases my hand. "I have an idea. I have to go. I'll see you tonight."

"Dad, what is it?"

"I'll tell you tonight."

I hear the door slide open.

"Mr. Lee." It's Petra, one of my nurses. "Just a moment."

The nurse and Dad speak in hushed voices. Soon two more voices that I don't recognize join the conversation. I try with only partial success to stifle my annoyance at being left out.

"Allison," Dad says.

"What is it?"

"The police are here to talk to you. About the attack. They just want to ask you a few questions."

"The police? Seriously?" My voice quavers. "I don't remember anything."

Dad takes my hand. "It's okay, baby. Just try to answer their questions. They're here to help."

The cops introduce themselves as Detective Nora Wolf and Detective Hal Caine. They apologize for disturbing me and claim they have every intention of tracking down my attacker.

"You don't have any idea who attacked you?"

Detective Nora asks.

"No."

"You didn't notice anyone following you? You don't have any memory of your attacker?" Detective Hal asks.

"I don't remember anything after leaving Noodle House," I say.

The detectives ask a few more questions, then wrap up the interview.

"Your father has my card," Detective Nora says. "Give us a call if you remember anything."

"Good luck with your recovery," Detective Hal says, and the detectives leave.

Dad squeezes my hand. "You did a good job."

"I didn't tell them anything."

"That's not your fault. You did your best."

Dad is about ready to leave, but I insist that he text Dalia to come visit me.

"Are you sure? You need to rest," Dad says.

"Dalia and Haji will distract me. All I do is obsess over my eyesight. Daddy, please."

Dad sighs. "Okay. But I'm going to check with the nurses first. Be back in a sec."

Dad returns a few minutes later with positive news.

"Thanks, Dad." I smile in anticipation of hearing the voices of my squad.

"I just texted Dalia," Dad says. "I need to go. I'll be back this evening."

"Can't you stay until my friends arrive?"

"I have an idea that might help you. Maybe. I need to speak to some people."

"What's this great idea? Tell me."

"It's a total longshot, Allison. If it's not a trip down

the rabbit hole, I'll tell you all about it tonight. Just don't get your hopes up. For now, get some rest before your friends show up."

"Fine." I cross my arms over my chest, feeling tension from the various cords and tubes hooked up to me.

We say our goodbyes, and Dad leaves. Why can't he just tell me about his great idea? Doesn't he realize I'm grasping at any lifeline no matter how tenuous?

I search the bed for the touchscreen music player Dad gave me the other day. He loaded *Jane Eyre* onto the device so I won't fall behind in school. In English, at least. I listened to the book last night and discovered the narrator's voice is a wonderful soporific.

My fingers brush against the cool glass front of the device. I find the wire for the earbuds and fumble the buds into my ears. Dad disabled the passcode, so opening up the device is as easy as finding the home button below the touchscreen. The audiobook app is right above the home button. I move my thumb up over the screen and tap it once. I wait a couple seconds, chewing on my lower lip. I tap the screen again.

"Yes!" I say as the voice actor starts reading Charlotte Brontë's masterwork. Easy peasy lemon squeezy.

I set the device down next to my hip. My eyelids droop shut as a description of Thornfield Hall escorts me to slumberland.

"Allison." The voice of James intermixes with the book's narrator. "Allison, are you awake?"

My eyes open, and I tear the earbuds out. "Yes. Wide awake."

"You have guests. Is that okay?"

"Definitely. Send them in."

"Allison," Dalia says. "I'm here with Haji. I was so excited when I got your dad's text."

"Hi, Allison," Haji says. Casters roll across the linoleum. "We're really sorry about what happened to you. We would have come sooner——"

"But you weren't allowed visitors," Dalia says.

It's so awesome to hear their voices. It reminds me that I'm not alone. My squad is pulling for me.

"Is it true? You're blind?" Haji asks.

I swallow. "Yes."

"Damn," Haji says under his breath.

"That is so horrible," Dalia says and takes my hand. "We're so sorry."

"What happened? We heard you were attacked," Haji says.

I shrug. "I guess. I don't remember, honestly."

"Who would've attacked you?" Dalia asks.

"I have no idea. I don't think the police do either. They were just here earlier. Asking me questions I can't answer."

"There have been lots of attacks around Tahoma University lately," Haji says.

"Can one of you help me with this? I'm listening to *Jane Eyre*." I fumble with the music player. I don't like being reminded I don't remember what happened to me. It's creepy. Anything could've happened. Anything.

"Sure," Dalia says and pauses the audiobook. "What's your prognosis?"

I catch them up on my time in the hospital.

"My dad has an idea that might help me see again. I think," I say.

"Seriously? That's so great. What is it?" Dalia asks.

"Yeah, what?" Haji says.

"I…I don't know." God, that sounds lame.

A very uncomfortable silence follows. I can imagine my friends staring at me with pity. I don't want their pity. I want to see again.

Haji saves us all by deftly changing the subject. "The climate march was last Friday. It was dope. Dalia did a great job helping to organize it."

"Oh, I missed that. I'm so sorry I didn't make it. I know you worked really hard to make the march happen," I say.

"You upset her," Dalia says.

"What?" Haji asks.

"She's crying, Haji. Geez. It's okay, Allison. You need to concentrate on healing. Don't worry about us."

"It's not his fault," I say, wiping the tears. "I'm afraid I'll never take photos again. I wanted to photograph the march."

They fill me in on what's been happening at school, which inevitably leads to talk about the Homecoming Dance. Dalia and Haji attended without dates with a group of friends. Sounds like they had a fantastic time. The conversation reminds me that Leslie asked Jason to the dance.

"Did either of you see Jason?" I ask, trying not to sound jealous.

"Yeah, he and Leslie were dancing all night long. I think they really hit it off," Haji says.

My face flushes.

"Sorry," Dalia says and quickly adds, "He's a nice guy. He'll probably figure out she's mean and dump her."

"You mean Allison has a thing for…oh," Haji says.

Thinking about Leslie reminds me of her ugly behavior in the girl's locker room and how vulnerable I felt. Now, being blind, I'm even more vulnerable. If I don't have the bravery to tell my friends what she did, the shame will crush me. After a deep breath, I tell them what happened in the locker room.

"Wow," Haji says. "That's not cool. I've heard my share of racist BS, and that's not cool. You shouldn't have to deal with that."

"That bitch," Dalia says. "She's lucky I wasn't there. I would've socked her in the nose."

My squad comforts me. Dalia gives me an embrace made awkward by the medical equipment. They stay with me until my dad shows up with a salad for me.

"I'm going to tell him what she did to you. He needs to know," Dalia whispers to me before she leaves.

I nod. "I know."

Dad helps me eat a salad from the cafeteria. It's sweet of him and embarrassing at the same time. The peppery salad dressing is delectable on the spring mix. Grape tomatoes explode in my mouth like little flavor bombs. He asks about my friends, but I'm not much of a conversationalist. I'm distracted with thoughts about Jason.

I scour my memories of the time we'd spent together over the years. Had he ever said anything overtly racist? I don't think so. One time last summer he tagged along with my squad while we shopped at Pike Place Market. He made a derogatory remark about a homeless man. I ripped Jason a new one over that, and he had apologized profusely, even buying the homeless man a sandwich. The gesture had impressed me at the time, but now I fear he is like Leslie deep down inside.

In the back of my mind, I wonder about earlier in the afternoon when Dad said he had an idea to help me. What in the world was he referring to?

"Are you thirsty?" Dad says. "I have some orange juice."

"Sure," I say and purse my lips.

There is a crack of a safety cap opening, and I feel the cool plastic of a juice bottle press against my lips. I let the orange juice fill my mouth. Some dribbles down my chin as the bottle leaves my lips.

"Sorry, Allison," Dad says. "I got carried away."

I hold a finger to my lips for silence. I slosh the citrusy fluid around my mouth to savor the sweetness a little longer. Finally, I swallow the juice.

"You can clean me up now," I say.

He wipes away the liquid with a napkin.

"So did you find anything out? That might help me?"

Dad sighs. "I don't want you to get your hopes up."

"You've already raised my hopes. Now you're not going to tell me anything?"

"You're right," he says and draws a deep breath. "I called in a favor with Dr. Woolworth. She's coming by tomorrow morning to examine you and maybe order some tests. She might—emphasis on might—be able to help. Her work is experimental. Some of it is not cleared for use on people." He pauses, sighs twice, then continues. "We'll see. If nothing else, she can provide a second opinion on your condition."

"Dr. Woolworth can make me see again? That's awesome!"

"I didn't say that, Allison. Please, please, don't get carried away. I don't know if she can help you or not. Hey, do you want to listen to the Sounders game? We can listen to it on the radio app on my phone."

"You bet." How can I say no? Some of my best memories are of screaming my lungs out next to him at the stadium.

He tunes in the game, but I'm hardly listening. I'm daydreaming about how much better it will be to watch soccer live after Dr. Woolworth restores my eyesight.

Chapter 5

I summon a nurse to help me to the bathroom. I had drunk a lot of orange juice. I don't need help taking care of my business, but someone needs to unhook me from the IVs and various monitoring apparatuses and hook me back up when I'm done.

After the nurse reattaches the equipment to me, I shift on the mattress trying to get comfortable. My head is so woozy after the trek to the bathroom I can't follow the play-by-play of the game.

"Goal!" the announcer shouts followed by thunderous applause.

"We won. We won," Dad says. "Allison? What's wrong?" He kills the radio. "Your head?"

"I'm just a little light-headed," I say.

"Gosh. Sorry about that. I was too wrapped up in the game. You need some rest."

Dad helps me prepare to listen to *Jane Eyre*. He sets the automatic timer to stop the narration after thirty minutes. I put the earbuds in my ears, and he kisses me on the forehead, then leaves to go take care of stuff at home while I rest. The voice actor whisks me to sleep in under five minutes.

Something startles me awake. I have a pounding headache, so I surmise I haven't been asleep for long. The only sounds are the buzz of machinery and the distant drone of forced air. I sense a presence in the room with me, something predatory and kindred.

"Hello?" I say and wince at how tremulous my voice sounds.

No response. Not even the scuff of a shoe against the linoleum.

The other presence reaches out to me, like an astral hand that I sense via some kind of sixth sense. It brushes against me with an electric touch and penetrates my skin. I gasp. The presence spreads through me like quicksilver. Sweat bursts from my pores and runs down my face. I'm feverishly hot and shivering. The presence brushes up against something hidden in the recesses of my being. A jolt of anger and physical prowess shoots through me, then dissipates as quickly as it came.

"Leave me alone." I paw at the bedding for the call button, but I can't find it.

"Help!" I scream. "Help!"

"Daughter," a voice whispers into my ear so ephemerally I don't know if the word is real or imagined.

The door to my room slides open, then shut, and the presence fades. I stop trembling, and I'm not burning up anymore. Goose bumps form on my clammy skin, and I shiver. My hospital gown and bedsheets are damp from sweat.

I feel disgusted and violated and afraid. I call for help again, but no one comes. I sit up in bed, feeling cables and tubes pulling at my arm and a discombobulating rush of vertigo. I search the bedding and tangle of cords for the wire leading to the call button. I find the overlarge button dangling from thick cords and jam it with my thumb.

I sit on the bed, holding the call button in a

quivering hand. Who had been in the room, and what had the stranger done to me? Why the hell did the stranger call me daughter? My mother disappeared years ago. Why would she return now? It's not like she has any way of knowing I'm in the hospital. Unless she keeps tabs on me in secret, but that's just a girlish fantasy. She's gone. She abandoned me. Whatever I just experienced must be some kind of dream or nightmare, an aftereffect of being bludgeoned with a club.

After several minutes, the door slides open, and I hear the jovial voice of James. "You call?"

I let out a breath. Part of me wants to cry and tell him that something otherworldly happened to me and that I am afraid. But I don't. He sounds unconcerned, like someone going about his business as usual. If I say anything, he will believe that I suffered a nightmare or am batshit crazy.

"I need to use the bathroom." I lift my arm with all the protuberances. "Unhook me?"

****

I'm exhausted and ravenous the next morning. I had a crap sleep, and for some reason, I'm craving meat. If I don't eat meat, I'm going to die of starvation. That's how I feel. Not normal. I gave up meat a year ago. Meat production produces tons of methane and nitrous oxide, two greenhouse gases. I want to be part of the climate solution. Net zero carbon. But my craving is crazy intense. Just the thought of meat makes me salivate. Maybe I'm still growing? Being sixteen, I'd given up on adding a couple of inches in height months ago. When an orderly stops by to take my breakfast order, I ask for fried eggs and every side of meat available.

The orderly returns with my food, which ends up smelling more appetizing than it tastes. The eggs are oversalted, the bacon slathered in enough grease to clog the arteries of an entire football team, and the sausage is of the institutional variety. Petra stops by a little while later to check in on me and asks if I need help eating. I decline the offer of help since I've already begun the laborious task of feeding myself.

"You're sure you don't want help?" Petra asks.

I imagine a middle-aged woman in blue scrubs with her arms crossed before her chest and an eyebrow arched to show incredulity. Her hair, dark brown with a few errant strands of gray, is up in a bun or maybe a beehive. Yeah, Petra is a woman with a beehive hairdo.

"I'm good. I need to learn how to do this. It could be months before my vision is back."

"I admire your moxie, Allison," Petra says. "I also can't stand the egg yolk running down your chin. Let me clean it up, and I will leave you to it."

I swallow the bacon I'm chewing. "Okay."

She gently cleans my chin with a napkin. "There. All better."

Petra is good to her word and leaves me in peace. I set down my fork on the plate and reach a hand for my cup of coffee. I'm a coffee-a-day kind of girl as in a pot of coffee. I love my brew, so I've been avoiding the hospital java for fear of disappointment. But after my visitation last night, or whatever it was, I'm desperate for caffeine. My fingers brush up against a paper cup, warming from the radiant heat. At least the drink is hot. The kitchen staff got that right. I grab the cup and bring it toward my lips. I blow across the liquid and feel the hot steam against my cheeks.

The door to the room slides open.

"Don't drink that, Allison," Dad calls.

"I know, but I didn't sleep well."

I hear Dad walk across the room.

"Hi, Allison."

I breathe in sharply. "Joe! You came to see me."

"I brought you some brew from that joint you like. The Obsidian Roast," Joe says. His voice is a melodious baritone. In a different life, Joe might be a DJ for a radio station that plays jazz.

"Joe, you shouldn't have."

"I'll take that," Dad says and removes the paper cup from my hand.

The next thing I know, I'm breathing in the rich aroma from a sixteen-ounce cup of dark roast from The Obsidian Roast. The coffee tastes strong and dark, just the way I love it.

The caffeine perks me up, and I tell Joe how my portrait of him won the grand prize at the photojournalism contest.

"My old face," he says. "Man, you really must be the world's best photographer, because I know I ain't winning no beauty contests."

He chuckles, and I laugh. My dad even joins in the laughter. My mirth, at least, is fleeting.

"Joe, what happened? When I was attacked?" I ask and feel proud that I keep my voice steady.

Silence long enough to be uncomfortable follows my question.

"Maybe you don't want to relive that right now," Dad says.

"Relive what? I don't remember anything. Just tell

me. I need to know. Without knowing, I'll never be able to understand why this happened to me. Why I can't see either of you even though you're right in front of me."

"Okay. I'll tell you." Joe clears his throat. "I heard a scream. I knew it was you and came running. I saw a man standing over you with some kind of club. Maybe a lead pipe. I started raising hell. Hollering all kinds of nonsense that I haven't said since Afghanistan. Must've scared him. He took off like he had a rocket up his ass. I wanted to chase him down and put the hurt on him, but he was way too fast. Besides, I saw you crumpled on the ground, unconscious. I figured you had a phone in your pocket, so I pulled it out and dialed 911. The medics and police arrived a few minutes later."

I shake my head. Listening to the tale is like watching a bad horror movie. The action happens to someone else, and I don't feel any fear. All my dread is reserved for the creepy presence that visited me last night. That I remember in vivid detail. I consider telling them about it, but I don't. It must have been a silly nightmare.

"The last thing I remember is leaving Noodle House with spicy ramen to go," I say.

"Maybe not remembering is for the best," Dad says.

"I wish I can forget what happened in Afghanistan," Joe says.

"Maybe," I say, knowing that I want to remember.

A little while later Joe makes an excuse to leave. I beg him to stay longer, but Dad reminds me Dr. Woolworth will be here soon. I exchange goodbyes with Joe and tell him not to be shy about visiting again.

Dad and I wait for Dr. Woolworth together.

"Dad?"

"Yes?"

"You don't stay in contact with that woman, my mother, do you?"

"No. Why do you ask?"

"Just curious is all."

Chapter 6

Dad holds my hand as Dr. Woolworth gives us the rundown. Dr. Maywood is in the room too, but so far remains silent.

"I reviewed your MRI," Dr. Woolworth says. "There are indications of optic nerve degeneration. Regretfully, this means your blindness is likely permanent."

"No," I say and let out a sob. Dad tightens his grip on my hand.

"Can anything be done?" Dad asks.

"A treatment exists that might restore Allison's eyesight," Dr. Woolworth says. "I've been working on it for the past five years at the university. It's experimental and is just entering the clinical trial phase. Allison, if you, with your father's permission, agree to undergo the treatment, you will be the first patient. There is no guarantee of success."

"That point is worth reiterating," Dr. Maywood says, her tone as pedantic as an irate high school principal. "The proposed treatment was only approved for clinical trials three weeks ago. It is meant to treat anophthalmia and severe ocular trauma. You, Allison, do not suffer from either condition."

If I could see, I would glare at Dr. Maywood. She is snatching away my one lifeline.

"Anophthalmia?" I say, my tongue twisting as I

mispronounce the strange word.

"Absence of the eye," Dr. Woolworth says. "A birth defect."

"Oh." I wince at the thought of never having been able to see. Taking pictures while walking the streets and green spaces of Seattle has been an integral part of my life since Dad bought me my first camera, a used digital rangefinder, when I was ten. I took pictures of everything, even the ubiquitous seagull droppings along the waterfront. Within a year, I had worn out the camera's shutter.

"My colleagues and I believe the MRI is inconclusive," Dr. Maywood says. "It does not show nerve degeneration."

"I can't see. I want to see again."

"Rest. Be patient," Dr. Maywood says. "In all likelihood, your eyesight will return."

"Will it or won't it?"

"There are no guarantees," Dr. Maywood says. "But undergoing radical surgery will not restore your eyesight."

The words radical surgery capture my attention. Radical isn't a word I like in conjunction with anything involving a scalpel and me.

"It's true. Your eyesight might return on its own," Dr. Woolworth says. "Don't feel like I'm pressuring you to undergo treatment."

"What does the treatment plan entail?" Dad asks.

"I want to know about this radical surgery," I say.

"I can walk you through the treatment plan step-by-step so you know exactly what you're agreeing to," Dr. Woolworth says. "Would you like that?"

Without hesitation, I say, "Definitely."

"Okay," Dad says. "That way we can decide if the treatment is right for Allison."

"Jane," Dr. Maywood says. "This is wrong, and you know it."

"It's her best chance at having her eyesight restored," Dr. Woolworth says.

"You are allowing your desire for prestige to cloud your judgment," Dr. Maywood says, and her high heels click and clack against the floor. The door slides open.

"That's not true," Dr. Woolworth says. "It's Allison's and Raymond's choice. Not your choice and not mine."

"If you insist on going through with this, I will stop you," Dr. Maywood says, and the door slides shut.

I'm still annoyed that Dr. Maywood is so negative, but the vehemence of her opposition gives me pause. Even the idea of a minor, run-of-the-mill procedure gives me the heebie-jeebies.

"Why is Dr. Maywood opposed to the treatment?" I ask.

"Yes, why?" Dad says. "I didn't realize there is so much resistance to your work."

Dr. Woolworth sighs, and casters roll across the floor. "It's because the surgery is radical. Dr. Maywood is right about that. It involves removing your eyes."

My stomach clenches, and I tighten my hold on Dad's hand. "Remove my eyes? How is that going to restore my eyesight?"

"Allow me to explain," Dr. Woolworth says. "Removal of the oculus uterque is the first step. That is followed by installation of the prosthetic eyes. The prosthetics will function like regular human eyes."

"Prosthetics?" I ask.

"Yes. This technique has been done on mice with great success," Dr. Woolworth says. "Not only do the mice have their eyesight restored, their sight is better than before."

"Mice? That doesn't fill me with optimism," I say.

"It shouldn't," Dr. Woolworth says. "At the end of the process, you could be left blind with two worthless prosthetics."

I'm tempted to back out. I don't want to suffer through surgery for nothing.

"What do you think, Allison?" Dad says. "Do you want to hear more?"

I draw a deep, cleansing breath. I want to see again. I want that more than I've ever wanted anything in my life.

"I want to hear more," I say.

Dr. Woolworth launches into a detailed explanation of the procedure. First, my oculus dexter will be surgically removed. Who knew the medical community had such a lit name for the right eye? Once my eye is removed, the damaged portion of my optical nerve will be carefully snipped away and replaced with an ultrafine filament that connects to my nerve and the prosthetic. I will be injected with the swarm of nanobots that will complete the connection of the filament to my nerve and speed the healing process. After a period of recovery that lasts a few days, I will be fitted with the prosthetic oculus. Once it is proven that I can see, I'll be scheduled to have my oculus sinister replaced. Oculus sinister. Wicked.

"After surgery, you'll be closely monitored. Your prosthetics might have to be adjusted for optimal performance. There will certainly be a period of orienting yourself to the prosthetics. I have no idea how long that will take. Perhaps several months," Dr. Woolworth says.

"Several months," I say. What would I be doing? Running into walls? If the surgeries were successful. If. If. If. So many unknowns. "What's the chance of success?"

"In the laboratory with mice, we achieved a success rate of sixty-five percent. That's from total blindness to eyesight fully restored to normal levels or better. Another twenty percent only had partial restoration of their eyesight. This means that sight was only restored in one eye or the restored vision was less than optimal in one or both orbs. Fifteen percent were total failures. That success rate won't necessarily translate to clinical trials. Most experimental surgeries are never approved for use on the general population."

"Would you undergo this surgery?" I ask. "Would you let your child undergo it?"

"Yes, but I wouldn't sleep at night."

"What do you think, Dad?"

"Can we have time to think about it?" Dad asks.

"Of course," Dr. Woolworth says. "Please make the decision soon. The nanobot treatment will halt the nerve degeneration. The more nerve saved, the higher the chance of success."

"I want the treatment," I say.

"Are you sure?" Dad asks.

"If I'm having surgery, I want the greatest chance for success. I need to see again."

"Well, there's lots of paperwork to fill out," Dr. Woolworth says. "You should know, due to the nature of the surgery, there may be a few more hoops to jump through. A medical ethicist will likely visit you to discuss the operation."

Dad and I ask a few questions about the medical ethicist. Dr. Woolworth assures us the ethicist will just make sure we both know what I'm getting myself into by talking us through the procedure.

"Dr. Woolworth, am I making the right choice?" I ask.

"Yes. Yes, you are."

"You're certain?"

"I don't deal in certainties, Allison, only probable outcomes. I believe the treatment plan is the only avenue with a high probability to restore your eyesight. Otherwise, I wouldn't be here."

I nod, wishing I could see her expression and body language. Being blind makes talking face-to-face as impersonal as speaking over the phone or messaging.

Dr. Woolworth takes her leave, and soon a hospital official shows up with the paperwork. The official, a woman named Pam with a high little-girl voice, launches into an explanation of the various forms. Without being able to see, I can't follow the conversation. Thank goodness Dad is here.

When Pam leaves, I'm ready to fall asleep. I have a headache, and making the decision to opt for surgery has left me emotionally drained. I tell Dad to fill out the paperwork by himself while I sleep.

"You're sure? This is your life," he says, his voice sharp and insistent.

"I've made my decision. I'm not going to change my mind."

Dad wakes me up when the bioethicist drops by in the afternoon. My stomach growls while Dr. Jordan

Ellison walks us through the procedure. He speaks in a practiced tone of faux concern that makes me grind my teeth.

"I'm familiar with the treatment plan," I say, interrupting Dr. Ellison. "Dr. Woolworth already told me all about it."

"Nevertheless, now we have to discuss it. Thoroughly," Dr. Ellison says and picks back up in his spiel with hardly missing a beat.

His droning monotone is about as engaging as a grass-growing competition. I start yawning.

Dr. Ellison pauses his speech. When he speaks again, his voice is intense. "You understand your eyes will be removed? It's a big decision."

I want to scream that I've made my decision and my father supports it and that I'm sixteen, practically an adult, and there is nothing Dr. Ellison or anyone else can say that will change my mind. "Of course, I understand. I want the procedure. I want to see again."

Dr. Ellison finishes the interview with a few more questions and asks me to sign some paperwork. Dad helps me sign. Finally, the bioethicist excuses himself, and it's just Dad and me again. I'm starving, but I'm too upset to eat. Dad insists on grabbing me something from the cafeteria anyway.

"Just a salad. Something with meat," I say.

"Back on meat? I thought I saw some sausage on your breakfast plate. That's great," Dad says.

"I have this craving. I don't know why."

Dad returns with a Caesar salad. I poke at it with a fork and eventually choke down a few bites with his assistance. Dad plays public radio on his phone. The stories about cataclysmic climate change and endless gun violence and political deadlock aren't what I want to listen to right now. At my insistence, he tunes in the local classical station. Soon I zone out to the music of Mozart and Mendelssohn and other long-dead fellows.

It's dinner time when Dr. Woolworth makes an appearance. I'm finishing my salad from earlier in the day, and Dad is eating a slice of pizza.

"Good news," Dr. Woolworth says. "Your surgery is scheduled in two days."

"Wow. That's great." I set down my fork, my appetite on vacation.

"That's it? No delays?" Dad says. "Dr. Maywood didn't gum things up?"

"Dr. Maywood made her concerns known, but Dr. Ellison is satisfied you both understand the risks of undergoing an experimental procedure and greenlighted the surgery," Dr. Woolworth says. "There is nothing Dr. Maywood can do to prevent the operation from moving forward."

I barely sleep over the next two days. Anxiety gnaws at me like an insatiable rat. Dad is as restless as I am. He tries to make small talk and read to me and get me to listen to the radio, but I'm unable to relax.

They come for me in the wee hours of the morning since the surgery is at six a.m. Just before orderlies wheel me out of the room, Dad kisses me on the forehead. His BO is as skanky as a teenage boy's, but I manage to smile instead of grimacing.

"I'll talk to you in a few hours," he says. "I love you."

"I love you too."

When I'm wheeled into the operating room, my mind churns over the possible bad outcomes. What if I wake up in the middle of the surgery? Will I feel Dr. Woolworth pluck my eyeball from my head? What if the surgery is a total failure and I'm left blind for the rest of my life?

"Allison," Dr. Woolworth says and squeezes my shoulder. "We're going start in a few minutes. Try to stay relaxed. You're doing great."

"Will I see again?" I ask, remembering doing photography and seeing my friends and enjoying all the wondrous colors of everyday life.

"We have a great chance of success, Allison," Dr. Woolworth says. "I need to step away for some final prep."

The disembodied voices of the surgical staff hover above me, and I smell their sweat right up until a mask is fitted over my face, and the anesthesiologist tells me to breathe in deeply.

Chapter 7

I wake up groggy.
I can't see.
Why can't I see?
"Allison, are you awake?"
I don't recognize the voice.
"What happened?"
I feel and sound like my mouth is full of mush. I try to turn toward the voice, but I move like I'm encased in jelly.
"You just had surgery. You're in the recovery room. Your vitals look good. Oh, Dr. Medina is here."
Machinery buzzes, and the smell of antiseptic is thick and strong. Dr. Medina, the anesthesiologist. The surgery. The first surgery of…I don't remember. Two? Three?
"How do you feel, Allison?" Dr. Medina asks. I recognize her polished, professional tone with a slight accent that I can't place.
"Loopy."
"What was that?"
"I feel like crap."
"I'm sorry to hear that. You should start feeling better as the anesthetic wears off," Dr. Medina says and rattles off some medical jargon that's obviously not meant for me to understand. "Dr. Woolworth will be in to see you soon."

"I want to talk to my dad."

"After Dr. Woolworth sees you," Dr. Medina says, and a hand gently squeezes my forearm. "It won't be long."

Dr. Medina leaves, and the nurse tells me to rest while I wait on Dr. Woolworth. Rest. Yeah, right. I only want to know one thing, and I want to know it right now. When will I see again?

My head starts to itch. I'm becoming progressively more aware of something wrapped around my head. A bandage? I ask a nurse when she drops by to check on me.

"Yes, there is a bandage around the surgical area."

Well, this bandage must've been devised by a demon from the ninth circle of hell. My skin beneath the bandage itches like I have hundreds of mosquito bites, and if I turn my head, the material abrades me.

When Dr. Woolworth deigns to show up, she runs through some niceties while checking my charts or something.

"Am I going to see again or not?" I interrupt her.

"I sincerely hope so, Allison," Dr. Woolworth says. "So far, the operation is a success. Right now, you need to concentrate on recovering."

"How long will that take?"

"It's hard to say. The injection of nanobots will speed your recovery. I don't know by how much. Be prepared for up to two weeks."

Great. A fortnight. "What about this bandage? It really itches."

"No, it's too soon to remove it," Dr. Woolworth says. "I'm sorry it's bothering you, but the itching is a good sign. It means the nanobots are accelerating the healing process."

My lips perk up into a smile. "The nanobots are working? That is totally lit!"

"So far that seems to be the case. We'll have a better idea in a couple days."

Not long after Dr. Woolworth leaves, I'm wheeled back to my room. A few minutes later, Dad shows up. I smell coffee on him and ask about it.

"Nothing you'd like," Dad says. "Cafeteria coffee. Hot but weak."

I take a deep breath. "Smells great, though."

"You want some?"

"Nah, need to sleep." I'm still woozy, and worse, I swear a T-rex has its jaws locked around my head and is in the process of detaching it from my shoulders.

I shift in bed and even try counting sheep to relax, but the T-rex is about to make my skull burst like a melon. Soon I'm moaning instead of sleeping.

"What's wrong?" Dad asks.

"My head," I groan.

"Call the nurse. Time for pain meds."

I hit the call button, and a few minutes later, Petra shows up. I tell her my issue.

"Too soon. You still need to wait for another hour."

"I'm dying here."

"What's your level of pain on a scale of one to ten? One being minor irritation and ten being you must be hospitalized due to the pain."

"Ten, obviously. I'm hospitalized."

"Listen to the comedian." Petra laughs mirthlessly. "I'll page Dr. Woolworth."

Maybe Petra does page Dr. Woolworth right away,

but I have to wait for the longest, most pain-filled time of my life before she shows up. She listens as I explain how a long-dead carnivore has my head in its jaws. She doses me with a painkiller via an IV drip, and boy is it a good one. The dinosaur is still killing me, but I don't care anymore.

****

I slip into sleep. When I wake, Dad provides me a salad with chunks of chicken since my meat craving is as strong as ever, and orange juice. After I eat, we talk for a few minutes and listen to the radio until I fall back asleep. I don't know how long I slept when I wake up in utter misery.

I stir restlessly, wanting nothing more than to rip the bandage from my head to tear at the hundreds, no thousands, of mosquito bites that I swear are hidden underneath it. I beg the nurses for more meds. James and Petra are relentless.

"No."

"You're being weaned off the medication."

"Sorry. Doctor's orders."

I stew, unable to get comfortable no matter how I turn my head. Desperate to escape the pain and itchy discomfort, I try to think about something, anything that might take my mind off my immediate agony for a few minutes. My thoughts turn to Jason. Did that dolt dump Leslie?

"Dad, can you text Dalia? Maybe talking to my friends will take my mind off, you know, the T-rex."

"Are you sure that's a good idea? I think you need to rest. You've been...waspish of late," Dad says.

Waspish. Dad's diplomatic way of saying that I've been a bitch. It's true. Every time he's tried to distract me from my throbbing head, I've thrown shade.

His phone starts playing "Ode to Joy," his ring tone. Despite my general bad mood, I smile. It's a fleeting moment because doing so makes the bandage abrade my skin. God. He's right. I'm too waspish to interact with my friends right now.

"Hi, Mom. Dad. Yes, I'm here with Allison. She's awake. I'll put you on speaker." Dad lowers the phone and whispers to me. "Last time they called, you were asleep. Try to be polite. They're worried about you."

I'm a bit insulted. I always treat my grandparents with the utmost respect. He turns on the speaker, and I talk with them for several minutes. They're worried out of their minds and want to hear my voice. I start yawning, and Dad steps outside to continue the conversation. Before he returns, I'm falling asleep.

****

I'm eating oatmeal for breakfast that tastes overly sweet and possesses a chalky texture, like instant oatmeal from a packet. I'm getting pretty good at eating blind. I estimate eight times out of ten, I maneuver the spoon from the bowl to my mouth without any spillage. With a napkin in my offhand, I can wipe up the oatmeal running down my chin when I have a mishap. Enjoying the little wins keeps me sane.

It's the third day since my surgery. The pain is getting better, but it's still there, a constant throbbing. Dad is with me but has mentioned twice already that he should head in to the office to check in. Honestly, he's probably right. We've been in each other's company far too much lately, and I'm not a joy to be around.

I'm scraping the oatmeal from the bottom of the bowl when Dr. Woolworth shows up.

"How long until the bandage comes off?" I demand without preamble.

"Today. This morning, in fact," Dr. Woolworth says. "Just as soon as I'm done with my rounds."

"Seriously." The spoon slips from my fingers to clatter into the bowl. "That's great. Did you hear that, Dad?"

"I certainly did."

"You're going to stay, right?"

"You bet."

"Don't get too excited," Dr. Woolworth says. "I'm going to check the surgical area. More than likely, you'll need another bandage."

"But the nanobots—"

"The nanobots do speed up the healing process. Just don't get your hopes up too high. Recovery in three days will be remarkable, very remarkable," Dr. Woolworth says.

Dr. Woolworth leaves, and I'm left waiting to have the bandage removed. My excitement almost makes me forget my discomfort. Soon I'll have a prosthetic oculus dexter. I'll be able to see again. Take photos. See my friends. Not just talk to them. Really see them. I'm as excited as a toddler on Christmas Eve.

What if Dr. Woolworth looks at the wound and decides something is wrong? What if I'm not a viable candidate for the prosthetic? What if Dr. Maywood is right? What if Dr. Woolworth has been selling me snake oil the entire time? I don't want to believe that, I really don't, but my manic mind is jumping from insane highs to desperate lows every time a neuron fires.

"Dad, what are you doing?" I ask.

"I'm reading," he says.

"Can you read to me?"

"Sure. It's an academic journal. Nothing as exciting as *Jane Eyre*."

I laugh and grimace. "I fall asleep listening to that."

"I know," Dad says and starts reading aloud.

The journal article is about some mumbo jumbo concerning quantum computing. I don't try to follow it. I just listen to the sound of his voice. By the time Dr. Woolworth returns, I'm no longer a nervous wreck, and I'm ready to face the music, whether it be joyful or a death dirge.

Dr. Woolworth and James help me sit up in bed. Then the doctor unwraps the bandage. It's a slow, careful process. Some of the aching dissipates as the pressure from the wrap releases. The air is cool against my skin.

"The surgical area looks great," Dr. Woolworth says. "How do you feel? Any discomfort?"

"It's itchy. My head hurts, but not too bad," I say.

"A T-rex isn't detaching your head from your shoulders?" Dr. Woolworth says dryly.

James and Dad chuckle.

"No, you scared her away." Of course, the T-rex is a girl. Her name is Leslie Chapman.

"Good. I think we can fit the prosthetic oculus dexter today. We can do it here in the room. No need to schedule the OR. This is good. Really good," Dr. Woolworth says.

"I'll be able to see again? Today?"

"Yes, Allison, you will. For now, we'll let the incision site air out. In twenty minutes or so, James will apply an eyepatch. It will be a couple hours before the prosthetic is ready. I'll need to go back to the university to run final diagnostics at the lab and arrange for transport."

More waiting. I. Want. To. See. Right. Now. Still, I'm hanging ten on a wave of bliss. I'm in such a good mood I even joke about being a pirate after James puts on the eyepatch.

It's evening before Dr. Woolworth returns. I expect bad news. To my relief, it's not. She ushers my dad out of the room, then walks me through the procedure: first local anesthetic, then cleaning the wound, and finally the installation of the prosthetic. I can't wait.

I feel a pinch, like a flu shot, where my right eye should be when Dr. Woolworth administers the anesthetic. After that, I don't feel any discomfort, just pressure as she works.

"All done," Dr. Woolworth says. "Now, we wait for the local anesthetic to wear off. Then we'll find out how the prosthetic works."

"What? More waiting!"

Chapter 8

"Can you see anything?" Dr. Woolworth asks.

"No." Goose bumps cover my arms, and I shiver. "Should I be able to see?"

"No worries. I'll connect my tablet to the prosthetic." Under her breath, Dr. Woolworth adds, "Great."

"Is something wrong?" I ask, my voice rising an octave with every word.

"I just need to try something," Dr. Woolworth says.

"I hear you're a Sounders fan," James says. "Did you hear about their win over the Portland Timbers?"

"My dad and I listened on the radio."

"My son and I are huge Sounders fanboys. He wants to play for them. He's only six. Oh, Dr. Woolworth is ready."

"Sorry about that," Dr. Woolworth says. "The prosthetic's wireless is finicky. I sent the command for the prosthetic to run a diagnostic. It will only take a minute. Could be something got jostled in transport or installation."

"So if I jump up and down, my eyes will stop working?"

"No, no. If you get hit in the head with a soccer ball or…" Dr. Woolworth says and sighs.

I bite down on my lower lip until I wince.

"Are you okay? Are you having pain?" Dr.

Woolworth asks.

"All good," I lie.

"James, hold my tablet. I'm going to try a hard reset," Dr. Woolworth says. "Allison, I need you to stay still. You'll feel pressure against the prosthetic."

"Hard reset?" My throat is constricting. A hard reset? That's like something you do to a phone when it's totally screwed up, and you're one step away from sending it in for repair.

"The prosthetic isn't detecting a connection to the neural filament," Dr. Woolworth says. "I know the filament is functioning. I tested it before installation. A hard reset should resolve the issue."

My dreams flicker and fade like lights during a brownout. If I can't see, I can't pursue photography, my first and greatest love. I'll always be the blind girl, the disabled girl, the girl who was assaulted. I'll need to learn to read braille.

I feel pressure against my eye socket.

"Okay," Dr. Woolworth says. "It will take five minutes for the prosthetic to reset."

James talks to me about the Sounders. He knows way more about soccer than I do, and I'm glad for the distraction. Dr. Woolworth interrupts his analysis of the Sounders' midfield. Perfect timing on her part. I'm a fan, not a superfan.

"Can you see any light?"

Electric tingling shoots through my body. "Yes. Yes. I see the light. I see it."

In the center of my vision is a bright pinprick in the black. It's not much, but it's enough to give me hope that Dr. Woolworth isn't a snake oil salesperson. My dreams stop waning and come back into razor focus.

"Excellent," Dr. Woolworth says. "Your eyesight will continue improving. It will clear up in a couple of hours."

Dr. Woolworth and James leave. Dad is allowed back in the room.

"How is your oculus dexter?" Dad asks.

"I can see light and dark," I say. "The prosthetic gave Dr. Woolworth some trouble, but it's working now."

"That's wonderful, Allison."

My field of vision is progressively becoming brighter with more gradation between light and dark. It's like staring through a thick fog just after sunset when you can tell there is stuff out there in that gray soup, but you can't tell what.

"Do I look dope?" I ask.

"Of course," Dad says.

"Can you tell which eye is the prosthetic?"

"Let me look. Hmmmm. Honestly, I can't tell."

"I don't look disabled?"

"No."

"Good." I don't want anyone's sympathy. At first, I wanted to know why I was assaulted, to understand why I suffer blindness. Now that my vision is being restored, I couldn't care less why I was attacked. "I look normal? I don't look like a dork?"

"You look like you, Allison. Perfect."

"Now I know you're lying."

"You look perfect to me. You'll see. Once your vision clears up, you can look in the mirror."

"Did you just move? I saw you move."

"You did? That's great."

"You moved?"

"Yes, I walked from your bedside over to the chair."

"Oh my God, I saw you move."

I squeal like a little girl who finds every present she's ever wanted underneath the Christmas tree. I giggle as smudgy colors and blurry shapes materialize around the small hospital room. It's like I'm looking through a semitranslucent shower curtain into a bathroom shrouded in steam.

"I can see you in the chair, Daddy. You're wearing a maroon shirt."

"That's great. It's really working."

I gaze around the room, observing the indistinct medical equipment and nondescript walls. There is something rectangular and black attached to the wall near the ceiling across from the foot of the bed.

"Is that a TV? Where is the remote?" I ask.

With a ten-gigawatt smile plastered on my face, I watch my maroon blob dad rise from the chair and lumber toward the TV. He retrieves the remote, and the TV comes to life.

"Thanks a billion," I say when he hands me the black, rectangular remote.

I channel surf as my vision sharpens. It's wonderful. It's fun. I settle on watching a Mariners' game. I'm soon disabused of the notion that I'm watching the Mariners. In reality, it's a playoff game between two teams from back east. Once I can read the players' names on their jerseys, I know it's time to look in the mirror.

I swing my legs off the bed.

"Don't you want to call a nurse?" Dad asks.

"No."

I slip from the bed, and my feet touch down on the cold floor.

"Do you need help?"

"I can make it on my own."

I cross the ten feet or so to the bathroom, the IV pole's casters squealing as I pull it along. There is a mirror above the sink. I stare at my reflection. I'm blown away, and in a good way. I smile. Dad is right. I can't tell the prosthetic is fake. Even the iris is the same brown as my left eye. Normal. Such a relief. I was so sure I'd look strange and that everyone would remember I was assaulted when they saw my eyes or at least wonder what had happened to me.

Closer inspection reveals that I can't see any blood vessels in the prosthetic's sclera. I shrug. After the novelty of my prosthetics wears off, I doubt my peers will pay enough attention to me to notice.

Otherwise, I don't look terrible, considering. That's not to say that I look snatched either. The right side of my head around the eye socket is swollen and bruised. A red scar runs from somewhere beneath my hair down the left side of my forehead to terminate just above my eyebrow. I make a disgusted *ugh* and crinkle my nose. That's from being hit on the head.

I try to remember what happened that stormy night. I shake my head. Nothing. It's frustrating and comforting at the same time. I don't want to feel the abject fear that I must've felt, but I don't like having a blank space in my past like someone erased the security footage. Anything could've happened. Anything, and I'll never know.

"Do you want to video chat with your grandparents?" Dad calls.

"Sure," I say and head back to the bed.

Dad turns off the TV and makes the call. Granddad answers after the second ring and calls over Grandma. The small phone screen is blurry, but I can see by the smiles lighting their crinkly faces that they're thrilled I'm recovering. I don't really track the conversation. I'm already looking forward to seeing my friends, and my head is starting to throb. I lie back in the bed and hit the call button for the nurse.

James enters the room about five minutes later, and Dad makes for the exit.

Dad says, "No, Dad, don't buy any tickets until she's out of the hospital. I don't know when that will be."

James ambles over to the bed. He is short and barrel-chested with a bald head and a bushy red mustache.

"You can see?" James asks.

"Sure can. My head is throbbing, though."

James looks at me and the nearby medical equipment. "Looks like the IV tubing is kinked. Move your arm to the left. Good. Let me adjust this. There. The medication is flowing. You should start feeling better soon."

"Thank you so much. You're a lifesaver."

"I aim to please." James saunters to the foot of the bed. "How many fingers am I holding up?"

"None."

"Good," he says, smiling. "And now?"

"Five."

"I'm going to page Dr. Woolworth. She'll want to know your vision has returned. If you don't start feeling better in twenty minutes or so, buzz me again. Okay?"

Dad is in the chair reading when Dr. Woolworth comes to check on me. She's a tall woman, willowy, with curly brunette hair chopped off at the midpoint of her neck. She wears glasses with thick circular lenses. She doesn't look like she wears any makeup, or at least not much. The sparse makeup, dorky glasses, and poor hairdo don't detract from her natural good looks. I can't tell how old she is. She possesses an ageless beauty like an old-time movie star.

Her gaze lingers on my father for maybe a half-second longer than a mere glance as she enters the room. He is too engrossed in an academic journal to do more than nod his head in acknowledgment of her presence. While she examines me, I admire her long, graceful fingers that are devoid of rings. Dad is always helping Dr. Woolworth with her research at the university. What is the nature of the research? Hanky-panky? That hardly seems possible.

Dr. Woolworth gives my right eye the all-clear and leaves, promising to schedule the surgery for my oculus sinister as soon as possible. My dad and I discuss my hopes and dreams now that my eyesight is restored. Photojournalism, of course! Despite my excitement, I'm soon yawning. It's late, and I'm exhausted. I think my dad is too.

"Thanks for being here," I say, my eyes fluttering.

"I'll always be here for you, baby." He stands and kisses me on the forehead. "Try to get some sleep."

The next morning, I wake up more rested than I remember feeling since I entered the hospital. I order up eggs with all the sides for breakfast, and I'm able to eat by myself without any spillage. It's so great to be able to see. It's amazing how much easier it makes everything. Now, if only my eyesight made the food taste better…oh well, can't have everything.

Dad is munching on a bagel and sipping hospital coffee. I'm so jealous. I'd do almost anything for a cup of brew. A good cup. I'm not quite desperate enough to try the hospital coffee yet, but I'm getting close.

I ask Dad about my phone. It's at home, so I ask him to message Dalia, which he does. Turns out it's a Saturday morning. It's easy to lose track of time in the hospital. His phone pings with her response that she will be over in an hour or less with Haji in tow.

"Is it okay if I go for a run? I figure you don't want me around when your friends show up," Dad says.

"Sure. You haven't been running for a long time."

"Only once since you were hurt. When you went in for surgery. I couldn't just sit around and read or do nothing. I was too worried. I can make a quick stop by my office too. I have some paperwork to sign."

"Enjoy yourself. Don't rush back," I say.

I channel surf while waiting on my friends to show up. Nothing engaging is on, so I keep channel surfing, but my head still throbs, and I have mild vertigo. I decide watching TV isn't helping with my vertigo, so I kill the flatscreen.

I lie back on the bed and stare at the ceiling. Maybe closing my eyes will help me feel better, but I'm too thrilled to see again to do that. I space out, my mind a blank slate, until I hear a knock on the door.

"Allison?"

It's Dalia's muffled voice. I smile and sit up in bed. "Come in."

The door opens, and Dalia rushes inside. I've never been so overjoyed to see her neon pink hair.

"Allison!" she squeals and runs to the bedside with her arms wide open. "Can I hug you?"

"Yes," I say, and we embrace.

She is gentle and careful, and I'm awkward and clumsy with the IV dangling from my arm. It's the best hug I've had in a long time, maybe ever. Haji is in the room holding a cup of coffee, along with another person I didn't expect. My breath catches in my throat, and I glower at Jason.

"Sorry," Dalia whispers. "He was working with Haji on that dorky school blog and insisted on tagging along."

Dalia and I break our embrace. My head swirls like a dinghy bobbing on a violent sea.

"Your dad said you can see. Can you? Can you?" Dalia says.

"Yeah, can you?" Haji says. "Your dad filled us in on the surgery. A prosthetic eye! That is far out. This coffee is for you—from The Obsidian Roast."

I grab the proffered cup. "Thank you. I'm dying for a coffee." I take a sip. Ambrosial. "So good. Thank you, Haji." I set the cup down on the bedside table. "I can see." I gesture to my eyes. "Can you tell which one is fake?"

"Your eyes look identical," Haji says.

Dalia and Jason peer at my orbs and shake their heads.

"It's my right eye. The oculus dexter," I say.

I give them a rundown of my painful recovery and the upcoming surgery.

"Geez," Haji says.

"Ouch," Dalia says and winces.

"I survived one surgery. I'll survive the next," I

say. "Next time Leslie sees me, she can bully me for having fake eyes."

I laugh at my joke, and so do Dalia and Haji, bad taste or not. Jason, though, flushes and stares at the floor. His reaction tells me all I need to know. I'm tempted to call him out for going to the dance with a racist hater. Instead, I clench my jaw and keep my lips sealed.

"Leslie is really sorry about what she did," Jason says, the words coming out in a torrent. "She's not racist. She doesn't hate you. She's just jealous. That doesn't make up for what she did. She knows it, and I know it."

Jason stares at me. His expression is stricken. Dalia and Haji both look like they'd rather be somewhere else.

"So you're an apologist for a racist hater," I say. Jason's face turns bright red as I speak. I'm not sure if it's from embarrassment or anger, and I don't care. My head hurts, and my heart is broken, and the triumph of my returning vision wanes. "Get out. Go tell her the girl with the ugly slanted eyes doesn't want to see you again."

"I'm not dating her. I went to homecoming with her, but that's it. I told her I couldn't date someone who hurt one of my friends like that," Jason says and turns for the door. He opens the door and pauses in the doorway. "I'm sorry. I really am. I didn't mean...it doesn't matter."

Jason leaves. My friends stare at me. I turn away from them and gaze at the ceiling, wondering if I even care that he is not dating Leslie. He went to the dance with her, and that was a betrayal.

Chapter 9

I'm in surgery the following Monday. Just like the first operation, it goes flawlessly, and within three days, Dr. Woolworth installs the prosthetic oculus sinister. A week after the second surgery, I'm discharged from the hospital on Halloween of all days.

I'm ecstatic to go home in time to see the trick-or-treaters and hand out candy. Just a few weeks ago, I feared I'd never see again. Now, everything I see is fresh and new and beautiful. I want to take in everything from sunrise to sunset to a moonlit night sky.

My body undermines my plans. My head still throbs, especially if I move around too much. I take a prescription-strength ibuprofen. I have a month's supply of prescription opioids, but Dad and I decide it's best I avoid the opioids unless I'm desperate for relief. I'm disappointed but not surprised that I spend Halloween in my room with a pounding headache, unable to sleep from the doorbell ringing until about nine thirty.

Dad returns to work the next morning, and I stay home by myself. I spend most of the a.m. sleeping and trying to read *Jane Eyre*. I read the book using my eyes, my prosthetic eyes. Whoever thought something so mundane could be so awesome? Still, reading that gripping tale puts me to sleep.

It's eleven o'clock when I wake up with a pounding headache. I drag myself downstairs in search of ibuprofen and food. I open the refrigerator to find an unopened package of chicken sausage. Hunger pangs give me cramps. I'm hungrier than I thought, and my meat craving hasn't abated one iota. I pull out the chicken sausage and a carton of pulp-free orange juice and place both on the counter.

My stomach roars like a half-starved dragon, and I heat up all five sausages in the microwave. Then I pour myself a glass of orange juice and down an ibuprofen. The microwave beeps just before I finish tidying up. I retrieve my meal, then head to the dining room. I consider the TV for a moment before deciding against turning it on. My head hurts so badly my eye sockets literally ache. So I inhale the sausages in silence. My stomach knots and grumbles. That's surprising. I just ate enough sausage to tide me over until dinner.

I amble back to the kitchen and throw open the fridge. I don't find more meat in the refrigerator, so I check the freezer. Nada. My usual fare, yogurt and vegetables and the like, isn't appealing, so I head back to my room and lie down. I'm expecting Haji to swing by after school to help me with homework, and Dalia will come over after cross-country practice, so I had better rest.

By mid-November, I'm feeling well enough to go back to Cascadia Prep. Dalia and Haji come by to walk me to school. It's still dark out, and a freak November snow dusts the ground. Snow isn't falling as we trudge across the yard, but more is forecasted to come down later in the day.

"Thanks for walking me to school," I tell my

friends as we turn onto the sidewalk. "I really appreciate it."

"We couldn't let you walk to school alone when it's black out," Haji says.

"I'm sure you don't want your dad to drop you off on your first day back," Dalia says. "That'd just be embarrassing, right?"

"Definitely." I had a long argument with my dad about him driving me to school the night before. He's worried about me walking alone in the dark (please) and that I'll run out of energy due to the physical strain of walking the half-mile to school (again, please).

My friends complain about the dark as we tramp down the sidewalk. I'm honestly not bothered by the darkness. I don't know, it seems like I can see better in low light than before.

Up ahead, the snow-covered sidewalk juts unevenly. Haji's foot catches on the projection, and he catapults forward, shouting an expletive. He lurches and windmills his arms. I reach for him, and so does Dalia, but it's too late, and he goes sprawling onto the sidewalk.

"Haji, are you okay?" Dalia and I ask in unison.

"Jinx," Haji says in a strained voice. He pushes himself up to his hands and knees. "Ouch. What did I fall over?"

Dalia kicks the snow from the uneven path. "The sidewalk."

"You seriously didn't see that?" I ask.

"How could I in the dark? Jeez," Haji says.

Dalia helps Haji up, and he brushes the snow from his clothing.

I turn to Dalia. "Did you see it?"

"The uneven sidewalk?" Dalia asks.

"Yeah."

"It's dark."

I smile and laugh. Both of them look at me.

"I think I have night vision."

Haji's eyes go wide. "Seriously? That is totally lit."

"From the prosthetics?" Dalia asks.

"Yeah!"

"Well, you let me know if I'm going to trip on anything."

I act as a guide for the rest of the trek, navigating us safely over the snowy terrain. We are marching across the school parking lot when a wave of vertigo washes over me. My hands go to my forehead, and I do a stutter step to maintain my balance before halting.

"What's wrong?" Dalia asks.

"I'm dizzy," I say. I feel nauseated too. "I need to sit down."

Dalia and Haji take me by my upper arms and guide me into the school. The spacious common room with its soaring ceiling is just as crowded as I remember. The mob of people flow like water around me, and their chattering only makes my vertigo worse. My friends guide me to a long stone bench abutting the staircase. There is a narrow space for me to sit smack dab between two boys of linebacker proportions.

"Thanks," I say and sigh. Maybe I'm rushing back to school, but being cooped up all day at home gives me cabin fever.

"Haji, get Allison a cup of water," Dalia says.

"Ummm...sure," Haji says and strides off into the crowd.

"Are you okay?" Dalia asks.

The linebacker on my left shifts his bulk to glance at me.

"I think so. Being off my feet helps."

"You're sure you're okay? I can text your dad."

"Don't you dare. I'm fine." I notice the linebacker is staring at me. I face him. "What?"

He blinks his eyes twice and points at me with a finger that is as large as my hand.

"You're...you're Allison Lee. The cyborg." The linebacker turns to his friends. "Guys, this is Allison Lee."

The jocks surround me. They ask questions and take pictures with their phones. My head is swimming.

"Back off. Give her some space. Can't you tell she's not feeling well?" Dalia says.

The big linebacker next to me raises his hands. "Sorry. Sorry. Come on, guys, leave Allison alone."

After a few more pictures, the group breaks up. The linebacker stands up and ambles into the crowd. He pauses and faces us.

"Sorry. I didn't mean to upset you," he says and turns away.

Dalia sits down next to me.

"Everyone knows what happened to me?"

"You haven't read the *Cascadia Weekly*, have you?" Dalia asks.

"I've been too busy trying to catch up on homework," I say.

"Here's the water," Haji says, weaving through the crowd. He holds a red plastic cup up high over his head. He comes to a halt before us. "Sorry it took so long. I had a heck of a time finding a cup."

"Haji," I say with feigned sweetness and take the

cup. "Did you write an article about me for the *Cascadia Weekly*?"

Haji's eyes bug out, and he gives me a curdled smile. I take a sip of water and wait for his reply.

"Yes."

"Did you mention my prosthetics?"

"I did." Haji drops his gaze to the floor.

"You should've asked." I'm mad, but I'm not super mad. Haji doesn't need to know that.

"Sorry," he says.

I gulp the remaining water and thrust the empty cup at his chest. He takes the cup. "Come on, Dalia, let's head to class."

Mr. Leonard, the algebra instructor, makes a big deal about me being back in class. After the linebacker incident, I'm prepared to answer his questions and those of my classmates. I can't wait for my fifteen minutes of celebrity to blow over and to just go back to being Allison Lee, the girl who flies under the radar most of the time.

By lunchtime I'm tired. After lunch, another bout of vertigo hits me on the way to American history class. I stop in the hallway, leaning against the lockers for several minutes before I'm steady enough to continue. By the time I get to class, I'm late.

Mrs. Higgins, the matronly history teacher, pauses her whiteboard lecture to stare at me as I walk to my seat at the back of the class. "Miss Lee, so good of you to join us."

My peers watch me as I walk between their desks that are arrayed with parade-ground precision. I take my seat and pull out a notebook and pencil from my backpack. Mrs. Higgins flashes me an insincere smile and continues the lecture.

Choosing the back of the class as my stomping ground in American history wasn't one of my best ideas. Mrs. Higgins loves to use the whiteboard, loves it. Her handwriting is cramped and jagged and often illegible. If you don't catch what she is saying, you're screwed. Asking her to repeat something is a surefire way to suffer a feisty retort. To make matters worse, I'm having a hard time catching up on my American history coursework. Too much reading for a girl who tires easily.

I gather Mrs. Higgins is lecturing on the post-Civil War south, carpetbaggers and sharecroppers and the like. But between my woozy head and my inability to read her writing, I can't follow the lecture. It would be so much easier to read her handwriting if I sat at the front of the class. My vision goes momentarily out of focus then sharpens, the whiteboard appearing closer than before.

"Holy shit." I can read Mrs. Higgins' handwriting. This is savage. My prosthetic eyes just zoomed in like a zoom lens on a camera.

I belatedly notice Mrs. Higgins has paused her lecture and is glaring at me with narrowed eyes. My peers turn in their seats to stare at me, some aghast, some indifferent, and more than a few smirking. I shrink in my chair.

"Is there something you'd like to share with the class, Miss Lee?" Mrs. Higgins asks.

I feign a cough. "Sorry. Fighting off a cold."

Mrs. Higgins frowns at me for a moment then resumes the lecture.

On Wednesday after school, Dad picks me up to

take me to the medical robotics lab to see Dr. Woolworth. Since being discharged from the hospital, I've been going to the lab for a checkup once a week. It's a nerve-racking drive. Overnight snow that lasted until about six a.m. left a half-inch of the white stuff blanketing the city. Even with such a puny snowfall, the city's response is already catching criticism. With more snow forecasted, people are expecting a winter of playing bumper cars. Still, Dad manages to get us to a parking lot on the university campus without incident.

We trudge from the parking lot to the modern glass and steel Robotics Technology Center, RTC for short. The sky is an ominous steel gray.

"How is your first week back at school?" Dad asks.

"Tiring," I say.

"Well, at least you're learning about your prosthetics' different abilities."

"They are pretty cool."

I had told him about the night vision and zooming. He was totally impressed, like a kid with a sweet tooth in a candy store.

The interior of the RTC is as sleek and modern as the exterior. The heat is blasting inside the building, so I strip off my heavy coat and carry it in my arms. The lab is on the second floor, so we head to the elevator.

The medical robotics lab is a sterile white facility chock-full of exotic equipment and computers. Dr. Woolworth and her graduate students all wear white lab coats. The lab gives off the vibe of being a movie set for a sci-fi or techno-thriller.

I sit down in a chair, and Dr. Woolworth examines me.

"No infection. The bruising is gone, and so is most

of the swelling," Dr. Woolworth says. "This is excellent. Really excellent. So you're back at school this week? How's that going?"

"Fine overall. I do tire easily and sometimes get dizzy."

"Are you still having headaches?"

"I do, but not as bad as last week."

"Good. Just make sure you don't overextend yourself."

She hands me over to a graduate student who quizzes me about my prosthetics performance. He's quite impressed to learn I discovered the night vision and zooming functions. In less than twenty minutes, the examination is done until the following Wednesday.

On Saturday morning, Dalia comes over, and we brave the falling snow to walk to our favorite coffee shop, The Obsidian Roast. I'm feeling far better now and want to get out and about to somewhere other than Cascadia Prep. The Obsidian Roast is a small, artsy joint that serves strong coffee and delicious baked goods. We know the baristas by name, and they know ours. After gorging ourselves on cinnamon rolls and slurping twenty-ounce coffees, we march through near whiteout conditions to the university.

We head for the Chapel Library off the quad to study with Haji. Over an inch of snow hides the red bricks of the quad. The snow falls dry and thick, quickly filling in our footprints. We enter the library and walk to a chamber like a cathedral with a high vaulted ceiling, book-lined walls, and long tables. The room is only sparsely populated with studying students, so we easily find an empty table and sit across from each other.

We decide to work on algebra while we wait for Haji. We're deep into working quadratic equations when someone loudly clearing their throat makes me nearly jump out of my seat. We both look up, searching for the disturbance. I half expect the culprit to be Haji.

It's a tall and absurdly thin man standing just inside the entrance to the reading room. I recognize him as Dr. Radcliffe from the many faculty functions I've attended with Dad over the years. I stare at him, entranced, not believing what I'm seeing.

"Allison, is something wrong?" Dalia whispers.

"No," I say and drag my gaze back to the quadratic equation written in my notebook.

Dalia resumes talking about strategies to solve the equation, but I barely register a word. My gaze is lured back to Dr. Radcliffe like a particle inexorably pulled into a black hole. My eyes widen, and my jaw slackens. Furrowing my brow, I blink, desperate to clear the mind-boggling absurdity from my vision.

Chapter 10

Projecting from Dr. Radcliffe's body is a shimmering golden dragon, the European variety complete with sparkling golden scales, talons, and green wings. The dragon fades and flashes in and out of existence. The tail, the bulky body, and leathery wings pass through the wall as if all are insubstantial. This is insane asylum madness. I must be hallucinating, or maybe it's my prosthetic eyes. Not a single person, and there must be at least fifteen people in the library, notices the beast. On top of that, the dragon doesn't make a sound. There is no way an animal of that size can be silent in such a confined space.

I don't know if I should hope it's my eyes or not. If it's not my eyes, I'm a nutter. If it is my eyes…it's too terrible to consider.

I draw a shuddering breath and chew on my lower lip. The hairs on the back my neck stand up straight, and my body tenses like prey ready to flee a predator. I want to look away from Dr. Radcliffe and the craziness glimmering all around him, but I can't.

"Allison. Allison."

I tear my gaze away from the professor, but I still glimpse the dragon's glimmering golden light in my peripheral vision.

Dalia stares at me in evident exasperation. "Did you hear anything I just said?"

My gaze shifts back to Dr. Radcliffe and the draconic projection surrounding him. A student walks straight through a foreleg. My mouth drops open.

"What is it?" Dalia asks and turns in her seat to face Dr. Radcliffe. She turns back to me. "Do you know him?"

"Know who?" I shift my gaze to Dalia, long enough to catch her puzzled look, then look at Dr. Radcliffe.

"That old man you're staring at," Dalia says. "Are you okay? Is he the one who attacked you?"

I stare at my friend. "What? No. How would I know? I don't have any memory of that. That's Dr. Radcliffe. He knows my dad."

I see golden scales and a red cardigan right behind Dalia. I look up and feel like my prosthetics are going to pop out of my head. Behind Dalia is Dr. Radcliffe and the twinkling winged beast.

"Oh my God," I whisper.

A spectral golden forefoot with foot-long white talons passes straight through Dalia's chest.

"What?" Dalia says. "You look like you've seen a ghost."

Dr. Radcliffe stares at me from behind rimless spectacles. He is holding a thick book at his side. I try to meet his gaze, but my eyes keep flicking up at the looming dragon's head, staring down at me with yellow eyes split by black pupils.

"You're Raymond Lee's daughter," Dr. Radcliffe says. "Wait. Don't tell me. Alice."

I shake my head. Dalia faces the professor.

"Hello, Dr. Radcliffe," Dalia says. "Allison was telling me all about you."

"Oh, that's right. Allison. How could I forget? And who are you, young lady?"

"Dalia."

"What a lovely name. Your hair. Pink like a dahlia," the professor says and hefts the book he holds. "Well, I will let you young ladies get back to it. Good day."

Dr. Radcliffe inclines his head, but the dragon stares at me without even blinking once. Dalia says goodbye, and I manage to splutter a word or two. Dr. Radcliffe turns away, and so does the flickering dragon. I watch them walk to the entrance, the dragon passing through tables and chairs and coeds with equal ease. Dr. Radcliffe walks through the doorway, and his draconic companion goes through the wall.

I rub a hand against my temple. What in the hell did I just see? Dalia gripping my hand startles me out of my contemplation. Concern is written on her face as plain as a fast food joint's menu.

"What was that all about? You're freaking me out."

I shake my head, trying to be nonchalant. "It's nothing. Let's get back to work."

"That wasn't nothing."

"I'm behind in algebra. You said you'd help."

"Fine. Be that way. I'm only your BFF."

Despite her feistiness, Dalia tries to help me. The only problem is my mind keeps straying from complex algebraic equations to the ethereal dragon. It had looked at me. Its talons had passed through my best friend. I must've imagined it. That had to be it, didn't it? Either that or the prosthetic eyes somehow caused me to hallucinate. Was there even any difference?

"You're not paying attention again," Dalia says.

I focus on her face. She is arching an eyebrow at me.

"Sorry," I say, standing up. I close my math book and shove it into my backpack. "I need to go to the RTC to see Dr. Woolworth."

"Now?"

"Yes, now," I say and put on my heavy winter coat. I swing my backpack over my shoulder. "Tell Haji I'm okay. I just need to get my eyes checked."

"It's Saturday. No one will be there."

"Dr. Woolworth is. My dad is helping her out."

"Wait. I'll come with you." Dalia stands up and starts packing up her things. "I'll message Haji to meet us there."

Dalia follows me into the swirling snow and icebox cold. A handful of people brave the storm to trudge across the quad. The snow must be nearly six inches high, so marching through it is hard work. I soon find myself tiring. Dalia notices I'm slowing down and starts telling me about this boy Devin that she met at a climate march while I was in the hospital. I watch her out of the corner of my eyes. Her breath steams in and out, like smoke escaping a dragon's mouth.

"I really wish you were there. You would've loved it," Dalia says.

"Loved what?"

"The Dark Matter Electrica concert. Our favorite group. Never mind." Dalia stares at me with incredulity. "You're out of it today. Did you listen to anything I said?"

"You met a boy named Devin."

"What color is his hair?"

I hesitate too long.

"Well?"

"Fire engine red."

"Allison, you're not listening. His hair is purple."

"Hey. Wait up!"

I turn toward the voice. Haji is plodding down a path between trees and waving to us. He is decked out in skinny blue jeans, a heavy black seaman's coat, and a bright red beanie covers his ears.

"Haji," I call and dramatically wave to him like he's my long-lost brother who I haven't seen in years. With any luck, his presence will save me from Dalia's well-meaning concern.

"What's going on?" Haji asks when he joins us. He walks on my right side, so I'm in between my friends. The snow crunches underneath our boots.

"Allison wants her eyes checked," Dalia says.

"Seriously?" Haji says. "Why?"

"You wouldn't believe me if I told you." I inwardly wince as soon as the words leave my lips. Remaining silent would have been better than saying that.

"Try us," Haji says.

I don't respond. In the distance looms the Robotics Technology Center, rendered as an impressionist painting by the falling snow.

"Stop shutting us out," Dalia says. "Something has you spooked. I mean, what's up with that Dr. Radcliffe?"

"Huh? Who is Dr. Radcliffe?" Haji asks.

"Presumably, an associate of Allison's father," Dalia says. "Rather creepy. Gives off the same vibe as Mr. Leonard."

I give Dalia a disgusted look. "Ewwww."

"Really?" Haji asks.

"He is a bit creepy," I say.

A gust of wind howls through the trees and between the university's buildings. Branches shudder, and clumps of snow fall onto the path. I look overhead, expecting snow or maybe even a branch to fall toward me. I lose my balance and stumble and crash into Haji. He catches me in surprisingly strong arms.

"Allison, are you okay?" Haji asks.

I try to push away from him, but he holds onto me, steadying me.

"I'm all good. Just a little light-headed."

Dalia gets in my face and stares at me. Her nose is bright red from the cold, and a snowflake rests on her nose ring. "We should get you inside. Take my hand."

Haji releases me, and Dalia takes my hand. She wears gloves. I wish I had the foresight to wear some. My fingers are popsicles. My light-headedness turns into vertigo, and my head twirls like the falling snow.

When we reach the Robotics Technology Center, I flop down on the first bench we come to. I shut my eyes, willing my head to stop spinning, and enjoy the warmth slowly bringing my hands and cheeks back to life.

"How you doing?" Dalia asks.

"Better. I suffered a bout of vertigo. Give me a minute."

My squad talks in hushed tones. I open my eyes and spot them in my peripheral vision a few feet away. They lean close together, their heads nearly touching. I have the distinct feeling they're talking about me. Do I dare tell them about the dragon, or will they think I'm crazy?

I stand up and don't move for a moment to make sure the vertigo has passed. I head to the elevator. Dalia and Haji follow, catching up to me as I wait for the door to slide open. The elevator dings, and we climb aboard.

We find the door to the lab unlocked. I open it and see my dad sitting on a stool in front of a computer. Dr. Woolworth stands at his shoulder. She's not wearing her usual lab coat, which is on the counter next to the computer's monitor. The black jeans and a matching sweater she wears show off her trim figure. She must be thirsty, not that my dad notices. He looks engrossed by whatever is on the screen.

"Dad. Dr. Woolworth," I call.

They both look up and face us.

"Allison, what are you doing here?" Dad says. "Hi, Dalia. Haji."

I explain that I'm afraid my prosthetics are malfunctioning. Dr. Woolworth tells my friends to wait outside and sits me down in a chair. Dad comes over to watch, worry evident on his face.

"What do you mean malfunctioning?" Dr. Woolworth asks.

"My vision was blurry."

"I'll run some diagnostics," Dr. Woolworth says.

Dr. Woolworth retrieves a tablet from the counter and pokes at the screen with an index finger. Dad squats down in front of me.

"How do you feel otherwise?" he asks.

"Tired," I say.

"No vertigo?"

"A little, but only after walking through the snow. I'm fine. My vision was just a little blurry in the Chapel

Library."

Dad glances over his shoulder at Dr. Woolworth. She looks up from the tablet, then turns her gaze back to the screen.

"You need to be careful not to overexert yourself, Allison," Dr. Woolworth says. "After what you've been through, it is to be expected that your body will take time to recover. It's okay to take time."

"I don't like you being out in the snow," Dad says, his tone becoming more stern with every word. "Once you're done here, I'm taking you home. I don't want you going out anymore this weekend."

"Seriously?" I ask, although it's not a half-bad idea. At home, I won't see dragons emerging from the walls. At least, I hope not.

"Well, Allison, the prosthetics check out okay," Dr. Woolworth says. "You were in the Chapel Library?"

I nod.

"The lighting isn't great in there. That might've caused the prosthetics to go out of focus. It's hard to say." Dr. Woolworth sets the tablet on the counter. "If it happens again, call me immediately. It might help if you can tell me exactly what you're experiencing as it's happening. You have my pager and cell number. Also, if you experience any other aberrations, we can remove the prosthetics—"

"Remove! No way." I shake my head. "Anything is better than not seeing."

Dad takes my hand and squeezes it.

Dr. Woolworth holds up her hands and says in a calm voice, "Not remove permanently, Allison. Remove the prosthetics for servicing. Think of it like taking your car to the shop."

"Okay," I say, frowning. "Just like taking the car for service."

Chapter 11

Dad insists on driving me home after Dr. Woolworth is done examining me. He wants me to rest. I beg him to allow Dalia and Haji to come over to study. They're game—they know I'll brew a pot of Grit City Roast to keep us well-caffeinated. If I'm by myself, I'm afraid I'll obsess over Dr. Radcliffe's spectral dragon. Dad relents. Being an academic makes him susceptible to arguments related to keeping up in school.

The four of us trek toward the parking lot. A cold wind stirs up the fallen snow and burns my cheeks. The white stuff is halfway up my boots and turns my toes into ice cubes. As we near the parking lot, Dad unlocks the hybrid. The car makes a loud beep and flashes its headlights. We clamber inside, Dad and I in the front, my friends in the back.

My dad looks out the front window and sighs. There's not much to see other than a sheet of white. He is about to jump out of the car when the driver's side backdoor opens.

"No worries, Mr. Lee," Haji says. "I got it."

Haji uses his arm to brush the snow off the windscreen then hops back inside the vehicle. Dad powers up the car and puts the heater on full blast to warm us up and defog the windows.

Dalia and Haji talk about how the arctic blast might

interrupt school next week. I try to keep my teeth from chattering. When Dad backs out, the car slips and slides like it's trying to gain traction on an ice rink. The car gets stuck when Dad stops to shift from reverse to drive. The wheels spin, making a god-awful sound, but the vehicle doesn't move. Feeling the queasy dizziness of vertigo coming on, I shut my eyes and pray to God and Allah and Buddha and any other deity who might be listening for the sensation to pass.

"Do you want me to get out and push, Mr. Lee?" Haji asks.

"Not yet," Dad says.

"You should've let me walk home," I say and sigh.

"Just give me a second. I got this," Dad says, and I hear him unbuckle his seatbelt and open the car door. "I went to graduate school in Wisconsin. I know how to handle a vehicle in the snow."

"You went to graduate school in Wisconsin like twenty-five years ago. I'm sure you remember everything from back then."

"Give me a chance," Dad says.

I'm not sure what he does, probably digs out the snow from beneath the tires. When he gets back inside, the car gains enough traction to get going. I open my eyes and yawn.

"See," Dad says and glances at me. "I told you I know to handle a vehicle in—"

"Mr. Lee, watch out!" Haji yells from the backseat.

Dalia lets out a shrill scream just as Dad slams his foot on the brake. I'm catapulted forward and backward in my seat like a frigging pinball. The car slides over the compact snow and ice, coming to a stop I swear less than a foot from a blue and red streak barreling down the main road. It's a tow truck using the roadway like a dragstrip.

Dad's grip on the steering wheel is white-knuckled. "Jesus Christ."

"Concentrate on the road, Dad."

Dad draws a deep breath and says, "Yeah. Yeah. Eyes on the road. You hear that, kids." He looks in the rearview mirror. "Always pay attention to the road while driving." His attempt at a teachable moment is met with stony silence.

After that, Dad pays attention to his driving and gets us home without incident. Just as good as making it back alive, I've fought off the latest bout of vertigo.

"I think I'll walk back rather than try my luck on the roads," Dad says. He pulls down the sun visor and uses the attached remote to open the garage door.

"I think that's for the best," I say.

"Don't exhaust yourself," Dad says.

"I won't," I say and throw open the car door.

I climb out and shut the door. Dalia already waits for me just inside the garage. Haji stops beside the driver's side door as my dad hauls himself out of the car.

"That was one heck of an exciting ride, Mr. Lee. Thanks," Haji says.

I turn to Dalia and whisper, "Why does he always brown-nose my dad? I don't get it."

Dalia shrugs. "Haji is always nice and respectful to everyone. He's extra respectful to adults. Not just your dad."

"I guess."

"I'm serious. He treats my mom and dad exactly the same."

"Hurry up, Haji, we're freezing," I call and wave. "Bye, Dad."

Haji hurries into the garage, and Dad waves then trudges down to the sidewalk. I lead my squad to the door from the garage into the house proper. We pause at the entrance to strip off our coats and boots, and I hit the garage door button. We go inside, entering the kitchen.

I hand my backpack to Haji. "Go set up on the dining room table. I'll start some coffee."

I retrieve my personal supply of Grit City Roast and burr grinder from the cabinet. I set the grinder on the counter and open the bag of beans, breathing in the rich, smoky aroma.

Smoke.

Fire.

Dragon.

I shut my eyes and shake my head. Don't think about Dr. Radcliffe and the shimmering dragon. Don't.

Once the beans are ground, I start up the coffee maker and head to the dining room. Dalia and I battle multivariable quadratic equations while Haji powers up his laptop to work on something else. During my time in the hospital, Dalia learned several new techniques for unraveling the equations, which she tries to impart to me with the patience of a kindergarten teacher. I'm far from the ideal pupil since visions of an incorporeal dragon keep distracting me. It's a relief when I hear strident beeping from the kitchen announcing the coffee is brewed.

I push back my chair that makes a loud scraping noise against the wooden floor and stand. "Everyone want coffee?"

"Do you even need to ask?" Dalia bats her eyes at me.

Haji looks up from his computer, considering. He drinks far less coffee than Dalia and me. "Yes, please. Warm me up."

He rubs his hands together as if to warm them.

"I'll help you." Dalia follows me into the kitchen.

I snag three maroon mugs emblazoned with green Ts from the cabinet above the coffeemaker. I set the cups on the counter and pour the coffee. I take a sniff of the aroma rising with the steam from the black gold and smile.

Dalia grabs two mugs and heads back to the dining room table. I follow, pausing in the opening between the kitchen and dining room. Dalia sets a coffee down beside Haji, and he mutters his thanks. She continues back to her seat, and Haji remains engrossed in his work. He sits with his back to me so I can see what he is working on over his shoulder. It's not homework. He is changing the layout of a post for the *Cascadia Weekly*. He is resizing photos from football games and sprinkling the images throughout a lengthy article. The credit for practically every photo goes to Leslie Chapman.

"What are you working on, Haji?" I stride to my seat and set my mug on the table with a loud thump.

He looks up at me. "I'm summarizing our horrible football season and offering my analysis of what we need to do to improve in the standings next season. That's one thing you didn't miss out on. Believe me. We weren't taking home the bacon. It was painful to watch."

"Looks like Leslie took some nice photos for you,"

I say and take my seat.

Haji squirms. "The *Weekly*'s top photographer was sidelined."

"I told you," Dalia says and glances at me. "I warned him not to use her pictures. I told him he'd be better off using pics from his phone."

"The *Weekly*'s readership expects top-notch photography. It's what sets the *Weekly* apart from other school newspapers."

"How can you keep working with her? After what she did," I say.

Haji stares at the table. "I'm sorry, okay. From now on, I'll only use your photos. Nothing from Leslie."

"I'll hold you to that promise," I say. "But you know, I'm really disappointed in you, Haji. I thought you of all people would understand what Leslie said and did are completely unacceptable."

"At least I'm not dating her."

Dalia half laughs, half snorts into her coffee, then starts coughing. She slams her mug onto the table. Between coughs, she says, "As if she would ever date you. She only knows you exist because you're the editor of the school newspaper."

Haji holds up his hands. "That's true. I don't deny it."

"Who is dating her?" I ask.

"Dating who?" Haji says.

"Don't play the idiot."

"Just let it go, Allison. Let's enjoy the coffee and get back to algebra," Dalia says.

"Jason is going out with Leslie," Haji says.

"What? After he swore that he wouldn't." I feel betrayed, again. Maybe I shouldn't. I mean he did go to the dance with her knowing full well her reputation as a mean girl.

"That's just a rumor," Dalia says.

I face her. "You know about it too?"

"It's not a rumor," Haji says. "Leslie told me. Straight up."

"And why would she tell you that?" Dalia asks. "Are you besties now?"

"Forget about it," Haji says, waving a hand dismissively. He turns his gaze back to the computer.

Forget about it. Easy for Haji to say. Jason hadn't broken his heart. Leslie hadn't spouted a racial slur in his face. I pick up my coffee and take a sip. The hot liquid scalds my tongue a wee bit, but it still tastes wonderful. Before my next sip, I blow gently across the dark liquid. The steam rises over my face, like a warm, moist cloth. To hell with Jason and Leslie.

"Basketball season is starting up soon." I turn my gaze on Haji. "You promise to use my photos exclusively for all the games?"

Haji meets my gaze. "That's what I said."

The tension eases after that, although it never completely dissipates. We're a squad, a family. We can have disagreements and set them aside. Dalia and I power through algebra fueled by two cups of coffee apiece. Then all three of us turn our attention to American history, sharing notes and regaling each other with stories about the horrible Mrs. Higgins.

Four hours and a pot of coffee later, we're done for the day, our brains fried. We wander into the living room and look outside onto the swirling snow and the dark, ominous sky. In the front yard, the branches of the cherry tree sag under the weight of the snow.

We sit around talking, mostly about school and Devin. Dalia can't seem to get him out of her head. She has a date with him tonight, pizza followed by a movie. After about an hour, there is a break in the weather, and my friends decide to head out before it gets dark.

Without my friends to distract me, my thoughts turn back to Dr. Radcliffe and his draconic projection. I need to veg out. I sprawl on a chair in the dining room and turn on the TV. After allowing it to warm up, I stream episodes of an old sitcom. Even that frill doesn't completely distract me.

Dad comes home several episodes later. I turn off the TV and follow him into the kitchen, where he is preparing to cook pasta.

"Do we have meat?" I ask.

"We do," he says as he puts the pot on the stove and starts the burner. "I bought some turkey meatballs from the store."

"Thank goodness," I say.

"Still craving meat," Dad says and smiles. "Maybe you're going to shoot up. Grab the meatballs out of the freezer for me."

"I doubt I'll be doing much growing." I dig out the meatball package from the freezer and place it on the counter. "Say, Dad, do you know anything about Dr. Radcliffe?"

Dad looks at me. "Sure. I know Dr. Radcliffe. Everyone does. He's been around forever. In fact, I think you met him last year. Remember, you came with me to a faculty potluck."

"We saw him at the library."

Dad walks across the kitchen to the pantry. "Really. Speaking of the library, how is your vision?

92

Any issues?"

"No, my eyes are great." I rap my knuckles against the countertop. "Knock on wood."

Dad comes out of the pantry, smiling and holding a bottle of red sauce. He loves that old expression.

"No vertigo?"

"Nah. Tell me about Dr. Radcliffe."

Dad narrows his eyes. "He teaches medieval history. He is world-renowned for his knowledge of dragon lore, as I recall."

A tingle races down my spine. That has to be a coincidence, doesn't it?

"He has worked at the university for years. He must be nearing retirement. He has a reputation of being eccentric. I don't know much else about him, honestly. Why the sudden interest in Dr. Radcliffe? You've never mentioned him before."

"He said hi. He knew who I was and introduced himself. I just couldn't remember anything about him."

After dinner, I go to bed early, claiming tiredness, which is true. I'm exhausted, physically at least. My mind, perhaps fueled by an excess of caffeine, keeps playing images of Dr. Radcliffe and the dragon moving through the library. It's like an animated gif plastered in front of my eyes.

I don't know how many hours have passed when I finally give up on sleep and roll out of bed. I walk through the dark to my desk and open my laptop. It's easy with my prosthetics. The time in the corner of the screen is 1:18 a.m. God. I'm not getting any sleep.

I open up a web browser and type in Tahoma University's URL into the address bar and punch enter. I navigate around the website until I find the faculty homepage for Dr. Frederick Radcliffe, a tenured professor of medieval history. There is an old picture of him as a younger man. Not much in terms of what classes he teaches or any kind of personal information. There is, however, an email address below his picture. Radcliffe@tahomau.edu. I copy the address.

I have an old email account that I rarely use. I set it up when I was maybe twelve or thirteen for no reason other than I could. As best as I can remember, it has no truthful personally identifiable information included as part of the account. I login to the email account after two tries to guess the password. I create a new email message and paste Dr. Radcliffe's email address into the text box. In the subject line, I type: *I know what you are.*

Chapter 12

The pointer hovers over the send button.
Send.
Don't send.
Send.
Don't send.

Why am I doing this? I need to think this through. Maybe I should sleep on it. I click on the save draft button then close my laptop. It's 1:35. In the morning. Thank goodness, there is no school tomorrow. If I don't sleep until noon, I'll be a zombie all day.

I flop down in bed. The mattress squeaks under my weight. I throw my head back against the pillow and squeeze my eyes shut. In under a minute, I'm staring at the ceiling, obsessing over Dr. Radcliffe and his ephemeral dragon. *I know what you are.* Do I know what he is? Is he a magician? A dragon in disguise? Or, and this is the most likely scenario, I'm crazy, and he's just a college professor.

What will sending the email get me? No response, more than likely. Will that tell me anything? The message might be blocked by a spam filter. Or he might delete it without reading it. What if he reads it? If he's just a professor, he won't reply unless he's lonely or weird, the kind of person who follows anything down a rabbit hole. If he is something other than an ordinary college professor, he won't reply. Why would he? Why risk revealing himself over an email? What if he responds, and he is a magician or something else? Why would he reply in that case? To protect himself? Yes, to protect his secret. Contacting him might put me in danger. It might put my dad and friends in harm's way too.

I roll onto my side and shut my eyes, ready to let go of my obsession with Dr. Radcliffe and get some much-needed sleep. I end up flipping and flopping like an asphyxiating fish. Unable to get comfortable, I sit up and growl. Rest is not in the cards. Much to my surprise, the prospect of danger excites me. I'm drawn to it. Something predatory stirs deep within me.

I slip out of bed and pad across the room to my laptop. I don't bother sitting down. I just flip open the machine and glance at the time. 2:01. Damn. I access my ancient email account and open the draft email to Dr. Radcliffe. The professor might be dangerous, he might toast me up with dragon fire and eat me for a snack, but I'm not the prey in this scenario—he is. I hit send, close the laptop, and snuggle underneath my blankets. Warm and cozy, I'm asleep within minutes.

I wake up the next morning with a pounding headache. Why did I email Dr. Radcliffe? Stupid. Stupid. Stupid. I lie in bed restless, for how long I don't know, until I give up on falling back to sleep. I drag myself out of bed and go to the window. I pull open the blind. Still dark out, the only illumination is from porch lights and distant streetlamps.

Sighing, I trudge across my room and flip the light switch next to the door. I know I won't be falling back asleep. I flop down at my desk and open my laptop. It's 6:18 in the morning. I hardly slept a wink. 6:18. That's about an hour before sunrise. I glance at my camera bag on the floor next to the desk. I haven't been out shooting photos since I came home. Too much homework to catch up on. I need something to keep my mind off Dr. Radcliffe, and photography might be the ticket.

After checking my email and finding no response from Dr. Radcliffe, I go through my morning routine: showering, brushing my teeth, and searching the bedroom floor, including underneath the bed, for clean clothes. I end up in skinny black jeans and an oversized white sweatshirt with a goth black kitty emblazoned on the front. I inspect myself in the mirror over my desk and smile. I look savage. The scar above my left eye has faded to a thin white line from my hairline to my eyebrow. It makes me look like a femme fatale. That's just dope.

I turn away from the mirror to grab my camera bag but stop. I look in the mirror again, inspecting the scar. I run my middle finger down it. Someone had hit me with a freaking lead pipe or the equivalent. My lips form a grim line. Who left this mark on me? I think back to that stormy night, leaving Noodle House with the soup for Joe. I try recalling what happened after leaving the restaurant. I shake my head. I don't remember anything about the attack, and I'm glad about that. Yet there is part of me, perhaps the scarred femme fatale, who wants to meet my assailant for a second time in the dark, only this time I'm the predator.

I grab my camera bag and tromp downstairs to raid the freezer for the remaining turkey meatballs. The package contains eight. I heat up all eight. While the microwave drones, I make coffee. Just the smell of the grinding beans perks me up.

I sit at the dining room table for breakfast. After downing a second cup of coffee, I'm ready to head outside. I grab my heavy black winter coat, purple scarf, and black stocking cap from a closet by the front door. I rush back to the kitchen and take my camera out of the bag. The cool metallic and rubberized body of the mirrorless digital camera feels familiar in my hands. I turn the camera on, checking the battery life and the amount of free space on the two SD cards. Full battery power. Enough space on the cards for 2,000 shots. I smile, looking forward to heading outside, despite expecting to suffer from the biting cold.

The front yard is my photographic playground. I capture the sun as a starburst, backlighting the snow-laden branches of the cherry tree. Icicles hanging from the gutter catch my eye. The icy stalactites gleam golden in the light, almost like sparkling jewels. It reminds me of the glittering scales of the astral dragon. Don't think about Dr. Radcliffe or his dragon. Don't.

I bite my lower lip and notice my fingers are about as nimble as the icicles. I'm not wearing gloves to better manipulate the camera's controls, the sacrifices an artist must make. I shoot for another twenty minutes or so, creating a visual scrapbook of the morning before the cold drives me inside. I rush to the kitchen where I find Dad sipping coffee while oatmeal simmers on the stove.

"Out taking pictures?"

"Yup, it's a beautiful morning."

I race to the sink and turn on the faucet to hot. I put my hands under the water. As the liquid warms up, feeling returns to my numb digits.

"You want oatmeal?" Dad asks.

"I already ate," I say and add self-consciously, "All the meatballs. Can you stock up on meatballs and garlic chicken sausage next time you're at the store?"

"Sure," Dad says, looking me up and down. "Have you grown taller? The way you're eating, you must be getting ready to grow."

"Do you have to comment on my eating habits?" I dart from the kitchen, ignoring his reply.

I stomp upstairs to my room and leap into bed and bury myself underneath the blankets to continue warming up. I peruse the photos I took using the LCD on the back of my camera. Most of the pictures don't cut the mustard, but several of the icicles catching the morning light are savage. Something about the golden reflection imprisoned in the frozen water is captivating just like the glimmering scales of Dr. Radcliffe's draconic companion.

I frown, staring at my camera. Can this device capture an image of the dragon? That seems unlikely, but what do I have to lose by trying? Maybe my mind, but I already feel like I'm losing that.

The following week is Thanksgiving. I start a personal tradition. Every morning as soon as I stumble out of bed and every afternoon as soon as I arrive home from school and every night before I go to bed, I check my email for a message from Dr. Radcliffe. Nada.

On Wednesday, I trudge across the grounds of Tahoma University on the way to my regular appointment with Dr. Woolworth. My dad isn't with me because he is at SeaTac to pick up my grandparents, who are flying in from Florida for the holiday. I'm excited to see them live and in person. Video chatting is great, but there's something special, primal even, about being hugged by your grandparents. Plus, I can't wait to show off my prosthetics. Haji is bundled up beside me, keeping me company.

"Aren't we headed to the RTC?" Haji asks.

"Not yet." I motion for him to follow me. "I have a couple of things to do first."

"Are you going to be okay?" Haji says. "This is where...you know..."

"I was attacked?"

"Yeah, that."

"Honestly, it doesn't bother me at all. No flashbacks. Nothing."

"Well, if you do. Have any flashbacks or something, I mean. We can talk. You know, if that'd help."

"Of course. But no worries. No disturbing emotions. Nothing. Seriously, I'm one hundred percent PTSD free."

The homeless encampment is partially hidden by the shrubbery near the base of a towering Douglas fir. I'm worried Joe might not be there. When the weather becomes too cold, like everyone else, he tries to stay indoors. As we get closer, I can see a few people milling among the shrubbery and between the ramshackle tents and tarps that serve as sparse shelters against the elements.

"Joe!" I yell and break into a jog made awkward by my boots clomping in the heavy snow. Haji makes a disgruntled sound and follows with a clumsy gait.

A tall, broad-shouldered man emerges from the bushes, disturbing the snow as he passes through the branches. His skin is almost as dark as the heavy black coat he wears that is dusted with white flakes. For a hat, he wears a safety orange beanie. He keeps his hands tucked inside the pockets of his coat.

"Allison," Joe calls. "Allison, it's good to see you up and about, girl."

I pull up in front of Joe, and Haji stands next to me, huffing and puffing.

"You can see? By God, you can really see again?"

"I sure can see." I introduce Joe to Haji, reminding them that they've met before. Then I give Joe a quick synopsis of my experiences at the hospital and since.

"Holy cow. It's a miracle, Allison. It really is. A miracle," Joe says, shaking his head. His eyes are watery.

"Come celebrate Thanksgiving tomorrow at my house," I say.

"I don't know, Allison. I—"

"Joe, you're family. You just have to come. You saved my life. Come around two in the afternoon."

Joe breaks into a smile. "I'm sure glad I saved you, girl." He grabs me in a bear hug, lifting me up until my feet dangle above the snow. "You sure it's okay? Your papa be all right with me coming over?"

"Of course, he's always happy to have you over."

"All right then," Joe says and sets me down.

"Two in the afternoon, okay. Turkey with all the fixings."

"Damn, girl. You know I'll be there. The way to a man's heart is through his stomach."

The invitation made, we make small talk for a couple of minutes, then I make an excuse to move on. Joe gives me a goodbye hug and shakes Haji's hand. I lead Haji across the lawn past the war memorial flagpoles and a vast red brick building that looks like it could be a dormitory or an insane asylum. We skirt the quad with its cherry trees bending under the weight of the snow and pathways hidden by a thick white quilt.

"Where we headed now?" Haji asks.

"I want to swing by the Historia Building."

"The Historia Building?"

"It houses the history school. There is a professor there I want to see."

"Seriously? Why?"

I pat the camera bag on my shoulder. "I want to take pictures of him. He is sort of an eccentric-looking old guy."

The ancient building housing the history school is warm, almost uncomfortably so after being out in the cold and smells musty. We tromp down the narrow hallway that is well lit by banks of LEDs recessed in the ceiling. A few students move swiftly around the hall like they have somewhere to be. I swing my camera bag around to my chest and unzip it and pull out my camera. I pop off the lens cap and check the battery, just in case. One quick shot of Dr. Radcliffe, hopefully capturing his draconic companion as well. Then I'm out of here.

My hands are clammy when we reach his office. I check my camera settings, spinning the ISO up to 3200 and setting the machine for shutter priority. I set the shutter for 1/80 of a second. That should get me a bright and in-focus image despite the poor lighting. One downside of my camera, one that under ordinary circumstances I don't care about, no popup flash, and I don't have the money to buy an accessory flash.

I'm about to knock on the door but stop short,

crinkling my nose. I face Haji. "Do you smell something?"

"Smell what?" Haji asks.

I sniff the air. "I don't know. Like a rotten egg smell? It's faint."

"I don't smell anything."

"Must be my imagination." Just relax. One quick shot, and you're done.

I turn back to the door and raise a fist to knock on the surface that's covered with notes and posters advertising the goings-on in the history department. Haji points to a white sheet of paper taped to the very center of the door. In prominent black letters, the note on the sheet reads: *Out all afternoon for faculty meetings. Come back tomorrow for office hours.*

I knock on the door anyway, and, of course, there is no answer.

"What time is it?" I ask.

Haji takes out his smartphone. "4:17."

I sigh. "Damn. Okay. Let's go. My appointment with Dr. Woolworth is at four thirty. I'll have to catch Radcliffe another day."

Chapter 13

After my appointment with Dr. Woolworth, Haji insists on walking me home.

"You know I can see in the dark, right?" I ask.

"I know. But you were attacked. On the university grounds," Haji says.

"Thanks for reminding me."

"Sorry. I didn't mean to upset you."

"It's okay, Haji. You know, I bet one day people will opt to have themselves upgraded. I mean, my prosthetic oculi are savage."

"That will be so cool. I'm totally game. Like new feet. I read a story about a guy, I think he's a professor at an Ivy League school, who has these artificial feet that make it easier to climb rocks. Like free climbing."

After twenty minutes or so, we turn onto my street. Haji offers to help me with my American history assignment, which I take him up on. The night is young, and I know I need to write one hell of an essay to earn a good grade from Mrs. Higgins. That woman hates me more than ever since I've returned with my cybernetic eyes. I have a sneaking suspicion she doesn't like Asian people, but she's too careful to say anything out-and-out racist.

When we reach my house, Dad's hybrid is in the driveway. Apparently, he successfully navigated the wintry roads to bring my grandparents safely to our abode. To be honest, I'm relieved. After he nearly slammed into the tow truck, I've been wondering how little he remembers about driving in Wisconsin during the winter.

"My grandparents are here," I say. "Just a warning."

Grandma and Grandpa are in the front hallway to greet us when I open the door. My grandparents grab me in a tight embrace, and Grandma plants a wet kiss on my cheek. They ask me about my prosthetic eyes.

"They are awesome. Can you tell my eyes are fake?"

My grandparents squint at me. Grandpa gets right up in my face, and I smell the coffee on his breath.

"No." He shakes his head. "Look real to me."

"Who is this young man?" Grandma asks, smiling at Haji.

"Is this he your boyfriend, Allison?" Grandpa asks.

My face flushes. Before I can splutter a response, Haji answers. "No, we're just friends. I'm here because Allison graciously offered to help me with some homework."

"Oh, leave the children alone. They need to study," Grandma says.

"I'm just making conversation," Grandpa grouses as he ambles toward the living room.

Haji mounts the stairs, taking two at a time. I move to follow him when Grandma catches my eye. I stop, thinking she has something to say. Instead, she winks at me and flashes a wicked smile. I swear my prosthetics nearly pop out of my head. Grandma takes my forearm and pats the back of my hand.

"Play hard to get, dear," Grandma says. "It drives

the boys crazy. Don't play too hard to get, though. It's okay to be frisky. Just not too frisky. You'll do fine."

Grandma releases my arm and gently pats my cheek that must be about as burning red as a ripe tomato. She turns and heads to the living room. My grandmother just told me to be frisky. Ewwww.

I hope Haji didn't catch that. The second-floor hallway creaks from overhead. That'll be him walking to my bedroom. He probably didn't hear Grandma. I dash up the stairs before anyone else can sideline me to offer up free advice.

"Hey," Haji says when I enter my room.

"Sorry about that," I say. His laptop is out on my desk, and the homework assignment is open on the screen. "My grandparents have trouble with boundaries."

"No worries," Haji says and smiles.

I crinkle my nose, smelling something.

"Do you smell anything?" I ask.

Haji glances at me. "Umm…no."

I sniff the air again, detecting a mixture of eucalyptus and menthol with an undercurrent of sweat. Where do I recognize that odor from? A dark figure flashes in my mind's eye, arm raised overhead, holding something. Holding…a club or a lead pipe. I gasp. The muscles across my upper back and chest tighten painfully as if I'm being crushed by a giant's gnarled hand.

"What is that smell?" I say, voice shrill.

The pipe whistles through the air, water droplets flying off its surface. My throat constricts. I gulp for air and stumble over the unwashed clothes strewn across the carpet. I use my hand to catch myself against the wall and stand there feeling displaced like I have one foot in my room and the other on the damp grass of Tahoma University on that storm-ravaged night.

"Are you okay? What's wrong?" Haji comes to my side and puts a hand on my shoulder.

The stench of eucalyptus and menthol rolls off him, thick and strong. I back away, glaring at him until his hand falls away.

"You stink. Stay away from me. What is that damn smell?"

"It's a new body spray. I just put some on, so you won't smell my BO."

"Go wash it off."

Haji stares at me dumbly.

"Now!" I point to the hallway.

Haji nods. "Okay. Okay."

He darts from the room. I stagger to my bed and flop down. That smell. I don't remember the details, like my assailant's face or anything like that, but I do recall how it felt to turn around to find a shadowy figure stalking me, ready to attack. I shake and start crying for the first time since I've had my prosthetics installed.

Haji returns to the room with my dad in tow. I'm sobbing uncontrollably. They stare at me like a pair of idiots, which makes me cry even harder. There is nothing they can do for me, and that makes it worse.

"Allison," Dad says and rushes over to the bed. He sits next to me and puts an arm around my shoulders. "Are you okay? What's wrong?"

I'm crying too hard to get any words out.

"She started complaining about my body spray, Mr. Lee," Haji says. "She screamed at me to wash it off. When I came back to the room, she was crying like this. It's so unlike her. I was scared, so I came to get you."

I choke back sobs. "The body spray. What is it?"

Haji stares at me in puzzlement. "It's just something I picked up at the drugstore."

"What's so important about the body spray?" Dad asks.

"Whoever attacked me was wearing that body spray." I clench my fists at my sides. Anger, hot and terrible, mixes with my fear. I want to scream and pound the walls. I want to punch someone. "I'm certain of it. I remember the attack now. No details, but I remember."

As I talk, Haji goes to my desk and digs around inside his backpack. He pulls out a spray bottle.

"Here it is," Haji says.

The bottle is black with bold gold lettering, stating: *Manscape Bodywhiskey*. An italicized subscript reads: *hide the odor, attract the ladies*. I laugh so hard that I snort. They both look at me, Dad incredulous and Haji embarrassed.

"Hide the odor, attract the ladies? Seriously? The asshat who attacked me was wearing that?"

"It's very popular," Haji says.

I laugh even harder. He sounds defensive. He actually sounds defensive. The tension eases from me. This is just too funny.

"I researched it. Really," Haji says.

"Read all the reviews, did you?" I smirk. "Oh, I believe you."

"You remember something? About the attack?" Dad says.

"Don't get excited. It's not much." I fill them in.

Grandma calls from downstairs, interrupting my tale. "What's all that ruckus? You need something, Ray?"

"Allison thinks she remembers something about the attack," Dad calls.

"Do you hear that, George?" Grandma says.

There is a pause. Then Grandma says in an even louder voice, "Allison remembers something about the attack."

"You better call those detectives," Grandpa bellows from downstairs. "Get that goddamn ne'er-do-well behind bars."

My grandparents continue their conversation in loud voices. The stairs creak.

"Is there anything else?" Dad asks me.

I shake my head. "I just remember a tall, dark figure. Maybe wearing a trench coat. That's it."

"That's something," Haji says, his voice rising. He makes a fist with his left hand and smacks it against his palm. "You should contact the police. That's something for them to go on."

"I don't know—"

Grandpa interrupts me. "Contact the cops." He and Grandma huddle in the doorway. "Every little bit of information helps. Every little bit."

Dad snags his cell phone from his pants pocket and pulls out a card for Detective Nora Wolf. He calls the detective, who must answer on the first ring.

"Hello, Detective Wolf. This is Raymond Lee. My daughter Allison is remembering something." He pauses and takes a breath. "Yes. Here she is."

Dad hands me the phone. I'm very aware of

everyone staring at me like I'm an actor on a stage.

"Hello. Detective Wolf?"

"Hello, Allison. We met at the hospital."

"I know."

"You remember something about the attack?"

I tell her what I remember.

"A dark figure in a trench coat," Detective Wolf muses. "Do you remember any specifics? The assailant's height? Build? The color of the coat?"

"No. Like I said, what I remember clearest is the smell. Oh, and he had a lead pipe. I'm pretty sure about that."

"Okay. That confirms what we suspected about the weapon. Now, the smell. Manscape Bodywhiskey. You're sure about that?"

I explain about Haji wearing it and the flashback, adding, "It's a very distinctive smell."

"I know. My son uses that body spray. Thank you for the information. If we make any progress, we'll contact you. Of course, if you remember anything else, call us. Good night."

After the incident with the body spray, Haji goes home with strict instructions not to wear the body spray around me ever again. While eating dinner with my family, I wonder why he decided to wear the body spray in the first place. That is so unlike him.

Dalia and I exchange text messages on the subject. She assures me that it is just something high school boys do. Devin does. She gives me the full scoop on her dates with Devin and hints, not very subtly, that I should snag a boy so we can double date. With everything going on in my life right now, a boyfriend is out of the question.

110

It's all hands on deck for Thanksgiving. The kitchen is buzzing with preparation starting at about nine a.m., and that's with Dad having ordered a ready-made Thanksgiving feast from O'Hannen's Grocery down the road. Cooking is not really my thing, but helping my grandma make homemade rolls isn't that bad. She's kind and loving and doesn't bring up anything related to friskiness. My worry disappears as I knead the gooey dough and discuss school with her.

Joe rings the doorbell at two p.m. on the dot. He possesses an impeccable sense of time. I suppose it comes from all the years he spent in the military.

"You never said nothing about having family over," Joe says when I answer the door. Apparently, he caught a glimpse of Grandpa through the front window. "I don't know. I don't know."

Joe walks in place and keeps his hands underneath his armpits. His breath smokes from his mouth like a steam engine. There is a biting chill in the air that stings my cheeks.

"Joe, come on," I say. "They'll love you. We're letting all the heat out. Come in."

"Allison, who is it?" Dad asks.

"He's not expecting me? Allison—"

"Oh, Joe. Come in. Come in."

I glance over my shoulder. Dad is standing in the hallway.

Joe shakes his head. "No. No. I can't impose, Mr. Lee. Just stopping by to wish Allison here a happy Thanksgiving."

"Joe." Dad crosses his arms in front of his chest. He puts on a mock stern professor face. "It's never an imposition to have you here. Especially after you saved

Allison. In fact, she started to remember about the attack." I shoot him a dirty glare. "Sorry. Not something we necessarily want to talk about."

Joe looks at me. "Remembering something about the attack, huh? I'll stick around, but you need to tell me what you remember."

My grandparents are welcoming to Joe, and he listens attentively to my grandfather's innumerable ghost tales from South Florida. The dinner turns out fantastic, especially the rolls. I eat three slathered in butter. The rolls are so light and fluffy they melt in my mouth. Joe and I compete over who can eat more turkey. I win. It seems my meat craving still refuses to abate. While Dad and Grandma prepare the pumpkin pie in the kitchen, I run to my room to retrieve my grand-prize winning photo of Joe and my camera.

"So this is the photo your dad has told me so much about." Granddad holds the photo up to the light, his eyes narrowing. "You did a great job on the exposure. Wonderful shot. Is this of you, Joe?"

"Sure is. Your granddaughter, she's a wizard. I know I don't look that good in real life." Joe chuckles.

Grandma comes in from the kitchen burdened with two plates of pumpkin pie topped with whipped cream. "Joe, you are a plenty handsome man. Have some pie."

Dad follows Grandma with three more plates. Everyone is so relaxed and happy. I start snapping pictures. By the time everyone has finished their pumpkin pie, I've shot dozens of photos.

After dinner, Joe insists on helping to clean up. The two of us take dishwashing duties. Once my family retires to the living room, Joe questions me about the assault. I tell him what I remember and begin to shake.

I set the glass I'm holding down in the sink out of fear I might break it with my bare hand. I take a deep, shuddering breath in an attempt to tie down the rage rising up from my guts.

"What's wrong? You fearful?" Joe says. "If you're upset, say no more."

"Not upset, exactly. Angry," I say through gritted teeth. "Give me a sec." After a few deep breaths, I tell the remainder of what I recall.

"Manscape, huh?" Joe says. "That beanpole friend of yours is wearing that?"

I finish washing the glass and hand it to Joe. "It's surprising. It's totally unlike him to pay attention to stuff like that."

Joe laughs. "Allison, I can tell you why he's putting on bod spray, girl. He's into you, plain as day."

"Haji? No way."

"Maybe you're just too innocent in the ways of the male of the species to notice the signs." Joe sets down the dried glass. He points to his eyes. "I took one look at him yesterday. Shit. He's smitten."

Chapter 14

That evening I check my email before going to
bed. Nothing from Dr. Radcliffe.

Having the grandparents over means sharing the
one full bathroom in the house. It's not bad when it's
just Dad and me. The half bath downstairs suffices in
an emergency. Grandpa takes forever to brush his teeth
and floss and do whatever else he does to keep his gum
disease from getting worse. Grandma doesn't rush in
the bathroom either, so I'm waiting and waiting to take
a shower. I try to work on my essay for American
history, but stray thoughts about Haji or Dr. Radcliffe
or the assault keep breaking my concentration. It really
sucks.

Instead, I download photos from my camera to my
laptop and fire up the photo editor. I browse through the
images from last Sunday morning, a handful from
earlier in the week, and ones I took today of Joe and my
grandparents and Dad. I look closely at one I took of
Joe about ready to take a bite of pumpkin pie. He's
smiling, showing off crooked teeth and laugh lines. He
looks genuinely happy. I want him to be joyful and not
to struggle through life. I understand him better now,
his battle with PTSD, after reliving the assault. It's
haunting, and I know I'll never be able to smell
Manscape Bodywhiskey again without being
transported back to the attack.

By ten thirty, my grandparents are done in the bathroom. I can finally shower and do my evening routine. I'm in my pajamas and tucked in bed next to my giant kittycat stuffy by eleven. I'm exhausted, and I want to sleep, but my mind is still plagued by errant thoughts, mostly of Haji. Joe must be wrong. Haji can't possibly be into me that way. We've been friends forever. He is like a brother to me. He and Dalia are the siblings I never had. Still, as drowsiness fogs my mind, I decide Haji is handsome, despite his klutziness. If he ever grows into his frame, he will turn heads. His almond skin is smooth and unblemished, and his raven black hair is thick and lustrous. Running my hands through his silky hair would be wonderful.

Dad and I drop off my grandparents at the airport on Sunday afternoon. I'm sad to see them go, it's been a great visit, but I'm glad I'll only have to share the bathroom with Dad. The school week begins with no response from Dr. Radcliffe. I suppose he's not going to respond, but I keep checking my email every night.

By Thursday, I've finished my essay for Mrs. Higgins, just in time too. I'm confident I'll get a decent grade, probably a solid B. I grind my teeth, though, certain my work would earn anyone else an A, but she does have it out for me. I've done my best to avoid Haji for most of the week except while in the presence of Dalia to keep things from being too awkward. In the afternoon, he corners me in a crowded hallway between classes.

"You're coming to the basketball game tomorrow, right? We're playing Emerald High." Haji talks so fast I'm surprised he isn't tongue-tied.

"Of course. I need to get some shots for the

Weekly." I join the river of students meandering to classes.

"Wait, Allison." Haji grabs me by the forearm.

"Personal space, Haji." I pull my arm free.

"Just…just." Haji stumbles over the words. "Can I walk you to the game?"

My lips form a straight line. The awkwardness between us is painful. Yet he is my friend, a great friend. As long as he understands that…my gaze shifts to his dark, wavy hair. I really like his hair.

"I won't wear the…" He drops his voice to a whisper. "Body spray, I promise. I threw it out."

"Okay. Come get me at—"

"The game is at seven. I can swing by at five thirty, and we can grab something to eat."

Don't push your luck, buddy. "I have to study. I'm still behind in some of my classes. Maybe we can do something with Dalia on the weekend."

Haji's shoulders sag. He almost looks like a hangdog. I'm sorry for him.

"If she's not busy with Devin."

Over the past week, the snow finally stopped, and the temperature warmed, so when Friday evening rolls around, Haji and I tromp through a slushy soup. Somehow slush gets inside my midcalf-high rain boots, and icy tingling makes me wince. Haji is oblivious to the cold and in good spirits, speaking about the goings-on at school and the chances of the basketball team making it to the playoffs. We only have to dodge spray from cars twice, and soon the bright lights of the high school shine in the distance.

The gymnasium is a standalone structure next to the impressive stadium with its covered bleachers capable of seating several thousand fans. People are arriving for the game, trekking through the slop to the gymnasium, a long, narrow brick of a building.

At the door, we flash our student press credentials to the pimply faced freshman and Mr. White, an English teacher, who are working the ticket booth. The light inside the gymnasium reflects off the polished floor and the gleaming wooden bleachers. A sizable crowd has come out for the game, especially the Cascadia Prep fans. Both teams are warming up. The scents of popcorn and hot dogs hang in the air. People slurp pop from straws and pose for selfies. It's almost a carnival atmosphere.

The Cascadia Prep Titans wear blue shorts and white tank tops. Emblazoned across the shirts are the name of our school along with a cartoonish giant. On the other side of the court are the Emerald High players in green and white. A green silhouette of the Space Needle adorns their shirts.

I sling my shoulder pack around to my chest and pull out my camera. I check the battery and the capacity of the SD cards. All good.

"I'm heading to the press box," Haji says and waves to me. "Catch up with you later."

I glance up from my camera. "Sounds good. Wait. Take this."

I hoist my camera and bag from my shoulders so they're only around my neck. I take off my heavy winter coat and hand it to Haji.

"Keep track of this for me. It's hot in here."

"Got it."

I watch him walk away through the crowd. The press box is a folding chair at a table out in front of the bleachers where Mikey, a Cascadia Prep senior and game commentator, has the sound equipment set up. He also runs the digital scoreboard from a tablet.

A head of long blonde hair catches my gaze. Towering over most of the crowd is none other than Leslie Chapman with her camera dangling by a strap from her neck. I'm about to turn away when she leans down toward someone. It's Jason. They kiss. On the lips. It's just a quick smooch, but still. I turn away and wind through the crowd toward the restrooms in an alcove next to the bleachers. I thought I was over Jason, but the betrayal still stings like a slap across the face.

Don't cry. Pull yourself together. Leslie wants you to cry. She wants you to break down. Don't. Don't.

The door to the restroom swings open, and a diminutive Latina in an invisible cloud of flowery perfume walks out. A DSLR with an 80-200 mm zoom lens dangles from her shoulder. She wears a green Emerald High hoodie.

"Allison! Back photographing the games? That's awesome. I heard about what happened…anyway, it's great you're back."

"Hey, Margot. It's great to be back. I really missed this. Taking pictures."

Margot leans close to me and whispers, "I have to know if it's true…are your eyes like…like robo-eyes?"

"Yeah," I say. The high school photojournalist community is small, so I'm not surprised Margot has heard about my prosthetics. Heck, Haji probably filled her in on everything. But that's okay. Margot is good people.

Her eyes bug out. "Seriously? No way." Her eyes narrow as she looks at my orbs in concentration. "Look real to me. How's your eyesight?"

I smile. "Freaking better than ever."

I tell her about my enhanced night vision and zooming eyeballs. Her mouth drops open into a small O.

"That is the most savage thing I've ever heard," Margot says.

A buzzer sounds, followed by Mikey's baritone announcing that the game will start in five minutes.

"I better get out there," Margot says and flashes a quick smile. "We're going to destroy you guys. Good luck with the pics."

I slide into the restroom. People are rushing out of stalls to wash their hands and head out to the game. I go to the one empty sink and admire my savage green hair and prosthetic eyes in the mirror. What does Leslie have that I don't? Jason, I suppose, but he's not much of a catch. He approves of her racist attitudes, or he wouldn't be with her. A lousy bottom feeder, that's what he is. I smile at my reflection then speed walk out to the game.

I position myself behind the basket just in time to catch our first fast-break. Leslie is there, blazing away with her high-end DSLR. I ignore her, drop down on one knee, and bring my camera to my eye. Focus and shoot.

"Crap," I mutter, lowering the camera.

The shutter speed was way too slow. I check the image on the LCD, a blurry mess. I forgot to spin up the ISO. Such a rookie mistake. I spin up the ISO to 3200 and turn my attention back to the action. Emerald High just scored. Margot is right, they're going to murder us.

As the game progresses, I start getting some nice

shots, at least I think I do. I won't know for sure until I view the pictures on a computer screen.

Leslie keeps glancing at me, like repeatedly. She looks like she wants to talk. About what? There's nothing I want to talk about with Leslie. Honestly, it's all I can do to concentrate on photographing the game and not spin around and sock her in the mouth. A ferocity is boiling in my gut, and keeping it in check is not easy.

The game ends with an Emerald High victory, just as Margot predicted. I make a beeline for the press box, moving against the crowd heading for the doors. Leslie heads me off. Groaning, I try to step around her, but she sidesteps to block me.

"Let me by," I say.

"Allison, I need to talk to you," Leslie says in a loud voice to be heard over the din.

I meet her blue-eyed gaze with a glower. "I don't want to talk to you. Ever."

Anger blazes in her eyes. That's the Leslie I know.

"I'm trying to apologize. For…for everything."

I clench a hand into a fist at my side. I see an opening in the crowd and dart through it. I glance over my shoulder, buffeting people on either side of me. Leslie doesn't follow. She turns away and meanders with the milling crowd toward the exit.

I find Haji sitting with Mikey in the press box. Mikey is gigantic, more a bespectacled bear than a teenager. He's being recruited by universities across the country to play linebacker.

"Hey, Allison, Haji was telling me all about your prosthetic oculi. Oculi is a wicked word," Mikey says and stands up. "I'm super glad you're back at school. I hope the cops catch the asshole who attacked you. See you around. Later, Haji."

I say goodbye to Mikey as I put away my camera. Haji hands me my coat, and we leave. He walks me home despite the fact I remind him that I can see perfectly fine in the dark. Intellectually, I know it's black out, like really dark, especially when we are away from the streetlights. But, to me, it looks like twilight opposed to night. It's pretty awesome.

I enjoy Haji's company, and it bites that one day soon I'll have to break it to him that I will never be his girlfriend. He rants about the deficiencies of the Cascadia Prep basketball team and what he would do to make improvements if only he were the coach. It helps pass the time and keeps me from fretting about my issues.

Haji walks me all the way to my house before saying goodbye. As I wave good night to him, I wish he isn't such a sweet guy and wonderful friend. It would be so much easier to reject him if he were a jerk. I bite my lower lip. Maybe, if I luck out for once in my life, it won't come to that. Haji will fall head over heels for someone who wants to talk sports and get all cuddly while watching corny sci-fi flicks with him.

I go inside to discover Dad has stayed up waiting on me to make sure I arrived home okay. We exchange greetings, and I break the news that my school lost. He commiserates, and then we both head for bed. Before I can sleep, I have to check my email, not that I expect anything.

When I see the email from Dr. Radcliffe, I swear I have palpitations. "Oh my God."

My hand shakes so violently I can't control the

computer with the trackpad. I take a deep breath, hold it for a second, and let it out.

I shut my eyes and whisper, "Just open it. Get it over with."

I open my eyes to narrow slits. My hand quivers, finger bouncing over the trackpad, but I manage to click on the email. My body vibrates like a struck cymbal as I read the message: *Come to the Chapel Library's reading room tomorrow at 10 p.m. Alone.*

"There's no way I'm going alone." I snag my cell phone off the desk.

I chicken peck out a message to Dalia and Haji on the flip phone.

—*The Obsidian Roast tomorrow. Breakfast. 9 a.m. Must talk.*—

Chapter 15

The rain falls from a slate gray sky to patter against the pavement. The roads are still a slushy mess with mounds of snow piled high up against the curbs. In places, the sidewalk is hidden under a hard-packed crust of dirty snow. A cold breeze stirs the skeletal branches of deciduous trees and chills my exposed cheeks. I keep my head down, walking fast over the terrain toward The Obsidian Roast.

I arrive at the café before my friends. A few people occupy tables around the joint, enjoying steaming cups of java and sugary baked goods or croissant sandwiches. The warm air blasting from vents is welcome after suffering the cold on the walk over. I stride to the front counter, smelling the glorious scent of fresh coffee infusing the air.

Sipping coffee and nibbling on a cinnamon roll, I stare out the window onto the dreary day. What will my friends think when I tell them Dr. Radcliffe is followed around by a shimmering, semitransparent dragon? Insane. Nut job. Crazy lady. Half the time, I'm convinced that I'm a crackpot, so why should Dalia and Haji think differently?

Maybe I'm making a mistake. I shouldn't tell them anything. I shouldn't get them involved. What if Dr. Radcliffe is a magician or a dragon or has a dragon following him around? What will happen when three high school students show up to snap some pics? Despite the cozy temperature in the café and wearing my heavy winter coat, goose bumps form on my arms.

I take a sip of coffee, enjoying the dark, bitter brew. I stare at the water droplets on the window, each a self-contained little planet reflecting the larger world, and try not to worry.

"Allison."

Haji stands in the doorway, waving to me. I smile and wave back, and my stomach clenches. Will telling him about Dr. Radcliffe put him in danger? I chew on my lower lip.

Haji strips off his coat as he walks to the table. He drapes the coat over the back of the chair across from me.

"Oh, you already ordered," Haji says. "You waiting long?"

"I got here fifteen minutes early. I had trouble sleeping last night."

"Are you okay?"

"All good."

Haji's eyes narrow. He shrugs, then lines up to order. I watch him pull his phone out of his back pocket and begin to text. No doubt he is telling Dalia that something is up with me. I regret messaging them last night, and I regret even more emailing Dr. Radcliffe in the first place.

Haji comes over, carrying a scone on a plate. He sits down across from me.

"Did you order anything to drink?" I ask.

He grins. "Chai latte. With soy milk."

His smile broadens when I roll my eyes. I've tried to turn him into a regular coffee drinker, but he still prefers tea with steamed milk.

"So what's up?" Haji asks.

I shrug and sip my coffee.

"That text last night. What is that about?"

"We should wait until Dalia arrives."

"About Dalia," Haji says and checks his phone. "She's going to be late. She was up half the night chatting with Devin."

"They seem serious. Have you met him?"

"Once. He's an organizer for the climate marches. That's how they met. You know the big march that happened while you were in the hospital? I met him there."

I sigh, put off that Haji knows more about my BFF's boyfriend than I do. That's the worst part of what happened to me, having my life stolen. Instead of being out in the world with my squad, I had been in the hospital. I tense, rage and ferocity stirring deep within me. I breathe in sharply at the sudden, irrational urge to punch something. What is going on with me?

"I look forward to meeting him," I say through clenched teeth.

Haji looks at me quizzically. I try to smile, but I'm afraid I must look like I'm snarling. I'm just so...so angry.

"Is everything all right?" Haji asks.

"Yeah, yeah." I laugh, and it sounds forced. "So tell me more about Devin."

Haji shrugs. "He's a little full of himself."

A barista flutters over and sets down a giant, steaming mug of tan liquid in front of Haji. "Your chai latte, sir."

Haji glances at the barista, who is flashing him an

enticing grin. "Thanks."

The barista rushes back to the counter to attend to more customers.

"She's cute," I say. "I think she's new. What's her name?"

Haji stares at his tea. "She's okay."

"Her name?"

"Danica. I think."

"You do know her name. You should talk to her. Introduce yourself," I add in a whisper. "If you ask her out, I'm certain she'll say yes."

Haji shakes his head, picks up the mug, and blows across the hot liquid. A cloud of steam travels out across the table then upward to dissipate into nothingness. He takes a sip of his latte. He sets down the cup and looks at me with a serious expression. Don't say it, Haji. Don't declare your love for me, not here, not now. I don't have the time or energy to deal with that.

"Allison, I—"

"Allison. Haji. Sorry I'm late."

It's Dalia to the rescue. I let out a breath and unclench my jaw. Dalia sits down on the chair in between us, pink hair bobbing. She brushes her hand against mine.

"I'd be even later if Haji hadn't texted me. I had such a hard time getting up this morning. I was up most of the night talking with Devin. I won't see him all weekend. His parents are dragging him to Portland to visit family," Dalia says. There is a loud dinging from her coat. She bounces in her chair and pulls out her phone from a pocket of her coat. "That's him. I'll go order."

Haji takes a bite of his scone. I sip my coffee and look out the window. The cold and drizzle fit my mood.

Dalia returns with a steaming mug of black coffee in one hand and her phone in her other. She manages to sit and set the cup on the table while jabbing her phone with a thumb.

"There," she says with a pout and sets the phone on the table. "Devin just left."

The phone dings again, Dalia snaps the device off the table with the speed of a diving raptor. Her eyes widen, and she giggles. My gaze meets Haji's. He smirks and takes a big bite out of his scone. I love Dalia, but this is getting a little over-the-top. I really need to meet this Devin. Just a text from him makes my BFF lose her mind.

"Sorry about that," Dalia says and places her phone on the table. "So, Allison, what was that message about last night?"

Dalia and Haji stare at me. I wring my hands, then belatedly hide them under the table. Contacting them was a mistake. I don't want them involved or thinking I'm a nut.

"Yeah, what's up with that?" Haji says.

I shift in the chair that creaks under my weight and take another sip of coffee.

I shrug. "Nothing. It wasn't anything. I just thought it'd be nice to hang out."

Dalia leans forward. "You never get up this early on the weekend just to hang out, and neither do I. What's going on?"

"I'm the only early riser here," Haji says between bites of scone. "You only get up this early on the weekend for cross-country meets. Tell us. Is it something to do with your prosthetics malfunctioning?"

My eyes go wide. I stare at my food and rip off a hunk of the pastry and stuff it into my mouth.

"That's it," Dalia says and smacks the table with an open palm. The cups rattle, and a bit of coffee splashes out of her mug onto the tabletop. "Tell us. What's wrong? We're your squad, Allison. We're here for you."

Her phone dings, and her gaze darts to the device. Thank God for Devin. The Inquisition is over. Instead of answering the text or whatever, Dalia powers down her phone and slips it into a pocket of her coat. Her gaze meets mine.

"We're here for you."

I swallow the hunk of cinnamon roll. Haji stares at me expectantly. Maybe it's okay if I tell them what's bothering me. Perhaps they'll tell me that I'm under stress or that the prosthetics are malfunctioning, and that I'm not crazy. Maybe that's what I need to hear. Or they'll tell me to check myself in at the nearest mental hospital.

"It's nothing. Really." I shake my head. "I shouldn't have messaged you guys."

"Allison," Dalia huffs.

"Tell us," Haji pleads. "Especially if I can use it in the *Cascadia Weekly*."

I glare at Haji. "If I tell you anything, you have to promise not to tell anyone and not to print a word of it anywhere, especially the *Weekly*."

Haji drops his chin to his chest and rubs the back of his neck with a hand.

"You and that damn school blog," Dalia says and shakes her head.

"I prefer online periodical."

"Periodical," Dalia says and rolls her eyes.

Haji shakes his head and takes a sip of tea. "Okay. My lips are sealed, and I won't write about anything I hear today."

"What he said." Dalia nods her head toward Haji.

"Do you remember Dr. Radcliffe? From the library?" I ask.

"That creepy guy? The professor?" Dalia says.

Haji leans back in his chair and furrows his brow. "You mean the eccentric-looking guy you want to take a picture of?"

I move close to the table and look both of them in the eyes in turn. I whisper, "Yes, that guy. Here's the thing." I moisten my lips. My hands are clammy. I grab the warm mug of coffee and take a swig. "He's followed around by a dragon. I think I'm the only person who can see it."

Chapter 16

Dalia breaks out laughing so hard she goes red in the face. "Is this an April Fools? It isn't April yet."

My face heats up, and I stare at the table. Dalia's reaction is just what I feared. She thinks I'm a nut job.

"I don't think she's joking, Dalia," Haji says.

"Dragons? We don't live in a fantasy world, Haji. I know you want to, but we don't."

I look up. Haji is frowning, and Dalia is fighting back giggles.

"I'm serious," I say in a soft voice.

"You can't be." Dalia leans back in her chair and starts chewing on the tip of her right thumb.

"Maybe you should go see Dr. Woolworth," Haji says. "Is she working today?"

"I don't know. Maybe." I take another sip of coffee. "I'm not going to see her."

"You need to go see her," Dalia says. Her voice is strident, and she leans forward to rest her elbows against the table. "You need to tell her that you're hallucinating. Dragons. That's crazy."

"Not dragons," I say. "A dragon. Only one."

"It doesn't matter." Dalia sits up and drops her arms to her sides. "Dragons don't exist. Seeing dragons is not normal. It's like my grandma claiming she sees angels. Grandma is schizo."

"I'm schizo now?" My face grows warmer, and my

voice is shrill.

"That's not what I mean. You need to go see Dr. Woolworth."

"Maybe we should all calm down," Haji says. He makes a pushing down motion with his hands.

I look around the café, afraid we're creating a scene. People might hear us. Decide that I'm a schizophrenic nut. Thank God. No one is paying attention to us.

"Nobody is saying anyone is crazy," Haji continues. "We're just concerned. I have a feeling there is more to this tale. Maybe, Allison, you can share the rest with us?"

Dalia crosses her arms in front of her chest. She nods. "Okay. This is a judgment-free zone. Let's hear the whole story."

I take a gulp of coffee, followed by a deep breath. I'm on the edge of a yowling chasm of madness. Either my friends can pull me back, or they can let me fall. I stare into my nearly empty cup as I speak, admiring the air bubbles floating on top of the black brew. I tell them everything, from seeing Dr. Radcliffe and his draconic companion in the library to emailing and then unsuccessfully stalking the professor and finally his response to meet tonight at the Chapel Library.

The tale told, a weight is lifted from my shoulders, the vise crushing me in its iron grip loosened. I look up at my friends, a ghost of a smile on my lips. Dalia and Haji stare at me. My BFF's mouth hangs open, and her eyes are scrunched up in a puzzled squint. Haji, his usually smooth forehead furrowed, leans back in his chair.

"Have you talked to anyone else about this?" Dalia

asks. "Like your dad?"

I sink in my chair like a lead balloon. I shake my head.

"Maybe you should. Talk to your dad," Dalia says and glances at Haji as if searching for support.

"I'm sure Mr. Lee will want to know about this, Allison," Haji says.

"It's not normal to see dragons," Dalia says.

"You don't think I know that."

I don't remember the last time I felt so judged by my supposed best friends. Telling them was a mistake. Beneath the tabletop my hands form into fists.

"Allison, we're just trying to help," Dalia says.

"You said, I'm schizo."

"I did not. Allison…"

I stand up and finish the lukewarm coffee in one enormous gulp and slam the mug against the table.

"Allison, don't leave," Haji says. "I believe you. What do you want us to do?"

I glare at Dalia. "She doesn't believe me."

"I didn't mean you're crazy." Dalia's eyes are moist. "Maybe…maybe it's the prosthetics or having been hit on the head. I don't know. The point is you need help."

Tears stream down Dalia's cheeks. She wipes at the moisture with her hands. I chew on my lower lip. I hate seeing my friend cry. She only has my best interest in mind. Perhaps, I owe her and Haji a second chance.

"Maybe I hallucinated the dragon, but Dr. Radcliffe still wants to meet," I whisper and sit down. "I don't want to meet him alone. Will you guys come with me?"

"Of course," Haji says. "I want to see this dragon."

Dalia shoots him a withering look.

"Not so loud, Haji." I glance around the café. "I don't want people thinking I'm crazy."

Dalia sighs. "I'll come. Who knows what kind of weirdo Dr. Radcliffe is? Just promise me, when we don't see a dragon, you'll seek help. You'll tell your dad or Dr. Woolworth or someone."

I nod and make the promise, although I fear that I will see the dragon, and they won't.

"When does he want to meet?" Haji asks.

"Ten p.m."

"Creepy. The library will be long closed by then," Dalia says.

I nod and begin telling them my half-baked plan.

****

The wind picked up in the late afternoon, blowing away the rain clouds. So as Dalia, Haji, and I cluster in the shadows cast by a building on the outskirts of the university quad, a bright quarter moon and stars fill the night sky. There is a chill in the air that makes me shiver and huddle closer to my friends. We fidget to help stay warm. Not that it works.

We've been standing here for nearly an hour, since nine p.m., hoping to spot Dr. Radcliffe entering the library. No such luck. All we've managed to do is freeze our asses off, and I mean that quite literally.

"It's almost time," I say. "Phones charged? Cell signals."

My friends pull their hands out of their pockets. Dalia takes off a glove so she can manipulate her phone. They both give me an affirmative. I sling my shoulder pack around to my chest and take out my camera. Battery is good. SD cards are in place and formatted. I pop off the lens cap and stuff it into a pocket. Finally, I spin the ISO up to 3200. If I get a chance to take a picture of the dragon, I want the image sharp. I slip the camera back inside the shoulder pack and zip it shut. I keep the pack positioned across my chest for easy access.

"It's time. Everyone ready?"

My squad nods and wishes me good luck. I start off across the square, but Dalia heads me off and throws her arms around me.

"Be careful," she whispers. "This guy is a weirdo."

"I will be," I say and return her embrace.

We release each other, and I continue across the slushy bricks. In places, compact snow and ice make me slide like an ice-skating elephant, but I manage to stay on my feet. I mount the stairs to the library, being extra careful not to slip. I glance to my left and right along the columns that form the façade before the entrance. It is an excellent location for an ambush.

I look overhead, scanning the gloomy surroundings. In a corner, I spot a camera. I bite my lower lip, wondering if I'm being recorded. We all know and discussed the risks. If we're caught trespassing or whatever, at least we're underage. I reach my hand for the door and grasp the cold metal handle. I pull, half expecting to find the door locked. It slides open with a loud squeal that sets my pulse racing. I pause in the doorway, taking a deep breath to help calm my nerves. Despite the warm air rushing out, I'm as chilled as a shrimp on ice.

I enter and pull the door shut behind me that closes with a loud click. My friends will follow after one minute now that I'm inside in case the entrance is being watched. I start to count down from sixty. I won't enter the reading room until I reach zero.

I look around the interior of the library. The entrance hall is dark, only illuminated by the faint light of the moon streaming in from high windows and the green glow of an exit sign. To my right are the dark stacks. To the left across a marble floor is the doorway to the cathedral-like reading room.

I tread toward the reading room.

"Ten," I whisper.

I stop about fifteen feet from the doorway, staring into the interior. On the far side of the room are rustic shelving and colorful books. Without my prosthetics, I'd probably have to strain to see them. With my prosthetics, the reading room appears more of a twilight than nearly pitch black.

"Nine."

I take a handful of steps, coming within ten feet of the entrance.

"Eight."

My mouth is dry.

"Seven."

My heart thunders in my chest so hard I imagine it makes audible thuds.

"Six."

I stride forward and stop just outside the high vaulted chamber.

"Five. Four."

I step into the doorway.

"Three."

My hands are clammy. I look around the room, my view cut off by the doorframe. I swear I see a faint golden glimmer on the floor. I gasp and blink, and the light is gone.

"Two."

My breathing is fast like I just ran up a flight of stairs.

"One."

Biting my lower lip, I cross the threshold into the room. To my left, I see the glittering scales of a gargantuan golden dragon with its leathery green wings pressed tight against its sides. The beast shimmers and fades in and out of existence. One second the serpentine neck looms overhead to nearly touch the vaulted ceiling and in the next second fades away. The same is true for the rest of the serpent's body.

There is a click, and a desk lamp flares to life. I breathe in sharply and hop in place. Sitting in a chair at the table, bathed in the lamplight, is Dr. Radcliffe. His elbows are propped up on the table, and his hands are steepled.

"Ah, Allison Lee," Dr. Radcliffe says and checks a golden wristwatch. "You, young lady, have an impeccable sense of time, so unlike most of your generation."

I gulp, only barely registering what he just said to me. I gawp at his draconic companion.

"Well, Allison, you want to talk to me. Here I am."

"Why…why is there a translucent dragon looming over you?" I stutter and fumble with my sling bag's zipper.

"Hmmm," he says and, placing his fingertips against the table, stands. "A fascinating question. Do I take that to mean that you do not know what I am?"

"How would I know what you are?"

I get hold of the zipper and start opening the bag.

Dr. Radcliffe, lips forming a hard, grim line, marches around from behind the table and approaches me. The dragon that almost seems to project from him follows, a forefoot that should crush the table passing through the wood as though insubstantial.

My hand wraps around the barrel of my camera lens. I hear a door slam from outside in the atrium. Good. My friends have arrived. Even if I can't get a shot off, they will. Dr. Radcliffe stops in front of me and places a hand that feels very human against my hand that holds the camera lens.

"Now, now, Allison. I think it is best if you come with me, my dear. Your friends in the hall. They will come also." He sniffs me, like a predator scenting prey. "Odd. I do not recognize your scent."

"You're sniffing me? You sicko! I'm not going anywhere with you."

I pull away, but he clenches my wrist. His grip is shockingly strong for a spindly old man.

"Let go of me!" I scream and thrash.

"Please, please, my dear. It would be a shame to break your camera. Ah, your friends."

"Let go of her," Dalia says.

I look over my shoulder. Dalia rushes across the room toward us with her gaze fixed on me. In the doorway, Haji takes images with his phone. I realize by where they focus their attention that they don't see the dragon.

"Run," I yell. "Run. Call the police. It's the dragon."

"Dragon?" Dalia says. "It's just that creepy old prof. Let go of her, you freak!"

Dr. Radcliffe tuts like a scolding schoolmarm.

"Calm down, children. I will hurt you if I must. Do not bother making phone calls. Cell signals are so easy to block."

Another voice, one I don't recognize, rings through the chamber. "No one move. You're all trespassing."

Dalia stops midstride and spins toward the voice. Standing inside the doorway behind Haji is a woman wearing a police uniform. He faces the officer and retreats from her. A shimmering silver dragon, half inside the room and half-hidden in the wall, looms above the police officer.

Dr. Radcliffe releases my wrist. "As I said, my dear, you and your friends are coming."

Chapter 17

"She's like you," I say, staring at the silver dragon projecting out of the police officer and the wall.

"Ah," Dr. Radcliffe says. "You really can see us. Interesting."

The officer, a petite woman, carries herself with military bearing. She sniffs the air. "These two are human," she says, her words clipped, and gestures to Haji and Dalia. "I can't place the other one."

"What's going on?" Dalia demands, her gaze shifting from Dr. Radcliffe to the officer. "Of course, we're human."

Haji fiddles with his phone and holds it up as if he's making a recording.

"Are you live streaming this?" I ask.

"No signal." Haji is deadpan. He's always like that when he's working on a story. That must be what he's doing now, playing at being a reporter.

"What should we do with them?" the officer asks.

"Bring them in. Allison Lee…" Dr. Radcliffe pats me on the shoulder. I wince. "…is a fascinating conundrum. I cannot tell what she is. The others, I am sure, will want to see her. Handcuff those two and come smell her."

"Handcuff?" Haji says. "Why?"

"Are we under arrest?" Dalia asks.

"Please, let them go. I'm the only one who can see

the dragons," I say, but Dr. Radcliffe and the officer ignore me.

Dalia and Haji look desperate, like one or both might make a run for it. The officer blocks the entrance, but surely there is an emergency exit somewhere.

"On the ground, or I'll tase you," the officer says.

"We're not resisting," Dalia says.

"I'm recording. I will send this to Channel 5. Police brutality," Haji says.

The officer gives Haji an incredulous stare that says more loudly than words that he is an idiot. In two quick, compact paces, she covers the ground between them, her draconic companion following, and snatches the phone out of his hand.

"Hey." Haji makes a grab for the phone.

The officer moves so fast I can't tell what she does, but it's effective. Haji doubles over, clutching his gut, and teeters to the floor. Dalia makes a run for the exit.

"Please, don't hurt them. Please," I say, fearing my BFF will be tased.

Something flies through the air and entangles Dalia's legs. With a cry, she belly flops on the floor with a loud thud and a whoosh of air. Whatever was thrown clatters to the floor and thuds against the base of a wooden bookshelf. I realize after a moment it's the officer's flashlight.

"Do not worry, dear, Ion did not hurt them permanently," Dr. Radcliffe says.

Ion zip ties my friends' hands behind their backs and warns them that any peep will earn them a savage beating. She swaggers over to me, like a gunslinger in a black-and-white cowboy movie. The shimmering silver dragon follows her. The serpent is inside the reading room, except for the tail that passes through the wall to disappear. The beast is long and lithe, not nearly as bulky and muscular as Dr. Radcliffe's dragon.

Ion looks me up and down. Her name badge reads Davenport. She leans close to me and sniffs my neck. She leaps back several feet, a startling, inhuman feat of athleticism, and hisses like a feral cat ready to pounce.

"Skaag. I smell skaag on her."

"Surely not," Dr. Radcliffe says, backing away from me and walking over to stand next to Ion. Their draconic companions intermingle in a vibrant shimmer of gold and silver. "I am intimately familiar with the noisome stench of skaags."

"You males have worthless noses." Ion glares at me, lips curling to show teeth. My pulse gallops. She might shoot me. "There is the musk of skaag on her. It's subtle."

"An associate then?" Dr. Radcliffe says. "But she does not smell human."

"I don't know what she is. A mutt, maybe. We should kill her and her friends."

"Video cameras are recording this," I say.

"No one will kill anyone," Dr. Radcliffe says. "And I disabled the security system."

"I bet you didn't disable the cameras we hid here earlier today," Haji says.

"Why you—"

"Ion, control yourself," Dr. Radcliffe says, his tone commanding. "Boy, we know you are lying."

"You're sure you don't want me to kill them?"

"If Allison Lee is a skaag operative, we must find out what she knows," Dr. Radcliffe says.

Ion hauls Dalia and Haji to their feet and walks in

between them, a hand gripping each by the upper arm. The doctor juts his arm out like an old-time gentleman escorting a lady.

"Do not try to run," Dr. Radcliffe says. "If you do, I do not know what Ion will do to your friends."

Gulping, I rest my hand in the crook of his arm. Ion leads us out of the library onto the ice-cold university campus. I hope to see someone, anyone, and call for help, but the bone-shattering chill is keeping all the night owls indoors. The freezing temperature doesn't seem to have any impact on Dr. Radcliffe or Ion. Their astral dragons follow them, glimmering and fading away only to reappear like shades in the night. I'm amazed no one else can see the beasts.

Dalia puts up token resistance that ends when Ion shakes her like a maraca. Haji begs the officer not to hurt Dalia and pleads with our friend to stop resisting. I'm too defeated to say or do anything. All I can do is hope the night doesn't end with the three of us dead.

Ion leads us to a Seattle PD cruiser parked beneath a streetlamp on Stevens Way. I panic. If we are locked in the back of the police cruiser, there is no way for us to escape. I make a run for it. Dr. Radcliffe's strong fingers burrow into my forearm, preventing my escape.

"Let go of me!" I scream. "Help!"

My resistance inspires my friends to fight back. They start screaming and thrashing. Ion, though, is more than a match for them, thrusting them up against the cruiser and opening the back door. From somewhere out in the darkness, a person complains about the ruckus.

"Seattle Police. Stay back," Ion barks.

The three of us are crammed inside the police

cruiser. We are relieved of our phones and me of my camera. My friends look as sullen and frightened as I feel.

"Are you guys okay?" I whisper softly.

"I'm not hurt. My shoulders are just sore," Haji says, shifting his weight to relieve the pressure against his shoulder joints from having his wrists bound behind him.

"My knee hurts," Dalia says, a knife's edge of panic and pain in her voice.

We fall silent when Ion slides into the driver's seat, and Dr. Radcliffe sits in the passenger seat. The cruiser's engine roars to life, and we're off. The forelegs of their draconic companions pass through the cruiser's roof and the dashboard. The bulk of the dragons' torsos are literally in my face and the faces of my friends. The gold and silver scales catch every hint of light from that of passing cars to streetlights and stoplights to sparkle with blinding brilliance. I squint. Still, the luminescence is glaring. Damn prosthetics. I need to know where we're going, not be blinded by semitranslucent dragons no one else can see.

"Are you okay?" Haji whispers. He is in the middle between Dalia and me.

"The light," I say. "It's giving me a headache."

"What light?" Haji says.

"Is something wrong with her?" Dalia asks tremulously.

A strident growl comes from up front.

"Quiet now, children," Dr. Radcliffe says. "Ion prefers silence in her vehicle."

Just when I'm about to shut my eyes, they adjust to the light with remarkable speed. The glimmering bodies of the serpents fade to a tolerable luminosity. I sigh. My headache dissipates, and I can see. Something just happened, perhaps like in the classroom when my sight zoomed in because I couldn't read Mrs. Higgins's handwriting. The prosthetics responded, at least I think they did, to my conscious thoughts.

Ion drives onto WA-520, then onto I-5 southbound. Even at this late hour, the main north-south corridor through the city is busy in both directions. Ion merges into the fast lane and jams the accelerator. She runs up on vehicles and weaves through the traffic.

The cruiser exits at 163B to the Sodo District, the beating heart of industrial Seattle. Soon the streets become a maze of warehouses that have been converted into artist lofts and other trendy venues. A few cars roll down the streets, and we pass a handful of people on the sidewalks. Soon the warehouses are just warehouses. There are fewer cars and no pedestrians. Deep in the industrial zone, the warehouses are rundown, some downright ramshackle. The streets are dark. If it weren't for my prosthetics, I don't think I'd be seeing much. The cruiser pulls up in front of one of the warehouses, a wide low building with peeling paint, busted windows, and a rusted door large enough for a box truck to drive through.

The cruiser rolls to a halt, and Dr. Radcliffe gets out, his shimmering draconic companion looming over him, and slides the warehouse door open wide enough for the cruiser to enter the dark interior of the building.

"I have a bad feeling about this," Dalia whispers.

"Maybe they won't kill us," Haji says. "Why drive us all the way out here if they plan to kill us?"

"Because it's abandoned," Dalia says, her voice a

scourge.

Haji recoils.

"Quiet," Ion growls. "Unless you'd like me to try out my new pepper spray."

The interior is dark except for the cruiser's headlights and the glimmer of the dragons' scales that don't seem as brilliant as earlier. It's so dim even the night vision of my prosthetics can't penetrate the entirety of the gloomy interior. The far corners of the warehouse remain a mystery to me, but what is visible is empty, almost. The only exception is a small table with a lightbulb dangling over it by a long wire up ahead. There is something on the table, but I can't make out what it is.

The cruiser slows to a stop in front of the table. The item on the table is a laptop. Ion gets out of the car and opens my door.

"Out," the officer says.

I obey and stand aside so my squad can pile out. Ion pulls a razor blade from a pouch on her utility belt and cuts my friends' cuffs. My gaze is transfixed by the silvery dragon projecting in all its immense majesty from the police officer. The beast is somewhere between the size of an elephant and some massive dinosaur, a sauropod I think they're called. The shimmering serpent's four feet are equipped with long white talons that appear as sharp as razor blades. Leathery wings are pressed against its sides, but extended, I suspect the wingspan is nearly as wide as the warehouse. The dragon glimmers and fades and reappears as if caught in a flux between realities like some mythical beast out of a fantasy or science fiction novel.

"What are you looking at?" Haji asks.

"A dragon," I whisper.

"Dragon? Where?" Dalia says.

"Right there," I say, pointing at the beast looming above Ion. "I wish you could see it. It's beautiful."

My friends stand on either side of me, gazing at where I point.

"I don't see anything," Dalia says.

"Me neither," Haji says.

"You're humans. Pitiful senses," Ion says. "Your friend. She is something else."

"Wait. You mean there really is a dragon here?" Dalia says.

The lightbulb above the table flares to life.

"Some questions, young lady, are best left unanswered," Dr. Radcliffe says from behind us.

My friends and I turn to face him. My mouth drops open. His draconic companion is truly colossal. Its long neck stretches nearly to the ceiling. The head is huge, a cross between a T-rex and a dog. Next to the pair of nostrils positioned at the front of the muzzle hang two thick green tendrils, like a drooping mustache. The mustache is the same green as the leathery wings pressed against the dragon's golden torso. A serpentine tail stretches out through the darkness, curling and undulating. The beast makes the warehouse seem small.

"Ah, Ion is contacting our compatriots. Come now, children, gather around the table," Dr. Radcliffe says and strides passed us. He heads to the table where Ion has opened up the laptop and is manipulating the device with the trackpad. "Everyone will have an opinion on what to do with the three of you. Come along. Chop-chop."

Chapter 18

Dr. Radcliffe sighs. "What is taking so long?"

"You know the connection is bad," Ion says, opening computer programs with the pointer. "What do you expect?"

My friends and I exchange bemused glances.

"You need assistance?" Dr. Radcliffe asks.

"You barely know how to turn on a computer, old man," Ion says.

"I see the experience of being a human police officer has not imparted you with respect."

Ion glances over her shoulder at us, and her face twists into a rictus smile. "If you possessed one iota of common sense, we wouldn't be here." She gestures at us. "I wouldn't have to smell these..." She shakes her head. "These stinking up-jumped monkeys."

Dr. Radcliffe paces in front of us. "Just get them on the screen."

Ion turns back to the computer. "We could kill them. We wouldn't even have to worry about disposing of the bodies. I'm hungry. I'll eat them."

My eyes go wide. Dalia's mouth is agape, and Haji clasps his stomach. I'd like to think the officer is joking. It'd be impossible for her to eat all of us, wouldn't it? Even if she's a serial killer psycho, but then I only need to look at the silver dragon coming out of her body and looming over us to know there are creatures present that could eat us.

"We are not killing anyone," Dr. Radcliffe says. "Not until we have a vote."

"Maybe that's why you failed. Too much voting, too little decisive action."

Our captors continue their verbal sparring. Ion brings up video streams on the computer. One video feed resolves into an old woman with a face as lined as dry, cracked mud and thick white hair. More video streams resolve, but I'm not paying close attention. I'm considering something Ion said earlier. She didn't claim her dragon would eat us. She said that she would eat us. Does that mean Officer Davenport and the insubstantial dragon following her around are one and the same?

"I have Tanis and Mauve," Ion says. "Hello, ladies. I'm here with Frederick, two wayward humans, and an aberration."

I stiffen. I'm no doubt the aberration. It seems I'll never fit in anywhere, and people will always judge me no matter what. Ion is the one walking around with a dragon projecting out of her body, yet I'm the abnormal one. Just once, I'd like to be the girl who doesn't stick out in any way, who's not a target for anyone, not for the Leslies of the world, or whatever our captors are. Rage bubbles inside me, a geyser ready to vent. Something alien, perhaps the presence awoken within me that night in the hospital, slams against the cage containing it deep within me, rattling the bars. My hands clench into fists.

"Mauve is online?" the old lady asks.

A young woman with short brown hair and glasses that make her look reminiscent of an owl answers. "Yes, I'm here, Tanis. Hello, everyone."

"Damn," Haji whispers. "It's a video chat. They're going to decide whether or not to kill us over a video chat. Holy cow. Holy cow."

"Where is Tatsuo?" Dr. Radcliffe asks.

"He's not joining," Ion says.

"Probably sleeping on a beach somewhere," Dr. Radcliffe mutters and in a louder voice says, "We will have to proceed without him. Are we in agreement?"

Ion and the women on videoconference voice their agreement.

"Show us the aberration," the old woman, who I think is Tanis, says.

Dr. Radcliffe gestures for me to come. "Stand here in front of the camera."

"Putting the aberration on display?" I ask.

Ion faces me, her expression hard. Her hand rests on the yellow grip of the Taser. I'm certain she will tase me, but Dr. Radcliffe places a hand on her shoulder.

"Aberration is a poor word choice," Dr. Radcliffe says. "Please, my compatriots want to see your face. That is all."

"Do what they say so they let us go," Dalia whispers.

"Since you asked nicely." I walk to the table, maneuvering around a shimmering silver foreleg.

The women on videoconferencing do not have draconic companions. Are they different from Dr. Radcliffe and Ion, or are their dragons invisible to the cameras?

"You can see dragons, girl?" Tanis asks.

"Do be polite, Tanis," says the younger woman. I think her name is Mauve. "Your name is Allison?"

"Yes, to both questions," I say.

149

"Are you hearing this? Dragons?" Dalia says in the background.

"What are you?" Tanis asks.

"What do you mean?"

"Are you human?" Mauve asks. She squints at me from behind her spectacles. "You say you can see dragons. Humans can't see us unless we reveal ourselves to them."

I shrug. "I saw Dr. Radcliffe and his dragon in the library a couple weeks ago. I saw a second dragon tonight when Ion showed up."

"Are you a magician?" Tanis asks.

"A magician?"

"Can you cast magic?" Mauve asks.

I shake my head. "I know what a magician is. I can't do magic. I wish I could."

"She has the stench of skaag on her," Ion says.

Mauve's eyes go wide. "Oh my."

Tanis grimaces. "She could be bait. To ensnare us."

"That's exactly what I told Frederick," Ion says. "He insisted on meeting with her anyway."

"I do not smell skaag on her," Dr. Radcliffe says. "But she does not smell human."

"We should kill them and be done with it," Ion says.

I want to throw up. Haji and Dalia beg for our lives. Ion, hand resting on the grip of her pistol, rounds on them and snarls to be quiet. I move to stand between the officer and my friends.

"Don't hurt them. Please. They can't see you. They're not a threat." I look to Dr. Radcliffe. "If you need to kill someone, kill me. Let them go."

"Don't you dare hurt Allison!" Haji yells.

Dalia screams something incoherent. Ion shouts back and draws her gun and thrusts me aside with an arm as stiff as a steel girder and takes aim at my friends.

Dr. Radcliffe strides between my friends and the officer. He holds his hands up as if gesturing for everyone to calm down. He speaks, but I can't hear him over the cacophony.

"Silence!"

The word is spoken by Dr. Radcliffe with inhuman ferocity and intensity, so loud that I cringe and throw my hands over my ears. My friends do the same, and even Ion winces. The sound reverberates through the warehouse. I stare at the golden dragon looming over Dr. Radcliffe. The beast stares down at me with unblinking black and yellow cat eyes. I swear there is a sternness to the beast's demeanor that matches Dr. Radcliffe's.

"That is enough," Dr. Radcliffe says.

"They're a threat to us," Ion says and points to me. "She can see us."

"Your answer is to kill them?" Dr. Radcliffe asks.

"Yes. Neutralize the threat."

"If I may speak," comes a voice from the computer. It's Tanis. "There is an alternative."

"Please tell," Dr. Radcliffe says.

"The aberration is a threat to us. That fact is indisputable, and we must not ignore it."

I clench my jaw so tight my teeth ache.

"However, we don't know how great a threat she is. We should endeavor to learn what she is and how great a threat she poses."

"She is obviously a threat. I can smell skaag on

her," Ion says.

"Do not interrupt me, youngling," Tanis says.

Ion cowers as if struck. "Yes, eldest."

"Skaags cannot see us while we ride the slipstream," Tanis continues. "Yet the aberration can."

"Stop calling me that. My name is Allison."

"Don't antagonize them," Dalia whispers.

"Do not interrupt me again, Allison," Tanis says. "She can see us, so we know she is not a skaag. She appears human, but Frederick and the youngling say she does not smell human, so we know she is not one. I propose we put a tracking spell on her. We track all her movements over a period of time. Once we are satisfied she does not pose an immediate threat or is being used by skaags as bait, we bring her in for a face-to-face meeting with all of us. Mauve and I will use magic to discover her true nature."

"I think that is a wonderful plan. Much better than killing them," Mauve says.

"Too dangerous," Ion says. "Tatsuo would agree with me. You all know that. He'd say we should eat them."

"Tatsuo is not here," Dr. Radcliffe says with a shrug. "Shall we put it to a vote? I put a tracking spell on Allison and her human friends, or do we allow Ion to eat them?"

"Why bother with a vote?" Ion says. "You're going to put the spell on them. Just do it."

Ion turns away from the proceedings and stomps back to her cruiser. The silver dragon follows her and appears to stomp its semitransparent feet just like Ion. The officer gets into the cruiser and slams the door. The dragon sits on its haunches, its forelegs passing through the roof of the cruiser and tail end going through the trunk.

Dr. Radcliffe appears unperturbed by the petulant display. "All in favor of letting the captives live and placing a tracking spell on them, raise your hand."

Dr. Radcliffe and the two ladies on videoconferencing raise their hands.

"That decides it," Dr. Radcliffe says. "You will live. For now."

"What do you mean for now?" I ask.

"We might reconsider our decision at a future date. It depends on what we discover about you and your friends."

"You won't discover anything about us to do...to do with these skaags that you fear so much."

"Yeah, we've never heard of them," Dalia pipes in.

"What is a skaag?" Haji asks.

Dr. Radcliffe's expression becomes grave. "Hope that you never discover the answer to that question, boy. Pray to whatever god or gods you worship that you never do."

"I'm atheist," Haji says.

Dr. Radcliffe arches an eyebrow.

"TMI, Haji," Dalia says.

"There are higher powers in the universe," Tanis says. "Some call these beings gods."

"What spell will you use, Frederick?" Mauve asks.

"Some good old-fashioned blood magic should suffice?" Dr. Radcliffe asks.

Tanis frowns and nods. "That will do."

Mauve pushes her glasses up higher on her nose. "There are better spells. Molineux's Tracking Charm for instance or—"

"Yes, yes, but those are the spells that can take hours to cast properly," Dr. Radcliffe says.

"True. Blood magic must be renewed once a fortnight, or it will wear off," Mauve says.

"Two weeks should be more than enough time for us to learn what we need to know," Dr. Radcliffe says.

"Do be careful, Frederick," Tanis says. "I hate it when you exit the slipstream inside that warehouse. You bump your head against the ceiling, and the whole place will come down."

"Don't squash our guests," Mauve says.

"I will endeavor not to," Dr. Radcliffe says.

Our captors keep speaking about magic, maybe. The conversation is technical, diving into details I can't track. I withdraw to stand with my friends a few feet from the table.

"Exit the slipstream? Squash us?" Haji whispers.

I shake my head. "I have no idea."

"Should we run?" Dalia asks.

"I don't think we'll get far," I say. "Ion will run us down in the police car."

"I can't run fast anyway," Haji says.

We both give Haji an incredulous look. He shrugs.

"I can't," Haji says.

"Please, your life is on the line. You can run fast," Dalia says, and I nod in vigorous agreement.

"Follow me, children," Dr. Radcliffe says.

My friends move to follow him, but I don't budge. "Why should we follow you? I don't want magic done on me."

Dr. Radcliffe gives me an exasperated smile. "I do not enjoy resorting to threats, but I will make an exception for you, Allison Lee. Come with me now, or

I will have Ion tase you. I do not need you conscious."

I bite my lower lip. The raging beast is bending the bars that contain it. Along with the anger, supernatural prowess rumbles inside me like a volcano ready to detonate. I widen my stance. I can take him. Overpower him and escape. I crack the knuckles of my left hand, then my right. If Ion tries to stop me, I'll overcome her too.

"Just do as he says," Dalia says. "You don't want to be tased. None of us do."

"Okay," I say and comply. I'm really just biding my time.

Dr. Radcliffe leads us away from the computer and the police cruiser. He stops about fifty feet away. He faces us and smiles.

"Now, children, stay back and do not try to run. We do not want any accidents."

Dr. Radcliffe's eyes go vacant and his body stiff. His draconic companion comes into sharp focus, no longer flickering and fading. Electricity buzzes in the air, and my skin tingles. Bolts of electricity arc as the dragon's forelegs and torso become substantial, solid. The scales shine as if each possesses an internal source of light. A rumble fills the warehouse in time with the rise and fall of the beast's torso. The sound is like the gush of a blacksmith's bellows. It's the dragon's breathing.

"Are you seeing this?" Haji asks.

"Oh my God," Dalia says.

The beast threatening to break free from its cage retreats, whining like a beaten cur. My sense of my unnatural physical prowess drains, leaving me trembling. In their place I know fear and the certain knowledge that no matter the hidden powers I may or may not possess, I'm no match for the monster standing before me.

Chapter 19

"What do we do?" Haji asks.

"Run?" Dalia says.

I'm too enthralled by the wonder in front of me to respond. Besides, my legs are leaden. How can we escape this huge, magnificent beast? It can bat us aside with a mere swipe of a forefoot as easily as a cat kills a mouse.

"Let's go!" Dalia yells.

Feet pound against concrete. In the back of my mind, a small voice screams at me to run for my life, but somehow, I know I can't escape the dragon. And, maybe if I don't run, just maybe the dragon will ignore my friends and concentrate on me. I'm the one it really wants, the only one who can see it while it rides the slipstream. Whatever that means.

A hand grabs me by the upper arm and pulls me away from the golden beast. It's Haji, his eyes wild with terror. He starts to run away from the dragon toward the back of the warehouse. He yanks me along with him. I scramble to keep from falling, and then I'm running. Maybe twenty feet ahead of us is Dalia, sprinting at full tilt. Haji lets go of my upper arm and grabs my hand. His palm is warm and sweaty and comforting.

A thunderous boom shakes the ground, and I swear the warehouse wobbles. I dare a glance over my shoulder. A golden forefoot, more a monstrous hand with an opposable thumb, reaches for Haji and me. At the end of each finger is a long talon as white as ivory.

"Watch out," I scream.

The titanic hand engulfs us, mashes us together, and lifts us into the air, struggling and screaming. I punch a rough scaled finger and yelp. My hand comes away bloodied from numerous abrasions. Haji is tougher than I am. He keeps beating against the hand holding us even though his appendage is awash in blood.

Haji and I are squeezed together so tightly the knuckles of the hand I hold press into my thigh. Haji's bony chest crowds against my abdomen and left breast until I can barely breathe. We are jittered, teeth and bones rattling, as the dragon lumbers with booming footsteps in pursuit of Dalia. I try to yell at her to watch out, but the words only come out as a strained gasp.

An enormous hand swoops down and snatches Dalia into the air. The dragon raises us up high above the concrete floor. The beast is luminous and hot as if every scale contains a microscopic star fusing atoms. Haji stops beating against the impervious scales and starts murmuring something, perhaps a prayer to his parents' god. Above the loud breathing of the beast, Dalia utters a piercing cry.

The dragon's breath is hot and stinks of rotten eggs. Thin coils of smoke escape its lips. It stares at us, eyes narrowing, and very distinctly shakes its head in the negative, the green tendrils drooping from its muzzle wobbling. Its grip tightens. I yelp, and so does Haji. We're being crushed, squeezed so hard our heads will pop off. Dalia lets out an earsplitting wail. Then the grip loosens, and the dragon sets us on the ground.

I crumple to the floor, shocked that my bones aren't pulverized. The concrete is like ice after the hellfire grip of the dragon. Haji slumps down beside me. Dalia is on the ground too, bawling herself hoarse.

I scramble to my feet and run to my BFF. I drop to my knees and cradle her head against my chest. She shakes and sobs like a small child.

"Leave us alone," I say to the dragon that might be Dr. Radcliffe if the professor even exists in any real sense. "Can't you see you're frightening us?"

The beast growls a rumbling sound that comes from deep in its chest, echoing through the warehouse. Dalia presses herself closer to me, clinging. The dragon starts making a series of complex sounds: grunts and hisses and growls and shrieks, each resounding. The very air shimmers and grows hot.

Haji shuffles to my side, never taking his gaze from the beast. "What's happening?"

I shake my head and raise my voice to be heard. "I don't know. Blood magic?"

"Whatever that is."

"Doesn't sound good for us."

"How is she?"

Dalia's gaze is fixed on the creature. She clings to me, breathing in ragged gasps.

"I don't know, Haji. She's not good."

Without warning, the dragon rears up onto its hind legs, extending its serpentine neck until its head nearly brushes the ceiling, and roars. The sound is so deafening we throw our hands over our ears, even Dalia. The dragon opens its mouth, revealing a red forked tongue and teeth the length of short swords dripping with saliva. The tongue lolls out of its mouth, almost like a dog's. The beast reaches a hand to its tongue and uses a talon to pierce the red flesh. A bubble of purple ichor blossoms from the puncture.

The dragon reaches for us. I cower, and Dalia whimpers, gripping me again, and Haji, that brave, brave boy, takes both of us in a protective embrace. The dragon hesitates then withdraws its talons. It comes down on its forelegs with a boom that shakes the entire warehouse.

The next thing I know, the dragon's face is in mine, and that moist, bloody tongue licks my forehead. It's like a supersized slobbering Great Dane with a red-hot poker for a tongue just slathered me. I grimace at the heat and gooey slime. Both are uncomfortable, but not so irritating I want to wipe at my forehead and make my hand slimy. Haji and Dalia are licked in quick succession, each left with saliva and a patch of purple blood on their foreheads. I stare at my squad with eyes that must be as wide as chicken eggs.

"There was purple blood on your forehead. It disappeared. I think it was absorbed into your skin," I tell them.

"The purple stuff absorbed into your skin too," Haji says.

Dalia wipes a hand across her forehead. It comes away with covered in viscous slime. "Oh my God," she whimpers. "Oh my God. Why is this happening to us?"

The beast backs away, then turns to lumber back toward the body of Dr. Radcliffe that appears as inanimate as a marble statue. As the beast nears Dr. Radcliffe's body, it fades and shimmers and becomes translucent.

"It's gone," Haji whispers.

"Thank God. Thank God," Dalia whimpers into my chest.

I don't say anything. I don't want to tell them that the dragon isn't really gone. Dr. Radcliffe's human form smiles at us and pushes his glasses higher up the bridge of his nose.

"That was not so bad, was it?" the professor asks.

None of us respond. Dr. Radcliffe and his golden draconic companion watch us huddling together until the police cruiser rolls up. Ion gets out of the cruiser, walks around to the back, and pops the trunk. Dalia sobs, and Haji hugs us tighter.

"What's going on?" I demand.

"We are going to clean you up, of course," Dr. Radcliffe says. "We cannot send you home covered in saliva."

Ion swaggers around from the back of the cruiser holding a white nylon bag with a red cross on its side.

"What are you? Are you even human?" I ask.

"Allison, if you do not know the answer to that question already, you have not been very observant," Dr. Radcliffe says.

****

I wake up the next morning in my bed with an ass-kicking headache. My eyes flutter. I groan. I've slept like crap, and that's putting it mildly. Every time I shut my eyes and sleep whisks me off to slumberland, dreams or nightmares or almost nightmares, I don't know what to call them, plague me. The Dragon Radcliffe, because after last night I'm convinced he is, in reality, a dragon, or at least something that happens to look like said mythological monster.

161

I shut my eyes, deciding a few more minutes of sleep is worth the risk of suffering another nightmare. My head feels like a star about to go supernova. I hover between semiconsciousness and sleep when I hear the door to my bedroom creak. I roll onto my side and open my eyes to cracks so thin I see my eyelashes. The doorway frames my father's tall, lean form. I snuggle into a ball and shut my eyes with the assumption that he's checking on me like I'm still a little girl and will soon go about his business.

"You finally came back," Dad says.

"What?" I say, voice mushy.

"You went to study with your friends at The Obsidian Roast yesterday in the morning," he says and flips on the overhead light.

I squint and blink, my prosthetics take a moment to adjust to the sudden brightness. "Dad, what the hell?"

He ignores my protest and marches across the room to sit down in my study chair. He twirls in the chair to face me. "You don't come home for dinner. You don't call. You don't text. I call you. You never answer. What's going on?"

I sit up in bed, yawning, and wipe the grit out of the corners of my eyes with my index fingers. "Can't you see I need sleep?"

"Long night, huh?"

"Really long, believe me. Can you go now? I want to go back to sleep."

"Not until you explain yourself."

"Explain what?"

"I called you last night. No response. I texted you last night around nine. I waited and waited. Well, guess who called me asking about Dalia at ten forty-five. Her mother. Where were you?"

"We were just hanging out. Dancing. Having fun." I yawn again and put a hand in front of my mouth.

It's too late when I notice it's my bandaged right hand I'm holding in front of my mouth. Dad stares at the bandages. I whip my hand back under the sheets.

"What happened to your hand?"

After the encounter with the Dragon Radcliffe, Ion had used her first aid kit to clean and bandage our wounds and wipe off the gooey saliva from our heads. The militant police officer proved a proficient and gentle medic.

"It's nothing," I say. Dad raises his eyebrows. "I tripped and fell walking home. It was dark out."

Dad scoffs. "I might've fallen for that before you told me your prosthetics have night vision."

"Come on, Dad. My night vision isn't perfect."

"Were you drinking?"

"No." I shake my head. I'm angry now. My head feels like it's going to burst like an overripe melon, I have a dragon tracking me with blood magic, and Dad won't give me a millimeter of slack. "I'm leaving."

Dad's voice rises. "Not until you explain to me about last night."

I stare at him. Maybe I look afraid because concern flashes across his face. The sad fact is I can't tell him what happened last night. Dr. Radcliffe and Ion warned us if we tell anyone about what happened, they'll need to intervene. Ion implied she has a hankering for human flesh. I don't know if that's true or just a line of bullshit, but after last night I know that either one of them could crush my dad like a gnat.

"Stop me," I challenge him and throw off the

blanket.

I'm wearing pink panties with black polka dots and an oversized black T-shirt with bold print across the chest: *Smile, You're on Camera*. I stand up and prepare to strip off my shirt.

"Allison, stop!" Dad says, looking away. He jumps out of the chair and makes a beeline for the door. He darts from the bedroom and slams the door behind him. "We'll discuss this later, young lady."

I drop my hands to my sides and flop onto the bed. I listen to him stomp down the hall. Boy is he mad. He never slams a door. I'm just glad he didn't call my bluff. I don't think I could really strip in front of my dad, no matter how much I want him to leave me alone.

"Ugh." Just the thought of doing that to him makes me sick to my stomach on top of my skull-cracking headache.

I'm desperate for coffee. I go to my desk and retrieve my phone. Our electronics had been returned to us last night, but only after Ion had deleted all the images and videos off our phones and my camera. I message my squad:

—*Heading to Obsidian Roast.*—

I check the date. Crap. I have tests tomorrow.

****

I arrive at The Obsidian Roast to find my squad already there. They have textbooks and papers and laptops spread over the table like they're good little students. I can tell by the way they lean close and whisper that they're discussing last night. I come over to say hi and discover that they've ordered me a dark roast in an extra-large mug and a piping hot cinnamon roll.

I sit and take a slurp of coffee. "Thanks for this. I really need it."

Dalia looks like she needs her coffee as much as I need mine. Her pink hair is disheveled, and she has big bags under bloodshot eyes.

"Did you sleep at all?" Dalia asks.

"Not well," I say. "Your hoop. It's at a weird angle. Let me fix it."

Dalia leans close, and I carefully adjust the nose ring with my index finger.

"There. Perfect," I say.

"Thanks."

Haji watches, chewing on an egg and ham croissant. His fingers are poised over his laptop's keyboard.

"Studying?" I ask.

"No," he says, shaking his head. "I just want to get your account recorded. I typed out mine last night, and I just finished taking Dalia's."

"I don't know if that's…crap."

I stare at Officer Davenport, who is standing at the entrance of the café. Of her draconic companion, I only see the forelegs and a sweep of tail out on the sidewalk. The rest of the beast is hidden by the walls and ceiling. The police officer hooks her thumbs in the front belt loops of her pants like a strutting cowboy. She meets my gaze and smiles predatorially. Without a second glance, she struts to the front counter.

"Oh, Christ," Dalia whispers. She looks like she's on the verge of tears.

"Gosh. I guess they really are tracking us," Haji says.

Ion marches to the exit with a sixteen-ounce to-go cup in her hand. She eyeballs us, her lips curling into a sneer.

Chapter 20

I breathe easier when Ion leaves The Obsidian Roast. She swaggers down the sidewalk in the cold December air. Steam escapes from her mouth like puffs of smoke. The diaphanous silver dragon projecting from the officer swaggers too.

"Is she like Dr. Radcliffe?" Dalia whispers.

"Yes."

"Can you see her dragon?"

"It's slender. Silver. Beautiful."

Ion hangs a left onto 43rd, crossing the street and disappearing from sight behind buildings.

"We need to get them on camera. As dragons," Haji says.

"How? We just go up to one of them and ask politely? That's crazy. Ion will shoot us," Dalia says.

Haji shrugs and takes a bite of his croissant sandwich. With his mouth full, he says, "I don't think Dr. Radcliffe will hurt us. He should be easy to find. We just need to hang around the university."

I rip a hunk off my cinnamon roll and dip it in my coffee, then shove the dripping, gooey delectation into my mouth. I follow up the food with a long swig of black gold. My head is still bursting, but the coffee and pastry have taken the edge off my headache. I lean over and unzip my backpack and take out my algebra book. I'm too exhausted and overwhelmed to think about the dragons right now.

"Seriously? You're going to study?" Dalia asks.

"We have tests tomorrow." I flip open the thick textbook. "You and Haji might be all caught up, but I was out of school for weeks. If I don't study, I'm going to bomb my exams."

"Can you give me your account of last night while it's still fresh in your mind?" Haji asks.

"I don't want to think about that right now," I say.

Dalia looks aghast. "How can you say that?" she continues in a whisper. "Ion threatened to eat us. She threatened to eat anyone we talk to about…about them. This is serious, Allison. This is way more important than stupid tests."

"Give me a couple hours to study," I say. "Then maybe I'll be ready to talk about last night. I know this might sound weird after last night, but I really, really, really don't want to flunk."

Dalia throws up her arms in disgust. "Give me a break."

Haji pats her on a shoulder. "Take it easy. Allison needs some time. We should study too. Life doesn't stop."

"Dragons, Haji, dragons," Dalia says.

"Please, I just need a little time to study," I say. "That's all."

"All right. You win. Life doesn't stop," Dalia says.

My friends allow me to study, although I'm not sure that they study. As I work quadratic equations, Dalia spends her time staring into space, and Haji is engrossed with something on his laptop screen. I can't complain, though. Dalia helps me when I ask for assistance solving some gnarly equations, and Haji purchases us a second round of coffee.

After an hour or so, Dalia loosens up a little, and we quiz each other on American history. Dates and events that we think will show up on the exam. After precisely two hours, Haji interrupts us.

"I have an idea."

I glumly stare at him. "We're busy."

"Give us five more minutes," Dalia says. "We're almost through the Civil War."

"Allison said two hours," Haji says, frowning, but falls silent and turns his attention back to his laptop.

Five minutes later, the laptop starts making an annoying dinging sound. I slam a hand against the table, rattling the cups in their saucers, and glare at Haji. He flinches.

"That is seriously annoying, Haji," Dalia says.

"Five minutes is up."

"Okay," I say. "What is it? This fantastic idea you have."

"Your prosthetics," Haji says. "Can they do recordings? You know, have some onboard memory."

"I don't know."

"Maybe they do. Like for diagnostics."

Dalia perks up. "That's a good idea. We should go see Dr. Woolworth. She working today?"

I shrug.

"Your dad didn't mention anything?" Dalia asks.

"All he did was yell at me about last night."

"Tell me about it. My mom and dad cornered me in the bathroom. I couldn't get out of the house fast enough," Dalia says.

Haji gives us a puzzled look. "Your parents gave you a hard time for staying out late?"

"We were out past curfew," I say. "Isn't your curfew like eleven?"

"I just told them I was with you two, and they were okay with that."

Dalia and I exchange a glance and roll our eyes.

Haji shakes his head. "Your parents are harsh. Allison, how about you give me your account of last night before we go see Dr. Woolworth?"

****

A cold wind rustles skeletal tree branches as we trek across the Tahoma University campus toward the Robotics Technology Center. I pull my heavy winter coat tight around me and put up the hood. It's midday, so a few people are out and about, mostly students burdened with backpacks or books thick enough to be religious tomes. The sky is a stunning azure, and the sun is warm against my skin, but to the northwest is an imposing wall of dark clouds stretching across the horizon.

"Might have snow tonight," Haji says.

I think about Joe and the other homeless people around campus and the city at large. The cold nights are hard on them, and there are never enough beds, especially for the men. I bite my lip, thinking I should track down Joe and invite him to spend the night at my place, but past experience tells me he will refuse the offer.

"That's good for you, Allison," Dalia says. "You'll have more time to study when school is canceled."

I nod, noncommittal. The truth is I want to go to school to have something to do that will keep me from obsessing over the dragons, maybe alleviate the sense that I'm being watched for a few hours. I don't think

Ion or Dr. Radcliffe will show up uninvited in one of my classrooms, at least I hope not.

The Robotics Technology Center is uncomfortably warm after the outdoor chill. I pause just inside the entrance, drop my backpack to the ground, and strip off my coat. Haji does the same, but Dalia shakes her head and keeps her coat zipped to her chin and her hood up. A few people sit, either reading or studying, at low white circular tables interspersed around the first floor.

"What if you do have a recording of the dragon?" Dalia says. "What then? Aren't we putting Dr. Woolworth and your dad in danger?"

"Maybe," I say. "But we have to fight back somehow. If we don't, they're going to walk all over us."

"I'll never be able to forgive myself if they do something to them," Dalia says and chews on the tip of her thumb.

"You're right. Maybe this is a bad idea," I say, frowning.

"It's too late to have second thoughts," Haji says. "We need video. Once we blow the lid off this thing, it will be too late for them to do anything. Everyone will know. The footage will be on Channel 5 tonight, maybe even the national news. We upload a video to the Internet, and I guarantee it will go viral like you wouldn't believe. Everyone will know. We just need the footage." He points at me. "That might be on the prosthetics."

"I don't know…" Dalia trails off as the door opens behind us.

A young couple, neither more than three years older than us, walk in holding hands.

"Excuse us," the girl says, a tall, snooty, athletic-looking blonde who reminds me of Leslie Chapman.

We move a few feet away from the entrance, clustering by a leafy potted tree.

"Ion threatened to eat anyone we tell," Dalia whispers. "She can show up any time."

"Quiet," Haji whispers.

"What?" Dalia and I ask at the same time.

"Jinx," Haji blurts, then stammers, "It's…it's Mr. Lee."

My shoulders sag. Dad is the last person I want to see. My father, bundled up in Patagonia fleece, enters the building.

"Hi, Dad," I say, putting all the faux excitement I can into my voice in the hope that might blunt his anger over last night.

He stares at us. After blinking several times, he says, "Hi, Allison. Dalia. Haji. Funny meeting all of you here. I was just thinking about all of you. Late night, huh?"

My shoulders tense.

"Later than we expected, Mr. Lee," Haji says. "It's my fault. I'm supposed to keep track of the time. Sometimes I get lost in the beat. Dancing is such fun."

I relax a little. Fortunately, we had discussed our cover story before leaving The Obsidian Roast. Dalia and I have a default story for missing curfew, out late dancing, so I'm confident Dad won't have heard anything contradictory from Dalia's mom.

"Huh, that so," Dad says, nodding. "Why are you kids here?"

I wince. I hate it when Dad calls my squad and me kids like we're still in diapers.

"I dropped some cash last night," Haji says. "We're hoping Allison's prosthetics recorded something."

I keep my face impassive. I have to hand it to Haji. He can think quickly on his feet. The lie sounds totally convincing.

"The prosthetics might have recorded something, but the memory is flushed every hour. Sorry," Dad says.

"You're sure?" I ask.

"I wrote the routine myself," Dad says. "You kids are welcome to come up to the lab, but Jane can't help you."

There he goes again, calling us kids. It makes me want to scream. Haji, polite as ever, engages Dad in conversation. Dalia starts tapping me on the shoulder.

I round on her and snap, "What?"

She startles, eyes wide and lower lip quivering. She points out the tall windows onto the campus. I look to where she indicates and gasp.

"Is that him?" Dalia asks.

"Haji, we have to go," I say.

"What? Why? Don't you want to go up?"

I grab the gangly boy by the forearm and pull him toward the door. I call over my shoulder, "Bye, Dad."

Dalia follows us outside into the bracing cold. I shiver, but I don't bother to stop to put on my winter coat as I march toward Dr. Radcliffe, who watches us approach some fifty feet away from a pathway on the far side of a patch of exposed grass. He is dressed for the weather, and his draconic companion stands over him, its head lost in the branches of a tall Douglas fir. My friends drop back and call for me to stop, but I ignore them.

Dr. Radcliffe watches me approach from behind his spectacles that I doubt he needs. I have a feeling that dragons have excellent vision. It's all part of a disguise, camouflage. The man before me is just an automaton, a mindless drone controlled by the shimmering monster riding the slipstream. I stop less than an arm's length from him, staring into his gray eyes and doing my damnedest to ignore the golden beast with its tail stretching down the path and into the shrubbery.

"Allison, good afternoon," Dr. Radcliffe says. An icy gust of wind howls through the campus. I grimace and shiver. "You must put on your coat, dear girl, or you will catch the sniffles."

"We didn't tell him anything, do you understand? My father, Raymond Lee, we didn't tell him anything. We didn't tell Dr. Woolworth anything either. You leave them alone. You tell Ion to leave them alone."

Dr. Radcliffe gives me a toothless smile. "It is good that you did not tell them anything. If you did, I might not be capable of stopping Officer Davenport from doing something…rash. Good day to you, my dear."

With that, Dr. Radcliffe turns his back to me and strolls away. His draconic companion follows, bathing me and its surroundings in twinkling golden light.

Haji and Dalia catch up to me. Both have their phones out and are taking pics of Dr. Radcliffe.

"Did you get a photo of the dragon?"

Haji holds up his phone. On the screen is a photo of a tall man walking in the snow. There is no sign of the golden dragon.

"Nada," Dalia says.

"Do you think your prosthetics recorded the dragon?" Haji asks.

"I doubt it." I shake my head.

"It might be worth checking," Haji says.

Dalia nods in agreement.

"No. It's too risky. He said if they suspect we've told my dad or Dr. Woolworth anything, Ion will kill them. Besides, if your phones can't record the dragons, my prosthetics probably can't either. I can see them for some other reason. Maybe because of this skaag thing they keep calling me."

Chapter 21

I stare at the algebra test, the variables and other mathematical symbols of an equation blurring into an indecipherable black-and-white slurry. I blink my eyes until the symbols start resolving into something decipherable. Only it's not a mathematical equation. It's a dragon with numbers, plus signs and equal signs spewing from its maw like fire. I slam my pencil against the desk and shut my eyes. When I open my eyes, I realize I have broken the pencil in two and glimpse Mr. Leonard along with several of my classmates glancing in my direction. Heaving a heavy sigh, I retrieve my spare pencil and turn my attention back to the test.

"Thank goodness," I murmur as I interpret the algebraic equation.

When Mr. Leonard calls time, I've answered every question, and Officer Davenport didn't burst into the classroom. All in all, not a bad first period.

I have two more classes before lunch. I worry about Dalia and Haji. We're all in separate classes. I don't think Dr. Radcliffe or Ion will try to do anything to us at school, but that doesn't keep me from chewing on my lower lip. Dr. Radcliffe showed up at the Robotics Technology Center right after my dad did. Anyone we tell about the dragons is lunch meat for Ion. What if they think we told someone when we didn't?

Damn. Damn. Damn.

. My third test of the day is writing a five-paragraph essay about *Jane Eyre*. Thank goodness I finished the book, despite its soporific qualities. All my lucid thoughts about the novel flit from my mind like startled birds. I stare at the college-ruled notepaper on my desk and obsess over hungry dragons.

"Fifteen minutes warning," the teacher announces.

I gasp. Has it really already been forty-five minutes? God. I still haven't scrawled a single word.

"What the hell," I murmur.

I scribble down five halfway coherent paragraphs that at least mention the names of the major characters and lack any references to dragons. At the end of class, I rush to the common area to find my squad.

I spot my friends at a circular table in a far corner of the common room away from the congregating crowd of students. Leslie and Jason hold court at a table surrounded by friends and sycophants. I take a circuitous route to my friends to avoid the lovebirds.

I pull out a chair that scrapes loudly against the floor and flop down on it. Haji, his lunchbox before him on the table, is already biting into his sandwich with gusto. Dalia hasn't even bothered to pull out her lunch.

I look around the room to ensure no one is close enough to overhear us. "No sign of Dr. Radcliffe or Ion?"

Dalia shakes her head.

Between bites of sandwich, Haji says, "Nope. We need to get one of the dragons to become visible like at the warehouse. Then I bet we can get it on camera."

"Seriously? Are you out of your mind?" Dalia says. "Anything we do will put us and our families in danger.

That dragon nearly crushed us to death."

"We have to do something." Haji sets his sandwich down in a glass container. He crosses his arms on the table and leans forward. "We need to fight back. I don't care if they're dragons or not. All we need is one picture or even better a video. Put it on the Internet, and the genie is out of the bottle." He leans back in the chair and mimes an explosion with his fingers. "They'll back off after that, believe me. Too much publicity."

Dalia looks at me, lips trembling. "You don't think that is a sane idea, do you? The dragon nearly killed us. Ion threatened to—"

"Quiet," I hiss and gesture toward the expansive common room.

Dalia glances over her shoulder and mutters an expletive under her breath. Winding his way between the tables is none other than Jason. When he sees us watching him, a smile splits his face, and he waves. I look away, my sense of betrayal like thousands of little needles pricking my skin all at once.

"Hi, guys," Jason says and pulls out a free chair. "Can I sit?"

I don't say anything, and my two best friends in the whole world warily watch me. Jason shifts, hovering next to the chair.

"I just want to say—" Jason takes a deep breath. "—I'm really glad you're back at school, Allison. Really. I'm sorry things haven't been the same between us since Leslie and I started dating. I'm just glad you're back."

"Why do you care if I'm back at school? Does your girlfriend need a punching bag?"

Jason looks stricken. "Allison, it's not like that.

Leslie...she regrets what she did. Honest. She's...she's super competitive. Just like me."

"She's a racist just like you."

His face turns red. I'm not sure if it's in embarrassment or anger.

"That's not fair! I'm not—"

"Leave Allison alone," Dalia says and turns in her chair to glare at him. "Leave all of us alone. We don't want anything to do with you. Right, Haji?"

"The shade Leslie threw, that's not cool. I have brown skin. I have heard it all, and it's not cool," Haji says.

Jason stands there glowering. Like most people, he doesn't like uncomfortable truths flung in his face. He looks every bit like an angry, entitled white boy unable to look himself in the mirror and appreciate how good he has it. Yet I can't help feeling I'm a little harsh on him. We all are. We have lots of shared history. You can't choose who you love. I didn't choose to have a crush on him for all those years. It just happened. If there is any logic to love, I'd have a crush on Haji, and we'd be together right now. It's become obvious Joe is right. Haji is totally into me. He's always throwing little sideways glances my way and trying to be alone with me. I'm sure he's looking for an opportunity to ask me out. But Haji doesn't set my heart aflutter the way Jason used to.

"Go away," I say. "I don't want to talk to you."

Jason heaves a heavy sigh, shoulders sagging, and walks away.

"Do you think he overheard us?" Dalia whispers. "Talking about the dragons?"

Dalia scans the common room. I'm suspicious she

is searching for signs of Ion or Dr. Radcliffe.

"I don't think so," I say. "Don't worry."

"Good," Dalia says. "He is a jerk, like totally. But I don't want him eaten."

Haji is already back to chowing down on the sandwich. With his mouth full of an amalgamation of bread and peanut butter and jelly, he says, "What do you think?"

"About what?" I ask.

"Photographing the dragons."

"It's too dangerous!" Dalia says.

"Haji, do you really want to risk death?" I say. "Or have someone you love killed? Dalia is right. It's asking for trouble."

Frowning, Haji nods and tears into his sandwich. After swallowing, he says, "You guys need to eat. Classes are about to start."

****

On Friday, an arctic blast from Canada makes the temperature plummet and brings snow. By the time school is out, a half-inch or more of the white stuff already blankets the sidewalk and makes driving treacherous. A school bus lost control while pulling into the school parking lot and slammed into a light pole.

The crash draws a curious crowd of high schoolers, including Haji and me. Dalia had already hopped into the front seat of an old two-door hatchback next to purple-haired Devin. The car peeled out of the parking lot, fishtailing on the slick road. I hope he doesn't flip the car with her in it.

Anyway, the pole is teetering precariously when administrative staff comes bustling from the office to set up a safe perimeter and demand we teenagers go about our business.

"Let's go. I'm freezing," I say to Haji.

"Yeah, the crash will bring the police."

I shiver at the mention of municipal muscle. We trudge to the sidewalk along the main road. I pause to unsling my backpack from my shoulders and pull out my sling pack containing my camera. The snow should make for a few interesting shots on the walk home. While I'm slinging my backpack onto my shoulders, a side door to the school building opens with a loud click that's audible even from the sidewalk despite the cars zipping by well over the twenty miles per hour speed limit.

"Don't look. It's them," Haji says.

Of course, I look. What else am I going to do? Leslie and Jason share a passionate kiss in a romantic winter wonderland.

"God," I say. "Let's go."

Just as we turn away from the school, a Seattle PD car pulls up to the curb. I grab Haji's hand. Snowflakes pass through the semitransparent silver dragon projecting out of the cop car.

"It's her," I say, clutching Haji's hand in a death grip.

The passenger side window rolls down.

"Get in the back," Ion says, her tone broaching no argument.

We dumbly stare at the irate officer.

"What are you waiting for? Get in."

I nod, and we obey. The tires spin as the car pulls away from the curb. Jason stands on the sidewalk, staring at us with a puzzled expression. I mouth the word help to him.

Then we're speeding away through traffic, and he is out of sight. Being in the cop car is discombobulating with Ion's shimmering dragon form passing through the vehicle, Haji, and me. A fading and reappearing portion of torso impales me without any effect other than being disconcerting. I try not to obsess over it for the sake of my sanity.

I regret attempting to ask Jason for help. What's he going to do? Call the cops? Ion is a cop and a dragon on top of that. Jason is a racist ass, but that doesn't mean I want him hurt or dead. I don't even want Leslie dead. I fear that's what will happen if he interferes.

"Where's your friend? The pink-haired girl?" Ion demands.

"We don't know where she is," Haji says.

Haji squeezes my hand, reminding me that I still clutch his. The cop car is warm, so I am very aware that his hand is icy cold. I pull my hand away and cross my arms before my chest, putting my hands underneath my armpits.

"Frederick will have to track her down then. Don't think she's going to get away."

Ion takes us to the nearest onramp for I-5 south. Even early in the afternoon, the freeway is packed with cars and semis. Ion curses and flips on her lights and siren. Soon we're darting down the shoulder at high speed, flashing by vehicles rolling through the falling snowflakes at no more than fifteen miles per hour.

Ion exits at the Sodo District. The snow picks up, creating a blurry haze that obscures everything. When we arrive at the warehouse, I'm unsure it's the same one as before until Ion pulls the car inside after opening the rusted sliding door. The cruiser rolls to a halt just inside the large building. Ion gets out and slides the door shut with a resounding boom.

Up ahead is the same table with a laptop on it as last time. What is new is a cluster of folding chairs positioned haphazardly before the table and three individuals, each accompanied by a draconic companion. The shimmering light from the beasts is almost hypnotic. I can't look away, nor can I slow my racing heartbeat that thrums like a race car engine. Dr. Radcliffe is conspicuously missing from the draconic crowd.

"What is it?" Haji whispers.

"Those people. They're dragons."

"What? No way. I'm going to message…"

Haji falls silent when Officer Davenport opens the driver's door.

"Message whom?" Davenport asks.

Haji glances at me with earnest puzzlement on his face and turns to the officer. "Message? What are you talking about?"

"Give me your phones. Now," Ion says and maneuvers around to the back door and opens it. She leans into the back, her draconic companion's foreleg and torso passing through the roof and side of the vehicle. She holds out her hand for the phones. "I can hear everything you say."

Haji nods and paws at his pants' pocket for his phone. I unzip my backpack, snag my ancient flip phone, and, flinching as my forearm passes through glimmering silver scales, hand it to Ion. With a trembling hand, Haji surrenders his smartphone.

"Any other electronics I need to confiscate?"

We shake our heads.

Ion slams the back door, slides into the driver's seat, and drives us to the gathered dragons. She opens the back door and orders us out, telling us to leave our bags, and demands the passcodes for our phones. Part of me wants to resist, wants to tell her to shove my phone up her ass, but I don't dare without Dr. Radcliffe here. We stand in the warehouse with the cruiser between us and the three newcomers.

"If I find out you texted anyone while you were with me, I promise you I will hunt them down and eat them. You do not want to mess with me. Is that understood?"

"Yes," Haji says.

"Yeah," I say.

An old white-haired woman, I recall her name is Tanis, walks around the police car to stand in front of us beside Ion. Her draconic companion is white like the snow falling outside, and its pale pink wings are pressed tightly to its torso. The beast is far smaller than Ion's long and lean dragon.

The old woman stares at me with pale blue eyes that seem to see right through me into my soul. I fidget under her gaze. Her draconic companion lowers its head that looks remarkably like a poodle minus the floppy ears and with glimmering white scales instead of hair. It stares at me with pink eyes that are as large as saucers and split by black vertical irises. The beast lunges at me.

Screaming, I flinch and grab Haji by the hand. My fingers burrow into his skin, but he doesn't pull away.

"What is it?" Haji asks.

The giant poodle face hovers mere inches from me, scanning me up and down from head to toe. I dare not move. I have the uneasy suspicion the dragon can exit the slipstream and bite my head off.

"The dragon has its face in mine," I say.

"Which one?" Haji asks.

Haji swivels his head toward Ion.

"Not her," I say.

Tanis stares at me with a wolfish grin. "So you are Allison Lee. I've looked forward to meeting you. Come here. I want to smell you."

I hesitate and look at Haji. He shakes his head in the negative.

"I won't hurt you, girl, not yet. Not until Frederick arrives, at least," Tanis says and looks at Ion. "Where is their companion? The girl with the pink hair?"

"She wasn't with them. Frederick will retrieve her."

"We will begin without him. There is magic on this girl. Magic I cannot easily penetrate. It will take time to unravel the spell or spells."

"The sooner you start, the sooner you're done," Ion says.

Ion swaggers around the back of the cop car, pausing to say, "I'm going to check these for any recent texts." She holds up our phones. "Calls, recordings, videos. All of it."

The officer swaggers out of sight.

Tanis speaks, her voice like a scourge. "I said, come here, girl."

She points to the floor less than half a foot in front of her. I release Haji's hand. He holds on to me, so I pull myself free. I move to where Tanis indicates.

"Please, leave my friends alone," I say. "I'm the one you want."

185

Tanis leans close to my neck, her long white hair draping against my arm, and sniffs. With a groan, she backs away.

"Well." Tanis scrunches up her nose. "You're not human, but you're not skaag either. It will prove fascinating to decipher what you are."

Tanis snatches my hand. Her skin is brittle, like old parchment, but her grip is firm as she half leads, half drags me around the cruiser.

"Hey. Let her go," Haji protests.

"It's okay, Haji," I say.

"Come along, boy, but don't interfere," Tanis growls.

"It's okay, Haji, really. Don't cause trouble."

Haji scowls but follows without argument. On the other side of the cruiser, Ion sits on one of the metallic folding chairs inspecting our phones. Two more people with sparkling dragons projecting out of them stand near the table with the laptop.

Chapter 22

Tanis leads me toward the man and woman standing in front of the table with the laptop. Their draconic companions intermingle in a brilliant fusion of sparkling green and coppery light that is so intense it takes my prosthetics a few seconds to adjust to the brightness. I recognize the woman with thick glasses and hair chopped off unstylishly just below the ears from the week before. From the neck up she looks owlish due her oversized circular glasses, even boyish. Her bosom and curvy hips are not entirely hidden by her baggy clothes and betray her sex. The man is tall with a military crewcut and a sumo wrestler's build. He wears a loud Hawaiian shirt and pink man capris.

Tanis indicates I should take a chair before her compatriots. After a moment of hesitation, I comply. What else am I going to do? I tried running from Dr. Radcliffe, and that got me squeezed within an inch of my life by a gigantic dragon. Now, I'm facing three of them, not to mention Ion. Owl girl looks harmless enough, but the sumo wrestler sneers at me, and I suspect Tanis will kill me without hesitation if she thinks I'm a threat.

"Sit down over there, boy," Tanis tells Haji.

Haji mutters a response, and a chair scrapes against the concrete and creaks when he sits. The old woman turns to her companions.

"This is Allison Lee," Tanis says. "I suggest you smell her. She's not human."

The man arches an eyebrow. "Is Ion right?" His voice is gruff, and he waves a hand at me. "This thing pretending to be a girl is a skaag?"

"I don't think so," Tanis says. "She is something else. I don't recognize the smell, but it's decidedly not skaag."

I chew on my lower lip and squirm. I'm seriously through being sniffed.

"You're making her nervous," owl girl says. "Should we introduce ourselves?"

The sumo wrestler scoffs. "She's our captive. We don't need to introduce ourselves to her. The less she knows, the better."

"Well, she probably already knows my name. It's your name she might not know," owl girl says and smiles at me. "My name is Mauve, by the way. In case you had forgotten. His name—"

The sumo wrestler interrupts. "Tatsuo. You probably already knew that. Frederick and the youngling are supposed to be our security experts, but they don't take security very seriously if you ask me. That goes for all of you. If this thing is an agent for our enemies, she knows too much." He waves a thick finger at me. "Far too much."

"She is under our power and has not been in contact with our enemies," Tanis says.

"As far as we know," Tatsuo says.

Mauve makes an exaggerated sigh. "If you're so worried, why are you even here?"

"I respect the chain of command," Tatsuo snaps.

"I suppose that's why you weren't on the call last

week," Mauve says. "Respect for the chain of command and all."

"I was indisposed," Tatsuo says.

"Regardless, we are here now," Tanis says. "Frederick will soon be joining us. Tatsuo, Mauve, please smell Allison Lee."

Scowling, Tatsuo ambles toward me. His draconic companion follows, breaking away from Mauve's, so I can tell that it's a bulky green beast with black wings and numerous slashes marring the glittering scales that might be scars. Mauve's copper dragon is long and lean, much like Ion's in appearance.

I cower in the chair and turn my head away from him.

"Believe me, this is worse for me than it is for you," Tatsuo rumbles. "Humans smell like shit. Whatever you are, I don't expect you'll smell any better."

He leans over me, his breath hot and heavy and carrying with it the scent of alcohol. As he comes closer, the odor of eucalyptus and menthol rolls off him like a rogue wave to drown me in its stench. I cry out, and my eyes tear up. That odor transports me back to Tahoma University on that dark and stormy evening. A gust of wind rattles the trees. A branch snaps and thuds to the ground. I sense the presence behind me and twirl around. Looming in the darkness is a silhouette armed with a pipe.

I scramble from my chair and stumble away to escape the stench, backing into chairs as I go. I can't outrun the memories seeping from my psyche's recesses.

Tatsuo scoffs. "What's wrong with you?"

I hold a hand out in front of me. "Stay back. That smell."

My stomach roils, and I double over, gagging. All that comes up is liquid since I didn't eat anything for lunch. There is a bitter taste on my tongue. Everyone is talking at once. Ion weaves between the folding chairs to stand next to Tatsuo. Her expression is angry, and she is snarling something I can't decipher in the multitude of voices.

"Please, that smell."

Ion is going to grab me and force me next to Tatsuo, but then Haji is there, wrapping an arm around my shoulders, helping me to a chair. He is shouting, and slowly everyone falls silent, even Ion. I press myself against his body, taking solace in his solidity and warmth.

"It will be okay," Haji whispers and continues in his normal voice. "I think it's the smell. Do you wear Manscape Bodywhiskey?"

"So what?" Tatsuo says.

"She was attacked by a man wearing that body spray. The smell gives her some kind of PTSD response," Haji says.

"It's true. I read the police report," Ion says. "You need to stay away from her, Tatsuo, until you wash that crap off."

Tatsuo throws up his arms and walks back to the table. "Good. I didn't want to smell her anyway. Your turn, Mauve. I'm not washing off my Bodywhiskey for that thing."

"You use something called Bodywhiskey?" Mauve asks.

"It's body spray," Tatsuo says. "It's trendy."

Mauve leans close to Tatsuo and sniffs loudly. "Not unpleasant."

Tatsuo shoos her. "Don't smell me. Go smell that thing."

Smiling, Mauve approaches me. "Don't worry. I eschew perfumes."

"One minute," Ion says and holds up my flip phone. "Why is Jason texting you about being picked up in a cop car after school?"

My mouth moves, but no words come out. My brain is frazzled after catching a whiff of Bodywhiskey.

"I saw Jason leaving the school when you picked us up," Haji says, his voice tremulous and sincere. "He probably saw you order us into the car. It's not every day someone sees their friends being hauled off by a cop."

I find my voice and a lie. "He's my boyfriend. He doesn't have any idea about you or any of this."

"Boyfriend?" Tatsuo says. "Give me the phone. I'll send a message that will put the young man at ease."

Mauve snickers. "Our Casanova."

"Casanova could have learned a thing or two from me. I've lived among humans for what, seven hundred years? At least six hundred of those as a man. Never once has anyone suspected my true nature." He holds out his hand. "Give me the phone."

Ion gives me a sideways look. "No, she's lying, Casanova. I did a background investigation on her. This Jason is definitely not her boyfriend." She points at Haji, then me. "If anything, these two should be together. They're not."

"Okay. I'll pretend to be a friend," Tatsuo says.

"We'll do it together," Ion says, swaggering around

behind me.

Tatsuo ambles toward me. I grimace in anticipation of catching another whiff of his nauseating body spray. He sees my expression and glowers but changes course to stay away from me.

"Now that we're done with that distraction," Tanis says. "Take a sniff."

"Oh, of course, of course," Mauve says and strides toward me. She smiles, almost shyly. "I'm terribly sorry about this. At least I don't smell. Could you…it's awkward. Sorry."

Awkward? Then it dawns on me. Haji is holding me. I gently push him away and sit up. Mauve's politeness is disarming, almost enough for me not to worry about the giant shimmering dragon towering over her. Almost.

I can't stop myself from cringing when she bends over to sniff me. She's dainty, taking a few discreet sniffs of my neck. Then she seizes me by the shoulders and buries her face in my hair. I fight back, grabbing her arms to wrench her hands away from me, but her limbs are as hard and unyielding as rebar.

"Stop!" I scream.

"Let go of her," Haji says.

Tanis's voice cracks like a whip. "Stay out of it, young man, or you will get hurt."

"She's hurting Allison," Haji says.

"She is not," Tanis says.

Mauve releases me and takes several steps back. I stare up at her in horror, feeling violated. Mauve meets my gaze, looking mildly embarrassed. Her copper draconic companion lowers its head to stare at me with yellow eyes. A forked tongue shoots from the beast's mouth to lick me. I flinch, unable to avoid it. The tongue passes through me then fades to nothingness as the dragon withdraws.

Haji comes to my side, hugging me to him. I can feel his heart hammering in his chest. God, what are we going to do?

"I can smell skaag on her. It's faint, but present," Mauve says.

From behind us, Ion says, "See. I told you. Can we kill them now?"

I shudder against Haji, and he whispers that everything will be okay. I want to scream at him to stop lying to me.

"Killing them is the best option," Tatsuo says. "It will be easier that way. Rip off the bandage."

"I'm not a skaag," I say.

Tanis shakes her head. "No, we can't kill them. Not yet. We must discover Allison Lee's true nature."

"I'm not a skaag," I insist.

Mauve glances at me, her expression annoyed. She brings a finger to her lips in a shushing gesture.

"Just because I smell skaag on her doesn't mean she is one," Mauve says. "For one thing, a skaag wouldn't be cowering. It would be killing us."

"Trying to kill us," Ion says.

I free myself from Haji's embrace and stand.

Mauve rolls her eyes. "Trying to kill us. The point is, she is not a skaag. She is something else. Something related, perhaps, something new."

"I'm not a skaag!" I scream and glare at the dragon people. "I'm not related to a skaag or any other weird monster. I don't know what you are afraid of, but I'm not it."

My voice echoes through the warehouse. No one says a word. Mauve looks like she swallowed a fly, but Tanis appears unperturbed.

"We know you aren't human," Tanis says. "You can make life easier for all of us by just telling us what you are."

I'm about ready to sob. Why won't they listen to me? Why do they think I'm a monster?

"Perhaps, she doesn't know her nature," Mauve says.

"It's possible," Tanis says. "I find it disconcerting we smell skaag on her. I will taste her. That's the only way to determine her nature."

From somewhere among her baggy clothing Mauve pulls out a curved dagger. Light gleams along its razor edge and sparkles in the colorful jewels encrusting the hilt.

"Taste me?" I gasp.

"Don't worry. This won't hurt much," Mauve says, advancing with the dagger held at her waist.

Chapter 23

I shrink in the chair, my eyes locked on the curved dagger at Mauve's side. It's so gaudy with red and green and blue and orange and purple gems encrusting the golden hilt that looks like part of a Halloween costume you'd buy off the Internet. The blade looks sharp enough to shave your scalp.

"What's going on?" I ask.

Haji stands and moves in between Mauve and me. His hands hang at his sides, forming fists.

"Haji, don't," I say.

Haji ignores me, damn male machismo.

"I'm not going to hurt her," Mauve says.

"Why the knife?"

"Okay, I'm not going to hurt her much. We just need a little blood, a shallow cut on the palm. That's all. Ion has a first-aid kit. She'll bandage the wound. I'm on your side. I don't want to hurt any of you. But you have to cooperate. The others—"

Tanis interrupts. "Boy, you were warned to stay out of this. Ion, restrain the boy." Tanis shakes her head in apparent frustration. "Handcuff him or something."

I hear Ion moving behind me into my peripheral vision. She is reaching for her utility belt.

Forcing myself to stand, I dart to Haji's side ahead of Ion. "Don't hurt him. I'll cooperate. Do whatever you need to, just don't hurt Haji."

My gaze moves from Ion to Tanis. The old woman appears stern, frowning, and I don't know how I can tell this, but her draconic companion seems relaxed, unperturbed. I know this with certainty, right down to my marrow. Maybe it's the fact that the dragon's pink eyes are hooded by white, scaly eyelids and the way it languidly flicks its transparent tail like a horse swatting flies. Ion is the complete opposite. Officer Davenport looks calm and competent, devoid of emotion, even her usual snarly disdain, as she stands at the ready with her cuffs held loosely in her left hand. She gazes at Tanis as if waiting for instructions. Her silver draconic companion holds its head low to the ground, mouth hanging open to reveal sharp white teeth dripping saliva. The dragon's unblinking eyes never stray from Haji.

I take Haji by the forearm. Beneath his winter coat, I feel his tense muscles. "Sit. I'll be fine."

"This isn't right," he tells me and shouts at Tanis. "Why can't you just leave us alone? We never did anything to you."

"Go sit. Mauve won't hurt me," I say, glancing at the dagger-wielding woman.

Her dark eyes look excited, and the diaphanous head of her dragon hovers just above hers with its forked tongue flicking in and out like a snake tasting the air. Already doubting my words, I crinkle my nose and stifle an *ugh* sound.

"You won't hurt Allison?" Haji asks.

Mauve smiles. "Just a quick slice across the palm. Not deep. I won't cut any tendons. I do this quite often. Magic, I mean."

I clench my jaw. Her assurances aren't putting me

at ease, but I can't let Haji know that.

Haji looks at me. "You're okay with this? Seriously?"

I shrug. "Does it matter? They don't need a dagger to hurt me."

Haji meets my gaze, his expression grim. Fear reflects in his eyes. I know he is remembering Dr. Radcliffe's dragon, or, perhaps in reality, Dr. Radcliffe in dragon form, crushing us in its talons. Swallowing, he nods and sits in the nearest chair.

Smiling, Mauve strides to my side and offers me her free hand. I bite my lower lip, my gaze moving from the humanoid Mauve to the dragon with its head hovering just above her. The beast is not being aggressive. It's displaying curiosity like a small child exploring a toy with all her senses. Of course, a curious child can't crush me like an ant and doesn't have a mouth large enough to tear my head off with a single bite. I take her offered hand in mine. Her skin is warm, on the verge of being hot.

Mauve leads me away from the table and chairs and the light from the LED bulb dangling from the ceiling by a long wire. The only light is from Mauve's glowing draconic companion and diffuse sunlight seeping in from cracks and holes in the roof. A few snowflakes fall through those cracks, twirling in shafts of light in their slow descent to the warehouse floor. Tanis follows us, keeping at a distance.

Mauve glances behind us. "Is this good?"

I don't hear Tanis's response, but Mauve squeezes my hand once and stops. She doesn't let go of me. Tanis comes around to stand before us. When she speaks, her voice is kind for the first time.

"Try not to startle, Allison. We don't want to hurt you. You are, of course, afraid. I'm sorry about that, but we must know what you are."

The air crackles with electricity and shimmers. Tanis's eyes go dead, her body as rigid as a corpse. Lighting flashes, and the dragon becomes solid and real, no longer fading in and out of existence. The beast rolls its shoulders and neck. Joints crack like splitting tree trunks. Its scales sparkle like thousands of dazzling stars.

My mouth is dry, and my prosthetics feel like they will pop out of my head. I'm vaguely aware of Mauve turning my palm toward the ceiling.

"This will hurt," Mauve says.

Fiery pain lances across my palm, and I gasp, involuntarily jerking my hand away from Mauve, but she holds it fast. The white dragon's huge poodle head comes face-to-face with me. The pink eyes split by vertical black pupils stare at me, hooded and ancient.

Mauve forces my arm toward the beast. Again I try to pull away, but the woman is too strong. The dragon's forked tongue shoots out, the warm, moist tip brushing across my wound so gently I barely notice it over the pain. The beast rears up and sits back on its haunches like a dog. With its eyes shut, it looks every bit like a yogi in deep contemplation.

The dragon remains sitting for a long moment that might last only minutes or stretch on for hours. My hand throbs, a pulsating, unrelenting pain. I grind my teeth, wanting to be strong despite my fear and frustration and physical torment, but unbidden tears stream from my eyes.

Mauve tries to comfort me, but she's awkward like

she's never comforted anyone before. I turn away from her, not trying to escape because I know that's impossible, only to avoid her ministrations and hide my embarrassment from tearing up in front of her.

The dragon rumbles a loud sound from deep within its chest. I tense and turn toward the beast. The rumble is followed by a hiss like steam escaping a teakettle. The dragon's pink eyes are open to slits and locked on to me. I draw a shuddering breath, feeling like I'm in the gunsight of a high-powered rifle. One twitch of an assassin's finger...*bam*...my head explodes like a shot watermelon.

"Oh my," Mauve says, and her grip on my wounded hand tightens.

"Ouch. You're crushing my hand," I say.

My tears dry up. I'm angry. Mauve is hurting me, and I don't like it, not one bit.

"Stop," I say, wincing. "You're breaking my bones."

The air shimmers, and the white dragon becomes translucent.

"Mauve, release her," Tanis says, her human form full of life once again.

"Sorry," Mauve says, releasing my hand and dropping her gaze to the floor. She takes two measured strides away from me.

"You are a puzzle, Allison Lee," Tanis says. "I can taste the skaag in you, our most hated enemy. We should strike you down where you stand."

"Why don't you?" I demand, my voice strident. I'm tired of being accused of something I'm not, something I know nothing about. "Just kill me and get it over with. Stop with the threats, just do it. All I want is for you to leave my friends and family out of it."

"We're not going to kill you," Mauve says.

I don't believe Mauve. Behind her thick spectacles, her eyes look as big as chicken eggs. She licks her lips, perhaps betraying nervousness. Her draconic companion towers over her. The beast's demeanor has changed. It's still curious, but the curiosity is tempered by something. Fear, maybe, but perhaps fear isn't right. The dragon is wary, if not afraid.

I stand straighter and thrust back my shoulders. I'm no longer just a caged curiosity. I'm a dangerous curiosity. My shoulders roll forward a little, slumping. Maybe being hazardous isn't a good thing. That might make these dragon people more likely to lash out. Regardless, my new sense of power makes me feel good, and with that feeling, the rage deep within the core of my being that brings with it limitless physical prowess stirs like a sleeper on the verge of waking.

"Your wound," Tanis says. "How is it? Does it hurt?"

Wound? Hurt? I look at my hand. It's stained with blood, but all that remains of the gash is a thin white scar running horizontally across my palm. How? I open and close my hand. No pain, not even stiffness. My puzzled gaze darts from Tanis, then to Mauve, and back to Tanis. I hold my hand out for them to see.

"What happened?" I'm not sure if I should be excited or horrified. Am I a creature from the fantasy books Haji reads? Am I a skaag? "My hand…the wound…"

The scabs on my hand and wrist from smashing my arm against Dr. Radcliffe's golden scales are gone, leaving behind unblemished skin. Impossible.

"The skaag in you is waking to defend itself," Tanis says. "Just as surely as the shock troops of the Empress are our baleful foes, we are theirs. You are not skaag alone, though. You are something else. A half-breed. I don't understand it. I never imagined it possible."

"Half-breed?" I whisper, remembering my encounter with Leslie in the girls' locker room. Fake she had called me. Ugly, half-breed, fake, aberration. It seems the dragon people only want to give me more reasons to hate myself.

"Tanis tasted both human and skaag in your blood," Mauve says, an undercurrent of awe in her tone. "You are a conundrum. For one thing, your skaag blood doesn't explain why you can see us riding the slipstream."

"You mean skaags can't see your dragons?" I ask.

"If skaags could see us while we ride the slipstream," Mauve says with a curdled smile, "we'd all be dead."

"What is a skaag? What am I?"

Mauve and Tanis exchange a look, the kind that adults do when they're not going to tell you something.

"We will discuss that when Frederick arrives," Tanis says.

"But—"

"We will answer your questions if and when we choose, Allison Lee," Tanis says.

Chapter 24

Mauve and Tanis escort me back to the others. Tanis instructs me to go to Haji, who is sitting on a folding chair. The dragons move out of earshot. They cluster together, speaking in hushed voices and throwing sideways glances my way. I chew on my lower lip, knowing I'm the subject of conversation. It feels like Leslie and her posse are making fun of me behind my back, only worse. Leslie and her friends won't kill me. Of course, you never know these days. There is a school shooting somewhere in the United States just about every week.

Haji looks up as I near and stands. Absolute relief is plastered across his face.

"Holy moly," Haji says. "Another dragon. Geez."

"They're all dragons, Haji," I say and flop down on the chair next to him.

The metal is cold against the back of my legs, and I shiver. As the afternoon progresses, the warehouse is becoming a freezer. I hug my arms to me for warmth. I keep my wounded hand awkwardly jutting out so I don't get the blood on my coat. Haji sits down next to me.

"Are you okay?" Haji asks.

"I guess."

"What did they do to you? I didn't have a clear view."

"I'm not sure. Tanis licked me."

"Is that blood? Mauve did cut you. Oh, man. How bad is it?" Haji reaches for my scarred hand.

I move my hand out of his reach. "It's not bad."

"Are you sure you're okay?"

"When I say it's not bad, I mean it. Who do you think you are? My boyfriend?"

Haji sits back in his chair, his expression hurt. "Sorry. I'm just worried. Was Tanis a dragon when she licked you?"

I nod, remaining noncommittal. I don't want to talk about what happened—just gross. I still need time to process the claim that I'm a half-breed and decide if I believe it or not. I'm not so naïve to believe every half-baked story I hear in person or on TV or even the Internet. Climate change isn't real? Give me a break. Why should the claim that I'm a skaag be any different? Then again, why would the dragons lie? Maybe the better question is, why wouldn't they? Then there's always my miraculous hand.

I turn back to Haji, who is staring at me with concern. "How long was I with Tanis and Mauve?"

Haji shrugs. "Twenty minutes, maybe? Why?"

I uncross my arms and hold out my bloodstained hand. "Mauve cut this hand."

"All that blood." Haji's gaze shifts between my hand and my eyes. "Where is the wound?"

"That's the weird thing. It's just a scar now. She cut me—"

"What scar?"

"Right there." I jab the fingertips of my scarred hand against his chest. "Look."

Haji takes my hand in his graceful fingers. His

touch is light against my skin and enticingly warm as he inspects my palm. "That's the thing, Allison. I don't see a scar. Blood, yes—"

"What?" I say, ripping my hand from his grasp. He's right. The white scar that was there just minutes ago is gone, leaving bloodstained but otherwise unmarred skin. I glance over my shoulder at the dragons. They still huddle together, whispering. Their draconic companions are coalesced in a brilliant light display that looks more like the center of a galaxy than anything vaguely reptilian. I turn back to Haji. "Mauve cut me. With the knife. I'm not joking."

"I believe you." Haji shakes his head. "Did they...I can hardly believe I'm going to ask you this. Did they use magic on you?"

"I don't know," I say, remembering what Tanis told me about the skaag in me defending itself, and my impression that something deep inside me is waking. Am I a half-breed? Do I dare share that possibility with Haji? No, I can't. Not now. I don't want to risk him looking at me like I'm some kind of freak.

The clank and boom of the warehouse door sliding open save me from further discussion of the nonexistent wound. Dr. Radcliffe pushes the door open, revealing a vintage model 4 x 4, probably from the 1990s, with its hood and roof caked with snow. Light pours in through the wide doorway along with a flurry of snowflakes.

"Do you think he has Dalia?" Haji asks.

"He wouldn't be here if he didn't," I say.

Dr. Radcliffe pulls the 4 x 4 inside, then gets out and closes the warehouse door. Our captors break from their huddle, their luminous draconic forms becoming distinct. They watch Dr. Radcliffe hop inside the 4 x 4 and drive it slowly toward us.

Haji sighs. "It's like living a MMO campaign."

"MMO?" I ask.

"You know, massively multiplayer online game. Before last week, when that dragon nearly squeezed our heads off, I couldn't imagine anything more exciting than living a campaign in real life, except maybe being the color commentator for the Super Bowl. How stupid is that?"

I shrug. "We all have dreams. I guess it's better when we don't live them."

"I'd still like to be a commentator for the Super Bowl."

"You'd be great," I say. "But how many plotlines contain attacks on the Super Bowl?"

"Killjoy."

The SUV stops next to the police cruiser. Dr. Radcliffe gets out. It's odd how I don't find it bizarre to see his dragon form coming out of the vehicle through its roof and sides and following the old professor around like a faithful dog. I shake my head. I don't want any of this to become commonplace. I want these dragons out of my life and to be nothing more than an unpleasant memory.

"Shoot," Haji whispers and points.

"What?" I look at the back door of the 4 x 4. "Oh no."

Two people have climbed out of the vehicle, Dalia and a boy with purple hair whose hand she clutches in a death grip. Dr. Radcliffe marches over to the other dragons and joins the discussion.

"They have Devin," Haji and I say in unison.

"Jinx," Haji adds.

I glower at him. "This isn't good, Haji. Devin is in danger."

"Old habit," Haji says with a sheepish grin.

"Do you smell something?" I ask and sniff the air. My mouth waters. "Pizza. Sausage and pepperoni."

"Food. Man, I'm starving," Haji says and starts moving chairs, so six are arranged in a semicircle.

Dalia and Devin, both grim-faced, walk toward us, each carrying a pizza box. I do my best to put on a brave face, smiling and waving to my BFF. She smiles in return, but it's only halfhearted.

Dalia and Devin set the pizzas down on two of the chairs. I jump out of my chair, nearly knocking it over, and throw my arms around Dalia in a tight embrace. After a moment, she hugs me back.

"I thought we had another week before they'd come for us," she stammers between gut-wrenching sobs. "I never would've gone out with Devin if I knew he'd come for us. Now Devin is in as much danger as we are."

"It's okay. It's not your fault," I whisper.

We hold the embrace, rocking back and forth. Haji joins in, wrapping his gangly arms around us. Devin watches, out of place, like a fourth wheel on a tricycle. After a spell, Dalia breaks the embrace and pulls her boyfriend over.

She grasps his hand and leans her head against his shoulder. "This is Devin. Devin, these are my best friends. Allison and Haji. You met Haji at the climate march, remember?"

"Hey. Of course I remember Haji." Devin and Haji shake hands. Then he shakes mine. His palm is sweaty, and his grip is overly tight like a macho man trying to prove something. "Allison, Dalia has told me so much about you."

"Likewise," I say, trying to keep my face blank. He smells distinctly of moldy socks. Most boys our age stink and are unhygienic, but Devin seems far to the right on the bell curve of teenage skank.

We sit down around the pizza. I make sure I'm as far away from Devin and his BO as possible without being obvious about it. I snag two slices of pizza, one in either hand. I devour one before I notice everyone staring at me. No one else has touched the food.

"What? I'm hungry," I say.

"I didn't know you like meat so much," Haji says.

"How can you even eat?" Dalia asks.

"You should eat too," I say. "Who knows when there will be another opportunity."

Devin shrugs and frees his hand from Dalia's. "Good point. Dig in, babe. You didn't eat lunch."

With some gentle encouragement, both Haji and Dalia start eating. I worry about my BFF. She takes one small slice and only nibbles at it. The boys eat with enthusiasm but not as heartily as me. Are my hunger and craving for meat due to the presence stirring deep within me? I push the thought aside, not wanting to dwell on it.

As we eat, Dalia fills us in with what happened to her and Devin. After school, they went to a film at the Arthouse Theater in the heart of the University District. About an hour into the movie, a stranger sat down next to Dalia. She thought it odd. There were dozens of seats available. Only when the lights came on after the film did she realize the stranger was none other than Dr. Radcliffe.

"I wanted to scream and run. I really wanted to, but I couldn't. I don't know why," Dalia says, shaking her head. "I could only do exactly what he told me to do. He said, follow me. That was it, I followed him."

Dalia looks at Devin.

He nods in agreement. "It was bizarre. I couldn't even talk. I felt like a robot. When he stopped at the pizza place, I thought we could make a run for it, but he told us to stay put and not to do anything. That's what we did."

Haji and I exchange a glance.

"Must be magic," I whisper, and Haji nods in agreement.

"Magic, huh? Holy crap." Devin leans back in his chair. His thick lips gleam with grease. "You all are into some weird shit. I mean, who are these people? What do they want?"

"How much does he know?" I ask Dalia and nod my chin toward her boyfriend. I don't want to tell him anything. I don't trust him, and I don't even know that I like him. What does Dalia see in him?

"He doesn't know anything," Dalia says. "There is something else I need to tell…"

Just then, the vehicles roar to life. The cop car backs up and does a one-eighty, heading for the warehouse door. The other dragons pile into the SUV.

"They're leaving?" I stand up. "This is our chance…"

Tatsuo ambles over to us with his massive draconic form lumbering behind him. He smiles, showing off perfect white teeth.

"What are you kids talking about?" he asks. "Anything you want to share with Uncle Tatsuo?"

The warehouse door creaks as Ion pulls it open. Not nearly as much light pours in from the outside as before. It's getting dark.

"Where are they going?" I ask.

"Pick up some items to work magic on you, Allison," Tatsuo says, his grin going even wider. "I'm just here to babysit. I'm not an expert on magic. Neither is Ion, but Frederick is afraid she might decide to eat you. Me? No need to worry. I don't have a hankering for human flesh. I prefer skaag, hot and bloody."

He winks at me, and his scarred draconic form stares down at me from overhead with its mouth hanging open to reveal razor-sharp teeth flashing in and out of existence. My stomach knots, and I regret having gorged myself on pizza.

"This talk about magic. That's bullshit, right?" Devin says.

"You're the extra, huh? You haven't seen Frederick," Tatsuo says and walks around us to stand behind Devin. He grabs Devin's shoulders in meaty hands. The boy squirms. "Well, you just sit tight, Mr. Purple-Hair. You're about to get an education as soon as my associates return."

Tatsuo's fingers bore into Devin's shoulders. Grimacing, Devin curses and struggles to no effect. I have the distinct impression the massive man can snap Devin like a toothpick.

"Leave him alone," I say.

"Sure. Whatever you say." Tatsuo releases Devin, then saunters over to the table with the computer.

"Are you okay?" Dalia asks and tries to take Devin by the hand.

"Don't touch me," Devin says, standing up. "I'm

leaving." He glares at Tatsuo. "That old man, the professor, has my phone. He better give it back or—"

Tatsuo glances over his shoulder. "Or what? Sit your ass down, Ace, before I come over there and give you a nice shoulder massage."

Devin looks at us for support and, finding none, sits down without another word. After that, we sit in sullen silence as Tatsuo plays on the computer. The screen is mostly blocked by his heavy shoulders, but it looks like he is checking out Hawaiian real estate.

Dalia leans close and whispers, "During the film, Jason messaged me. Said he is worried about you. I thought it was something about you being mad at him. He wanted to meet, so I messaged him that I was at the Arthouse. When we were leaving, I think I saw him."

I put my finger to my lips and whisper, "He can hear us."

Tatsuo turns, and his dragon form goes on high alert, peering into the darkness around the warehouse. "That's right, I can hear you. Smell you too. What—"

A tall girl darts out of the darkness and points something at Tatsuo. There is a hiss, and a spray hits him in the face.

"Run!" the girl screams.

"Leslie?" I say, slack-jawed.

Then Dalia is pulling me out of the chair, and we're running toward the back of the warehouse. With my excellent night vision, I see Jason in the darkness before the flashlight he holds flares to life.

"Come on. My car is outside."

Chapter 25

I'm running headlong, surrounded by my friends.
Dalia is ahead of me, holding my hand. Ahead of her is
Devin, his breathing making as much noise as a freight
train. In my peripheral vision to my left is Haji, his
lanky frame making him a graceless runner. I reach for
him, my fingers brushing against the back of his hand. I
clasp his hand just as a surge of physical prowess roars
through my body, making me feel light as a feather and
as powerful as a grizzly. I pull Haji along, then force
him ahead of me.

"Hurry," Jason urges us.

He stands near a door that I can see off to the left
along the far wall of the building. The door is ajar, and
a triangle of dim light shines in from outside to
illuminate the concrete floor and a small section of
sheet metal wall.

Haji is flagging, his breathing labored and his gait
even more awkward. I clutch his hand even tighter.

"Almost there," I cry. "Keep it up."

From behind us comes a bright flash and the
crackle of electricity. My skin tingles. There is a loud
crash and the crunch of metal. I dare a glance over my
shoulder. Arms pumping and legs overturning in perfect
form, Leslie sprints after us, but there is no escaping the
massive hand covered in green scales reaching for her.
Tatsuo snatches her, flinging her into the air. Leslie

somersaults upward, arms flailing and legs turning over like she is still sprinting over the ground. A scream of abject terror echoes through the warehouse. I don't know if I'm shrieking or if I'm hearing Leslie or Jason or someone else. Leslie's upward trajectory ends just below the ceiling, and she plummets, appendages whirling and hair streaming behind her like a golden pennant. I am about to look away, certain Leslie is going to strike the concrete floor and splatter like an overripe tomato, but then a second clawed hand catches her in midair and raises her up to a massive maw full of saliva-coated fangs and a blood-red forked tongue. Black smoke escapes the dragon's mouth to rise to the ceiling in small, puffy clouds. The beast's right eye is livid green split vertically by a long, black pupil. Where the left eye should be is a cratered ruin of mangled pink and blackened flesh.

Tatsuo roars, rattling the walls of the warehouse. It's enough to make me cringe and slow my stride. My friends slow too, and they're looking back to see Leslie held before the scarred dragon's gaping mouth. Leslie is covered in gooey spittle. She struggles against the giant hand holding her, but there is no way she can escape the beast's grip.

The threat is obvious—we either surrender to Tatsuo, or he will bite Leslie's head off. Part of me says to hell with Leslie, run, escape, let her die. She's a racist. What do I care about her? But the more decent part of me, the part of me taught by my father to respect people and the planet and life and to always keep an open mind, demands that I stop and sacrifice my freedom to save Leslie, even if she is little better than a stinkbug. There is another part of me, that thing deep inside me that is waking and disturbing the cage that holds it. That part of me sees Tatsuo's threat against Leslie's life as a battle challenge, a call to arms. In its dreams that are somehow oozing into my consciousness, the sleeper wants to slay Tatsuo with claws and teeth designed to pry aside the armored scales to expose the vulnerable flesh underneath. The sleeper's feral desires fog my own. Do I fight or surrender? Who am I? What am I?

"Stop! Stop!" I scream, slowing and pulling Dalia and Haji to a stop. "Stop! If we run, he'll kill her."

Devin, looking over his shoulder in terror, keeps running straight into Jason's arms. The two boys go down in a heap.

****

"You need to get over here now," Tatsuo shouts into the cell phone as he paces back and forth in front of us. His materializing and dematerializing draconic companion follows him.

We're sitting on the cold concrete among the ruined chairs and table, squashed pizza, and the laptop, its dark screen a spiderweb of cracks. All of it crushed by the dragon when it passed from the slipstream into the warehouse.

Tatsuo's face is puffy where the pepper spray hit him, and tears stream from his eyes. He takes no notice of the irritation like it's just the body reacting and not the man. He has confiscated Leslie's and Jason's cell phones. Neither one had the foresight to contact the police or anyone else for that matter. If they had called the cops, I have no doubt that would only have brought Ion.

"If that's the plan, you need more," Tatsuo says.

He stops pacing, his appraising gaze on Jason and Leslie. "The girl is tall, slender." A pause. "I don't know. How tall are you, blondie?"

Leslie whimpers and buries her face in Jason's chest.

Jason answers, "She is six one."

A few short weeks ago, I would have given almost anything to rest my head against Jason's chest and have him hold me. Now, I find the mere thought of cuddling with him repulsive.

"You get that? Six one," Tatsuo says and resumes pacing. "The boy is average."

I despise Leslie. She's a racist and entitled and just plain mean. Despite that, I feel sorry for her after her ordeal. I suppose being nearly crushed to death by a massive, winged reptile myself makes it easier to be empathetic, and she helped Jason try to save us. Who the hell knows why she did that? I wonder if she knows herself.

It's easy to guess why Jason tried to save us. Guilt, obviously. The guilt of being a bad friend and a closet racist. The guilt is a good thing for him. Maybe it means he's maturing and ready to dump Leslie. Then again, looking at them now, holding each other, I don't think he's planning on dumping her anytime soon.

Then there is Devin, Dalia's oh so brave boyfriend. Even my BFF gives him the cold shoulder after I had to drag him out from behind the wheel of Jason's beater with mismatched doors. After crashing into Jason, Devin had fought his way free and sprinted for the door and out into the swirling snow. He had made it to the car and was trying to put it in gear when Dalia and I reached him. It was dark out, the only light from the headlights of the car, but I could see everything I needed to with my prosthetic eyes. The physical prowess had still been with me then, and even the locked driver side door couldn't stop me from catching my prey. I smashed the window with my fist and dragged him out by his hair and flailing arms. I flung him to the ground and growled at him not to move and turned off the vehicle.

Devin cowered at my feet, holding a hand before his face like he was afraid I'd thump him. Red droplets splattered the white snow. He had good reason to fear, for as I stood over him the craving to taste bloody, raw meat pounded through my body. I shuddered, and I swear, I could have thrown myself on him and started tearing into his neck like a vampire. But I didn't. My prowess abandoned me, and I stumbled back inside the warehouse, leaving Dalia to deal with her boyfriend.

"How's your hand?" Dalia asks.

I look at her questioningly.

"Your hand was bleeding. When you dragged my worthless boyfriend out of the car. I can't believe he was going to abandon us."

I hold out my hand.

Dalia inspects it. "I thought your knuckles were cut?"

"Mauve cut her with a knife," Haji says. "Allison has miraculous healing abilities."

Dalia raises an eyebrow inquisitively. Tatsuo has finished talking on the phone but still paces before us, not more than five feet away.

"Okay, I'll fill you in." I start retelling what had happened to Haji and me. He fills in some details, and I even tell Dalia and him about being tasted by Tanis and her determination that I'm some sort of half-breed monster known as a skaag. They listen with rapt attention, and if they judge me, I can't tell. Unburdening myself to my squad makes me feel like I've jettisoned some of the detritus that had been holding me down.

"Wow," Dalia says after I finish the tale. "Wow."

"This is so cool, Allison," Haji says. "You're like a monster—a doppelgänger or something like that."

"Haji," Dalia scolds. "That's not nice to say."

"That's okay," I say. "Maybe, if I'm a monster, I can save us. You know, it takes a monster to fight monsters."

"Allison, it doesn't matter what they say," Dalia says and takes my hand in hers. "You're not a monster."

"I hope you're a monster, Allison," Haji says. "That is savage! You have superpowers. Now we just have to learn how to unlock them."

****

We huddle in the cold for an hour or more before Dr. Radcliffe and company show up. The dragons gather around us, their human forms looking disapprovingly at the newcomers and their draconic forms coalescing into a nebula that is nearly blinding in its brilliance.

"Do we have enough for all of them?" Dr. Radcliffe asks.

Mauve steps forward from the group. "Stand up, please. All of you."

None of us are quick to comply.

"Stand up, children. Before you make Uncle Tatsuo angry," Tatsuo growls.

We scramble to our feet. I'm not sure who is the fastest, Devin or Leslie. Maybe it's a tie.

Mauve walks over to stand in front of me. She looks me up and down. If she had a measuring tape, she could pass as a seamstress measuring my proportions.

"Can you explain what you're doing?" I whisper to her. "We're frightened. Tatsuo turned into a dragon and nearly killed Leslie. We don't want to die."

"You were warned not to tell anyone about us," Mauve says. "We don't want to die either. Our anonymity keeps us safe."

"Stop fraternizing with the prisoners," Ion barks.

Mauve is about to retort, but Dr. Radcliffe speaks. "Do hurry, Mauve. We have a long night ahead of us if we do not want people to notice the children are missing and start snooping where they should not."

Mauve gives me an apologetic smile and moves on to Dalia.

"I still say we kill them," Ion says. "I'll eat their bodies. Bones, clothes, even their shoes. No evidence. It'll be just like old times."

I gulp. Dalia grabs my hand and quivers. Haji moans, and there is whimpering that might be from Devin or Leslie or Jason or some combination of them. I can't blame them. They're newbies to the dragon game and don't realize the threat to eat us is an empty one. At least, I hope it is. Dr. Radcliffe doesn't chide Ion like he has in the past. Instead, he stares at me like the patron of a butcher shop inspecting a side of meat. He turns to Tanis.

"Are you sure we should awaken her true nature?" Dr. Radcliffe asks.

"I'm not," Tanis says and strides toward me. "But if she proves dangerous, there are five of us and only one of her. Slaying her won't be difficult."

Chapter 26

"Come with us," Dr. Radcliffe says.

Tanis and I follow him away from the dim light cast by the LED. I glance over my shoulder at my squad, the dragons, and those three other teenagers who aren't my friends. Tatsuo paces in front of my peers, who are clustered together. Ion and Mauve are emptying paper bags from the back of the SUV. They place the bags on the concrete floor at the edge of the illumination provided by the single bulb.

"Clay," Tanis says.

"You bought clay?" I ask. A dozen or so paper bags are arrayed on the floor. "Why so much?"

Dr. Radcliffe chuckles. "All in good time, Allison. You do not expect us to reveal all our secrets at once, do you?"

I look at Tanis, who only gives me a sly smile.

"Who are you? What are you? Why can I see you as shimmering apparitions while the others can't? Why me?"

We come to a halt halfway between the center of the warehouse and the back wall. I suppose for someone with regular eyes it would be a murky gloom, but between the light given off by the translucent dragons and the night vision capabilities of my prosthetics, I might as well be out in the midday sun.

"We spoke about your disturbing ability to see us

while we ride the slipstream," Dr. Radcliffe says. "We have a plausible if improbable explanation."

"More of a theory," Tanis says.

"Are you going to tell me or not? You've kidnapped us and threatened our lives. I think I deserve an explanation of why this is happening."

Tanis stiffens. Dr. Radcliffe smiles avuncularly.

"We believe it is an unexpected outcome of your prosthetic eyes and skaag blood. It is something we do not understand. The human eye cannot penetrate the slipstream, and neither can a skaag's. Ordinarily, human devices, even a highly sensitive scientific apparatus, cannot penetrate the slipstream. You, however, can see us. You could not see us, I assume, prior to having your prosthetic eyes?"

"You've been a dragon forever, right? Like at the faculty gathering last September, were you? A dragon, I mean."

Dr. Radcliffe nods.

"I couldn't see you then."

"We do not like having our true nature revealed to an outsider," Dr. Radcliffe says. "Our enemies hunt us even now as they have for hundreds of years. They will kill us without hesitation."

"What's that have to do with me?"

"You're part human and part skaag," Tanis says. "Humans and skaags shouldn't be capable of interbreeding."

"Yet here you are," Dr. Radcliffe says.

I remember the ghostly visitation I experienced at the hospital. The sense that whoever or whatever intruded upon my rest woke something alien hidden deep inside me. Then came insatiable hunger for meat and the fury that somehow never seemed entirely my own. Earlier this evening my body healed itself with remarkable speed, and for a fleeting time I possessed immense physical prowess. Somewhere in my core, the sleeper stirs, rattling its cage.

"You feel it, don't you?" Tanis says and takes my hand in both of hers. Her hands are warm, almost hot. "The wound is gone. Preternatural healing is a skaag trait." She rubs my palm with her thumbs. "The skaag in you is fighting to emerge. It's kept in check by powerful magic."

"How do you know?" I demand. I don't want to be a monster. I don't want to be me either, the half-Asian girl abandoned by her mother and the butt of every joke and offhand remark of the popular girls. I don't want to be the girl who pines after a boy only to lose him to a racist. I don't want to be me, but that doesn't mean I want to be a monster. How can I even be one? My dad is just a college professor, an ordinary guy.

My gaze darts to Dr. Radcliffe. No, Dad is not like him. He's not a monster. Never. I know him, and I'd know if he is a skaag. I would. I can't say that about my mother. I don't have a single memory of her. She's always been the mysterious woman who abandoned me long ago while I was a helpless infant. No, that's not possible. That's asylum-level insanity. There's no way my mother is a skaag. I'm not buying what these dragons are selling. No way.

I bite down on my lower lip, remembering that astral presence that claimed me as its daughter at the hospital. No. That had to be a dream, didn't it? Maybe? Then again, not that long ago I consigned dragons to fairy tales.

"Are skaags like you? Do they look human?" I ask.

"They can look human, but they are not like us. They are shapeshifters, able to alter their appearance to look like your kind," Tanis says.

My lips tremble. Maybe my mother had a good reason to abandon my father and me. Maybe she never expected to become pregnant.

"Is my mother…" I whisper, then shake my head. "No, I'm jumping to conclusions."

Inside me the sleeper stirs and, with the stirring, the certainty that my mother is indeed a skaag. I fear I might weep in front of Tanis and Dr. Radcliffe. I want to be impervious to the emotions bubbling inside me, but I feel like I'm tumbling down an abyss. It's a helpless feeling, like your feet have slipped out from under you, and there's nothing you can do to stop your fall.

"When I tasted your blood," Tanis says, "I detected three things. Human blood, skaag blood, and magic, thick and strong. A powerful sorcerer doesn't want you or the world to know you're a skaag."

"My mother. She is a skaag," I say, knowing from the sleeper that there is truth to my words. "She worked the magic to protect me."

"Possibly," Dr. Radcliffe says, nodding. "Your father is not a skaag. His smell would have given him away long ago. He likely never suspected your mother was anything other than human. Of course, with magic at play there are other possibilities."

"Other possibilities?" I ask.

"The man you consider your father might not be your biological father," Tanis says with uncharacteristic gentleness.

"No." I shake my head. "He's my father."

"Magic can alter human perception," Dr. Radcliffe says.

"He's my dad. You'll never convince me otherwise. I...I need time to process this."

I try to pull away from Tanis, but her hands clench mine with a force that belies her aged appearance.

I wince. "Let go. You're hurting me."

Tanis releases me, and I back away, opening and closing my aching hand. I want to flee. I don't want to be a monster. I want to be anywhere other than here with these dragons and their problems. If the rage inside me wakes and fills me with physical power, I can escape. Jason's car is still parked behind the warehouse with the keys in the ignition. A burst of incredible speed, and I will be through the door before they can stop me. I've never driven in the snow. I've never even driven without my dad. But I can't let that stop me.

I glance back at Dalia and Haji, who huddle together so close their shoulders touch. My chest aches.

"You need not worry," Dr. Radcliffe says. "As long as you cooperate, your friends are safe."

I face him. "Why should I trust you?"

"It would be an easy thing for me to allow Ion to kill all of you," Dr. Radcliffe says with a bemused smile. "If I give the word, she will eat you. Flesh and bones and clothes. No one will ever know what happened to you. As near perfect a crime as possible."

"Why don't you do that then? Why all the threats?"

Dr. Radcliffe raises an eyebrow and glances at Tanis then back to me. "I thought it would be evident why we have not killed you. Despite your reaction when you see us pass out of the slipstream into this world, we are not monsters. We are civilized. More civilized than humans. Humans are on the cusp of disaster. Consider the greatest existential crisis humanity faces. Anthropomorphic climate change. Humans are destroying this planet's ability to support life. It is a scientific fact, yet some politicians claim that it is a hoax. My people faced similar circumstances millennia ago and overcame the challenges. We adapted by learning to live in harmony with nature instead of attempting to conquer it at every turn. For that, we reaped the rewards. Our civilization spans planets, stars, dimensions. We do not destroy life without cause. You must forgive Ion. She is young and afraid and a soldier. It is in her nature to deal with problems by crushing them. She killed dozens of skaags before fleeing to Earth."

Dr. Radcliffe continues speaking, but his words smear. Deep inside me, the sleeper wakes and throws itself against the bars of its cell. The cage rattles. The bars bulge but do not break. Its strength flows into me as a trickling stream that builds into roaring rapids.

Tanis says something to Dr. Radcliffe. She backs away from me, and Dr. Radcliffe marches toward me. His looming golden draconic form follows him, fading in and out of existence. Animalistic fear seizes me as his dragon form nears, yet the fear is tempered by something out of place—confidence. Confidence that I can match the dragon in combat.

I retreat, but Dr. Radcliffe snatches me and pulls me around in front of him to face Tanis. He is behind me now, his hands clamped down on my upper arms. The old woman stares impassively at me as the air around her crackles. An electrical arc sizzles from the crown of her head to zap the ceiling. More arcs emanate from her body. My skin tingles as her dragon form shimmers into existence.

The white beast stretches its neck toward the ceiling, joints crackling like popcorn. A clawed hand lifts the humanoid Tanis, who is stiff as a granite statue, off the ground and sets her aside out of the way. The dragon turns her large, pale pink eyes on me. The sleeper throws its writhing black body against the cage. The bars clatter and buckle. I tremble. I convulse. Only Dr. Radcliffe's strong hands keep me upright.

My lips curl into a snarl, and I battle against his indomitable grip. His long fingers cut into my skin like steel manacles, yet I fight against him, spurred on by the torrent of fear and hatred and hunger gushing from the sleeper.

I throw my head back like a wrecking ball, clipping the bottom of his chin. He grunts and stumbles. The sleeper hurls itself against the cage. Metal strains and squeals and cracks. A thick, black, serpentine body squirms between the bars. The bars burst from the stress. I gasp, my eyes going wide. A jolt of physical prowess with the kick of gallons of adrenaline surges through me. I lift my right foot and slam my heel into Dr. Radcliffe's ankle. His joint pops. Pain shoots up my leg, but it's mere diagnostic feedback.

Dr. Radcliffe grunts and wobbles. I wrench my right arm free, then my left. Fingers brush against me, then fall away. I'm ready to run, but the ancient white dragon blocks my way. She might be smaller than Dr. Radcliffe and Tatsuo, but she is still bigger than an elephant. Her pink leathery wings are outstretched, reaching either wall of the warehouse. I spin around just as more electrical sizzling fills the air. Lightning flashes in my peripheral vision. Electricity arcs. A golden hand slaps me, rattling every bone in my body. I strike the ground, and my breath whooshes out of me. I scramble, but Dr. Radcliffe's scaled hand pins me to the floor.

I struggle against clawed fingers as thick as tree trunks. I growl in frustration. I should be able to escape. I should. The sleeper can overcome these monsters. It's why I was made with the desire and attributes to slay dragons. Only something is wrong. The sleeper is out of the cage, but it is still trapped, held in check by an invisible, unconquerable force. The sleeper shrieks, and I scream. The sleeper throws itself against the translucent netting entangling it, and I writhe.

Dr. Radcliffe's massive head fills my vision, golden lips curling up to reveal fangs the length of short swords. His hot breath stinks of sulfur, and wisps of black smoke curl between his teeth. His mouth expands into a gaping chasm with bright flames burning in its depths. Writhing, I flail my arms against his golden scales. My hands come away bloody as the scales rip my skin and the fabric of my coat.

Still pinning me to the floor, Dr. Radcliffe withdraws his head, giving Tanis space to move her bulk over me. She holds a claw coated in steaming purple ichor above my chest. The hand holding me shifts, grip loosening. I wiggle my torso and shuffle my feet, winning free but only for a moment. The hand tightens around my waist. At the same time, the ichor-stained claw inches toward my chest.

The sleeper shrieks, and I scream. "No!"

The purple claw pierces my clothes and pricks my skin. Flames burn through my body. The invisible netting melts, freeing the sleeper. With sickening squelching and loud cracks, bones break and burst from my skin in a red torrent. Organs rend and reshape like works from the imagination of a mad origamist. There is no pain, only a sense of movement. Then agony explodes, expanding like a supernova. A blood river floods my vision, transforming into a pulsating white that withers to black.

Chapter 27

The freezing concrete floor wakes me. Frigid air burns my lungs. I sit up in the darkness. My squad and the others sleep nearby. I roll my neck, trying to work out a kink, and the flimsy blanket covering me falls away. Oh my God, I'm naked. Where are my clothes? Goose bumps form on my arms. I wrap the blanket around myself. The material is crinkly and metallic, like an emergency blanket. It's a wonder I haven't frozen to death. I wrack my brain for what happened to me, turning up a blank.

I scan the warehouse, still amazed by my prosthetics' low light capabilities. About twenty feet away, the concrete floor is blackened, maybe even melted. Strange. The cop car is gone, but the SUV and a navy-blue minivan with a rusting hood are parked nearby. A golden glow emanates from the side of the vehicle opposite to me. Stretched out beyond the front bumper of the SUV is a golden serpentine tail flickering in and out of existence. Dr. Radcliffe.

I gasp, and my jaw goes slack. Memories of confinement and fear and rending pain slam into me like a rogue asteroid. I tremble. The sleeper ripples through me, staying beneath the surface and in the shadows, still cowed after last night. What did he and Tanis do to me? What did they do to us? God. That explains my clothes, shredded by my body during transformation. Lips trembling, I stare at my arms, remembering bones rupturing from my flesh with bloody gouts of gore. How can my skin be unblemished?

Dalia stirs on the floor at my feet, and her eyes flutter open. She rubs the grit from her eyes.

"Allison?" she says, her voice mushy. "You're awake. Are you okay? After last night—"

I kneel next to her. "Do you know what they did to me?"

Dalia sits up. "No, they wouldn't let us watch. Dr. Radcliffe and the old woman—"

"Tanis," I say.

"Yeah, that one," Dalia says, nodding. "They turned into dragons. It was frightening. The noise." Her eyes become distant, and she gulps. "Horrible shrieking and roaring. Dr. Radcliffe spread out his wings so we couldn't see anything. I wanted to go to you…Haji did too, but that nasty Tatsuo wouldn't let us."

As if his name disturbed him from his slumber, Haji rolls from his side onto his back. "Dalia? Who are you talking to?"

"Allison is awake," Dalia says.

"Allison?" Haji's eyes flash open.

Haji sits up and smiles. He leans over and embraces me.

"I'm so glad you're okay," he whispers. "When they brought you back…I was so scared. We all were. You were covered in blood and your clothes…I didn't look. I mean, I looked away. I…"

He says more, but I'm lost in my memories. I push him away. I remember the purple-stained talon hovering over me like a guillotine's blade. I pull the blanket aside to expose my chest where Tanis stabbed me with her claw.

"Haji, don't look," Dalia says sharply.

"I'm not!"

My skin is stained with blood, red except for a single streak of purple between my breasts. The sleeper recoils at the sight of the purple ichor. I wince at the memory of my organs shifting and expanding and contracting like a diabolical surgeon eviscerated me and took my insides for trophies. I tremble. How am I alive?

I'm not human. I'm something else. I double over and retch, only vaguely aware of my friends scampering away to avoid the half-digested pizza spewing from my mouth onto the concrete. Dr. Radcliffe and Tanis and the other dragons weren't lying. I am a monster, a skaag.

"Allison, maybe you should lie down," Dalia says. She stands over me, her face contorted in a worried frown. She wraps the emergency blanket around me. Haji hovers at her shoulder.

"Ah, you are awake. Excellent," Dr. Radcliffe says.

Radcliffe stands in front of the SUV and gestures to me. His draconic form looms behind him, translucent and glowing.

"Come, Allison, I have clothes for you. Quickly, now. There is no time to waste. You have a busy day ahead. We all do."

****

Ion's South Seattle townhouse is cramped with six teens and four dragons sitting around the small living room. Dalia, Haji, and I occupy the pale blue carpet in front of a huge flat screen TV. Jason and Leslie sit together on a lounge chair, their arms enveloping each other. I'm proud that I can look at them without a pang of jealousy.

Devin sits by himself. He made overtures to Dalia on the ride over from the warehouse, but she is still giving him the cold shoulder. Dr. Radcliffe, Tanis, Mauve, and Tatsuo occupy the couch in human form. Their draconic companions coalesce into a luminous aura that looks like a space telescope photograph of a distant nebula. On the coffee table in front of the couch are the remains of breakfast, sweet bun crumbs and half-empty coffee cups. Speaking only for myself, the pastry was delicious, and the coffee tasted like used tractor tires coated in cowpie and pesticide.

On the ride over in the minivan, my fellow captives filled me in on the purpose of the clay.

"Golems," Haji had said, his voice full of excitement usually reserved for sports and the *Cascadia Weekly*.

"Like straight out of Jewish folklore," Jason said. When everyone had looked at him, he added, "I took a world religion class over the summer. For college credit."

Haji described how Mauve had sculpted replicas of each of us using red and blue and green clay. The entire time she had chanted in a guttural language no one understood. When she completed the sculptures, a drop of blood was taken from everyone and wiped over the crude mouth of their doppelgänger. Then Mauve crossed over from the slipstream and heated the clay people with dragon fire.

"We went from being miserably cold to hot as hell in an instant," Leslie said.

I was not interested in anything Leslie had to say,

231

but everyone nodded in agreement with her, even my squad. It made me feel left out. They had bonded while watching the creation of the golems.

"Dragon fire is seriously hot," Devin said.

His observation did not make me think any higher of his intellect, but it did explain the melted concrete I saw earlier.

"They let us stand outside to escape the heat," Dalia said. "Dr. Radcliffe carried you."

"Like a baby," Haji added.

"Was I naked?" I asked, aghast.

"I think so, but we couldn't see anything," Devin said, sounding disappointed. "You were covered in that space blanket thing."

I breathe easier knowing the boys hadn't seen me in my birthday suit. Had Haji seen me nude when I woke up this morning? My face flushed, and I avoided looking at him. I don't like the other girls seeing me half-dressed in the locker room for PE or cross-country. *Ugh*.

When they had been ordered back inside by Tatsuo, the golems were complete. Our doubles were no longer rudimentary statues made from a mishmash of multicolored clay—they were exact replicants of each of us complete with clothes that more or less matched our individual styles.

"They made us listen to the golems speak to make sure the voices sounded correct," Haji said.

"Those things sound exactly like us," Dalia said. "It was creepy. I was glad when Ion and Tatsuo got the van."

It turned out Ion drove off in her police cruiser with Tatsuo. The roly-poly man returned with a minivan, which the creepy golems had piled into, except for the Jason and Leslie look-alikes. Those two headed to the warehouse's back exit, presumably to take Jason's car. After that, everyone had eventually fallen asleep, although Devin claimed with pride that he only pretended to slumber.

For my part, I had slept through the entire drama.

****

The dragons have been talking among themselves, quite animatedly, but I can't hear a word. We watch the inaudible spectacle unfold like a silent movie from the last millennium. Tatsuo and Dr. Radcliffe are positioned at opposite ends of the couch. The men argue while Tanis and Mauve are stuck in the middle. Both the women look uncomfortable. Tatsuo's fleshy hands are clenched into huge fists resting on his knees. He looks every bit like a sumo wrestler ready to piledrive his opponent.

"I can't hear them," Devin says. "Can anyone hear them?"

That's Devin for you, always quick to point out the obvious.

"Not a thing," Jason says.

"It's bizarre," Leslie says and snuggles closer to Jason. "It looks like those boomers are screaming at each other. We should hear something. What do you think, baby? Magic?"

"Maybe. I don't know what to think anymore," Jason says.

"It has to be magic, right?" Haji asks me.

I shrug. "What else could it be?"

Tanis involves herself in the argument and appears to have brought calm to the proceedings. Neither

Tatsuo nor Dr. Radcliffe look happy. Instead, they appear like eager prizefighters in their respective corners. It seems male dragons, at least, I assume they are male, suffer from the same flaws as human males.

"Are they voting?" Haji asks.

Only Dr. Radcliffe doesn't raise his hand. The old professor throws up his arms in evident disgust and begins to lecture his cohorts.

"It's a draconic democracy," I quip.

Dalia and the boys laugh. Leslie flashes me an irritated look. Apparently, she isn't as secure in her relationship with Jason as she appears. It's not like I plot to snatch Jason away from her, but her insecurity pleases me nonetheless.

Without warning, I can hear the dragons. Tatsuo is chuckling and smiling as smug as a well-fed cat.

"Well, I better get to it then," Tatsuo says. He places his open hands on his knees and stands. He points and glares at each of us in turn. "You kids better stay on the straight and narrow. Do what Dr. Radcliffe and the ladies tell you. We clear?"

We nod and mutter affirmative responses. Devin says something nasty under his breath. Tatsuo must have heard the expletive too because he glowers at Devin, who cowers under his gaze.

"I'm glad we have an understanding. You don't want to see Uncle Tatsuo mad." Tatsuo smiles.

He ambles from the living room into the narrow hall, whistling an old tune. Beach Boys, maybe? The front door opens and closes, and he is gone.

"Frederick, it's our best chance to face them at a time and place of our choosing," Tanis says.

Dr. Radcliffe waves aside her comment. He stares

at me. "Allison, come with me. I have something to show you."

He stands and walks to the kitchen that is separated from the living room by a countertop bar. I move to follow, but Haji grabs my hand.

"It's okay." I squeeze his hand.

He nods once and releases me.

Dr. Radcliffe stands in the middle of the small kitchen, staring at his smartphone. He glances up when I enter.

"Look at this." He hefts the phone.

I stride over to his shoulder, passing into the glowing light of his draconic hind leg. The rest of the dragon's body passes through the walls and ceiling. I blink several times as my prosthetics adjust to the shimmering light. On the screen is something serpentine like a Chinese dragon only oily black. Two short, powerful legs are visible complete with hooked, yellowish talons. Its one visible eye is closed like the beast is unconscious on a concrete floor. I stiffen. The sleeper who no longer sleeps quivers.

"Is that…" I gulp. "Inside me?" I ask tremulously.

Dr. Radcliffe nods. "It is you. The skaag." He shakes his head. "Or half-skaag. I am sorry for what is to happen next. I do not agree with it, but I was outvoted."

Chapter 28

After two very uncomfortable days inside Ion's townhouse, Dalia, Haji, and I sit in the back of a dingy minivan driven by Dr. Radcliffe. Tanis rides shotgun, and Ion sits in the back, eyeballing us as if she suspects we'll try to escape or something equally stupid while the van zips up Highway 101. If I look at the radiance of our captors' draconic forms for long, I start to get a headache even with my prosthetics, so I spend most of my time looking out the window. Occasionally, a semitransparent leg or wing obscures the view, but it is still better than looking at the glowing dragon parts inside the vehicle.

Rain pelts the roadway, dings against the roof, and almost overwhelms the windshield wipers. To the west, I glimpse the slate gray vastness and whitecaps of the Pacific Ocean between towering firs, hemlock, and spruce. To the east, the coastline gives way to the wilderness of forest and mountains known as the Olympic Peninsula.

Our captors haven't been forthcoming about where we're going or why. I suspect it has something to do with the argument between Dr. Radcliffe and Tatsuo two days earlier because it was a call from Mister Roly-poly last night that set this road trip in motion.

"Where are our friends?" I ask for what must be, let me see, the twentieth time.

"They're not your friends, so why do you care?" Ion says, as snarly as ever.

The trip is doing nothing for Ion's mood. All she does is answer my questions without really answering them and complain about our stench. Honestly, we can't smell that bad, even Haji. We all showered before piling into the van. Ion made us.

"I'm still concerned about them," I say. "Jason and Leslie came to save me."

Ion rolls her eyes. She points to Haji and Dalia, who sit on either side of me. "These two are your friends. That's why they're here. Just in case you decide to step out of line, I'll bite their heads off."

Dalia and Haji squirm. I don't blame them. After living in her townhouse for two days, we learned Ion is very literal and more than happy to follow through on her threats. She warned us the first night that if anyone tried to run off, she'd tase them. Well, guess who tried to run off? Jason and Leslie. I'm surprised Devin didn't try to escape too. Anyway, Ion caught them trying to crawl out a bathroom window and tased them both. Leslie puked all over the bathroom floor.

Dalia speaks up. "Devin is my boyfriend. I'm worried about him. Mauve seems okay, but I don't trust that Tatsuo guy. He is mean and creepy."

Ion gives Dalia a look that drips *oh, really*.

"Okay. Ex-boyfriend, but I'm still worried about him."

"I'm friendly with Leslie and Jason," Haji adds.

I elbow Haji in the ribs. If he wants to have a chance of one day being my boyfriend or even just staying my friend, he had better rethink his level of friendliness toward Jason and especially Leslie. Just because they came to rescue me doesn't mean I plan to forgive either of them.

"I said friendly, not friends," Haji says sheepishly.

Dr. Radcliffe pulls the van over at a turnout. Cars rush by, exceeding the fifty mile an hour speed limit.

"Ion, your turn to drive," Dr. Radcliffe says and puts the van in park.

Outside in the rain, the two dragons argue. I can't hear what they say over the pounding rain and the roar of passing vehicles. After a couple minutes, they climb back into the van. Dr. Radcliffe sits in the back with us. He is soaking wet, but he doesn't even wipe his glasses that are covered in water droplets.

"Mauve has taken your friends to a safe location," Dr. Radcliffe says.

Ion pulls out onto the highway, spinning the tires on the slick pavement.

"But Tatsuo…" Dalia says.

Dr. Radcliffe holds up a hand for quiet.

"Tatsuo is not with them. He is waiting for us at the rendezvous."

"Where is the rendezvous?" I ask.

"And where is this safe location?" Haji asks.

Dalia nods in agreement. The three of us stare at Dr. Radcliffe, who smiles unperturbedly.

"Don't tell them anything," Ion says.

A gust of wind howls, buffeting the van. Ion fights with the steering as the van veers off the road. The wheels run over the bumper strip, shaking the vehicle and making my teeth clatter. Ion corrects for the wind gusts, and the van swerves back onto the smooth pavement.

"Pay attention to your driving," Dr. Radcliffe says.

"They deserve to know what is happening. They are in danger."

"The less they know, the better," Ion says.

"We discussed—"

"It's a mistake to tell them anything," Ion snaps, pounding one hand against the steering wheel. "We don't owe them anything. Allison Lee is a skaag!"

I shudder at the reminder that I'm not human. Dalia wraps her arm around my shoulders, and Haji takes my hand. My friends have done their best to accept and comfort me since that fateful night in the warehouse when my true nature was revealed to me. They haven't seen the picture of my skaag form, and I haven't told them about it. I'm afraid if they know I'm a monstrous, black-as-crude-oil Chinese dragon, they'll fear me. How couldn't they be frightened? I am. When I think about the power that filled me when the sleeper stirred inside me, I'm amazed. When I think about the power that might fill me now that it's awake, I tremble.

"What is a skaag?" Haji says. "You're magic-wielding dragons. If you're afraid of these skaags...holy cow. Are these things like the end of the world badasses or what?"

Dr. Radcliffe looks about ready to speak.

"Frederick, anything we tell them might be used against us later," Ion says and scowls at us in the rearview mirror.

"Youngling, you forget your place," Tanis says, speaking for the first time on the drive. "Frederick is our leader and your elder. You will treat him with respect and deference."

"I'm in charge of security—"

Tanis growls and hisses inhuman sounds. Ion

stiffens, her hands clenching the steering wheel, her knuckles turning white.

"Yes, Grandmother," Ion says in a formal tone and lapses into sullen silence.

"Grandmother?" Dalia says. "They're related?"

"An imperfect translation of their relationship," Dr. Radcliffe says. "Tanis is…an adoptive mother to Ion. Ion's parents were civil servants. They were arrested and executed in a purge while Ion was a baby."

"That's horrible," I say. I think of my fear of losing my dad. That's why I'm here. They threatened his life. I can imagine what it is like to live without parents, acrimony and longing intertwined to leave a taste in the back of your mouth that is sometimes sweet and always sour. "I'm so sorry."

"Don't be," Ion says. "My parents were fools. They spoke out against the Empress. They should have expected reprisal."

"Youngling, things were different before the rise of General Bale. Your parents never expected to be arrested and executed," Tanis says, her voice soft and sad yet firm. "None of us understood what was happening until it was too late. Now, be silent. I do not wish to hear you disparage your parents."

"Is that why you're here? On Earth," I say. "Because the Empress and General Bale want you dead? They sent the skaags to hunt you down?"

Dr. Radcliffe nods. "Skaags hunt us and other rebels across the multiverse."

"Did you just say the multiverse?" Haji says, releasing my hand and leaning toward Dr. Radcliffe. "As in multiple universes?"

"You have heard us mention the slipstream. It is a

realm between universes. We dragons can ride the slipstream, crossing in and out of it at will."

"How?" Haji asks.

Dr. Radcliffe winks and smiles. "The ability is innate to our physiology."

"Can skaags ride the slipstream?" I ask, imagining an army of oily black lizards materializing out of the ether.

"Yes and no," Dr. Radcliffe says. "Skaags cannot enter and exit the slipstream at will. They must rely on openings in the slipstream, gateways. Similar to what you might call wormholes. These gateways are stable for a while and then collapse. A great deal of magic, science, and technology are dedicated to predicting the location and stability of these gateways."

"So if one formed here...skaags could invade?" I ask.

"In theory," Dr. Radcliffe says, nodding. "It depends on the duration and stability of the gateway. Two skaags are already here. They have been here for thirty years. One is known as Mark Cassidy and the other as Druk."

At the mention of Druk, Ion hisses. More is said, but I'm lost in mental calculations. Thirty years ago. Mark Cassidy. Druk. Neither name means anything to me. My mother's name is Jing Lee, or at least it was when she bore me. I suppose if she is a skaag, Jing Lee is simply an assumed name. Her real name might be anything, maybe Druk.

How long did Dad know that woman before I was born? Eight years, maybe? They met while he was a Ph.D. student in Wisconsin, and she was an exchange student from a university in China. I suppose being an exchange student was all made up, a cover story. They didn't get married until my dad landed a position as an associate professor at Tahoma University. I was born three years later. I'm sixteen, so that's twenty-four years ago. It makes a certain amount of sense. This Druk arrived on Earth thirty years ago, took six to establish a false identity and whatever else skaags do. Then she seduced my father, had me, and abandoned us.

Dr. Radcliffe is deep in an explanation about how the dragons need to be tethered to a dimension outside of the slipstream to survive, which makes them vulnerable to the skaags.

I interrupt him. "Is Druk my mother?"

The question ends the lecture. The only sounds are the ring of the rain off the van, the growl of the vehicle's engine, and the dull roar of passing cars. Dr. Radcliffe stares at me then looks down at his hands.

"Druk is female."

The van swerves. I'm thrown in my seat, and so are Dalia and Haji. A horn blares. Dalia yelps. Even Dr. Radcliffe sways precariously. Tires squeal, then the van abruptly comes to a halt along the side of the road.

Ion turns in her seat, facing me. Her eyes are full of unfettered loathing. I cower under her gaze, and I feel the sleeper retreat to somewhere in the recesses of my being. It's not Ion's anger alone that scares the sleeper. It's the anger in combination with being outnumbered by the dragons three to one.

"Let me have my revenge," Ion growls. "Blood for blood. Every second I'm near her, I'm reminded what Druk did to Alec. It was hard before when I only suspected. Now that I know that she is a half-breed and must be the child of that monster, it's intolerable. Don't you understand?"

I hear the grief in Ion's words.

Tanis places a hand on Ion's shoulder. "Youngling, your brother's death is not this child's fault."

"His name is Alec. Why won't you say it? After he died…you have never said his name."

"It causes pain," Tanis says.

No one says anything. Tension permeates the interior of the van. Then to my shock Ion begins to cry.

"Perhaps it's better if I drive," Dr. Radcliffe says.

****

The rain stops, but the clouds are omnipresent as we continue north. Ion curls up on the floor in the back of the van and whimpers. I keep catching myself staring at her. For the first time since meeting her, I realize she is more than just a snarling monster. She is young and fragile and lost and powerful. She is not that different from me.

I unbuckle my seatbelt. Dalia is asleep, but Haji isn't, and he grabs me by the arm.

"What are you doing?"

"She's hurting."

"Ion is dangerous," Haji whispers, his eyes bulging and his grip tightening on my arm.

The sleeper emerges from hiding. I discern the distinct scent of everybody in the van, and my pulse races. I can break Haji if I choose. It's both exhilarating and frightening.

"She hasn't hurt us."

"What about Leslie and Jason?"

"She could have killed them, Haji. She didn't. Let me go."

243

Reluctantly, his hand drops away. "Be careful."

I kneel next to Ion, passing into the shimmering light of her dragon form. The brilliant light makes my head throb, so I narrow my eyes to slits. I place a hand against her arm. Her uniform is still damp from the rain, and heat radiates from her body. Bathed in the glimmering brilliance of her draconic form, I lie down next to her and wrap an arm around her shoulder. She doesn't stir, but the sleeper inside me does.

The sleeper wants to strike out, kill before it's destroyed. I draw a shuddering breath, tamping down the animalistic urge to fight. I might not be human, but I'm not skaag either. I'm something else.

At some point, the cozy warmth radiating from Ion puts me to sleep. When I wake up, the van is stopped, Ion is gone, and it's dark out. Haji snores softly with his head pressed up against the window. Dalia is curled into a ball on her seat with her head resting against her flattened hands.

I push myself up, careful not to make any noise. I look out the window and see Tanis and Dr. Radcliffe sitting at a picnic table. Their draconic forms flicker in and out of existence and are obscured by the surrounding trees. With the aid of my night vision, I quickly surmise we're at a wooded campground.

I make my way to the front of the van and exit out the passenger side door. I shut the door softly so as not to wake my friends. Dr. Radcliffe and Tanis face me. My stomach growls.

"Ah, you are hungry," Dr. Radcliffe says. "I forget how often your kind needs to eat."

"The human or the skaag?" I ask.

"Both," Dr. Radcliffe says. "I would call Ion to

bring food, but I do not have a cell signal."

"We can survive without food for a little while but not without water. We need water," I say.

"This campground has water," Tanis says and gestures toward a dark building obscured by the trees.

"Drink your fill, then rest," Dr. Radcliffe says. "Tomorrow, we will kill Mark Cassidy."

The sleeper roars inside of me, filling me with a desire to lash out. I'm not sure if I want to attack the dragons or Mark Cassidy or both. "You tell me that and expect me to rest?"

Dr. Radcliffe shrugs. "Sorry."

His unblinking gaze never leaves me. Tanis stares at me too. It's unnerving. They know I'm conflicted. I march down a narrow footpath through the woods toward a building that I can see is a bathroom facility. Outside of the building near one of the entrances is a water faucet. I kneel next to the faucet, turn on the tap, and slurp cool liquid. Some water runs down my chin to splash against my sweatshirt. The fine hairs on the back of my neck stand on end. The scent of eucalyptus and menthol wafts on the breeze rustling the tree branches.

Chapter 29

The familiar scent of Manscape Bodywhiskey transports me back to the university's lawn. The banshee howl of the wind fills my ears. From overhead a tree branch cracks and thuds to the grass. I spin to face a silhouette.

My breathing is shallow and ragged, my body shuddery as I pull my lips away from the water cascading from the faucet. I'm about to call for help, but I hear a twig snap behind me and to my left. Maybe ten, fifteen feet away. I remember the lead pipe whistling through the air. Never again.

Nonchalantly, I turn off the faucet and remain kneeling. Beneath the scent of body spray is a distinctly male odor of sweat and testosterone. Shoes crunch against gravel, so soft no ordinary human would hear it. He's no more than five feet away now.

I surge to my feet, twirling to face my assailant. He gasps, eyes widening, pupils dilated. He is tall and cadaverously gaunt. Greasy blond hair covers his crown, and a few stray wisps fall across his brow. His long black trench coat hangs on him like the Grim Reaper's cloak. He doesn't hold a scythe or lead pipe— he grips a cleaver.

Leering, he dances forward, slicing the cleaver through the air. His preternatural speed shocks me. My heel catches against the piping for the faucet. I stumble and involuntarily scream but stay on my feet. The blade slashes mere centimeters from my throat.

Dr. Radcliffe shouts, and I hear feet stomping from the trees. In my peripheral vision is the glow of the oncoming dragon. Cadaver man raises the cleaver overhead. Before he can hammer it down, I grab his bony wrist. He snarls and hisses, and his mouth opens wide to reveal brown, chipped teeth. He lunges toward me, his mouth clacking shut short of my nose. A stinking mixture of alcohol and cigarettes from his maw washes over me.

"I can't fail twice," he says, spraying spittle that splatters against my face.

He swings his free hand against the side of my head. The blow rings my bell as if I've been hit with a sledgehammer. My vision goes red, then black, then clears. I don't let go of his cleaver arm. Cadaver man swings his cleaver arm up and down with a force that belies his skeletal build. He's more like a linebacker or silverback gorilla, lifting me bodily off the ground and slamming me back down onto my feet. I almost lose my grip on his wrist, but then the sleeper's power surges through me like an electrical current. My fingers buzz with unbridled strength, and my hands tighten with bone-crushing intensity.

Cadaver man keens and scrambles backward, pulling me along. Gravel crackles beneath our feet. The cleaver clatters to the dirt. He swings his free hand like a wrecking ball against my forearms, once, then twice. I pull my arms away before the third blow lands. I lose my balance and, arms flapping, thump onto my butt.

Cadaver man spins away and runs into the woods, cradling his injured wrist. I snatch the cleaver and vault to my feet and hurl the blade. The knife spins through the air. My aim is true. It's about to strike him between the shoulder blades, then he disappears. The blade carves into a tree trunk, quivering.

I scan the surrounding forest, but even with my prosthetics, I can't see him. All that is left of the cadaver man is the cleaver and a hint of eucalyptus in the air. Panting, I pace back and forth, hyped up on so much adrenaline I want to punch something or scream or…

"What happened?" Dr. Radcliffe asks.

I face him and scream, the sound coming out more like the roar of a dragon. I collapse to the ground and start crying, glad to still be alive and scared half to death by what I just survived and terrified by the knowledge I would've ripped cadaver man limb from limb given half a chance.

Dr. Radcliffe kneels beside me and wraps an arm around my shoulders and wipes the tears and spittle from my face. Being enveloped by his glowing draconic form makes me feel like the finale of a fireworks display is going off in my head. I clench my eyes shut, which stops the explosions and makes it hard to keep crying for long. I manage to blather my account of what happened.

"I think it's the same man who attacked me on the university campus," I say.

"He disappeared?" Dr. Radcliffe asks.

"He ran into the woods. I threw the cleaver at him and…" I shake my head. "He vanished."

Dr. Radcliffe stands up. "Stay here."

He walks away, and I open my eyes. He's beside the tree with the cleaver in it.

"Are we still in danger?" I call. "Should we go back to camp?"

"Tanis is in camp. Your friends are safe," Dr. Radcliffe says and wrenches the cleaver out of the tree trunk. He examines the oversized knife. "I believe you encountered a magician."

"Wait a minute," I say, trying to wrap my mind around what Dr. Radcliffe said. "That guy is a magician? Is he human?"

"From your description, I believe so."

"You're telling me humans can use magic?"

"Yes," Dr. Radcliffe says. "There is a small human magical community. Most, but not all, are beholden to Mark Cassidy."

"The dude who almost permanently blinded me is a freaking wizard! It never occurred to you that might be something to tell me. What the hell, Dr. Radcliffe?"

"I never suspected the man who attacked you on campus was a magician. But...perhaps, you are right," Dr. Radcliffe says. "You must forgive me. Forgive all of us. We masquerade as humans, but we are not humans. Our lives are lies, and we do not surrender our secrets easily. It is easy for us to forget that you are not part of our world as much as we are not truly part of yours."

"I shouldn't be surprised." I sigh. "Dragons. Are there any other fairy tale creatures I need to know about?"

"Fairies died out a hundred years ago," Dr. Radcliffe says seriously. "Habitat loss. Over logging."

"Some things never change."

We share a moment of thoughtful silence.

Dr. Radcliffe clears his throat. "The magician must

be an agent for Mark Cassidy. Otherwise, he would never dare attack you, not while you are in our care."

"Unless he didn't know you're a dragon," I say.

"He knew. That is why he ran. That is why he used this." Dr. Radcliffe hefts, then discards the cleaver.

"I think I broke his wrist. Maybe that's why he ran," I say.

Dr. Radcliffe shrugs. "Perhaps. He could have stunned you or killed you with offensive magic, yet he did not. Instead, he enchanted himself with a simple spell granting increased strength and speed. He could have cast that miles away, far outside the range of my magic detection ability. He wanted to remain inconspicuous. He only dared use magic here to escape. We must leave. If Mark Cassidy does not know our location, he will soon."

****

"Do you have a cell signal?" Dr. Radcliffe asks.

The van sputters along, the engine sounding worse than it did yesterday. The roadway is dark in between the towering trees. Overhead, the moon backlights an ocean of spectral clouds.

"Not yet," Tanis says. "You need to get back on the highway."

In the back, I tell my squad about my encounter with the magician. They listen, occasionally yawning and wiping the grit from the corners of their eyes.

"Humans can use magic?" Haji asks.

"I guess so," I say.

"That is so cool," he says. "Do you think I can learn?"

I shrug.

"Most human magicians are born into a coven and

begin training as children," Tanis says.

"Bummer. My parents aren't witches," Haji says.

"If you saw the magician, you'd think differently." I shudder. "He was scruffy—"

"I can do scruffy," Haji says.

"In a cadaverous sort of way," I add.

"About that magician, it's too bad you didn't break his neck," Dalia says.

"Dalia," Haji chides. "How can you wish someone dead?"

Dalia scoffs. "Like you've never wished anyone dead. He attacked Allison. Twice. He almost killed her the first time. She was in the hospital for weeks."

I wish I possess more of Dalia's fierceness, although I suspect wanting someone dead is far different than carrying out the deed. Yet I had thrown the cleaver at cadaver man's back. If it had struck him, he might've died. I'm woozy, and my stomach tightens. Maybe killing isn't so hard. Perhaps it's far easier than I ever dared imagine.

"Pull over," Tanis says. "I have a signal."

The van swerves onto the shoulder, crunching the loose gravel, then coming to a stop with a squeal of wet brakes.

Tanis dials. "What should I tell her?"

"We are compromised and need to switch vehicles." Dr. Radcliffe takes out his phone and pulls up a map. "We are heading to Forks for gas, and the humans need food."

"Thank goodness." Haji rubs his stomach.

"Ion, we're compromised," Tanis says into the phone.

"I'd kill for a cup of coffee," Dalia whispers, and I

nod in agreement.

Tanis relays Dr. Radcliffe's instructions to Ion. I can hear the officer's voice shouting from the receiver.

"She's not happy," Tanis says.

"Just tell her to meet us at Forks," Dr. Radcliffe says, glancing at the map on his phone. "We will be there in forty minutes. About 4:20 a.m."

"No wonder I feel like crap," Dalia says.

****

Dr. Radcliffe pulls up to the pump at the first gas station he finds in Forks, a community slowly fading into the oceanic fog. Two vehicles are parked in front of the minimart, a sedan with peeling paint and a mud-splattered pickup. Dr. Radcliffe swivels in his seat to face us.

"Go get some food in the minimart," he says and hands me two crisp twenty-dollar bills.

My squad and I pile out of the back of the van and make a beeline for the minimart. The clerk, half-asleep and bored, glances at us when we enter, then goes back to playing on his phone.

"Bathrooms?" Dalia asks.

"Head to the beer fridge, then hang a left."

We march to the beer fridge then turn down the hallway, stopping at the one unisex bathroom, which is occupied. The recessed light fixture in the ceiling buzzes. After five minutes, the toilet flushes. Five minutes later, no one has emerged.

"Give me the money. I'll go buy some munchies," Haji says, holding out his hand. I slap the twenties onto his palm. "You guys want coffee?"

"You kidding me? The coffee here is going to be horrible," Dalia says. "Get me a soda. Something diet."

"Same," I say.

Haji saunters off.

"Get candy too," Dalia calls after him.

"Got it."

The toilet flushes for a second time.

"Thank God," I say.

"I hope it's not much longer," Dalia says and starts squirming. "I'm going to pee my pants any minute."

The sound of running water comes from the bathroom. Dalia's squirming has become a tap dance. It's painful to watch and makes me more aware of my urge to empty my bladder. I start squirming too. A hand dryer starts up.

Ten seconds pass.

"Come on," Dalia grumbles.

The hand dryer turns off. There is a clank, then the dryer starts again.

"Still waiting?" Haji calls.

He stands by the beer fridge laden with bags of chips and candy in one arm and three diet sodas in the other.

"Yeah," I say.

"Tanis is coming. I'll pay and tell her you're waiting on the bathroom," Haji says and strides from view.

The hand dryer stops, and after a moment, there is the click of a deadbolt. The hinges squeak as the door opens. I tense, catching a whiff of menthol and eucalyptus beneath the strong stench of human defecation.

"You?" cadaver man whines in the bathroom doorway, still cradling his injured wrist.

I ball a fist and sock him on the jaw. All my half-

253

breed power is surging through me. He crumples under the blow, his head smacking against the off-white tile floor with a juicy slap. Shaking out my aching hand, I stare at him. He doesn't move.

"He attacked you?" Dalia asks.

"Yeah," I say.

He's still not moving, and I'm afraid I've killed him. Part of me doesn't care that he is dead. He's just a sack of meat and bone, something to feed on. That's the sleeper. The rest of me is repulsed by the fact he might be dead.

Dalia steps forward and kicks him hard in the ribs. Cadaver man groans and curls into a ball. I let out a puff of air.

"What do we do now?" she asks.

"I don't know." I look toward the fridge. "Thank goodness."

Tanis stands by the fridge, looking at us quizzically. I motion for her to come.

Tanis stares at the cadaverous man. "This is the magician?"

"Definitely," I say. "What do we do now?"

"We take him with us and question him," Tanis says.

"They have security cameras," Dalia points out.

"We have magic," Tanis says. "Don't worry. Ion is almost here. She and Frederick know how to deal with security footage."

"I really need to pee," Dalia says.

I shrug, still feeling the sleeper's power. I grab cadaver man and drag him into the hallway. He's heavier than he looks, but I am more than up to the task.

I glance at Dalia. "You first."

Chapter 30

The minivan blasts out of Forks on Highway 101 North. Ion lead foots the accelerator. I have no idea what she and Dr. Radcliffe did to the clerk or the security footage at the minimart. The clerk was alive when we pulled away, even waving at us from the store window. Strange that he should seem so jolly after Ion showed up spitting mad and tased him. I thought for sure she was going to kill him. I was scared, and so was my squad. Even Dr. Radcliffe and Tanis appeared perturbed.

It's getting lighter now. The low marine layer is as slate gray as a blackboard. Between the backseats of the minivan, Dr. Radcliffe kneels on the floor and leans over our captive. He slaps the man's gaunt cheeks. The man moans, shaking his head back and forth, but remains unconscious or is doing a good job pretending.

Dr. Radcliffe slaps the man again, a solid smack. "Wake up."

"He's faking." Dalia scoffs and levels a kick against the magician's swollen and bruised wrist.

The man's eyes bulge open, and he writhes and cradles his injured wrist against his abdomen. "Okay. Okay. Stop. No torture. Please."

He rasps like a five-pack-a-day smoker. In the confines of the van, his stench, which is an amalgamation of Manscape Bodywhiskey, cigarette smoke, alcohol, sweat, and week-old morning breath, hangs in the air like a feral musk. His nervous eyes rotate in their sockets, his gaze never resting anywhere for long.

I yearn to sink my talons into his chest and dig out his heart. I pine to bury my fangs in his throat and tear it out. As he lies dying, I'll lap his blood.

"Can I sit up?" he asks, his voice quavering.

I gasp and violently shake my head to exorcise the repulsive imagery flitting before my mind's eye like devil birds. I'm not a killer. I'm not. I don't want to become one, no matter if the sleeper is in me or is part of me or whatever. I won't kill. Haji reaches for me. I glare at him, and he backs off, expression worried and hurt.

Dr. Radcliffe nods. "No magic. I have a dampening net in place. If you try to break it…"

"No, sir," cadaver man says, shaking his head.

"Why did you try to kill me?" I demand.

He cowers. "I was paid."

I clench my jaw, combating the urge to break cadaver man's other wrist. He shrinks under my glower.

"Nothing personal," cadaver man says.

"Who paid you?" Dr. Radcliffe asks.

"You know who. Not getting paid enough for my trouble." He raises his injured wrist.

"Who paid you?" Dr. Radcliffe asks again.

"If you don't know, I ain't telling. My employer don't abide failures or traitors."

"What's your name?" I ask.

He licks his lips. "Gore."

"Well, Gore, who do you work for?" I ask.

Gore smiles coyly. "Like I said. You don't know,

it's best I don't tell."

Dalia aims a second kick at Gore's wrist. He turns away from her, but too late. She lands a glancing blow, and he howls.

Ion laughs. "Good interrogation technique. Keep it up. He'll talk."

"You talk, or I'll keep kicking," Dalia says. "You tried to kill my best friend. Now, talk."

"Okay. Okay," Gore whimpers, tears leaking from his eyes. "I'll talk. Just no more kicking, okay? It's not like health insurance comes with my job." He looks at me. "I tried to kill you, twice. Failed, didn't I? First time, just dumb luck that man came to your rescue before I could finish the job. Hell, dumb luck you survived that blow to the head. Should've killed you. I should know." His eyes become cold. "I've offed people with a lead pipe before. I know how it's done. But you ain't no girl. You're something else. Mark Cassidy, yeah, that's who I work for, never told me you're a supernatural something-or-other." Gore shakes his head. "Good old Mark. All he says is he has a problem he wants me to fix. Good money and premium heroin for the job. The kinda heroin that makes you feel magic, get all tingly like electrical current running through your body. He even gave me a hit. Premium." His eyes become distant, and he smiles as if reminiscing. "Good stuff. Real good, top-shelf. All I needed to do is off this little girl and make it look like a mugging. Easy, he says. Easy my ass."

"Heroin?" Haji asks.

"The drug increases human magicians' sensitivity to magic," Dr. Radcliffe says.

Haji grits his teeth, looking askance at Gore.

"Maybe I don't want to be a magician."

"Don't sell it short until you get a taste," Gore says.

I wave a hand for silence. "Did Mark Cassidy tell you why he wants me dead?"

"Nah," Gore says, shaking his head emphatically. When I frown, he adds, "Do you tell the hired help everything?"

"Dalia, kick him again," Ion says.

Dalia lines up another punt.

"Wait. Wait. I do recollect something," Gore says, cowering, his gaze locked on my BFF.

Dalia leans back in her seat. I'm not sure if I like this fearsome side of her. Judging by the sideways glances Haji keeps throwing her way, I think he finds this new Dalia troubling too.

"Answer the question," Dalia says through clenched teeth.

"He mentioned that he needed Allison Lee dead to smooth things over for Druk before the expeditionary force arrives," Gore says.

"Expeditionary force? What does that mean?" Haji says.

My pulse quickens. Smooth things over for Druk. The sleeper surfaces. My hand goes to my lips. My God. This is confirmation. Druk must be my mother.

Dr. Radcliffe leans close to Gore. "Any ideas?"

"How should I know? For certain, I mean. I can guess as well as you can. Expeditionary force means more skaags."

"Did he say when they are coming?" Dr. Radcliffe demands.

Gore vehemently shakes his head. "Just that

258

they're coming soon. That's all I know."

"Ion, what do you think?" Dr. Radcliffe asks.

Ion sighs. "My gut says we aren't going to get more out of him. Time to kill him or cut him loose."

"Come on, I answered your questions," Gore whines. "I'm just a down-on-my-luck magician."

"Tanis, it is too dangerous to keep all the children here. We cannot protect them all. Fly Dalia and Haji to Port Angeles. You can find a car there," Dr. Radcliffe says.

My friends and I exchange puzzled glances. Something fishy is going on here, but I, at least, am not sure what.

"Got it," Tanis says from the passenger seat.

"Start looking for a good spot," Dr. Radcliffe says.

"Roger that," Ion says.

"Good spot for what?" Gore moans.

Gore pleads for his life, whimpering and crying. He is so pitiful I start feeling sorry for him.

"Are you going to kill him?" I ask Dr. Radcliffe.

Dr. Radcliffe doesn't respond, but Ion does. "You bet I am."

"No, come on," Gore says. "You let me go, you'll never see me again. Or maybe I can help you. I'm a good magician, you know. All I need is some first-class big H. You going up against Mark Cassidy and Druk, you need all the help you can get."

Gore keeps babbling, but I stop listening to him.

"We should let him go," Haji says. "Killing is wrong. It makes us no better than him."

Gore points at Haji. "Yeah, listen to the Arab boy."

"What did you just call him?" Dalia asks.

"No more kickin', please." Gore shields himself

259

with his uninjured arm.

"This looks like a decent spot," Ion says.

The van whips over onto the side of the road. A diesel truck chugs by, its lights flaring in the morning twilight beneath the trees. Gore fearfully looks around the van.

"Decent spot for what?" Gore asks.

"Everyone out," Ion says.

We all pile out except Gore, who pleads for his life. I half expect Ion and Dr. Radcliffe to drag him bodily from the van, but they ignore him. We huddle together on the side of the road near the trees. In the distance is the dull roar of the ocean. The air is cold and misty, but at least it's not raining.

"You know what to do?" Dr. Radcliffe asks Tanis.

"I do," Tanis says. "Haji, take my hand. Dalia, take his hand. Good. I'm going to lead us down to the beach."

"What about Allison?" Haji asks.

"We just can't leave her behind," Dalia says.

A semi speeds by, sending up road spray that splatters against the minivan. I look at Dr. Radcliffe and hold his gaze.

"I have to stay. To make sure the skaags come. I'm the bait," I say. My squad is about to retort, but I cut them off. "I need to do this. Mark Cassidy wants me dead because…because Druk is my mother."

"Allison, what are you talking about?" Dalia says.

"Show them the picture," I tell Dr. Radcliffe.

He pulls out his smartphone, opens the photo app, and hands the phone to Dalia. My BFF's eyes go wide.

"What is that?" she gasps and shows the picture to Haji.

Haji gulps. "That's you?"

"That is inside me, or it is me." I shake my head. "I don't know exactly, but I know…" I remember the night of the visitation at the hospital, the presence I couldn't see. The immediate memory is chilling but also possesses a warm afterglow like the dying rays of sunset bleeding out on a distant horizon. "I think my mother visited me at the hospital. I know the dragons want to kill the skaags, and maybe that's how it will turn out, but…if I can meet my mother, talk to her…maybe she can help me understand who I am, what I am."

"We're not going anywhere," Dalia says.

The passenger side door to the van swings open with a loud creak.

Gore scampers across the highway.

"He's getting away!" Dalia hollers and lunges after him.

Haji keeps a tight grip on my BFF, stopping her pursuit. There is a loud crack of a gunshot. Gore staggers, blood blossoming from his shoulder, but he keeps running.

"Get them out of here. I'm going to chase him, make it seem like it's hard," Ion says and races across the road, smoking gun in hand.

"Do not worry," Dr. Radcliffe says, looking between Haji and me. "She will not kill him. We want him to escape. To pass bad intelligence to our enemies. We must leave. Someone might report the gunshot."

"But he knows where they're going," I say.

"No, child, I'll fly out over the ocean and head south," Tanis says. "Ion will remain here."

"I'm not leaving," Dalia says.

261

"Go," I say. "Please, for me. What I have to do will be easier knowing that you're safe. That both of you are safe."

Dalia throws herself into my arms, sobbing. Haji joins us for a group hug. My fam. We hold each other for a few seconds or maybe a minute. All I know is that it hasn't been long enough when Dr. Radcliffe pulls us apart, insisting it's time to leave.

Chapter 31

The gale-force wind blows the rain nearly horizontal. I wish I had my rain jacket that had been shredded when the dragons forced me to transform into a skaag or half-skaag, whatever. The black hoodie they gave me just isn't cutting it. I'm soaking wet and shivering cold. Dr. Radcliffe shows no sign of the weather bothering him. But that's because his human form is a golem, and the rain slices straight through his insubstantial draconic body.

The beach is utterly remote. It's a narrow strip of sand in between steep cliffs accessible by a harrowing, bushwhacking descent down a bluff. Most of the sand is occupied with massive, bleached logs large enough to crush cars. The tide is coming in, rumbling like a colossal hand dryer, the water grayish with ghostly whitecaps under a blanket of smudgy clouds. Soon, I fear, we'll be forced to ascend the headland. The oncoming tide will lift the killer logs from the ground, rattle them like giant dice, and send them careening onto the sand with earthshaking thuds or battering against the cliff face. Dr. Radcliffe might survive such an assault, but if I remain here for long, I'll be crushed or swept out to sea.

I manage to stop my teeth clattering. "Why here? This weather is miserable."

Dr. Radcliffe glances at me. His spectacles are

awash with rainwater. How can he see anything? I remind myself he doesn't need to see anything from his humanoid eyes. The golem probably doesn't really see anything. It's his draconic orbs that count, and I don't think those miss much. His long, serpentine neck is fully extended to tower over me. The green tendrils hanging from either side of his snout sway as his head swivels, scanning the sky and the headlands.

"The weather and location are perfect for confronting and killing skaags," Dr. Radcliffe says. "Skaags hate water. They cannot hold their breath."

"Face the enemy on the ground of your choosing," I say.

Dr. Radcliffe smiles and nods.

"I can hold my breath," I say.

"But can you in skaag form?" Dr. Radcliffe says. "I suggest you do not attempt to discover the answer to that question today."

Dr. Radcliffe scrutinizes the northern headland. His draconic gaze locks on the bluff too, his head no longer so much as twitching.

Scrambling down the cliff, knocking loose rocks, is a man dressed like he just stepped out of an outdoor outfitter's catalog. I suspect his jacket and pants and boots are waterproof. I wish I had his gear. I'm quivering in my waterlogged sneakers.

The man scampers over the driftwood giants, then drops to the sand. I squint against the rain, my prosthetics easily making out his inhumanly black eyes, like twin pools of glossy oil with only a thin white oval of sclera around the edges, and a deathly pale face that is all sharp angles. He possesses an undeniable feral splendor akin to a wild cat such as a serval. He stops before us about ten feet away. At his sides, his gloved hands clench into fists.

Dr. Radcliffe is unearthly still. His draconic form, while still translucent, no longer flickers in and out of existence. I have the uncanny feeling the beast is ready to explode from the slipstream.

"Frederick," the man says. "It's been a long time."

Over the blast of the wind and the ocean, I can hear the refinement in his resonant voice, a musical quality.

"Mark Cassidy," Dr. Radcliffe replies.

"Is this Allison Lee?" Mark asks.

"It is," Dr. Radcliffe says.

"Hand her over," Mark says. "And you can leave."

"Tell me about the expeditionary force," Dr. Radcliffe says. "Then you can have her."

I gasp and twist to stare at Dr. Radcliffe, a dagger of betrayal stabbing into my chest.

"You're going to hand me over for information?" I scream, my hands forming fists.

Dr. Radcliffe glances at me, only the man. The dragon's gaze remains fixed on Mark Cassidy. Behind Radcliffe's rain-speckled glasses, I swear his eyes are dismissive. The blade slices deeper into my chest.

I lash out with my fists and feet. My fists slam against Dr. Radcliffe's arm and torso with wet smacks. I kick him in the shin twice before pain sprouts in my toes, and I stop. My hands aren't hurt, so I continue my assault, a banshee wail of rage splitting my lips.

Dr. Radcliffe snatches me by the wrist, and he shakes me hard enough that I bite my tongue. Pain lances through my mouth, and I taste blood. Overmatched, I go silent and as floppy as an overcooked ramen noodle.

Dr. Radcliffe stops shaking me. Only his strong arm is keeping me from pooling on the sand like a wet rag.

"Are you done?" he asks.

I don't reply. There is nothing to say. Dr. Radcliffe is going to hand me over to Mark Cassidy, and I am powerless to stop him. The only light in my despair is the hope that my squad and my father are safe. Maybe it's a false hope, but it's the only buoy I have.

"Go ahead, kill her," Mark Cassidy says. "Saves me the trouble."

"No," Dr. Radcliffe says. "Tell me what I want to know, then Allison Lee is yours to do with as you please."

"Gore told you, did he?" Mark Cassidy shakes his head. "I know Gore isn't bright, but he's always proven a competent hatchet man. Guess those days are done. What do you want to know about the expeditionary force?"

"Why is the expeditionary force coming and when? Where is the gateway?" Dr. Radcliffe asks.

"Why would I tell you that? So you can collapse the gateway? I can't give out that information."

"You will tell me because Allison Lee is Druk's daughter."

Mark Cassidy flinches, then snarls. "So you deduced that, did you? The girl must die because she is an impossibility. She must die because General Bale will not tolerate her existence. If she is alive when he arrives, he will execute Druk. He'll likely have me killed too. That abomination is supposed to have died long ago." Cassidy gestures at me with a gloved hand.

That word, abomination, disturbs the sleeper. It

ripples underneath my skin, angry and afraid, and yearning for something...yearning for acceptance. I want this man, this skaag, to accept me for what I am. His rejection hurts, cuts deeper than when Jason decided to date Leslie. Deep down the sleeper—or the part of me that is the sleeper—desires acceptance and belonging above all else. If Mark Cassidy chooses to kill me, I'll die happy if he looks me in the eyes just once and tells me I have finally come home to my people, a safe place where I can be me.

I'm doomed to live and die as the reject, the freak with the fake eyes. The sad truth is that Leslie is right, righter than either she or I ever imagined. I am a fake, a phony, a sham. Even now, I don't know if I'm pretending to be human or feigning at being skaag. I'm like an actor so caught up in her role she can't separate reality from the script.

"Give me the information. I give you Allison Lee. I collapse the gateway. You kill the girl. We both win."

A shriek pierces the air, slicing through the roar of the wind and water. Overhead is a shimmering silver dragon, long and lithe, tumbling through the air, wings beating in a manic attempt to stay aloft. Wrapped around the dragon's torso like an anaconda is a burnished black beast with a blunt head and short, powerful legs. A skaag. Not just a skaag, my mother, the feared Druk, I realize with a chill that sets my entire body trembling. Do I want my mother, the woman who abandoned me sixteen years ago, to win or die? I don't know. I don't. It's hard to imagine the beast enveloping the dragon as anything other than a fiend from the darkest nightmares of the human mind. To think that I came from that monster makes me feel sad and alone.

I'm doomed to the life of a lone wolf, never really belonging anywhere or with anyone.

When I saw the picture of my skaag form, I thought I looked like a black Chinese dragon. The monster wrapped around the silver dragon is many times larger than me and looks like a cross between an eel and an alligator. Its maw opens wide to reveal row upon row of yellow fangs. The skaag clamps down on the serpentine neck of the dragon just before the beasts crash to the beach behind the logs with a ground-shaking thump.

"Ion!" Dr. Radcliffe shouts.

"Give me the girl," Mark Cassidy says, reaching out a hand. "Ion is dead. Druk has her. Neither you nor Tatsuo need to die. We know all about your pitiful ambush. Tatsuo will outflank me? Please. That fat, old wyrm doesn't remember how to fight. I'll dispatch you before he arrives. Together Druk and I will kill him. Sometime during the fight, Allison Lee will die. But it doesn't need to happen that way."

Behind the logs come shrieks and roars and thuds and something that sounds like the crackle of lightning. Silver and black bodies rise up, writhing above the skeletal tree trunks, then thunder back to the earth hard enough to shimmy the driftwood over the sand.

"Let me kill Allison Lee while Druk is occupied. You can leave," Mark Cassidy says, taking tentative strides toward us.

Dr. Radcliffe's gaze shifts between Mark Cassidy and the battle. His draconic gaze never leaves Mark, until a green dragon larger than a jumbo jet swoops over the headland behind the skaag. Dr. Radcliffe releases me, and I crumple to the sand just as electricity arcs through the air, making my skin tingle.

The sleeper roars to life inside me, its energy powering my appendages. My arms and legs whirl. I scramble across the sand toward the driftwood logs. I barely avoid the draconic body parts materializing into solid mountains of scales and muscle.

I throw myself against a log. A bright flash blinds me, and a crack reverberates in my ears. It feels like my brain is colliding against the inside of my skull. After that, all I hear is a buzz. The ground shakes. My vision clears.

Dr. Radcliffe, now a dragon, is laid out on the sand, unmoving. Black smoke rises from his golden scales near the base of his neck. I smell his burned flesh. His golem stands stiff as a statue in front of him.

Mark Cassidy the man is gone. In his place, is a gargantuan alligator eel with yellow electrical arcs crackling along its body. It swims through the air like a shark cutting through the water. Dr. Radcliffe is about to die. I understand this with an animalistic certainty that doesn't come from the human part of me.

Then I remember Tatsuo lumbering through the sky. Surely, he will rescue Dr. Radcliffe, and maybe he will save me. I don't know why he would, but he might, and I know I don't want to die. I look skyward, finding the scarred green beast with its raven black wings bearing down on Mark Cassidy. Tatsuo is so slow, too slow to prevent the skaag from slaying the draconic leader. I know, with excruciating detail, just how the skaag will do it. He will dig his hooked talons underneath the scales damaged by the electric pulse. With great effort, for a dragon's hide is the best armor known in the multiverse, it will pry back the golden scales, tearing them away from the vulnerable flesh underneath. Then...

A shriek and a roar penetrate the buzz in my ears. Tatsuo and Druk somersault through the sky, locked in deadly battle. Electricity arcs and a gout of flame lances from the dragon's mouth, so hot my skin warms even though I am hundreds of feet away.

On the ground, Mark Cassidy is over Dr. Radcliffe, finishing the laborious process of slaying a dragon. Should I do something? No, let him die. What could I do anyway? Throw sand in Mark Cassidy's oily eyes? Let Dr. Radcliffe and Tatsuo die, just like Ion who must already be dead. What have the dragons done for me, other than threaten my life and the lives of my loved ones? That's all they've done. They are getting what they deserve.

Thoughts of my loved ones stick in my mind, like a shard of potato chip stuck in your throat. Ever present, an annoyance, sometimes sharp and painful. Where is my squad? Where did Tanis take them? Dr. Radcliffe and Tatsuo know. Ion knew. Everyone who can tell me where they are will soon be dead. More than that, Mark Cassidy and Druk won't be happy with finishing off these dragons, will they? They will hunt down Tanis and Mauve next. They will hunt down my friends as a result. Watching Mark Cassidy pry up Dr. Radcliffe's scales, and Druk struggle through the sky, clawing Tatsuo and being clawed, I know they won't give a damn about Dalia and Haji or anyone else.

Mark Cassidy is not a skaag to leave a job half done. After he kills me and the dragons and my squad, he'll eliminate my father. Maybe he won't do it himself. Perhaps he'll send Gore or some other heroin-addicted assassin beholden to him, but he'll see it done.

I surge to my feet and charge across the sand toward Mark Cassidy and Dr. Radcliffe. A bestial shriek tears from my lungs. I don't have a plan. I expect to die. But I'm not going to sit by without putting up a fight. I'm not trying to protect Dr. Radcliffe. I'm out to protect Dalia with her pink hair and Haji with his long, graceful fingers and loving eyes, and my dad with his goofy smile and soccer obsession. I'm fighting to save my people.

Mark Cassidy's black eye locks on to me. His blunt head swivels to face me. Yellow electricity arcs over his body. A bolt shoots toward me. I'm blinded, and something burning hotter than a furnace lances into my chest. My clothing bursts aflame. I'm incinerating, facing the oblivion of death, but then the sleeper explodes from inside me, rending my flesh and rearranging my organs in an agonizing instant as long as an eternity. With the emergence of the sleeper, my flesh no longer burns. I don't sprint across the sand. I fly. I'm literally flying!

I slam into Mark Cassidy's face with a loud squelch. It's like I just ran full tilt into a brick wall. My body aches from the impact. But I've moved him. I've knock him off Dr. Radcliffe into the surf of the oncoming tide. He's panicking, at least I think he is, so I keep pushing against him, willing myself to shove him out into the ocean.

If Mark Cassidy chose to fight back, I think he'd quickly kill me, but he doesn't fight. He squirms, and his claws scramble over the sand and rock, and he struggles to keep his head out of the water. I try to keep my body above him, hoping to weigh him down so he can't take to the air, and I keep pushing, straining against his bulk until finally the hand of the tide grabs us and pulls us out into the deep water.

I paddle my four stubby legs, but I sink beneath the waves, and salty water fills my mouth, rushing down my throat to my lungs.

Chapter 32

I taste the seawater in my mouth. The brine is far more intense on my skaag tongue than any flavor I have ever experienced. It makes me feel both more alive and less human, as if my skaag senses are opening an undiscovered sensual world.

Tendrils of ice spread through my chest, burning everything they touch. My lungs expel the water, but I draw in more. I can no more stop breathing than I can will my heart to cease beating.

My legs thrash in the water. I'm trying to dog paddle, but instead of surfacing, I'm sinking. At least, I think I'm sinking. Maybe not. Everything is murky, opaque liquid filled with floating debris that appears like dust levitating near a sunlit window.

My hind legs touch something hard and slick and undulating. I swivel my eyes and catch a glimpse of a sleek black body barely visible in the liquid gloom.

The veins of ice are spreading throughout my body, making my gut go frigid and turning my limbs into leaden diving bells. Desperate to live, I plant my legs and push off with all the force my dying body can muster.

I torpedo through the water, up or down, I don't know. I pray to a god whose church I never attended. Let me breathe again. Just grant me one last chance at life. Let me feel Haji's warm, graceful fingers against my hand. Let me dance with Dalia to an electronic beat in a crowded rave once more.

My head breaks the surface. Before I can hack the liquid death from my lungs, I drop beneath the choppy water. Jesus Christ, this is so unfair. I'm drowning! Just five minutes ago, I was flying. I can fly. Why am I drowning when I can fly?

Part of my mind remains eerily calm. It's not the loudest voice in my head, but it remains rational, a neutral observer. It points out that I can't swim as a skaag, but as a human, I most certainly can.

Body throbbing, head woozy, eyesight going black around the edges, I cling to that thought like it's a life preserver. As a human, I know how to swim. I know how to hold my breath. Maybe I can survive. But how do I transform?

Clenching my eyes shut, I will myself to transform like a child trying to will a horse in a paddock into a magical unicorn. Without preamble, my body implodes. Organs shrinking and rearranging, bones cracking, muscle shredding, and sinew snapping. Water is expelled from my lungs. Even in my half-dead state, the pain shocks me back to life. Kicking my legs and windmilling my arms, I resurface and suck in air. My lungs burn, but a breath of air has never felt so good. Water splashes into my mouth, and I spit it out. I bob like a bit of plastic detritus beholden to ocean currents.

My entire body aches. Rain lashes my face. My limbs are rice noodles as I tread water, barely keeping my head above the surface. I need to find land before my arms and legs give up, but all around me is the ocean as limitless as an ever-expanding universe.

From somewhere distant off to my left, I hear a

dragon's roar. The battle. The battle on the beach. Spitting saltwater from my mouth, I swim toward the sound, each stroke a desperate struggle to stay afloat. My limbs ache and spasm. I'm losing the battle against the ocean's current.

The voice, the rational one, tells me it's time to end my suffering. My body is as worn out as a disintegrating paper towel. Fighting extends my torment without purpose. It's okay, sink beneath the waves and welcome the cold oblivion of death. My muscles will no longer feel like they're being ran through a meatgrinder, and my joints will no longer be fiery pokers inserted between my bones.

"No," I gurgle, spitting saltwater. I've survived too long to give up now. I want to see my friends and Dad again. "Keep going. Keep going."

I can still hear the shrieks and roars of combat. I think I'm heading toward it, but it sure doesn't seem any closer. No. Don't worry about the distance. Concentrate on moving your arms and legs.

Something is odd. No rain. I can see the rain ahead of me and to either side, but none falls on me. I sense something overhead just before I glimpse a golden hand with long white claws encompassing my entire field of vision reaching for me.

****

"Duane Hathaway of Forks provided us with this exclusive video that he claims shows a dragon battling a supersized snake," says a female voice.

The voice intrudes on my consciousness. I'm discombobulated, dislocated. I swear that voice sounds like the Channel 5 newscaster. Am I dreaming? I must be dreaming. The last thing I remember, I was sinking beneath the waves, icy saltwater filling my lungs.

A man's voice. "It was like a scene from a monster movie."

Monster movie? I'm breathing, at least. Not drowning then. I don't feel water lapping against my skin. I'm not in the ocean. Moaning, I open my eyes to darkness. My prosthetics quickly adjust to the dimness. Mattress springs gouge my back. I sit up, stiff and groaning. The mattress squeals as I move.

The newscaster's voice. "Here's the video. You be the judge."

I hear two sounds that I recognize. A roar and a shriek. Both distorted, yet distinct.

The man's voice again. "That giant snake bit the dragon's head clean off. Decapitated it. The body is probably still down there. Go investigate. You'll see. If the snake didn't eat it. You'll see."

"We're sending a news crew to the remote Olympic Peninsula beach..."

"Ion," I whisper, an arrow of sorrow piercing my chest.

Ion was angry most of the time and threatened my squad and me more than once, but that was all bluster. Wasn't it? Most of it? My hands ball into fists when I think of her growling that she'd bite our heads off and eat us. She didn't have to do that. She was a dragon who could force us to do whatever she wanted without resorting to threats. Ion was a bully plain and simple, and I'm glad she won't be hounding us any longer. But I still feel bad about her death. At least, she went down fighting. Like a warrior. Like a soldier. Dr. Radcliffe had said Ion was a soldier, had been one for most of her life. She died as she had lived, battling to the bitter end.

"Are they going to find Ion's body?"

A smile cracks my face at the sound of Dalia's voice. I swing my legs off the bed onto the carpet.

"Not her dragon body. We have enchanted our bodies, so they will fade into the slipstream minutes after death. They may find her golem, but without her life force to sustain the magic powering it, it will crumble to dust within a few hours or days on the outside."

That voice belongs to Dr. Radcliffe, who had been prepared to hand me over to Mark Cassidy for information. The bastard. He'd been ready to let that skaag murder me. Not threaten to kill me. Not be like, oh, I'll bite your head off if you don't do as I say. No, Mark Cassidy would have killed me given half a chance, I have no doubt, and Dr. Radcliffe had been ready to let him do it in exchange for information. My life for freaking information. I stifle a scream and pound at the mattress with my fist instead. I don't know who's out there, and I don't want them to think I'm a weirdo.

To calm myself, I stand up with the intention to pace the small bedroom but end up discovering my sling bag at the foot of the bed. I kneel down next to it and open the main compartment to find my camera. I run my hands over the cool metal and rubberized body, turning the device on and off. Everything is in order. Smiling, I return the camera to the bag and zip the compartment shut.

I stand and start pacing. I'm a bit wobbly, so I steady myself against the shelving lining the walls. The shelves are full of well-worn volumes with names referencing magic. My gaze lingers on the word

Wiccan. Doesn't that have something to do with magic? I run my finger across the spines of the books. I used to think people who believe in magic, like really believe, were lonely people looking for something to have faith in or plain nut jobs. Turns out I was wrong. Dragons are real, and they have magic. Maybe the contents of these books aren't so far out. A grumble from my stomach ends my contemplation. A pang of hunger grips my abdomen.

I take a moment to make sure I'm decent. I don't know who I will find out there, and I don't want to die of embarrassment. The dragons have been known to drape me in an emergency blanket, so I better take stock of my attire. I'm dressed in some sort of a yellow and blue nightgown, covered to my knees. That's a relief. I can face the world like this. Oh God. A cartoon character with a toothy grin and bulging eyes is emblazoned across the chest of the gown. My stomach clinches and growls. Placing a hand across my belly, I know it's time to eat.

I shuffle down a narrow hallway past a couple of shut doors to the living room where everyone is gathered around a flatscreen TV. When I say everyone, I mean everybody except Ion and Tatsuo. I stand in the opening onto the room along the same wall as the TV. Everyone turns their attention all at once from the television to stare at me. Talk about feeling like you're on display, and me dressed for the occasion.

"Allison!" Dalia and Haji shout in unison. They both leap off the loveseat they're lounging on and make a beeline for me.

Jason, Leslie, and Devin sprawl on the worn wooden floor in front of the TV. They scramble to avoid my stampeding squad. Mauve smiles up at me, a genuine smile I think, from a recliner next to the loveseat. Behind the loveseat stand Dr. Radcliffe and Tanis, who both stare at me, their visages expressionless.

Dalia and Haji embrace me in a group hug, and they start telling me how glad they are that I'm alive and recovering.

"Where am I?" I ask. "Have I been out for long?"

"We're at Mauve's house," Haji says. "In Olympia."

We break our embrace.

"You've been asleep since you arrived last night," Dalia says.

Jason, Leslie, and Devin have stood and joined us in a small gaggle. I spare the other three a quick glance. They all look well, and I'm glad for that, but that doesn't mean that I want to see them. I want to eat and go somewhere with my squad and leave all of this behind.

Squinting, my gaze darts for a moment to Dr. Radcliffe. He stares at me as if he can see straight into my mind and read my thoughts. A pulse of anger makes me tense and clench my jaw. I don't think I'll ever forgive him for offering me up as the sacrificial lamb. It was supposed to be an ambush, not an exchange.

"I think you slept for like fifteen hours straight," Dalia says. "You want to eat something?"

"I'm starving," I say.

****

Mauve's house is larger than Ion's townhouse, but it's still cramped with nine people. The dragons don't let us leave. I guess we're waiting until the whole thing with the video on the news blows over. It doesn't. The news crew doesn't find Ion's or Tatsuo's dragon bodies, but they do find Tatsuo's golem, which promptly disintegrates into dust live on TV.

Turns out their golems don't have to eat, so the kitchen and pantry are pretty sparse. Luckily, Mauve is a great jailer, more than happy to go shopping for her prisoners. We don't starve—in fact, we eat pretty well.

The best is when she buys coffee. She already has a coffee maker that I don't think has ever been used. My squad and I drink coffee by the pot. I fill them in on what happened to me and learn Tanis flew them here after the encounter with Gore. They don't remember anything about the dragon flight because Tanis used magic to put them to sleep. Something about not wanting panicked passengers. Anyway, they've been here with Mauve, Jason, Leslie, and Devin since they landed. We stay up late and fall asleep in front of the TV. The others do much the same, Jason and Leslie canoodling and Devin pretty much on his own. On the second day, I start feeling sorry for Devin. Watching Jason and Leslie snuggling is enough to make anyone sick, and I'm sure it serves to remind Devin of what he had only a few days before with Dalia.

All this happens under the ever-watchful eyes of the dragons. Tanis and Dr. Radcliffe are stoic. Maybe that's how they mourn the loss of Ion and Tatsuo. Mauve is manic. She is solicitous almost the point of being over-the-top and then will just stare into space silently for an hour or more.

By the third day, we're getting cabin fever. To entertain us, Mauve pulls out a fantasy card game. Haji and Devin know how to play it, but nobody else does.

"I bought these hoping to play with Tanis and Ion, but they weren't interested," Mauve says. "I wish…"

"Wish what?" I ask.

"I wish Ion was still with us," Mauve says with a wan smile. "Tatsuo too."

"I'm sorry," I say and mean it.

We spend the morning learning to play and talking. I even find myself talking to Leslie. Neither of us is particularly interested in the card game, so we talk cameras. I don't know that I forgive her for what she did or like her, but I can't hate her. Not anymore.

Dr. Radcliffe's cell phone rings, a loud and insistent dinging. He takes the phone out and stares at it. "Tanis, Mauve, Allison, come with me. The rest of you. Stay here."

I tense.

"What's going on?" Haji asks.

"I don't know," I say. I'm curious to know who's calling, but I don't want to be alone with the dragons, especially Dr. Radcliffe.

"You don't need to go with them," Dalia whispers.

Mauve waves insistently at me to come from the doorway to the kitchen.

"I should go. So one of us knows what's going on," I say.

"Allison, don't let them push you around," Leslie says. "You're strong."

"I won't."

I follow the dragons into the kitchen. Dr. Radcliffe and Tanis stand at the table. Mauve stays in the doorway to watch everyone in the living room.

Dr. Radcliffe has answered his phone and turned on the speaker. I'm shocked to hear Tatsuo's voice piping from the device.

"I don't have long. Druk is coming." Tatsuo's tone is strained and bitter.

"What happened? Where are you?" Dr. Radcliffe demands.

"Back home on Maui. Linked up to my backup golem. I survived by hiding in the ocean. I waited until I thought they were gone, then I took off for home. Turns out, Druk was still around. Hiding. She followed me. I think she hoped I'd lead her to you."

My mother, the hunter, the killer. I fear becoming my father, but right now that doesn't seem like such an unfortunate fate. At least he isn't a murdering monster.

"You said she is coming," Dr. Radcliffe says. "Get out of there."

"I'm too weak to escape using the slipstream," Tatsuo says.

"Fly. Get out of there now, soldier. That is an order," Dr. Radcliffe shouts into the phone.

"It's too late, Frederick. Don't worry. I accept my fate. Now, listen carefully. While I was hiding in the ocean, I kept close to shore. Kept my head near the surface. Mark Cassidy didn't drown. He managed to stay close to the surface until Druk plucked him from the water. I overheard them talking, Mark Cassidy and Druk. Mount Rainier. That's where the gateway will open."

"Where on Mount Rainier?" Dr. Radcliffe asks.

"The—"

Tatsuo is interrupted by a shriek reminiscent of what I heard on the beach. The cell connection goes dead.

Chapter 33

Dr. Radcliffe sets the phone down on the kitchen table. I chew on my lower lip, unsure why I'm even here. I mean, I know why I'm a prisoner in the house, but why am I in the kitchen with the dragons? As if I'm one of them. I'm not. I'm a skaag or half-skaag or whatever. I don't know what I am. What I do know is this: Mark Cassidy wants me dead, and Dr. Radcliffe is ready to hand me over to him.

"We must assume Tatsuo is dead," Dr. Radcliffe says.

"I agree," Tanis says. "At least we know Druk is in Maui."

My mother, the killing machine. What does that make me? I haven't killed anyone, but I could. I could have ripped Gore's arms off with my bare hands. Is that my destiny? To become a killer just like my mother?

"She will trace the call," Dr. Radcliffe says and lifts the phone in both hands. He snaps the device in half and places the ruined remains on the table. "It will not take long. We must leave. Did either of you share your cell numbers with Tatsuo?"

Tanis shakes her head in the negative.

"No," Mauve says from the entrance to the kitchen.

"I hope she kills all of you," I blurt.

"You wish me dead?" Mauve says.

I turn to her, the only dragon who has ever been

kind to me or any of us. Yet when I see her shimmering dragon body projecting from her golem, I'm reminded that I don't really know her. Her friendliness and concern and very human goofiness might all be an act, like the good cop in a good cop, bad cop routine.

"Dr. Radcliffe was ready to hand me over to Mark Cassidy," I say, words staccato. "Don't tell me you didn't know."

Mauve's mouth drops open to form an oval. She blinks several times behind her thick glasses. Glasses that she doesn't need. A prop. Part of the deception to make her appear human.

"No." Mauve shakes her head. She looks beyond me to the other dragons. "No, Allison Lee was meant as bait, nothing more. You promised to keep her safe. You promised not to sacrifice her."

I turn back to the other two dragons.

"I did not—" Dr. Radcliffe says.

Tanis interrupts him. "Do not judge our leader, youngling. You weren't there. Ion—" Her voice cracks with raw grief, and she gasps. "—died on that beach. I raised her from the time she was a hatchling...I'm sorry. I need to be alone."

Tanis leaves the kitchen. Dr. Radcliffe and Mauve allow her to go. From the living room come the voices of my fellow prisoners. I don't know how I should feel about the deaths of Ion and Tatsuo. I always knew them as the ones who wanted me dead the most. Yet they are dead, and I still live in part due to their sacrifices. I can't say I'll miss either one of them, but Tanis's palpable grief is like a punch to the gut. I can't help feeling sympathetic for her. But it also reminds me that the dragons are weaker now than they've ever been.

Are we better off with them, or should we try to escape? Sure, our jailers can always track us using magic, but maybe if we flee now, they'll be too preoccupied mourning their losses and avoiding my mother to recapture us.

Mauve joins us at the table. "Well? Did you lie to me? Did you plan to hand Allison Lee over?"

"I did not intend to hand Allison Lee over, at first," Dr. Radcliffe says, voice aggravatingly matter-of-fact. "However, once Mark Cassidy confirmed Gore's information regarding the expeditionary force, I was ready to hand Allison Lee over in exchange for the gateway's location."

"You planned to hand me over all along," I say.

"I did not," Dr. Radcliffe says. "But I would have to glean the location of the gateway. You are but one life, Allison. If the skaags invade this planet, millions will die. At best, humans will face extinction. At worst, humans will be enslaved or used as food stock. Skaags, as I am sure you have discovered, have a great appetite for meat in all its many forms. I am sure their delicatessens will stock human meat. Exchanging you to gain the location of the gateway seemed like a bargain at the time. And, I hoped, a vain hope indeed, the ambush would succeed and that you would live, but it did not go as planned. I do not deny that I was willing to sacrifice you. For the greater good."

"Don't pretend you give a damn about humanity," I say through clenched teeth. "All you care about is saving your own hide."

"That is unfair."

Dr. Radcliffe's lips downturn in a frown, and I must admit he looks sad. His draconic head projects from the ceiling, its wide eyes looking down at me. The green tubes on either side of his snout hang toward the floor like a drooping mustache. There is something reproachful in the dragon's visage that is hard to quantify. It's reminiscent of a loyal dog's expression after being scolded by her master.

"I have lived among humans for over a thousand years," Dr. Radcliffe says.

I raise an eyebrow.

"It's true," Mauve says.

"I used to eat humans," Dr. Radcliffe says. "All the tales of dragon slayers are false. I toyed with and then killed and ate all who dared oppose me. In those days, I traveled the slipstream often between my universe and this one. I battled my enemies and returned here to lick my wounds. I was always hungry and angry and alone. Over time, I brought more of my brethren here to hide and plot our next move against the Empress. Earth, in many ways, is an ideal world for us. The atmosphere and climate are hospitable. Food is readily available. Its existence was unknown to our enemies. We did not advertise our presence to humans, but neither did we hide as we do now. I have lived, as I do now, a dragon riding the slipstream attached to a humanoid golem for nearly seven hundred years, Allison. I am fond of humans. In some ways, I am as much human now as I am a dragon. Here." He taps his chest with a hand. "And here." He taps his head with a finger. "I dream of one day returning to my dimension. I do, but...I know that day may never come. This is my home for now, and I will protect it even if it means sacrificing my life and the lives of my people. I ran once long ago. I could run again, but I will not. If the expeditionary force reaches Earth, humans will suffer. I do not want that. I will die protecting this planet and all the life on it."

"Why should I believe anything you say?" I ask. "You threatened me, my friends, my family, all to protect yourself and your people."

"Is it wrong for me to want to protect my own?" Dr. Radcliffe asks.

I'm about ready to scream, but Mauve speaks. "You must understand, Allison. We were shocked that you could see us riding the slipstream. Frightened. Not all of us have a positive view of humanity. I'm sorry for everything we've done to you."

"That still doesn't explain why you're telling me all of this," I say. "You're sorry. So what?"

"You are half-skaag. If you possess the ability to discharge electricity like a full-fledged skaag, you can collapse the gateway. We also can disrupt the gateway using dragon fire. The bottom line is, we need your help. I must warn you, collapsing the gateway is a death sentence. One of us," Dr. Radcliffe says, his gaze shifting from me to Mauve and back again, "will not survive the coming days if we succeed."

"Stop more of those snake monsters from invading my planet, I'm in," Dalia says.

"Me too," Haji says.

I turn to the kitchen entrance. Dalia, Haji, and the others fill the entryway.

"We're all in," Leslie says. "Right?"

"How can we help?" Jason asks.

"Yeah. How?" Devin says.

I look at them, especially my squad. I don't trust the dragons, but I sense the truth in what they say about the skaags. More skaags won't be good for humanity. I have no doubts about that. The yearning for meat, the hunger, I understand that intimately since the sleeper woke inside me. The expeditionary force must be stopped. To keep my friends and my family safe.

I turn back to Dr. Radcliffe. "How do we find the gateway? We don't even know how much time we have."

"Tanis and I will leave for Mount Rainier. We will scout for the gateway as dragons. We will risk detection by humans and skaags, but that is a risk we must take. We might not be able to get a precise location for the gateway. For that, the rest of you may need to explore on the ground. It will be risky. Mark Cassidy knows we are aware of the gateway, and he will be guarding it."

****

Dr. Radcliffe and Tanis leave in a two-door hybrid with plans to drive toward Mount Rainier for the remainder of the day and begin their search as dragons at night. The snow from a few weeks ago is completely gone in the lowlands, but it's still cold, often freezing at night and warming during the day as weather system after weather system rolls in dumping rain. The TV news reports winter storm warnings for the Cascades. I wonder how the dragons will fare both in the compact car and later flying through the frigid skies.

The rest of us sit around the kitchen table with Mauve, making plans. Dalia graciously prepared an entire package of chicken sausage for me. I chow down unabashedly as the others discuss what to do. Only my squad has seen the picture of my skaag form, but everyone present is aware that I'm not exactly human. So why bother being dainty?

"We can't go up into the mountains without proper

clothing," Leslie says.

"That'll cost money," Devin mutters. Dalia uses her laser eyes on him, and he adds, "I'm just saying."

"Don't worry about money," Mauve says. "I have a credit card. How many of you can drive? Without the minivan, I'm afraid we'll need two cars. Just so we're clear, I don't know how to drive."

"I can," Jason says.

"So can I," Devin says.

"We have cars?" I say.

"Yes, the SUV and an older car. I think you would refer to it as a beater," Mauve says.

Great. A beater. Perfect for heading into the mountains, but anything is better than waiting around here for my mother to find us.

"You're prepared," I say.

"Of course. We always knew the day might come when the skaags would be closing in on us," Mauve says. "Now, decide what you need, and we'll go buy it. Then we must leave for Mount Rainier. As soon as Druk learns our location, she will come in all haste."

I swallow a mouthful of sausage. "Won't she be worried about being detected?"

"Perhaps," Mauve says. "But that will no longer be her primary concern. In skaag form, she is almost completely impervious to attack by humans. With the expeditionary force coming, she may decide hiding her true nature no longer serves a purpose. I believe she will risk detection in exchange for easy kills."

"How long will it take Dr. Radcliffe and Tanis to find the gateway?" Haji asks.

"I don't know." Mauve shrugs.

"We can't camp out in the mountains in this

weather," Devin says.

"He's right," Dalia says, grudgingly.

"Maybe we can stay in a hotel. Is anything open in…what's that town outside the national park?" I ask.

"Ashford," Jason says.

"Yeah, that one," I say.

"Can I borrow your phone?" Jason asks Mauve.

"Can I trust you?" Mauve asks as she pulls her phone from a pocket.

"You can trust I don't want to put my friends and family in danger and that I want to stop the skaags from invading my planet," Jason says.

Mauve glances at me. I bite into a slice of sausage and nod. She passes the phone to Jason. He opens up the internet browser and starts typing with his thumbs. Leslie leans over to rest her hands and chin on the back of his chair. Leslie is no longer just the mean girl who might be a racist. She tried to save me from trans-dimensional dragons, and now she's fighting to save the world. If she makes Jason happy, I'm okay with them being together.

Dalia and I talk about everything and nothing at the same time. It's our way of coping, trying to avoid the reality that in a few hours we might be hunted down by my mother or be tromping through a frozen wilderness in search of an inter-dimensional gateway.

"I could really listen to Dark Matter Eletrica right now," I say.

"I know, right?" Dalia says. "I'm sure they have an electronic beat that captures how inter-dimensional travel must feel and all this other craziness." She shakes her head. "I'd kill to have my phone."

"I wish."

Haji pulls his chair up close to me almost like we're a couple. "What are you all talking about?"

"Can you give me some space?" I say, shifting my chair away from him. The chair's legs scrape across the tile floor.

"What?" Haji gives Dalia and me a puzzled look. "I can't join the confab?"

"Do you have to be such a Stan? Just don't sit so close to me."

Haji's eyes go super wide, and his mouth drops open. He looks like he might be about ready to say something, but instead he stands and retreats from the kitchen.

"Feeling salty?" Dalia asks.

"Not really. I just want my personal space."

"Well, that was a little harsh."

"Maybe." I shrug and bite into a chicken sausage.

If I'm honest with myself, Haji is growing on me in the boyfriend sense, kind of like a cute mushroom on a nurse log. Pretty soon, I'm either going to have to kiss him and hope I go on a wonderful psychedelic trip, or I'm going to have to tell him to seriously back the hell away. I don't look forward to either option. If I kiss him, I'm afraid I won't like the psychedelia. If I tell him off, I'm worried I will irrevocably harm our friendship.

After maybe five minutes, Jason says, "I can reserve a room. I need a credit card."

"Will we be safe there?" Haji asks from the entrance to the kitchen. "It's pretty close to Mount Rainier. If Druk is looking for us…"

"There are several hotels in town. All are almost fully booked. Quite a few people," Jason says.

"We know we're not safe here, and we have to get to Mount Rainier," I say.

"I'll get my credit card. Reserve the room, then we'll go shopping," Mauve says. "Are we agreed?"

Dalia looks dubious but nods anyway. Taking his cue from his ex, Devin shrugs noncommittally, then nods.

"Let's kill some skaags," Haji says.

Jason and Leslie look ready to agree with this sentiment, but I beat them to the punch. "One of those skaags is my mother."

"I didn't mean it that way," Haji splutters. "I just meant like…go team. Let's get pumped up."

"Is that so? Well, let me put this to you in terms you can understand, Haji," I say. "If we meet, I'm either going to kill her or she is going to kill me."

"That won't happen. The dragons will get her," Haji says.

As Haji is saying this, Devin is animatedly running his index finger across his throat. Leslie and Dalia stare at Haji aghast. Jason smacks a hand against his forehead in disbelief.

"Oh my," Mauve says, eyes widening behind her glasses.

I stand up, my chair scraping against the floor. "Sometimes, you are the most clueless person I've ever met."

I flee the kitchen before they can see my tears.

Chapter 34

We pile into two vehicles. Dalia, Haji, and I hop into the beater with Devin as the driver. The car makes a distinctive squeal, like tires spinning on pavement when Devin starts it up. The racket continues as he pulls out of the driveway of Mauve's sky-blue craftsman to follow the SUV.

"Fan belt is misaligned. Might need to be replaced," Devin says.

He and Haji, who is riding shotgun, talk about cars. I sit in the back with Dalia and stare out the side window at the well-maintained houses and bare trees along the road, trying to ignore Haji's voice; I'm still mad over his comment earlier. I hold my camera in both hands, idly moving my fingers over its familiar buttons and switches the way one might massage her own hand.

"What do you think we're doing at school?" Dalia asks.

"School? What do you mean?" I say, turning to my friend. Her neon pink hair is faded. Don't get me wrong, it's still neon pink, but it lacks its usual metallic luster. I'm sure if I examine myself in the mirror, I'll find numerous strands of black in my forest green mop.

"Our golems are at school today, right?" Dalia says. "Today is what? Tuesday, Wednesday? So easy to lose track. Anyway, it's not winter break until next week. I know that. I wonder what's going on at school…and at home. I worry about my family. What if the golem hurts my little sister? Or my parents? You know, like they realize it's not me or something. I wish I could call them to make sure they're okay. Just thinking about it is driving me crazy."

Dalia hunches her shoulders and chews on her thumbnail. I want to comfort her, but I don't know what I could say other than an outright lie. With everything else going on, I haven't thought very much about my golem and what it might be doing or not doing.

"What happens when your golem goes to see Dr. Woolworth? They're going to figure out it's not you, right? As soon as they try to run the diagnostics on your prosthetics, the cat will be out of the bag."

"I don't know. I guess I thought the golem would avoid anything that might expose it," I say. My prosthetics are so much a part of me now I hardly even notice them any longer. Night vision and even the zooming ability seem natural. "Mauve made the golems. I don't think she'd do anything that would hurt us or anyone else. Not on purpose." I wrap an arm around Dalia's shoulder. "She's different from the others. She's kind. She cares. I…I can talk to her. Make sure the golems aren't a threat."

Dalia smiles. "Thanks. We've all been worried about our families. We spent a lot of time talking about the golems while you were recovering. We don't talk to the dragons like you do. Mauve is nice, but…she's still one of them. I mean, they kidnapped us and threatened to kill us more than once."

I almost say that Ion and Tatsuo died to keep us safe, but I don't know if that's really true, and, regardless, they were our jailers. Instead, I heft my camera and say, "Take a selfie with me?"

"Sure." Dalia smiles, then playfully sticks her tongue out between her teeth.

I pop off the lens cap, turn the camera on, and spin the ISO up to 1600. We lean our heads together, and I hold the camera out in front of us with both hands.

"Say cheese," I say.

"Cheese," we say in unison, and I snap the picture—three shots, bracketing, of course.

We shift in our seats, and I hit the play button on the camera to examine the photo. Haji turns in his seat.

"Can I see?" he asks.

"No," I say. "Go back to talking cars and leave me alone."

Haji flashes a pained expression but does as he's told.

"You really screwed up," Devin mutters. "She is pissed."

"I know," Haji says.

I'm glad Haji realizes he messed up. Maybe that will keep him from being such a clueless ass again.

Staring at the picture on the camera's LCD, I realize I'm as haggard as Dalia. Our smiles are strained like you sometimes see on the news of people who are surviving in a war zone or a refugee camp. Just as I expected, my forest green hair is not as savage as I like. It's faded, and locks of black hair are prominent. Not that long ago, I wouldn't have been caught dead outside the house with my hair looking like this. Now, I'm happy I look human so that not everyone I encounter realizes I'm a monster.

"Let me see," Dalia says.

I tilt the camera so she can see the photo, which, of course, disappears. I hit the play button again, and the image fills the LCD. Dalia lets out a little sigh and touches her hair.

"This picture reminds me that you're always here for me," I say.

Dalia laughs. "It's funny. Just a few days ago, I dreamed all the time about graduating from high school, leaving home, going to college. Moving on. Now, I just want my life back the way it was."

"How do we go back to our old lives after this?" I ask.

"What choice do we have?" Dalia says, quizzically. "It's like you said. Life doesn't stop. We can't live like this forever. On the run. Under constant threat."

"I guess so," I say, but I don't know if that's true for me.

****

I'm not a complete neophyte when it comes to the outdoors, but I always find outdoor stores a bit overwhelming. Everywhere I turn is outdoor gear from kayaks to mountain climbing equipment, but no women's clothing other than cycling outfits. I'm eager to find something more comfortable to wear than Mauve's oversized jeans and sweatshirt. Dalia isn't familiar with the store either, but Leslie, who turns out to be a downhill skier, leads us up a wide wooden staircase to the clothing section full of coats and pants and other paraphernalia labeled waterproof, breathable, subzero, micromesh, etc. Leslie points out brands that will work well for hiking in a mountainous winter wonderland.

I head to the changing room, burdened with an

armful of winter clothing. I strip down and pull on a pair of all-weather pants with a fleece lining that are warm and cozy. Fits great too. I'm about to pull on a black thermal turtleneck, but I pause to stare at my midsection, remembering my bones breaking and muscles ripping as I transformed into a skaag. Dropping the shirt, I look for scars, deformities, anything that might reveal my true nature. I press my hands to my abdomen and stare down at my navel. Nothing. I gaze at myself in the mirror.

"Who are you? What are you?"

The bones in my arms snapped when I transmuted, burst from my skin. Now my skin is pristine. How? How am I even alive?

"Dalia."

"Don't talk to me, Devin."

They are right outside the changing room.

"We should get out of here," Devin says.

"What are you talking about? You don't even have keys to the car. Mauve confiscated those. Maybe you're too high to remember."

"Come on, you know I don't have any weed. This is a mall. We can slip away. Catch a bus or something."

"I'm not leaving Allison, Devin. Unlike you, I don't abandon my friends," Dalia says. "Besides, the dragons put some kind of tracking magic on us. That's how Dr. Radcliffe found us, remember? There is no escaping them. If you want to run away, don't let me stop you."

Devin continues wheedling away at Dalia as whiny as the toddlers I babysat as a tween. Their footsteps and voices fade into the general background din of the store. I finish trying on my clothes, discarding a few and keeping others. I leave the dressing room with two complete winter outfits and a fleece-lined waterproof coat.

I'm about to go downstairs in search of Mauve when Leslie calls to me from over by the shoes, or rather the hiking boots section. "Did you choose boots yet?"

Jason and Haji are with her. Seeing Haji gives me a pause. I look down at my feet. I'm wearing flip-flops. I stride over to the boot section, ignoring Haji, who smiles and waves at me.

"You definitely want something that will keep your feet warm and dry," Leslie says, pointing out several options. "Still mad at Haji?"

"A little," I say.

Leslie grabs an ankle high gray and blue boot. "Try this one first. I think this brand will keep your feet cozy warm in the cold. Do you want my advice?" Leslie looks me straight in the eyes. "On Haji?"

"Not really." I take the boot from her.

"Well, don't stay mad at him for too long. He's clueless, not an asshole."

About twenty minutes later, we are lined up to check out. It's a big bill, but Mauve pulls out a credit card and pays for it without blinking. I head to the bathroom to slip into clothes that fit while the others wait by the exit. Out in the parking lot, I motion to Mauve to hang back. She hasn't handed out the car keys to Jason and Devin, and I'm tempted to tell her what I overheard. But I don't.

"Are the golems you made of us dangerous?" I ask. "Will they hurt anyone? Like our families?"

A chill is in the air that I only feel against my

cheeks. My new winter gear keeps the rest of me warm.

Mauve's golem, dressed in loose-fitting jeans and a T-shirt, appears as unaffected by the cold as her shimmering draconic form. "Unlikely, but not an impossibility. The golems will defend themselves. As you know, they are physically stronger than any human." She smiles. "I'm only being honest. It's highly unlikely they'll hurt anyone. You shouldn't worry."

"What about my prosthetics?"

"You refer to your mechanical eyes?"

"Yes, I have appointments with Dr. Woolworth. She visually examines my prosthetics and runs a diagnostic. She can connect to them wirelessly using a tablet."

"I can understand your concern. Hmm…that would expose the golem. Its body is constructed of clay that is made to look human and is automated by magic. Certainly, it could pass a visual examination, but this diagnostic." Mauve shakes her head. "No. It would be uncovered."

I bite my lower lip and drop my gaze to the concrete. "What will happen if it's discovered?"

If the golem hurts Dad or Dr. Woolworth, I will die. The whole reason I've stayed with the dragons and done what I'm told is to protect those I care about.

"The golem is infused with a limited amount of your memories. It will realize Dr. Woolworth could expose it and will attempt to avoid her."

"Hey, we're waiting. Come on," Devin calls from where everyone waits by the vehicles.

"What if the golem is uncovered?" I ask.

"The golem will only defend itself against physical attack. If it's discovered…I don't know. What would you do if your father discovered your secret?"

My secret? Which one? "I wouldn't hurt him."

"Then as long as he doesn't try to hurt the golem, it won't hurt him."

"Good. Great. Our families are safe."

"Yes, Allison. I think so," Mauve says.

****

Devin merges onto the interstate northbound toward Mount Rainier. It's midafternoon, so the traffic is heavy but far from rush-hour conditions. The roadway is still damp from the last bout of rain, but overhead the sky is blue. More ominously, the sky to the north and east is full of dark clouds that look ready to dump buckets.

As Devin zips through traffic, he spouts off. "How come you're so friendly with the dragons, Allison? What the hell? What are you? Their little pet? They kidnapped us. Threatened to kill us. That Tatsuo...you know, I think he molested me."

"Seriously? I don't know about that. The molesting part," I say.

Devin responds with a string of curses, some bordering on racist.

"That's not cool, man," Haji says, jumping to my defense.

Dalia looks at me and rolls her eyes.

"Just because you have a thing for dragons—"

Dalia interrupts her ex. "Shut up, Devin. You're the one who can't be trusted."

"What are you talking about?" Devin demands.

"What is she talking about? I don't know," Haji says. "Maybe about you abandoning us at the warehouse?"

"Fuck you, Haji," Devin says.

"Is that the best you can come up with?" Haji says. "I've heard worse and more imaginative."

"Be quiet. Both of you just be quiet, please," I say, sick of listening to them argue. "Turn on the radio or something."

Devin snarls. "Whatever. Like—"

"Devin, do what Allison says," Dalia says.

"Fine," Devin says and punches the radio.

The radio is tuned to a local news station. The anchors are talking about recent events on the Olympic Peninsula. My mouth goes dry, and my palms clammy, as memories of the battle flash through my mind. The fight wasn't the worst part. The worst was being betrayed by Dr. Radcliffe and then nearly drowning. Despite my warm weather gear, I shiver at my body's recollection of the ice-cold seawater pouring into my lungs.

"Are you okay?" Dalia asks.

"Change the station," I whisper.

"Someone change the station. I don't want to listen to that," Dalia says.

"Come on, this is interesting," Devin protests.

Haji turns in his seat. His eyes meet mine. "Oh. Just a sec."

He switches the station, twirling the dial until it lands on a pop station Devin finds acceptable.

"Do you want to talk about it?" Dalia asks me.

"Not right now," I say. "Maybe later."

Instead, I tell Dalia and the guys about what Mauve said concerning the golems. The information eases their anxiety. I'm glad for that. My tension eases a little bit too, but I'm far from calm. I'm still haunted by the events at the beach and the certain knowledge that this expedition to close the gateway will lead to a deadly confrontation with my mother and Mark Cassidy.

I reach across the backseat and take hold of Dalia's delicate hand. She looks at me and smiles sweetly. From my place behind the driver's seat, I can see Haji's profile. I'm no longer mad at him. I know he didn't mean to make me angry or hurt me. He's genuinely kind at heart.

I fear for all of us, even Devin. We might not survive the coming days. My stomach roils with hatred for my mother and Dr. Radcliffe. Especially that damn woman or skaag, whatever. If it weren't for her, if she weren't a monster who chose to bear a mutt for a daughter, we wouldn't be living this nightmare.

Chapter 35

We arrive at Ashford along SR 705 outside of
Mount Rainier National Park no later than five o'clock
in the evening, but it's already dark out—at least, for
those without prosthetics. Rain patters against the roof
of the car and the gravel parking lot of The Rainier
Hostel. The sky is a continuous dusky blanket of
clouds, promising more rain tonight and snow on the
mountain. Not for the first time, I wonder how far we
will make it in the beater on roads covered in snow and
ice.

"Looks cozy," Dalia says.

The hostel is a long, low building, periwinkle with
yellow trim. Well-kept up, but not the Ritz.

"It's great for the boonies," Devin says and kills
the engine. "We used to come here with my dorky
cousins during the summer. I hope Jason reserved one
of the big rooms. There's a few that have five or six
beds."

"Only five or six?" Dalia says. "Oh, snap. One or
two short. That means you'll be sleeping on the floor."

Mauve asks Jason and Devin for the car keys.
Jason gives up his key without comment.

"What? Are you afraid I'm going to drive off?"
Devin protests.

"The thought did cross my mind," Mauve replies.

Devin throws his arms up in the air. He looks at us.

"Doesn't anyone else think this is total bullshit?"

"Devin, stop making a scene," Dalia says. "It's cold. Let's get inside."

"Screw this," Devin says and drops the keys into a mud puddle in the gravel parking lot. He stomps toward the hostel. The performance lowers my already poor opinion of his intellect. Mauve is a freaking dragon.

Mauve is about to fish the keys out of the water, but Jason beats her to it, muttering, "I got it."

We gather under the eave outside the office while Mauve and Jason handle the check-in. An enticing aroma wafts from the café. My stomach cramps with hunger pangs, and my meat craving hits overdrive. After registration, we head to the room to drop off our belongings.

"What room do we have?" Haji asks.

"Twenty," Jason says. "Five beds."

"For seven people," Dalia says with a glance at Devin. "You still get the floor."

"Jason and I can share a bed," Leslie says.

I stiffen. The thought of Jason and Leslie sleeping together is just...*ugh*. I hope they don't plan any PDA.

"Still one short," Dalia says.

We pull up at a purple door with a square window built into the top half. Jason produces a key and unlocks the door and leads us inside.

"I do not require a bed," Mauve announces.

"I'll take the twin by the window if that's okay with your majesty," Devin says with a snarky bow to Dalia. He flops onto the nearest bed, bedsprings squeaking under his weight.

The room is spacious. Dalia cranks on the heat, and baseboard heaters rattle to life. Leslie and Jason make a beeline for the queen bed. The rest are twins. I choose the one by the bathroom. A line forms at the bathroom since, except for Mauve, we're all desperate to relieve ourselves.

The café is an attractive space, all polished hardwood with a bar and plenty of seating. With the permission of the hostess, we move two tables together. My camera dangles from my shoulder dangerously close to the table's sharp edge. I twist my torso so the camera harmlessly careens off my side.

The menu only lists breakfast fare, but several of the omelets are chock-full of meat. We give our orders to a solicitous waitress who draws the eyes of all the boys, even Jason. His roving eyes earn him a hard punch in the shoulder from Leslie. His indignation and wincing don't win him any sympathy.

We fall into boisterous conversation. We talk about anything that doesn't involve dragons and skaags and wizards. Mauve merely observes.

"You know what?" Haji says. "I think the Sounders might be in the MLS Cup Final."

"Yeah," Jason says. "And we're missing out on that because of—"

Leslie punches him in the shoulder. "Maybe keep quiet about that."

We talk about the Seattle sports scene. I'm happy to talk about soccer. It brings to mind fond memories of time I spent with my father watching games at the stadium or on TV.

Soon, I notice Dalia has lost interest in the conversation and is staring listlessly out the window into the rainy gloom. I snap a picture of her with my camera. That brings her out of her stupor.

"I'd love some coffee from The Obsidian Roast right now," Dalia says.

"I know. Coffee, music, and dancing," I say.

I snap more photos as we discuss the things we miss. I concentrate on photographing my squad, but I even snap a few of Devin and Leslie and Jason. It's impossible to take a picture of Leslie or Jason without having both of them in the image. Everyone is cheerful, maybe even happy, except for Mauve—she looks pensive and keeps to herself.

I suppose our mood is a live-in-the-moment thing. In a few hours or days, we might be a partially digested slurry inside my mother's stomach. My picture taking draws the attention of Leslie.

"What ISO are you shooting at?" she asks.

"3200."

"How is the noise?"

"Not bad, really. Honestly, I'd rather deal with noise than use a flash."

Leslie tells me about a flash seminar she took with her father, who is an avid shutterbug. Leslie, coming from a well-heeled family, has several flashes to go with her high-end DSLR. I'm not quite green with jealousy, but I'm covetous of her equipment.

It takes the waitress three trips to bring all the food and drinks. I dig into my sausage and egg burrito and slurp hot chocolate, ignoring the conversation around the table in favor of my food. It tastes great after the long drive and takes the edge off my hunger. Since waking up after the fight at the beach, I'm always hungry no matter how much I devour.

An older couple walks into the café, a white-haired man speaking loudly to his companion about the disintegrating man and a dragon and a giant snake.

"Giant snake?" the woman, who looks a good ten years younger than the white-haired man, says. "More like an eel with alligator legs if you ask me."

Grimacing, I look away, trying to ignore them. Leslie and Dalia look at me questioningly.

"It's nothing," I say, shaking my head.

The old couple sit at the table next to ours and continue talking. With every mention of a dragon or eel or giant snake, I'm on the windblown beach being offered up to Mark Cassidy, then drowning in the infinite vastness of the Pacific Ocean. My insides tighten into an aching knot. Despite my appetite not being sated, I set down the remains of my burrito on the plate and wait for the others to finish.

****

Dalia and I sit on my bed. After we look at the photos I took at the café, I tell her about the horrifying fight on the beach. She listens, and Haji joins us, catching the tail end of the story about when Dr. Radcliffe snatches me with his talons out of the watery tomb. The others, thankfully, don't intrude. I don't think I could relive the battle with anyone except my squad and maybe Dad.

Haji, of course, wants to hear the whole tale, and I end up retelling it to him. It's therapeutic. Afterward, he and Dalia are contemplative and even anxious, but I feel unburdened.

Dalia yawns. She has dark circles under her eyes. "I'm going to bed. You should think about sleeping too."

I take her hand and squeeze it. "Get some rest. We can have coffee at the café tomorrow morning."

Dalia smiles, but it's only halfhearted. I suspect she lies down on her bed to brood over her anxieties. Haji and I stay up talking soccer. Before long, we're both yawning. When it is clear he has no plans to go to bed, I tell him I want to sleep, and it's time for him to go.

"I'm sorry about what I said," he says. "About your mother and the dragons and all. I didn't mean to make you angry or be insensitive. Sorry."

"I know, Haji. Good night."

"We can talk about something else. Something not sports-related. Seriously."

I yawn. "I need some sleep, Haji. Good night."

****

Someone shaking my shoulder startles me awake. My eyes pop open, and I'm immediately squinting and throwing a hand in front of my orbs. Mauve stands over me, her luminous draconic form filling the room, its head and neck passing through the ceiling and out of sight. The dragon is the only source of light in the room. I hear the heavy breathing of people in deep sleep. Snores resound from near the entrance. Figures that Devin is a snorer.

"It's not morning already, is it?" I'm slurring my words in my zonked state.

Mauve raises a finger to her lips and makes a shushing sound. She lowers her hand and whispers, "Come with me."

Mauve glides across the room to the entrance. She stands there with a hand resting on the doorknob and stares at me expectantly. The bed squeaks as I swing my legs off, and my feet touch down on the cold wood floor. I clench my teeth, raising my feet off the wood. I snatch my clothing from the foot of the bed and pull on heavy wool hiking socks and a pair of all-weather fleece-lined pants. I pad across the room to Mauve. By the door, I retrieve my coat and hiking boots. I have difficulty lacing up my boots, my fingers as slow as fat banana slugs. At first, I confuse the patter of rain against the roof for something caused by my pounding headache.

Once I'm dressed, Mauve opens the door onto the patio under the eave. I step outside and grit my teeth. It's a torrential downpour with huge droplets pinging almost like hail off the parked automobiles. Mauve shuts the door and joins me in staring into the night.

"I'm not going out in that," I say.

"You must," Mauve says and steps out into the rain.

"Why?"

Mauve turns to face me, impassive. I can see the entirety of her draconic form now, a lithe beast that is all neck and tail. The tail curls like a snake through the parking lot, passing through automobiles like a magician walking through a wall. The rain passes through the shimmering dragon to soak the golem, who appears as unaffected by the drenching rain as it is by the cold night air.

"You need to practice," Mauve says. Her round glasses are doused with water droplets. "You can't practice here. We will go into the woods. So no one sees us."

"You want me to practice changing into a skaag?"

"Yes, and I want you to practice discharging electricity. That's how you can disrupt the gateway if it comes to you preventing the invasion," Mauve says.

I bite my lower lip. Prevent the invasion. Sacrifice

myself to keep the expeditionary force from reaching the planet. My mouth goes dry. I don't want to be the one to collapse the gateway. I might be a pariah, a half-human mutt, but I want to live.

"None of this would be happening if your kind never came here." I hold my chin high. I try to look at both her golem and draconic faces at the same time. It's an aggravatingly impossible task.

Mauve shrugs. "Perhaps. Earth is an attractive planet. The Empress might have found it eventually regardless of Frederick and the rest of us fleeing here. The point is, we are here, and the skaags are coming, and we need your help."

I set my feet. I don't want to transform into a skaag again. It's painful, and last time I nearly drowned. I was only able to save Dr. Radcliffe because I caught Mark Cassidy off guard. I wouldn't stand a chance against him, let alone my mother, in a fair fight. They are three or four times my size and are experienced killing machines. I'm a malformed infant by comparison.

"I don't want to kill," I say. "I don't want to become my mother."

"I know," Mauve says. "I don't want you to kill either. I only want you capable of defending yourself and your friends."

"And you and Tanis and Dr. Radcliffe," I say, my hands curling into fists.

"Of course," Mauve says. "I hope…I want to be your friend, Allison. I…I came to Earth while I was very young. I've never lived as a dragon among my own kind. My entire life, I've ridden the slipstream, hiding among you humans, only daring to enter this world as a full-fledged dragon a few times a year in remote wildernesses. It's exhausting. I have a life. A human life. I'm a network engineer. I have co-workers, some who I even consider friends, but none of them know me. Not really, and they can't. It's stifling. The others don't understand. Even Ion didn't. She was always consumed by the desire for revenge."

My fists slowly unclench. Mauve is just like me, caught, not by choice, between two worlds. Like me, she yearns for understanding.

"I don't want to die," I blurt.

"I don't want you to die either," Mauve says with a melancholy smile. "I don't want any of this. I'm so sorry you've been dragged into this, Allison. Frederick wasn't lying about the skaags being bad for humans. If unleashed, they will wipe out humanity or enslave humans for food stock."

"How do you know?" Even as I say this, the sleeper stirs inside me, hungering for bloody meat. It doesn't care if the meat is human. In fact, I salivate. It's curious how human flesh might taste. I groan and spit. "Ugh."

"Are you okay?"

I nod, clenching my stomach with my hands. "Go on."

"I've seen footage of what they did to dragons."

Mauve's golem remains impassive, but I swear tears leak from the dragon's coppery eyes. The tears along with the sleeper's curiosity to try human flesh convince me.

"I'll come. The skaags must be stopped no matter the sacrifice."

Taking a deep breath, I step off the porch into the rain.

Chapter 36

The trees provide some protection from the rain, if not the damp. Everything is wet—the bare branches of vine maples and the leaves of the innumerable sword ferns and other shrubs blanketing the forest floor. The ground is muddy, swampy in places. I'm glad for my waterproof gear.

Mauve sets a fast pace through the trees as impervious to the branches and brambles as she is to the rain and cold. I struggle to keep pace, even tripping over a fallen branch hidden by the undergrowth. I windmill my arms and do a two-step to keep my balance. If not for the excellent low-light capabilities of my prosthetics, I would have already twisted my ankle in the murk.

We head up a steep incline, a leisurely stroll for Mauve but a hard slog for me. We come to a halt on a rock outcrop screened by tall conifers. Mauve's golem shows no sign of fatigue, and her draconic form gleams like a beacon in the darkness. I pant and clench the painful stitch in my side. She really did set a grueling pace, and maybe I'm still not fully recovered from the battle at the beach.

"Can you turn into a skaag at will?" Mauve asks.

"No. I don't know how I transformed at the beach. It just happened," I say, rubbing my side and trying to catch my breath between words.

"Interesting," Mauve says, staring unblinkingly at me from behind her glasses. Her dragon eyes watch me too, just as intently. "Frederick rescued you from the water, correct?"

"Yes. I was human when he rescued me, trying to swim to safety. I would have drowned. The current pulled me far from shore."

"So, while in the water, you transformed," Mauve says, steepling her hands and pacing before me. "Fascinating. Skaags are shapeshifters. The ability to alter their form is innate to their physiology. Much like how dragons can move in and out of the slipstream. You may find it magical. For us, it is simply a function of our bodies."

"Why aren't my prosthetics destroyed when I transform?"

Mauve stops pacing and shrugs. "I'm not an expert on skaag physiology." She smiles and resumes pacing. "Magic maybe."

I frown. A question for another day then.

"Do you remember anything about what spurred your transformation?" Mauve asks.

I drum my fingers against the sides of my legs and begin to pace alongside her. "When I transformed into a skaag, I was scared. I feared for my life. I feared for my friends and family. I knew as soon as Mark Cassidy killed Dr. Radcliffe, he'd come for me, my friends, and my dad. I knew I had to do something—" I draw a jittery breath. "—or everyone I care about would be dead. I transformed. It just happened."

"You were afraid, and your body reacted to defend you."

"The sleeper woke."

Mauve stops pacing. "What did you just say?"

I come to a halt several feet from Mauve and face her. "The sleeper woke. That's what I call it or used to call it. The presence inside me. The skaag. Before I came to realize we are one and the same."

Both sets of Mauve's eyes narrow. "Do you still sense this second presence?"

"I do. As part of me."

"And when you transformed back into a human, did it just happen or…"

The words hang in the air like a bad smell. Did I consciously transform into a human, or did it just happen? Remembering drowning makes me feel like I can't breathe. I don't want to remember the icy numbness caused by the seawater in my lungs, but I do. I half clear my throat, half cough, and nearly double over expecting saltwater to gush from my mouth. Of course, it doesn't. Just memories.

"Well? Did you consciously take human form or not?" Mauve asks. Her tone is demanding, almost prosecutorial. I'm beginning to not like this side of her.

"I…I knew I couldn't hold my breath as a skaag. I couldn't swim, but I knew I could swim as a human. So I concentrated on changing. I willed myself to change. I kept repeating to myself over and over again to be human. Eventually, it happened."

"Concentrate on transforming then. Make it happen," Mauve demands and strides to the edge of the outcrop.

I stop pacing, cross my arms before my chest, and glare at her. "Easy for you to say. You know what you are. You've probably been passing in and out of the slipstream all your life."

"Taking your fear and frustration out on me won't help you transform. You need to relax. Clear your mind and concentrate."

"Fine." I say and uncross my arms.

I close my eyes and try to concentrate on morphing into a skaag. The outcrop isn't as sheltered as the forest proper. The rain pummels me. Even with my hood up, liquid splashes against my cheeks. My clothing is fleece-lined, but it's still damn cold out. I don't know how long I've been trying to transform when, without preamble, the air tingles with electricity. My eyes shoot open. Electrical arcs crackle from Mauve as she emerges from the slipstream. One arc burns a patch of rock black, and another nearly grazes a treetop. I back away, a surge of trepidation making my muscles tense, and my eyes go wide. Intellectually, I know she won't hurt me, but my reactions are not predicated by conscious thought.

Mauve is a burnished copper dragon, long and svelte. On either side of her snout hang two black tentacles that end just below her lower jaw. The tentacles sway in the pelting rain. The dragon stares at me with coppery almost fiery eyes, split vertically by pupils as dark as black holes. I'm standing a good ten to fifteen feet away from the beast, but even still I can feel the heat radiating off her as searing as a blast furnace. She carefully picks up her golem in a clawed hand and moves the now statue-like human facsimile out of the way near the tree line. Then without warning, she spins toward me, her mouth a gaping maw full of gleaming fangs.

I scramble backward, losing my footing on the slick rock. My feet fly out from under me, and I land painfully on my butt and utter a yelp that I can't hear over Mauve's enraged shriek. The sulfurous stink of rotten eggs fills the clearing, and deep in Mauve's abysmal mouth are fizzing flames. Fear pounds through my body, then my bones are breaking, my flesh and sinew ripping, and organs violently rearranging. I utter a gurgling scream as pain expels cogent thought.

Mauve looms over me. She's about to burn me to death with dragon fire. My hide will defend me for a short time, but I'm not powerful enough to escape or defeat her. My head throbs, blood roiling. Stinging shocks sizzle over my black body, like static electric discharges. A yellow bolt shoots upward, nearly singeing Mauve's snout. The dragon pulls away and retreats across the rock in two long strides. Her claws go to her face. I realize, in surprise, that I might have hurt her. I don't know if I should be glad or afraid.

More electricity arcs through the air. Then Mauve is back to riding the slipstream once again, and her golem is full of life. I curl like a rattlesnake in the air, hovering just above the rock. I'm levitating, flying! This is so amazing.

"Just as I thought. An instinctual reaction to danger," Mauve says.

Ah, I can understand her even as a skaag.

"Go ahead. Try to transform back into a human."

I hesitate to follow the command. I want to remain a skaag a little longer, experiencing flight and the prowess of this body. All the scents of the forest and even the golem are sharp and distinctive. Even though I know it's impossible, it seems like I can hear each individual raindrop patter against my scaly hide. The water makes me nervous, irrationally so. Deep inside me something knots, perhaps my stomach. It's an uncomfortable sensation, like I'm suffering from norovirus. Still, I turn my head skyward, wishing to fly up and touch the stars. Rain plummets from the cloudy sky. A droplet strikes me in the eye, stinging like acid. A rumbling growl, an expression of annoyance, vibrates my chest.

Blinking, I turn my gaze back to the clearing. Mauve watches me. I try to will myself back into human form. It doesn't work. I growl again, body shaking, angry at myself and Mauve. I'm frightened that I'm going to be stuck as a skaag forever unless I try to drown myself again.

"Your friends will be up in a few hours," Mauve says. "You've shredded your clothes, so unless you want them to see you naked, you better hurry up."

My transformation is immediate and excruciating. I lie on the ground, whimpering and shivering. Rainwater runs down my naked body.

Mauve stands over me, smiling. "That confirms it. You transform instinctually in reaction to fear."

****

By our third morning at The Rainier Hostel, I'm dog tired. Even the steaming cup of coffee on the café's table doesn't perk me up.

"Are you getting any sleep?" Dalia asks.

It's just the two of us. Everyone else is still asleep except for Mauve, but she shows little interest in leaving the room during the day. The night is another matter.

"Some," I say. "The bed is uncomfortable."

Dalia takes a sip of coffee. "I'm sleeping great. Better than I expected. But...Devin did wake me up last night with his snoring."

She looks at me expectantly. I bite my lower lip. She must know I wasn't in the room. What do I tell her? Oh, I've been sneaking off in the middle of the night to go with Mauve to practice transforming into a monster that can shoot lightning.

"I noticed you have new boots and a jacket. You bought them at the outfitter across the road?" Dalia says.

I nod. After ruining my jacket, boots, and other clothing, I always make sure to strip before practicing transformation.

"You know, when Dr. Radcliffe brought you to Mauve's house, you were naked."

I snatch my coffee cup off the table to hide my blushing face behind it.

Dalia sets down her cup. "Don't worry. You were covered in a blanket. You transformed on the beach. You did in the warehouse too. I didn't see what happened, but afterward, your clothes were shredded."

I take a slurp of coffee. It's hot and flavorful, but not quite as strong as I like. "Mauve is taking me into the woods in the middle of the night to practice." I drop my voice to a whisper. "Transforming. Does anyone else know?"

Dalia shrugs. "I haven't said anything to anyone. Devin is just a kludge who is busy feeling sorry for himself. I don't think he'd notice. Jason and Leslie are too into each other to pay attention to anyone else."

I set down the mug. My hands are clammy. "Does Haji know?"

Dalia looks thoughtful. "Ordinarily, I don't think he'd notice your new jacket and boots. They look pretty close to what you had, but he does have eyes for you."

The aroma of fried bacon precedes the waiter bringing us our food. It's bacon and eggs for me, and a bagel with cream cheese for Dalia. I ask for a refill on my coffee and attack my bacon. I barely taste the meat as I swallow it, yet there is still something primally satisfying to scarfing it. By the time the waiter returns to refill our coffee mugs, the bacon is gone. Two fried eggs and hash browns remain on my plate, but I don't find either appetizing. Dalia has only taken two bites of her bagel.

"Still craving meat," Dalia says.

I look away, staring at the scuffed wood floor.

"Don't be embarrassed," Dalia says and adds in a whisper, "You're different."

I turn my gaze back to her and whisper, "After transforming, I hunger for raw meat."

Dalia chokes on her bagel. I'm ready to leap up and start pounding on her back, but she holds up a hand and swallows. "I'm okay. I'm okay."

"Do I frighten you?"

"No," Dalia says, sounding scandalized. "It's just...you used to hate meat. You were nearly vegetarian. That's all." She looks around the café. There are a few guests, but none sit very close, and most are engaged in conversations. "How goes the nighttime training?"

I glance around the café to make sure the waiter isn't nearby.

"I can transform at will," I say, leaving out how excruciating transformation is. I don't want Dalia to worry about me. "I can shoot lightning, but only when I'm threatened. But I'm becoming more powerful.

Mauve thinks I can do real damage with my lightning discharge. It's enough to collapse the gateway. I'm not practicing that anymore. Mauve is afraid it might attract another skaag."

Dalia's mouth hangs open. "No, don't sacrifice yourself. Let one of the dragons destroy the gateway."

"I don't plan to if I can avoid it."

Dalia leans forward, gaze intense. "You. Don't. Plan. To. Period!"

My lips form a grim line. "Dalia, I don't want to, really. It's just—"

"Allison! Dalia!"

It's Haji. He's breathless. He stomps across the diner to our table. His eyes linger on me. I look away. Dalia winks at me. Cringing, I grab my coffee and take a long swig, nearly draining it.

"We need to go," Haji says. "Mauve got the call."

Chapter 37

Rain drizzles from the sky, the water sheening on the roadway. The old beater rattles along, following the SUV out of Ashford toward the national park. Soon we roll past a hotel that features a giant waterwheel and Victorian-era architecture.

From what I gather, the plan is to drive as far as we can into the national park. Then we'll hike cross-country away from the road using snowshoes purchased at an outfitter. I've never gone snowshoeing in my life. Under different circumstances, I might look forward to the experience, but right now it just gives me something else to be anxious about. Once hidden from view, Mauve will transform into a dragon and transport us to the Grove of the Patriarchs in the southeast corner of the park. Somewhere hidden in the grove is the gateway.

"What's flying like?" Haji glances at me from the passenger seat. He's a perpetual-motion machine: legs fidgeting, fingers drumming against his thighs, and eyes swiveling in their sockets.

"Being carried by a dragon through the air?" I ask.

"Yeah," Haji says and screws up his face in a grimace. "I remember when Dr. Radcliffe picked us up in the warehouse. But when Tanis flew us over the ocean, she put a sleeping spell on us so we wouldn't panic."

"I don't remember anything about the flight," Dalia says. "One minute I'm at the beach. The next I'm waking up on a couch with Mauve looming over me."

"I'm not looking forward to this shit," Devin mutters.

"I don't remember much about it," I say. "You—"

"How can you not remember?" Devin scoffs.

"Would you shut up and let her talk," Dalia says.

Devin mimes what Dalia just said in a high-pitched whisper.

"If you're going to argue, I'm not saying anything," I say.

I stare out the window onto a broad pasture. I scan the field for cows or horses or some other livestock and find nothing.

"Sorry, Allison. We won't fight. We won't," Dalia says. "Devin, you should apologize."

"Come on, just say you're sorry," Haji says.

"All right. Fine. I apologize for being argumentative. I'll try not to be," Devin says, his grudging tone betraying his lack of sincerity.

But Devin did apologize, which is something I've never known him to do before. I turn back to my friends. "The reason I don't remember much is that I was half-drowned and—"

An ear-splitting shriek cuts through the clatter of the engine. The sound makes my head ring. Wincing, I throw my hands over my ears. The car swerves, barely avoiding the ditch. Up ahead, the SUV veers into the opposite lane, its brake lights burning red. People scream. Devin brakes hard, and I'm thrown forward and back in the seat like a ping-pong ball.

A bright flash nearly blinds me, followed by a

deafening roar that penetrates the buzz in my ears. The SUV flies into the air and lands hard on its side with a resounding crunch of metal, then slides off the road into the ditch.

"Pull over! Pull over!" I yell.

I'm thrown back in my seat as the beater lurches forward, engine whining. I turn to Dalia. Her gaze is locked straight ahead, and her eyes are bugging out. The car swerves, and I bobble in my seat. Haji is screaming and pointing out the windscreen. That's when I see my mother flying through the air, body undulating. Yellow electrical arcs running over her black body, she swoops over us. I look out the back window. She's heading for the overturned SUV. I scream at Devin to pull over, but the car careens onward.

Haji grabs the steering wheel, fighting with Devin for control of the shuddering car. A silver truck with outsized tires hurtles toward us in the opposite lane, horn blaring.

"Watch out!" Dalia cries.

Haji wrenches the wheel, and the beater swerves in front of the truck. Brakes squeal. A horn blasts. The truck clips the back end of the beater with a crunch of metal. Everything is spinning. I'm flung forward and backward. My camera somersaults from my hands, strikes the back of the seat in front of me, and clatters to the floor.

The car comes to an abrupt halt in the ditch. Haji and Devin don't move, laid out in their seats like strung-out junkies. Dalia is wincing, tears welling up in her eyes, and touching her temple with her right hand. I unbuckle myself and lurch in between the front seats.

"Shit. Shit! Shit!" I place my fingers against Haji's neck, feeling for a pulse.

I don't find one, and he's not moving. Devin groans. I glance at him. His head slowly rotates, and blood seeps from a gash on his forehead. I turn back to Haji, shifting my trembling fingers on his neck in a desperate search for the thrum of blood pumping through his body. I think of all the time we spent together studying and laughing and watching sports and dancing. All that time, I'd been so stupid. I had pined for Jason, who had never yearned for me. I never realized that the boy for me had been here the entire time. Why haven't I kissed Haji, at least once? Why?

"I can't find a pulse!" I scream.

From somewhere outside come reverberating roars and shrieks. Without looking, I know it is the racket of a dragon and skaag locked in mortal combat. I need to be out there, helping Mauve save us all from my mother. A calm comes over me, and I let out a breath I hadn't realized I'd been holding. I steady my fingers and detect a pulse, strong and steady.

I turn to Dalia. She looks stunned, eyes wide and lips trembling, but otherwise unhurt.

"Help them." I gesture to the boys. "Do you understand? Help them."

Dalia nods. I scramble to the backseat and try to open my door, but it's jammed. Out the window, maybe a quarter mile away, a lean copper dragon battles a massive skaag. I can't tell who is winning, but my money is on my mother. She is larger and fiercer than Mauve and rushes through the air with the force of an avalanche. I throw my shoulder into the door, and it squeals as it shudders open wide enough for me to squeeze out.

I sprint toward the battle. A man with a phone to his ear watches the confrontation from near the truck we hit. He yells at me as I run by, but I ignore him. My mother's serpentine body is wrapped around Mauve. Both beasts snap at each other, mouths clamping shut on air with resounding clacks. Electricity arcs over Druk's body, and a bolt shoots from near her head straight into Mauve's chest with a deafening crack. Mauve goes limp and thuds to the ground.

Leslie and Jason scramble out of the driver's side window of the overturned SUV. Both are bloody and unsteady but manage to drop to the roadway and scramble away. I race for Druk. Her mouth is gaping, revealing hooked fangs engineered for prying up dragons' armored scales.

"Hey," I scream, waving my arms overhead. I have to save Mauve. I have to. She might be the only being in the world who has an inkling what it's like being me. "Mother! Mother!"

I stop some twenty feet from the action and continue shouting. I know how sensitive a skaag's hearing is, so I'm convinced Druk is ignoring me. Just as she has overlooked me my entire life. She works her fangs underneath the scales protecting Mauve's slender neck.

"Transform. Transform damn you," I say. "Do it."

But for some reason I can't. I howl, trembling, angry at my mother for killing my friend and for abandoning me and myself for my impotence. Enraged, I pick up a clod of dirt and run toward my mother. At about ten feet, I fling the dirt wad. It hurtles through the air, bits of dirt and rock flying from it to plop against

325

the side of her head.

Druk turns toward me, releasing Mauve from her jaws. Her body is still entwined like an anaconda around the dragon. Her mouth hangs open in an approximation of a demonic smile.

"Now, I have your attention." I move side to side, arms hanging loose. I want to punch her in her ugly face. "That's right. I'm Allison Lee. The daughter you abandoned sixteen years ago."

She shoots toward me like an arrow fired from a longbow, half her body still entwined around Mauve. My body reacts—organs relocating, muscles ripping, and bones cracking all to be reassembled in an instant. My mother's jaws clamp down around my head. The pressure of her teeth against my hide is terrible. One ounce more, and I'm sure my skull will crack like an eggshell. With a violent twist of her body, Druk hurls me to the ground.

I flop against the grass and remain still. The part of me that is the sleeper knows that my mother is proving her dominance. As much as I hate her, as much as I want to fight back, I must submit, or she will kill me.

Druk lowers her massive blunt head to stare into my eyes. She sniffs the air like a gargantuan bull snorting. Her eyes narrow, menacing and considering.

"*Daughter?*" an asexual voice echoes in my head. "*You were at the beach.*"

"*I was,*" I say to the alien presence pressing against my consciousness.

Druk's body unravels from around Mauve. The dragon slumps to the ground. Mother shoots skyward, body rippling as she flies. I watch her, confused and full of hate, until she disappears beyond the distant, wooded ridgeline. That is exactly what she did when I was born. She abandoned me. God, how I loathe her.

Chapter 38

Once Mother disappears from view, I gradually become aware of my surroundings: the noise of vehicles, the distant blare of a siren, indistinct voices, and Dalia screaming for help. I lurch to my feet on short stubby legs and kick off. I'm hovering above the ground, body undulating like an eel.

Dalia and Leslie struggle to open the driver's side door of the beater. I see movement inside the vehicle. It's Jason, trying to push open the driver's side door from the inside. Haji is in there. My body tenses, stomach clenching. I have to save him, but in my peripheral vision, Mauve stirs. Her chest heaves and shudders. Her scales are blackened where the lightning bolt struck her, much the same as the wound inflicted on Dr. Radcliffe by Mark Cassidy. Radcliffe survived without aid. Mauve will too. She must because there's nothing I can do for her right now. My friends need my help.

I shoot through the air toward the crash site. More cars are parked along the side of the road. People stand around gawping, some with their cell phones out. I cover the distance to the crash in seconds and hover behind Dalia and Leslie. They stand in the ditch, pulling on the door handle to no avail. Through the cracked driver's side window, I can see Jason desperately pushing against the door. Devin, face awash

328

in blood, struggles with his seatbelt. Haji's eyes are closed, and he isn't moving.

Dalia glances over her shoulder and screams, throwing her hands in front of her face and cowering. Leslie looks too and starts screaming. It's me I try to say, but the words come out somewhere between a growl and hiss.

No. Not Dalia. She can't be afraid of me. She's my BFF, my squad, my people, my family. She has always accepted me, the good and the bad and my un-caffeinated bitchiness on the rare occasion I miss my morning cuppa. If she doesn't accept me, no one will besides my father. My transformation back into a human must be what it's like to be run through a trash compactor.

I kneel in the damp grass, panting and shivering from the cold. I'm tired and hungry, and the pain of transformation lingers. Dalia stares at me with bug eyes.

"Allison? That was you? Holy shit. The picture really doesn't do you justice. They need help."

"Christ. Your clothes," Leslie says and takes off her coat. "You're naked. Put this on."

I shrug into the coat and zip it up. It covers me to my knees. Dalia gestures to the beater. I need to act before the remnant of my prowess abandons me. Dalia and Leslie stand aside, giving me access to the door.

I take hold of the door handle and yell to Jason. "Push on three. One, two, three!"

I yank on the door handle with all my might. Metal squeals, and there is a loud pop as something fails. I stumble back, nearly losing my balance, with the door handle broken off in my hand.

"Move over as far away from the window as you can," I say to Jason and Devin. "I'm going to break the glass."

Jason moves so that he is sitting between the two front seats. Devin shifts in his seat, watching me with glazed eyes. I heft the door handle and hammer it into the window, which shatters from the blow. I use the handle to clear the remaining glass around the frame. I toss aside the hunk of metal and grab the inside of the door frame and wrench on it. My muscles strain and ache, but I feel something give, and there is a squeal of protesting metal, then the door bursts free from its hinges, and I stumble backward, holding it awkwardly in my hands. I drop it in the grass. People watch us from the roadway, some clearly videoing or photographing the scene. I flip them the bird before turning my attention back to the crash.

Jason and Devin try to operate the seatbelt.

"It's jammed," Jason says.

"Give me some room," I say. I take hold of the seatbelt and jerk on it until it snaps. "Get out."

I stand aside so Devin and Jason can scramble out of the vehicle. Devin sways and collapses. Jason goes to his aid. I enter the vehicle and crawl across the driver's seat to Haji.

"Haji. Haji." I take him by the shoulders.

He stirs, eyes fluttering open then closed. "Allison."

His voice is weak, barely a whisper. I'm so happy to hear his voice I lower my lips to his and kiss him. His lips are smooth and moist and cool. It's fleeting, but I feel a warm flush through my body. When I draw away, my chest shudders. I lick my upper lip and smile.

I've never kissed a boy before. It's not quite what I imagined—the circumstances certainly aren't—but it's savage. His eyes open a crack, and he smiles wistfully. We're the only people in the universe.

"All I had to do was almost die for you to kiss me," he says. "If I had only known…"

I kiss him again.

****

We huddle together on the side of the road above the beater in the ditch. Haji, his head in my lap, passes in and out of consciousness, sometimes muttering under his breath or groaning. Dalia is helping Devin wrap a makeshift bandage around his split brow. Leslie and Jason embrace each other in a bear hug.

"He needs help. He needs help," I say, but no one is listening.

My prowess has abandoned me, leaving me too physically exhausted to budge. My body shakes so hard it feels like my bones are rattling, and I'm nauseated. The gathering crowd surrounding us doesn't help either. They are more concerned with filming and taking photos and staring at me with googly eyes.

"Is that the girl who tore the door off the car?"

"Yeah, it is!"

"What's your name?"

I stare at the mob, too numb to speak. Haji might be dying in my arms. Mauve might be dead in the field, murdered by my mother. I start stroking Haji's raven hair. It's just as silky as I always imagined.

"Please don't die," I whisper.

"Hey, girl, I asked what your name is!"

The crowd is growing and slowly encroaching.

"Leave her alone," Dalia says, standing over me.

"If you're not going to help, leave her alone."

"I called 911!" someone yells.

"That car in the ditch hit my truck!"

"What's that giant monster over in the field?"

"You blind? A dragon."

"That skinny girl in the oversized coat. She's a monster. Like one of those things on Channel 5."

"Yeah! Yeah! What is she?"

"A freak!"

"A monster!"

"She's not a freak or a monster," Leslie snarls, coming between us and the crowd. She stands at her full height, looming over most of the onlookers. "But I am. If you're not going help, go to hell."

"Excuse me. Excuse me." A woman wearing a black hijab weaves through the bystanders. "I'm an ER doctor. Please, allow me to assess the injured."

Leslie's intervention and the arrival the doctor calms the crowd some. The sound of sirens in the distance might also have something to do with it. In short order, the doctor, who smells soothingly of lavender, has Haji lying flat on the tarmac and is assessing him.

"Your friend has a very bad concussion," the doctor says. "He'll need to be hospitalized for observation and to check for bleeding on his brain."

"No. No. Will he be okay?" I say and glance at Dalia who is tearing up. "He'll be okay, right?"

"With proper medical treatment he should recover," the doctor says.

She is about to move on to assessing Devin when a shriek splits the air. The crowd screams and points toward the field. Lumbering across the pasture is

Mauve with a steaming black scar on her chest.

The doctor's eyes go wide. "What in the world…"

"It's okay," I say. "The dragon is with us. She won't hurt you."

The doctor nods and gives me a strained smile and turns her attention back to Devin.

Leslie and Jason come to my side. Jason offers me granola bars and water retrieved from the SUV. Leslie gives me a pair of my own pants and a double layer of socks to keep my feet warm. I gratefully pull on the clothing, then start downing the granola bars and gulping water.

Two police officers show up with guns drawn, yelling at the crowd to disperse. We huddle together along with the ER doctor. The police approach, pointing their weapons at us. Leslie and Jason try to talk to them but are screamed at to stay down and keep quiet. From somewhere behind us in the field, Mauve roars. One of the cops starts shooting. I glance over my shoulder to see Mauve not more than twenty feet away with her wings outspread. The bullets, if any hit her, have no discernible effect. With a roar, she raises her head skyward and lets out a great gout of crackling flame.

The crowd, which hasn't totally dispersed, turns on the cops.

"You're making that thing mad, you dumbasses!"

"That's a dragon! Your guns won't do shit!"

Faced with a dragon and angry bystanders, the cops retreat to their cruisers across the road.

Mauve lumbers over to the ditch so she is right across from us. She glares at me with her coppery eyes, then turns her gaze toward Mount Rainier. The peak is barely visible above a forested ridge.

"I'm too weak. I won't be able to transform," I tell her.

She roars and snatches me in her claws.

"Okay. I'll come. Let me say goodbye."

"We'll take care of them. Go. Close the gateway," Leslie says and takes Jason by the hand. "We got this. Don't worry."

Jason nods. "We won't let anything happen to them."

For some reason, maybe her tone or body language or both, I know Leslie will do anything to keep my friends and even Devin safe.

"Thank you," I say and turn to Dalia.

"I'm going with you," Dalia says.

"You can't. You won't be able to do anything," I say and kneel next to Haji, who is unconscious. I kiss him lightly on his sweaty brow. "Pull through, Haji. You can do it. Don't give up."

When I stand up, Dalia is melting me with her laser eyes. "I'm coming. You say I won't be able to help? Like you'll be able to do anything. I heard what you said to Mauve. You're too weak to transform."

"I'm regaining my strength. Stay here. I need to know you're safe. Haji will need you when he wakes up."

"Haji has Leslie and Jason. What are you worried about? That I'll get in the way? I won't."

Chapter 39

Dalia and I are flying over the Nisqually Entrance to Mount Rainier National Park. Rain spits from the sky, but only a few errant drops strike me as I'm held close to Mauve's draconic chest. The heat radiating from her body keeps me cozy warm. The wind blows cold against my exposed cheeks, but it fails to fully dispel the stench of burned flesh rising from Mauve's wound. Still, flying clutched in a dragon's claws is a fantastic experience.

Whenever I glance at Dalia, her eyes are clenched shut. She is intimidated by heights. That's too bad because she's missing out on a drone's-eye view of the forest, the narrow roadway cutting through the park, and the milky glacial water of the Nisqually River. It is so savagely wicked I feel like I'm in heaven. The only thing I'm missing is my camera, which I left inside the wrecked beater.

My thoughts stray to Haji, and I clench my jaw. His brain might be bleeding. People die from that. He can't die. He can't. He has to live, and the gateway must be closed.

****

I huddle next to Dalia, Dr. Radcliffe, and Tanis beneath the snow-laden trees across a trickling stream from the Grove of the Patriarchs. A sturdy suspension bridge spans the water and marks the entrance to the

Grove. Snowflakes twirl on a frigid wind, obscuring the massive trees on the far side of the bridge.

I fear I will have frostbite on my toes. Double socks don't do much good when your feet are buried in the snow and you don't have the benefit of watertight boots. My hands aren't doing much better, but at least I keep them squirreled away in the pockets of Leslie's heavy winter coat.

"I can't feel my nose," Dalia whispers.

I glance at my BFF. She could go trick-or-treating as Rudolph the red-nosed reindeer.

"I told you not to come."

"Keep looking for the gateway," Dr. Radcliffe says.

I turn my attention back to the Grove. Even with my prosthetics, I can't make out much with the combination of fading light and poor weather conditions.

"What am I looking for again?"

"Did you take a head wound?" Tanis asks and sighs.

I wish Mauve is with us instead of Tanis, but she is several miles away at a hidden clearing, her golem having been damaged in the car crash. She waits to hear a dragon roar, upon which she will come to our aid.

"The gateway will appear as a bright tear in something. In a tree or in the ground or a large boulder. The light escaping it will have a yellow tinge," Dr. Radcliffe says.

"It might even be a gash in the air," Tanis says.

"Unlikely," Dr. Radcliffe says. "Such portals are unstable, unsuitable for travel."

I shake my head. "How am I supposed to see a

portal in the ground?"

"I hope you can see the light," Dr. Radcliffe says dryly. "Your prosthetics have excellent light-gathering capabilities."

"True, but I don't see any strange light," I say, my prosthetics zooming as I scan the trees on the far side of the stream. All I see is swirling snow and dark tree trunks. "Wait a minute." My prosthetics zoom in, my vision momentarily going blurry, then resolving into sharp focus. "Somebody is over there. Two people. I think they're arguing."

"Is it your mother?" Dalia asks.

"I don't know. I don't even know what she looks like in human form."

"You saw Mark Cassidy as a human. Is he over there?" Dalia asks.

"Maybe."

"Do you see any yellow light?" Dr. Radcliffe asks.

I sigh. "I need to move closer. Over by the bridge."

"Wait," Tanis says. "If they see you, we lose the element of surprise."

"They know we're coming. My mother might not fight us. When I confronted her, she fled. She could have easily killed me, but she didn't."

I face them, my prosthetics temporarily going out of focus as they zoom out.

"At first, I was angry that she ran," I say. Dr. Radcliffe raises an eyebrow in curiosity, and Tanis is impassive. Dalia places a gloved hand on my knee. "Abandonment issues. Don't ask. I've been thinking about it. I don't think she wants to kill me or even hurt me. If they're arguing, it might be about me. Mark Cassidy wants me dead for some reason. My mother wants me alive, as strange as that seems. I mean, she did abandon me, and she is a bloodthirsty monster. I don't know. Maybe it's just a crazy theory, but it's the best I have."

Tanis glances at Radcliffe and shrugs.

****

Dr. Radcliffe and I crouch in snow-shrouded bushes next to the trail leading to the suspension bridge. On the portion of the path leading to the span covered by the trees are distinct footprints that haven't been obliterated by the falling snow.

"You see those?" I ask.

"I do," Dr. Radcliffe says.

"I need to move closer."

I creep to the very edge of the tree line. I stumble, my toes burning in pain. I clench my jaw to keep from screaming. Dr. Radcliffe catches me before I crash to the ground. His hulking draconic form casts a warm yet eerie light over the snow. Wincing, I crouch in the bushes and start scanning the trees across the stream.

"I'm going to lose my toes to frostbite," I say.

Dr. Radcliffe kneels beside me. "I should not do this, but I do not wish harm to come to you."

"Do what?"

Dr. Radcliffe places his hands on my legs, and his draconic form does the same with its foreclaws. He mumbles words in a language I do not understand. His draconic form blazes, becoming as bright as the sun. I scrunch and shade my eyes, but the afterimage of that flare is burned into my brain. The light fades, and warmth flows into my feet. Life returns to my toes. I can wiggle them. Each toe is free of pain.

"Thank you," I whisper.

Radcliffe nods. "Now find the gateway."

I see movement at the edge of the Grove, one then two people. They're coming closer, perhaps walking toward the suspension bridge. Of the portal, I see nothing. Twigs snap behind us. Dr. Radcliffe turns toward the disturbance while I continue to search.

"I detected magic," Tanis says.

"I saved Allison's toes," Dr. Radcliffe says.

"If I could sense the spell, so will Druk," Tanis says.

Dalia kneels next to me in the bushes. "Are you okay?"

"I'm fine. Dr. Radcliffe did something to my feet," I say. "What the…"

A naked woman emerges from the trees to stand on the far side of the suspension bridge. She is short and svelte with black hair that falls to the midpoint of her slender neck. Even through the swirling snow, I can tell her features are distinctly Asian and mirror my own. I may well look very much like this woman in thirty years. I shiver at the thought. She is Druk. My mother.

I bolt to my feet and scamper through the snow toward the bridge. Druk watches me, unmoving.

"Wait," Dalia calls.

"Let her go," Dr. Radcliffe says.

Whatever else they say is drowned out by the gusting wind. The same wind makes the suspension bridge sway. I take hold of the freezing metal wires that serve to support the bridge and double as railing. Tentatively, I trudge across the bridge toward my mother. She strides confidently toward me, seemingly unimpacted by the falling snow and gusting wind despite her lack of attire.

We stop in the middle of the bridge, not more than an arm's length separating us. Around her dark eyes and mouth are fine lines. Her lips are a blood-red. She stares at me silently. Her black eyes with only the barest hint of sclera around the edges seem to observe every detail of my appearance. I'm waiting for her to say something, anything. Just a simple greeting. She doesn't have to say that she loves me or misses me or that she has regrets. I need her to acknowledge my existence with something other than her unnerving stare.

I break the silence first. "I'm here to collapse the gateway."

She raises an eyebrow, and her lips perk up in a ghost of a smile that doesn't reveal any teeth. "You can try. Although I advise against it. To collapse the gateway, you must be inside the slipstream. You will die."

"Why do you care? You abandoned me. Remember?"

"I've never wanted you dead, Daughter."

"Druk, you know what must be done."

Mark Cassidy emerges from the trees to stand next to the suspension bridge. He is dressed much the same as he was at the beach, like a model from an outdoor clothing catalogue.

"I won't hurt my daughter," Druk calls.

"She's an experiment, Druk," Mark Cassidy says. "A proof of concept. She's not supposed to be alive."

"I won't kill her, and neither will you," Druk says. "You swore to let her live all those years ago."

"He sent an assassin to kill me," I say.

Druk's eyes narrow, accentuating the crow's feet

around her orbs. Her lips downturn in a frown. She draws a deep breath, and, when she lets it out, she growls. The rumble comes from deep within her chest and is entirely inhuman.

"You tried to have my daughter killed?" Druk asks.

Mark Cassidy steps onto the suspension bridge. "I had no choice, Druk. General Bale knows she still lives. I don't know how. But he knows, and he ordered me to kill her. If she's not dead when the expeditionary force arrives, we all die. I don't want to die for a specimen, Druk, and neither do you."

"Never tell me what I want," Druk says.

She reaches her hands toward me. I flinch, retreating several steps. She moves with remarkable speed, clutching my shoulders in her hands. I gasp. She's not gentle. She could snap me like a twig if she chose. Her dark eyes stare into mine, fierce yet motherly, like a lioness tending her cub.

"I didn't abandon you by choice," Druk says.

Mark Cassidy advances across the bridge, slowly, cautiously, like a predator preparing to pounce.

"Is what he said true? Am I the result of an experiment?" I say, my voice tremulous as tears form in my eyes. It figures that I'm nothing more to her than a protozoan in a petri dish.

"It is. I was ordered to copulate with your father in an attempt to conceive. I used skaag and human magic to force conception. It worked."

My gaze flicks to Mark Cassidy. He is no more than twelve feet from my mother's back.

Without looking, she snarls. "Stay back, Mark."

Mark Cassidy halts, glaring at me, his black eyes predacious.

"Back away, Mark."

His face contorts into a sneer, but he obeys.

"Is that all I am to you, the result of a successful experiment?"

"No," she says, shaking her head vehemently.

She sounds sincere. Like she means it. Like she cares about me.

"As soon as I held you in my arms, I knew you were so much more than the result of an experiment and that I would do almost anything to protect you. Almost anything. I'll take no direct action against my people, Allison, not even for you. I swore oaths that I cannot break. I won't stop you from trying to close the gateway, but neither will I aid you. I suggest you allow your dragon allies to occupy Mark Cassidy while you close the gateway, if that is the destiny you choose. Goodbye, Daughter. In this life or the next, we will meet again. Be certain of that."

So fast I don't even have a chance to respond, she leaps off the bridge. I watch her fall toward the water. As she does, she transforms into a skaag, body rippling, and soars over the stream.

"Behind you! Look out!" Dalia screams.

I turn toward my BFF. Unbeknownst to me, she has followed me out on the bridge and stands only a few feet away. Her eyes are as wide as saucers, and spittle flies from her mouth as she screams and points a trembling finger at me. No, not at me, behind me, at Mark Cassidy.

Chapter 40

I vault toward Dalia with my hands outstretched. I grab her, forcing her to the bridge's snow-covered planks. She falls, screaming, and lets out an *oof* on impact. I pin her while the bridge wobbles as if caught in a cyclone. I wrap one arm around her and snatch a heavy gauge steel wire to keep us from toppling from the span.

Mark Cassidy barrels toward us in skaag form, mouth agape to reveal hooked fangs dripping with saliva and a coarse blood-red tongue. Electricity crackles over his sleek black body that bulges against the steel cables supporting the bridge. Once again, Mother chose the perfect time to abandon me.

The sleeper stirs inside me, ready to fight to the death. I fear that in a second I'll transform into a skaag and crush Dalia beneath me. Mark Cassidy is nearly atop us. A support cable snaps with a resounding twang, and the bridge lurches to the left. Dalia screams, and I gasp, my arms straining to keep us from sliding off the planks.

The trumpeting roars of the dragons pierce the air loud enough to set my ears ringing. Mark Cassidy changes his trajectory, soaring upward to engage his sworn enemies. There's another snap. This time the bridge pitches right. We slide across the snow. Only the stout cabling keeps us from falling into the icy water below.

I scramble to my feet, pulling Dalia along. "Run!"

The bridge jitters as we charge through the snow toward the safety of the grove. More cables snap, one shooting past my cheek, only missing me by inches. The bridge twists right, throwing us off balance. I regain my balance first and snatch Dalia around the waist. My physical prowess is upon me, and I hurl Dalia the remaining twenty feet to the safety of the trail. I take two long bounds, then leap and hear loud snaps followed by a resounding crash. I land hard in the snow, rolling into a crouch to absorb the impact. Still, twin lances of pain shoot from the soles of my feet up to my hips. I wince and blink back tears.

I sit next to Dalia in the snow. She's breathing hard and staring at the dogfight overhead. All three dragons battle Mark Cassidy, but even outnumbered, the skaag is far from overmatched. His long body entwines Dr. Radcliffe's golden torso, and his mouth clamps down on Tanis's shoulder. Mauve rakes his body with her claws, but with no discernable effect. Their shrieks and roars boom like thunderclaps.

"Never throw me like that again," Dalia says.

I gesture to where the bridge had stood but no longer does.

"I was running. I didn't need you to throw me."

Mark Cassidy's jaw unclenches from Tanis's shoulder, and the slender white dragon tumbles from the sky to thud to the streambed. His mouth misses closing around Mauve's neck, instead snapping air.

"We need to find the gateway," I say. "Can you walk?"

Dalia nods.

We stagger to our feet and tramp along the trail into the grove. I pause at the tree line and glance skyward to watch flames crackle from Dr. Radcliffe's maw. The jet of fire rakes Mark Cassidy's oily black body. The skaag screeches and releases Dr. Radcliffe to escape the flames. With great flaps of their wings, Dr. Radcliffe and Mauve pursue Mark Cassidy.

"Are they winning?" Dalia asks.

"I don't know. Skaags are made to kill dragons. That is our purpose."

"You're not one of them. You're my best friend. My sister."

Dalia takes my hand.

"They're doing their part. Now I must do mine," I say.

"Don't do it. You heard what the dragons said. You'll die."

I face Dalia. She stares at me entreatingly, eyes moist. I remember her reaction when she saw me as a skaag. She will never accept me, not really. She can't because I'm not human. I'm a monster. I don't blame her for that.

"I'll sacrifice myself to keep you safe," I say and smile.

****

"I can't see anything," Dalia says.

"Hold my hand." I reach for her.

Dalia takes my hand. Underneath the trees, it is dark, even peaceful if it weren't for the shrieks and roars of the monsters battling in the sky. I guide Dalia along a path blanketed by snow. Soon the path becomes a boardwalk, looping around towering conifers. Interspersed along the walkway are benches laden with snow and signs with words and pictures obscured by white quilts.

Dalia keeps up a constant stream of talk. I'm not paying much attention; I'm searching for the telltale light of the gateway. The gist of her speech is an attempt to convince me not to collapse the gateway, not to sacrifice myself, not to commit suicide. She doesn't understand. I'm walking toward a destiny that I choose. I'm the only one who can destroy the portal. Even outnumbered two or three to one, Mark Cassidy might win.

Ahead of us is a tree with a gargantuan trunk. The boardwalk encircles it. Around the edges of the trunk, I see a yellowish glow.

"There it is," I say and redouble my pace.

Dalia pulls on my hand, trying to slow me, but I tug free.

"Don't go," Dalia cries. "We can find the dragons. Show them the gateway. Let one of them destroy it."

"They're still fighting."

"They'll win."

I stop next to the tree, observing the eerie glow. A few more steps, and I will face my destiny.

"You think you have to do this, but you don't," Dalia says between sobs. "Don't leave me. You're my best friend in the world. I love you."

"I love you too. That's why I must do this. To protect you. To protect everyone. The expeditionary force might arrive at any minute," I say, not facing my BFF. I'm afraid if I do I won't have the strength to do what must be done. "Tell Haji I'm sorry I didn't kiss him sooner. Tell him I want him to be happy."

I stride toward the glow. Dalia screams and grabs

my arm, yanking hard.

"Let go," I say, not breaking my stride despite having to pull her along. "This is what I want. Didn't you hear my mother? I'm just an experiment. I'm not meant to be alive. This way my death will count for something."

"No!" Dalia screams.

I wrench my arm free and continue along the boardwalk until I'm facing a tall, jagged gash in the tree trunk from which the yellowish light spills out. I reach a hand toward the portal. When my hand crosses the threshold, it is lost in the light. I withdraw my hand and look at it in the glow. My appendage is unharmed by the passage in and out of the realm between universes. Full of wonder, I enter the slipstream.

I'm floating in a passage of light. Rushing air buffets me, neither warm nor cold, without moving me overmuch, and fills my ears with a deafening roar. Beyond the light is only blackness in every direction like a night sky bereft of stars. The passage is circular in shape, wide enough to drive a semi through, and it seems to continue forever as infinite as the nothingness surrounding it. At the very edge of my vision down the pathway, I spy black serpentine shapes swimming toward me like gargantuan eels through water.

I transform, bones cracking and muscles tearing and organs rearranging. I scream, the sound morphing into an animalistic shriek as my vocal cords elongate. Then I'm the sleeper, the half-skaag, staring down the expeditionary force. I know I don't have long, but I'm not sure how long. I try to produce an electrical discharge but can't. What can I do? If those monsters reach Earth, everyone I love will die. Humanity will end. I quiver, and electricity tingles over my body, but no matter how loudly I scream in my mind for my body to unleash an electrical discharge nothing happens.

I sense a disturbance in the passageway and see a faint ripple in the light emanating from behind me. I twist until my head faces the gateway. A human arm reaches into the passageway. No, Dalia. My innards turn to water, and my body aches so much I feel like I'm going to explode. I try to scream at Dalia to remove her arm, but my tongue and lengthened vocal cords can't make the sounds.

The tingling running over my body builds. It's happening. It's happening. Electricity arcs over my body, crackles in my ears, and a bolt shoots from me into the yellow light. It strikes something with a boom, and lightning flashes along the passage. The collapse begins, and Dalia still reaches into the portal, her arm inside up to the shoulder. No, if she enters, she will die. Only I'm supposed to die. Only I need to make the sacrifice. I rush toward her as the light collapses in on me, the passage growing narrower and the blackness closing in.

Without consciously willing myself to do so, I transform. The pain is incredible, as always. I reach for Dalia's hand as the gateway shrinks, barely wider than a human is tall. I mean to push her away, but she grabs me and pulls.

I tumble out into biting cold and Dalia's arms. We fall onto the snow-covered boardwalk. Dalia is crying and hugs me to her.

"What did you do?" I yell at her, trying to break free of her grip, but all the prowess has left me. "The gateway—"

"It's gone. It's gone," Dalia says.

It's then I realize the eerie yellow light no longer illuminates the snow. I look over my shoulder. The gash in the tree trunk is no longer there, leaving behind blackened bark in the shape of the portal.

"I did it. I did it." I face my friend. "You saved me. Thank you."

Dalia smiles. "I told you I can help."

Dalia pulls me to my feet, and we stand, clutching each other for a long time. My heart pounds in my chest, and my stomach growls with hunger, and my legs are so weak I'd crumple without Dalia's support.

"We need to find you some clothes before you freeze to death," Dalia says.

"I'm okay. Whatever Dr. Radcliffe did to save my toes is keeping me warm," I say.

I listen for the din of battle. I don't hear anything.

"The dragons?"

Dalia shakes her head. "I don't know. The noise stopped after you entered the portal."

"We need to go. They might need our help."

"Mark Cassidy might be out there."

"If he is, we're dead."

Dalia chuckles mirthlessly. "And I thought I was the optimist."

Dalia supports me at the edge of the grove next to the remnants of the bridge. Snow falls from the dark sky and melts as it lands upon the dragons gorging themselves on the eviscerated body of Mark Cassidy. Despite my ambivalence toward the beasts, I'm relieved that they all live. Tanis moves gingerly, and it looks like her left foreleg is broken. Dr. Radcliffe and Mauve are both injured, purple blood oozing from numerous wounds.

"They're eating him?" Dalia says. "Why didn't they come to the gateway?"

"They no longer detect it. They know I was successful."

The dragons pause in their feeding frenzy. First, Dr. Radcliffe, then the others lift their long serpentine necks skyward and twist their heads to face me. If they are surprised to see me alive, they give no indication as far as I can tell. Dr. Radcliffe growls and bobs his head. I need no translation. He is telling me job well done.

Chapter 41

It's dark out and sprinkling when Dr. Radcliffe drops me off in front of my house. I exit the vehicle and step onto the sidewalk with trepidation. My camera swings by the strap slung over my left shoulder. It's my first time home since the incident. That's what we're calling the affair, from the dragons kidnapping us to the various clashes climaxing with me collapsing the portal.

Reporters and cameramen converge on me from the numerous media vans parked up and down the street. Cameras click, and lights glare. I chew on my lower lip and keep moving. I wish I am one of the photojournalists. I'd much rather be snapping the pictures than being the photographic subject.

A reporter from Channel 5 thrusts a microphone in my face. "What happened at Mount Rainier?"

"No comment," I mutter, brushing past the reporters.

"The public deserves to know."

"Allison, is it true you're a shapeshifter?"

The reporters surround me on all sides, blocking my access to my driveway. I clench my hands at my sides. I'm ready to scream at the reporters. I'm ready to transform.

"This is my house," I say. "Let me by."

"Does your father, Raymond Lee, know what you are?" demands a reporter.

The temptation to punch the reporter in the face is almost too great to resist when a horn honks. I turn toward the sound. Dr. Radcliffe has parked his car in the middle of the street and jumps out. Calling to the reporters, he bounds over the hood, landing on the sidewalk next to me. His display of inhuman athleticism catches the attention of the journalists.

"I am Dr. Frederick Radcliffe, a dragon from a different universe," he says in a voice like a carnival barker.

The reporters who didn't see his feat of athleticism spin toward him at the mention of a dragon, eager to learn anything about the alien visitor and hopeful that they might convince him to reveal his draconic form. I'm happy for him. It turns out he loves giving interviews. I take advantage of the distraction he causes to run for the front door and ring the doorbell.

Of course, Dad doesn't open the door. Whatever scientific journal he's reading always takes precedence over something stupid like answering the door. He probably thinks I'm a reporter. This gives the actual reporters in the back of the scrum surrounding Dr. Radcliffe time to get a bead on me and start closing in like sharks that have caught the scent of blood.

"Everyone has gone through this. I can survive it. Dalia survived. Haji survived. Even Leslie and Jason survived," I mutter to myself.

Is Dad even home? I ring the doorbell again. I hope I fare better than Jason. He had almost been trampled to death by reporters. Only Mauve using the preternatural strength of her brand-new golem saved him. And then there is Devin. He loves the limelight almost as much as Dr. Radcliffe. He started talking to the media before he had even left the hospital. Haji talked too. Honestly, I don't blame either one of them. I mean, it's not like people hadn't been posting videos and photos of dragons and skaags all over the Internet.

I pound on the door. A journalist shoves a mic in my face, and the flare of a flash makes me squint.

"You know," I growl, "I can bite your head off. All your heads."

I shouldn't threaten people, but I do love the reporters' expressions of shock and indignation as they retreat a handful of steps. They don't stay frightened for long.

One shouts, "Did you just threaten us?"

Before I have to answer, the door swings open. I spin to face my dad and leap into his open arms. He hugs me to him and kicks the door shut. His embrace is the most wonderful I have ever received.

He releases me and locks the door. "I'm so glad to see you. Oh God. I was so afraid, Allison. Oh God."

I have rarely seen him so emotional and start to tear up.

"I'm sorry, Daddy," I say, sniffling. "I didn't mean to scare you. I didn't mean for any of it to happen. It just did."

"It's okay, Allison," he says and takes me by the shoulders. He kisses me on the forehead and on the cheek. "It's okay. You're home now."

I throw myself against him and wrap my arms around him. He hugs me back.

"Have you heard what they're saying about me?"

He squeezes me tighter. "Yes."

"It's true. Not all of it, but the gist of it is."

"I know."

"I'm a shapeshifting monster, Daddy," I say. "Do you still love me?"

"Of course, I do, Allison," he says and kisses my forehead again. "You're my daughter, no matter what, and I love you."

"You're not even mad about the golem?"

"No, why would I be? It disintegrated a couple days ago," Dad says.

"You weren't like shocked when that happened?"

"Well, yes. Not as shocked as Dalia's mom." Dad shakes his head. "I'm just glad you're safe. Come on. There's someone I want you to meet."

Dad releases me and takes my hand, leading me toward the dining room. I'm a little miffed. He rarely has guests, like once or twice a year. Maybe it's a bit harsh, but I feel put out, like someone is invading my privacy and purposely disrupting my reunion with my father.

When the interior of the dining room comes into view, I say, "What the hell?"

"Allison," Dad says, smiling as broadly as a tween who just received the latest video game console for Christmas. "This is your mother."

"I know who she is." I glare at Druk. "What are you doing here?"

She sits at the head of the table, looking much the same as last time I saw her in human form, except she's wearing clothes, a black power suit. I have to admit, she looks striking in a severe, military sort of way.

"Mark Cassidy is dead. The gateway is closed. It might take General Bale years to create or find a new one to Earth," Druk says. "For now, I am free to live as I choose."

Dad crosses the room to sit in the chair next to Druk. She places her hands on the table, and he takes hold of her hands. I feel queasy, like *ugh*.

"You know she is a shapeshifting monster, right?" I ask.

"Allison," Dad says, looking sheepish. "I hoped...we hoped...if we ever had to have this conversation with you...it would be under... ummm...different circumstances." He shakes his head and falls silent.

"Allison, your father has always known the truth about you," Druk says. "I told him everything after you were born."

I stare at them, mouth agape. It's just like my mother to barge back into my life after sixteen years and upend everything. I feel like I'm being strapped into a catapult, lit on fire, and flung into the air. I mean, my father knew that I'm half-skaag all this time and never said anything. He knew my mother is a shapeshifting monster and never bothered mentioning it. Holy shit. I should be screaming at them right now, ranting and raving, but I'm not. I also feel good, not quite happy or bubbly or...I don't know. Alongside the sense of betrayal, I feel more contentment than I have ever experienced.

"So we're like a...a family?"

"Yes," they say in unison.

I look at Dad. "You don't care that I'm a shapeshifting monster?"

"No," Dad says. "You're my daughter, period. Just don't go eating the mailman."

I don't crack a smile, and neither does Mother.

"That was supposed to be a joke," Dad says.

"Okay, I'll just shut up now."

I meet Mother's gaze and swallow. "You don't care that I'm mixed species?"

"I couldn't care less," she says. "You're my daughter."

Everything isn't hunky-dory, but knowing two people in the world know exactly what I am and one hundred percent accept me makes life a little more bearable. For now, that's enough.

I take my camera from my shoulder. "I'll go get my tripod. We can take a family photo."

Dad glances at my mother. She nods.

"Sure, Allison," he says. "Sure."

A word about the author...

Dan has wanted to write novels since first reading Frank Herbert's *Dune* at the age of eleven. A native of the Pacific Northwest, he often goes hiking with his family through mist-shrouded forests and along alpine trails with expansive views.

Dragons Walk Among Us is his debut novel. He plans to keep writing fantasy and science-fiction for many years. You can explore his blog at...

https://www.danscifi.com

CPSIA information can be obtained
at www.ICGtesting.com
Printed in the USA
LVHW022304050821
694500LV00008B/505

9 781509 236558